1

Muirh

CW01082327

?

A Paninaro imprint

www.paninaropublishing.co.uk

A catalogue record for this book is available from the British Library

ISBN - 13: 978 - 1916088535

Front cover image by Yoshi Kametani from his Muirhouse 'Plastic Spoons' collection.

Johnny Proctor socials :

Twitter @johnnyroc73

Instagram @johnnyproctor90

Dedicated to Leia Proctor

You've faced a year that 'no' kid should ever have to deal with but despite everything. I have not heard you complain *one single time* when it has come to Covid 19, that has been forced on us all. You really could teach some of the adults a thing or two about living through a pandemic, LG.

I always love and am proud of you but *never* more so than here in 2020 x

Acknowledgments

Thank you to everyone who has shown me the love and support through buying my previous trilogy and who now find themselves with this, my first stand alone novel, in their hands. You really have no idea just how much your support and your word of mouth - of my work - inspires me to bring more words your way.

@YourWullie on Twitter for providing inspiration my way for ideas for the front cover and to Yoshi Kametani for allowing me the use of one of the images from his 'Plastic Spoons' collection of images from Muirhouse, Edinburgh. Danny McInnes for being brilliant enough to agree to have his younger self immortalised on the front cover. James Riordan who, during what has been the most challenging year ever for us all, has been not only a good mate but also a much valuable source of information *and* inspiration.

And finally to Rachel. My best friend, muse and better half. Thank you for your patience, love and understanding (as always) and thank you for being the best "wifeager" I could ever ask for. Forever on hand to make sure that I eat, bandage hands up for me when they get sore from writing and generally being the difference between a novel consuming me entirely during the writing of it and it not. Love you, PP xx

Chapter 1

Strings.

'Got the fucking ball ref

He's standing there, faux incensed, theatrically making the shape of an imaginary ball with his hands in front of him. Meanwhile the Pickle and the Barrel's player is lying crumpled on the deck, just in front of him. Screaming out in agonising pain, with one of his legs going in two different directions.

To suggest that you'd won the ball. While the aesthetics right beside you - lying there on the ground as cast iron evidence - are showing otherwise. Well, it's always going to be a touch on the optimistic side, isn't it?

'ARRRRGGGHHHH YA FUCKINNN DIRRRRTTTY BASTAAAAAAARD'

Their number seven screamed out while banging his hand hard on the pitch as if by doing so it would replace the searing pain that was - by the sights and, without question, the sounds - racing through him.

Fuck, it was cold, that morning, though. The evidence of this being the fresh imprint of the Mitre that I'd taken flush to my thigh when blocking practically the first kick of the game from one of their players. You could just about make out the 'Made in England' imprint in a scarlet red shade across my skin, never mind the fucking Mitre logo, itself.

'No cunt asked you, Puff the fucking Magic Dragon.'

Sunny, sneering, shouted down at him - in reference to the steam that was piling out of the guy's mouth every time he opened it to scream or shout - as all of the pushing and shoving started. Whatever the ref had in mind for him - and I had a pretty fucking good idea, myself - it was going to take a bit of time before he would be able to clear a path between him and Sunny to dish out the punishment for the - and let's call it for what it was - assault.

I just happened to be looking in the direction of both players when it happened. Proper Eagle Eye Cherry visibility on it all, like.

One of the Pickle and the Barrel's players, number four, had laid it off to their number seven. Looked like he'd been wanting a bit of give and go with his team mate because he was right on the move again the moment he'd passed the ball. Pointing and shouting for a quick return. Being fair to their number seven. He'd been receptive to this and had been quick witted enough to send the ball *back* and in the required direction to set up their attack.

The issue was that this 'one - two' had been fully executed *before* Sunny had then decided to come through the back of their player, with the extra callous move of taking his studs right down the boy's ankle. You could see the tear in his sock as he rolled around on the pitch. That, hardly a surprise because I had never known Sunny to ever change the studs on his boots in all the years that I'd seen him play for The Violet. It had actually been a bit of a running joke amongst the lads that with the sharp pieces of metal that he had fixed to the underneath of his Adidas World Cup boots - masquerading as studs - he really should've thought about the wellbeing of his opponents and switched the studs for fucking Stanley blades.

'Got the ball? I could've grown a fucking beard in the time you made the fucking challenge?!'

I said to Sunny as I set about doing my bit and trying to diffuse the situation by getting in between him and a couple of their players who were, quite understandably, threatening to take his head off.

It was an incendiary filled few moments. Depending on everyone's reactions that followed the challenge. We were either going to have a bit of handbags and examples of players showing that their bark was nothing even remotely close to their bite *or* we were going to have a full scale twenty two player brawl there on the pitch. There was also the added fact that - with the game being at Muirhouse Park - this pretty much equalled that there would've been a lot *more* than just the eleven players on the pitch representing the Muirhouse side of things.

'Got there as quick as I could, Strings, mate.'

He replied back - taking a temporary moment out from his protestations over what even he must've known himself was coming - with a slight wink while I found a random arm knocking the side of my face through someone behind me stretching to try and grab hold of him.

We called him Sunny but that wasn't because of some bright and uplifting nature that he possessed which left a positive impact on those who were lucky enough to meet him each day. No, he earned that name on account of that while on the fitba pitch he resembled a tractor, pulling a caravan. It was Pete Doig that come up with the name before he retired. We'd been playing a pre season friendly against a team of under 16s - which was one of the most stupid fucking ideas I'd ever seen, putting cunts that sit in the pub or graft most of their life up against teenagers that do fuck all other than play fitba or pull the end off it in their rooms - and Pete had gotten sick of the amount of times he'd found himself being the only one tracking back and by the second half he'd let his frustrations get the better of him. When the Under 16s were making a sub he took his chance to let rip at Sunny.

'If I'd fucking kent that I was going to have a passenger today alongside me I'd have brought you a copy of Shoot and packet of Revels for the fucking journey. Every time I've looked for you today you've been nowhere to be seen. Slower than a fucking week in the jail, you ya cunt. Strikers are allowed to come back into their own half now and again, eh?'

That was Pete though. Fucking Muirhouse Violet legend, that boy. If he gave you the hair dryer treatment out there on the pitch or back in the dressing room. Didn't matter where or when. You took it.

By the time the match was over though - I lost track of the scoreline in the end, it was that bad - Sunny, previously known up to then as Grainger, had earned himself the nickname 'Sunny' on account of our city prison Saughton and how *nothing* was slower than time inside 'Sunny Saughton.'

I had no idea of the theatrics that were all taking place behind me - my prime focus being to stop Sunny from saying or doing anything further to inflame things while at the same time, stopping anyone from getting to him - but I could hear it all. An absolute cacophony of noise, expletives, squabbles and - in some cases - some unreal attempts at crafting a narrative that was at a complete odds of what had *actually* taken place.

'Cunt's making the most of it to get our man sent off. Poor form that, like. Don't fucking fall for it ref. The boy's fucking at it' I could make out Coffee, one of our players, shouting towards the referee who probably wasn't going to be hearing anything from anyone due to the incessant whistling that he was doing in a pathetic attempt at trying to stop all of the handbags that was going on around this one small area of the pitch.

'Making the fucking most of it? You fucking seen his leg, aye? One part's going for a shite and the other's going for a shave, for fuck's sake.' I heard this high pitched whiny voiced reply and was quick enough to turn around in time to see the player try to lay a hand on Coffee and promptly be put on his arse, courtesy of a deft wee head-butt from our midfield general. With the ref having tunnel vision when it came to grabbing a hold of Sunny he, of course, missed Coffee's own particular indiscretion. Which was just as well for Muirhouse Violet.

'Come a - fucking - head then, mon, ya cunts'

I took my eyes off Sunny for a second and there he was. Arms outstretched, offering all and sundry out, so to speak. He looked like he was acting out of pure basic instincts crossed with adrenaline. He'd done a particularly naughty thing, and knew it himself, but was now doing all he could to ride his way out from the situation. Specifically through fronting and suggesting that there was even worse to come from him if anyone was interested in finding out.

'I'll take it from here. Step aside.'

The more well spoken voice came behind me from the referee in an attempt at being authoritative that never quite achieved its target.

'There's no place for behaviour like that on my pitch. You're off, son.'

Without any fucking about whatsoever the red card was hoisted into the air with the referee's other arm pointing in the direction of the pavilion.

'Good decision, ref' I heard one of their players say with a small round of applause to go with it.

'You shut your fucking mooth' I heard Montana, one of our forwards, shout back at him.

'Who the fuck are you, like?' A different voice then chipping in.

In was in this moment that, with all the mini arguments going on that you could see it all for what it was. A bunch of men who - for the vast majority - had sunk copious amounts of lager the night before and should've been either still in their beds or, at the very worst. Sitting, absolutely hanging, attempting to get a fry up inside of them while piecing the previous night's goings on together.

Basically anywhere *other* than a fitba pitch.

'Fucking red?' Sunny's hands were glued stuck to the top of his head as he stood there with a look of mock amazement on his face.

'It was my first challenge of the match, and a strikers one, at that?!'

I couldn't help but have a wee laugh at how quickly the man had climbed down from 'getting the ball' to it being his first tackle of the game. That's the thing. It *was* Sunny's first challenge. Aye, the mythical first tackle where you're meant to have a free pass that allows you to commit anything from heavy petting to manslaughter on an opposing player, as long as it's the *first* thing that you do in the match.

Ask fucking Gordon Strachan and Jose Batista about first tackles and see what they say about them. Batista would probably say that he got the ball, anyway. Coincidentally though. Sunny and his red card two minutes into Muirhouse Violet versus The Pickle and the Barrel gave the game a certain Scotland v Uruguay complexion to it. And by that I mean that the stupid sloth like cunt had left us right in the fucking shit and facing playing practically the whole match with ten men.

Sunny had his own ideas on that though.

I'm not sure if it was all the jeers and personal insults that was flying his way from the opposition or the pompously arrogant attitude of the referee towards him. Could've been simply out of his own sheer frustration at making such a stupid fucking tackle and leaving his team mates with an uphill task, especially at a stage in the match where a ball had barely even been kicked.

Muirhouse Violet - and I include myself in that - were not what you could have ever described as being filled with primed athletes at their peak. They say that teams play better with ten men. Aye, *professional* fitba teams. Cunts like us needed a Sunny on the pitch not through possessing any form of technical skill or tactical nous but purely through being another body on the pitch that you could pass the ball to and give yourself a breather. He was also - to the team's benefit - an absolute bastard. And we could never, ever, have enough of *those* in our starting eleven.

Whatever the reason. He just flipped. Went from the innocent 'wasn't me' demeanor to psychopath in the blink of an eye. While he *should've* been making his way off the pitch he's lunging for the referee with outstretched arms like he's going to strangle the poor arbitrator. It took myself and another two of the Pickle and the Barrel's players to be the difference between a potential on pitch asphyxiation and any incident between player and referee that you would see on most pitches on a Sunday morning across Scotland.

Took Jock Hunter, our gaffer, along with a few stragglers who had been watching from the sidelines to come on and physically remove Sunny from the pitch. Manhandling and rushing him off towards the nearest bit of touchline they could find. Like you see bouncers when they're kicking someone out of a club.

'I'LL FUCKIN KILLLLLL YOU'

Sunny was shouting as he exited the pitch while looking around like a man possessed trying to fix his gaze on the referee.

I'm not sure how many reds he got in the end. I thought it had been four shown by the referee before Sunny had technically left the pitch but a few others in the team reckoned that he had actually been flashed it six times before play had eventually restarted. In the world of Sunday League. How many red cards you collect *matters*. The difference between four red cards and six can literally be the difference between a five year playing ban and a lifetime one.

What Sunny decided to do that morning, however, left any talk of what kind of a ban he was going to get handed down as all a bit, well, pretty pointless.

Give the boys credit, though. Despite the blow of losing a man so early on. We rallied around and took advantage of the confusion that had been hanging over the pitch for the previous five minutes by going a goal ahead a couple of minutes after the ref had got the game going again. Big fucking daftie, Bungalow, losing his man at a corner and with a slight flick of his head sending the ball right into the top shelf with their keeper stood there completely static, watching it go past him. I wouldn't go as far as to say that Bungalow had measured and planned for it as that would have been going far past what his actual skill set was capable of but it looked cool as fuck, all the same. I'll give him that.

'FUCKING CONSOLIDATION NOW, BOYS.'

Jock Hunter shouted from the touchline. Looking at no one in particular while tapping the side of his head with a couple of fingers. Making a show of asking his team to 'think about it.'

The following ten minutes was a torrid time though. Complete one way traffic and not in the direction that we wanted it to be going in. The team from Leith huffed and puffed but with just the right amount combination of experience and shithousery we were doing enough to keep them out. I remember saying to Sepp, our keeper, when he was down getting treatment after landing awkwardly from a jump.

'Take your fucking time down there, big man, we've only played around fifteen minutes and the fact that we've barely touched the ball for the last ten of them I'm fucking breathing out of my Richard Gere, here, pal.'

Half time looked like being a bit of an ask to get to never mind playing a full ninety minutes. Nothing worse than when you can't get the ball back from the other team, though. Drains you both physically *and* mentally. The natural reaction is, understandably, to just wipe some poor cunt out and send some kind of a message out but you can't be doing that stuff. Not when you've already lost a player.

I could probably go to hell for admitting this but when I saw the white Ford Transit driving across the playing fields in the direction of the pitch. Headlights flicking repeatedly from full beam to off, horn being intermittently sounded in such a way that it was giving me a sore head. Well, sorer. And there was Sunny. Sat behind the wheel, still in his Violet top, with a manic fucking grin on his face. Rather than view things as I should've done. That a still half pissed Sunny was driving erratically towards a group of people with fuck knows what kind of nonsense in his head and that there was a real possibility that things were about to go too far.

Instead, I felt that it was going to provide a much welcome breather.

Once everyone had clocked what was coming. Play - obviously - stopped. Play to the whistle? No, mate, I'll play to the whistle *or* if I see three and a half tonnes worth of metal and pure radge speeding my way, thank you very much.

In a situation like that, it's every man for themselves and how they're going to react to such a situation. Some scattered, some were like rabbits caught in headlights stood there seemingly glued to the muddy turf. Rossi? For fuck's sake? I caught a quick glimpse of him standing on the touchline talking to Barry Swanson, having commandeered Swanny's can of Tennents and snout that was lit. Standing there taking a swig out of the can and then following up with a big draw exactly in the way that you'd do if there *wasn't* a complete nut job driving a Jamieson's Electrical Services van at a not inconsiderable speed towards the general catchment area that you were standing in.

Gauging the direction that he appeared to be going in. All I could really do was make sure I was as far away from it as possible and stand back while watching and praying that Sunny didn't do anything *too* stupid. I mean, *more* stupid than driving a vehicle on to a public pitch on a Sunday morning when the public is out and about getting a bit of recreation in.

It was only once he was entering the field of play that I was able to get a closer look at him. Still hungover from the night before I hadn't been exactly quick on the uptake, plus, it had all happened so fast but once he was on the pitch I was able to see him with one hand on the wheel. Intensely pointing towards someone.

Of course, he was coming for the fucking referee!

This was a new one. In my years playing for Muirhouse I'd seen a lot of stuff that you would never, ever, see grace the professional game. That time the Rottie came out of nowhere - no owner to be seen or heard of - and through sheer ferocious aggression managed to stop the game for ten minutes because of it running from player to player trying to attack them. That game when I was running down the wing, head up and waiting on the ball being switched, and tripped up over a junkie who had OD'd right there by the side of the pitch. Police coming and arresting players during the match because of outstanding warrants. When some wee bastard had fucking poked a wasps nest and we all got stung during the resulting swarm.

There's barely anything that would surprise me at Muirhouse Park but give Sunny his dues. Ten out of ten for creativity, like.

I know that the very first thing that should pop into your head in a dangerous moment like that is for everyone's safety and for any decent cunt that's *exactly* how it is, me included. That still didn't stop my initial thought - literally as I was watching someone in a Violet shirt shoving a Pickle and the Barrel player out the way, courtesy of some kind of flying superman rugby tackle - of 'He's going to get a five year ban for this.'

I'm not sure if coming so close to killing someone had been the difference to Sunny or not but you saw a bit of brake lights going on after he had flown past. Not that he was done, though. Pretty fucking far from that, actually. Approaching the goals down at the other end of the pitch he took (his bosses) van into a handbrake turn leaving an almost perfect c - ironically - inside the D.

Then he kind of sat there, menacing like, and started revving his engine. Like that Stephen King film about the car. Kind of intimidating, like. There was still a bit of confusion surrounding the pitch. Anyone - players or fans - with a fucking brain in their head would've got themselves as far away to fuck as they could have but it doesn't work like that around Muirhouse. And besides, it's not like Sunny was ever going to run one of his *own* team mates down although you can never run out the possibility of mistakes being made.

The referee? That one, I wouldn't be as quick to offer guarantees over.

It was probably the ref's whole attitude to being the keeper of law and order that was his undoing because if there was *anyone* on the pitch that should've been making themselves scarce, it was that cunt. Look at how the ref's get protected in Argentina, Boca v River and that, proper riot shields over the head to protect yourself from the projectiles from above while this daft cunt is standing there blowing his whistle, apparently and through nothing other than guesswork on my part that he was abandoning the match.

Meanwhile Sunny was taking off again in the van back down the pitch looking like he was more interested in abandoning the *referee*. Once again, players scattered. Most just to be on the safe side. He was going a lot more slower though than he had been when driving down from the pavilion where all the players cars were parked. Slower and in much more control of things he headed straight for the referee. At first, the ref didn't look like he was moving but then you could see the change in his face. The fear that come down on him. The part where if you had videoed it you could easily have paused and pinpointed the exact moment where he realised that his original estimation that Sunny wouldn't run him over was possibly going to be out a little.

He turned and ran, Sunny hitting the brakes a touch so that he could adjust the direction he was taking the van in and stay behind the ref. Even for as hungover as I was that morning. It was pretty fucking obvious that all the ref needed to do was make sharp changes in direction and there wouldn't have been a chance for Sunny to keep on his tail. The ref hadn't realised this though and ran in a straight line with an occasional curve to the left or right but nothing close to being able to throw off the Transit. It literally was a schemie version of Benny Hill.

Sunny honking the horn repeatedly while going just slow enough not to run the ref over but fast enough to be constantly right on his arse. Even some of their players - the ones that hadn't come close to losing their lives - were laughing at it.

'SO, MA FUCKIN BEHAVIOUR ISN'T ACCEPTABLE, EH? WELL HOW'S THIS FOR BEHAVIOUR. MIRROR SIGNAL MANOEUVRE, CUNTO'

It was a bit muffled due to most of his window still being up but you could hear Sunny shouting and taunting the ref from inside the van as he chased him.

'YOU ARE THE REF - A SPEEDING AUTOMOBILE HAS ILLEGALLY ENTERED THE FIELD OF PLAY. DO YOU A. ISSUE A RED CARD? B. DO YOU CALL THE FUCKING AA? OR C DO YOU GET YOURSELF TO FUCK BEFORE YOU END UP IN A AND E?'

Sunny sounded like he was having the time of his life, inside there. 'May as well make the most of it now, pal' I thought to myself as I watched the van leaving tyre marks behind it on the mud bath of a pitch. 'You'll not be seeing any fucking more referees for a while.'

The man in black was starting to struggle a bit and you knew that the chase was pretty much over. Either Sunny was going to go all Mortal Kombat and finish the cunt or he was going to show a bit of mercy, with his point well made by then. Obviously. Sunny chose to be merciful. Well, in his own special way, like.

Having had enough of things. He swung the van out to the left of the ref. As if he was just going to drive around. Only, when Sunny got alongside him he drove slowly while he appeared to be saying something to him - why the ref was still running was any cunt's guess. Maybe just a bit freaked out by it all? - Whatever it was it seemed to be one way as it didn't exactly look like the referee was engaging. He looked like he just wanted this nightmare of his to be over.

Sunny duly obliging by surprising all of the onlookers by opening his drivers door at the optimum angle - and height through it being one of those high roofed versions - just perfect enough to wipe the referee out with the door and sending him flying onto the pitch. The mud splashing everywhere upon him hitting the ground. The door quickly closed again and you saw his arm stretching out the window and a big middle finger to the ref produced before he started to speed up again, back towards the direction of the pavilion. More intermittent horn peeping as he went.

Jock, the gaffer, was already over to the ref to launch into the charm offensive in relation to the disciplinary, singular *or* plural, that was no doubt going to be heading our way after the dust had settled. Making sure that he was ok, helping him up, profusely apologising for one of his players' conduct.

'It's really not like the laddie at all. He was saying that he's been having some worries about losing his job recently. Think it's probably the stress of it all getting to him and came out in a different way. He didn't mean nothing by it, the boy. Can't be easy when you've got a family?' Jock appealed. Doing everything but whip out a fucking violin. I mean? I was almost in tears myself and I already knew that it was a lot of fucking fabricated pish.

There was going to be nothing that an apology was going to solve after what had just taken place, though. No sweeping things under the carpet. No putting things down to it being Sunday League and boys will be boys. If the referee wanted to be a cunt - which he was - then chances were he was going to press charges, never mind lodge all the red cards he'd dished out with the association. And Jock Hunter was there trying to avoid losing Sunny from the match the next again Sunday?

'Tell you what, Strings, I think he might get a ten for this' Big Bungalow said as we watched Sunny drive off across the field and into the distance, making his way to getting on to the main road. Right about the same time we started to hear the police sirens coming into earshot.

'What? From the league or in Saughton?'

Both being very real possibilities. All I knew was we weren't going to see the radge in a Muirhouse Violet strip again any time soon.

Chapter 2

Han

'JACKIE, IF YOU DON'T GET YOUR ARSE DOWNSTAIRS NOW. YOU'RE GOING TO BE LATE FOR SCHOOL'

I made one last attempt at what I'd long since accepted to be the virtual impossible. Getting our darling son to listen to a single word that I say. It would be easier to get Sandy Whalley, Joe's mate who's a plumber with Edinburgh City Council and who has a talent for going MIA whenever it comes to doing any actual plumbing, to come around to Martello Court for us and fix our dodgy boiler than it would be to get our Jack to take a telling. *Especially* in the morning.

'COMING MAW'

He shouted back down the stairs to me, Fooling absolutely no one in the process. His chance of breakfast before school now long expired. His father, on the other hand, was already sitting there at the table flicking through The Record while waiting on me putting his breakfast down for him.

A woman's work is never done though, is it? I can only speak for myself, of course, but sometimes it feels like the men in the house think that is just a figure of speech. Just a classic example of some of the stuff that we have to do for everyone else in the house before we can even get ourselves dressed and fed before going out to our *own* jobs. Not that the men and adolescents in the house ever throw a thank you in your direction, of course.

'Oh fuck, this is *not* good.'

I heard from behind the newspaper.

'What's that, hun?' I asked, still with my back to him while juggling between stirring the baked beans and making sure that the toast wasn't burning under the grill.

'Chaos was brought to Muirhouse Park, Edinburgh, yesterday during a Sunday League pub match when a player who had been given a red card moments earlier returned back to the field in a Ford Transit van during a blood thirsty rampage, causing the match to be abandoned. The fixture between Muirhouse Violet and The Pickle and the Barrel, from Leith, descended into mayhem when the player, belonging to the home side, appeared to take his red card badly by getting behind the wheel of his electrical contractor's van and gatecrashing the pitch. Spectators and players alike were seen to flee the scene for their lives. Miraculously, no injuries were reported before the driver sped off. Police arrived on the scene soon after.

While unconfirmed at this point. The Pickle and the Barrel's assistant manager, Dean Brewster, appeared to be left in no doubt exactly who the guilty party was.

'It was that c*** Johnny Grainger. Wasn't happy with trying to break our boy's leg he had to then come back and try and wipe the rest of our team out. We've got a cup game on Wednesday night to be worrying about. I'll be taking this up with the authorities, don't you worry about that. If we don't feel like we're getting some form of protection when we come to places like Muirhouse then there's a problem and one that, obviously, is going to have to be addressed.'

John Hunter, manager of Violet was a lot less forthcoming. Conceding that while it was true that his player had been given a red card and that it 'was' the van that Grainger drove for his employers 'the van was travelling so fast that it was a little difficult to see into it and who was 'actually' driving.' Adding that 'it would be extremely out of character' had it in fact been - who is known to the team as - Sunny.

A police spokesman for Lothian and Borders police issued a statement late last night that read 'A man wanted in connection with the incident has handed himself into Drylaw Mains Police Station and is scheduled to appear in court on Monday.'

'Did I not tell you last night that I had a feeling that Sunny was going to be making himself famous? Fucking tabloids love all of that stuff, don't they?' Joe said, putting down the paper while assessing how close I was with the food.

'Tell you what though, Han. That fucking Brewster from The Pickle and the Barrel's some laugh though, eh? *'If we don't feel like we're getting some form of protection?'* The cunt's from fucking Pilton!' Joe laughed out loud at the cheek of him.

My husband *did* have a point. Securicor needs Securicor when they go into that part of Edinburgh.

'So do you think that was Sunny that handed himself in last night then?' I asked with my back to my husband while I laid his breakfast out on to the plate.

'Naw, I'd have thought that it was just some random who fancied a potential five to ten years on the inside,' his reply. One that left him lucky I didn't leave him wearing his scrambled eggs, bacon and baked beans.

'Sarcastic prick' I smiled at him with a pretend screwed up face as I put his plate down for him and planted a kiss on his head.

'Love you too, *darling*' he said picking up his cutlery while offering an air smooch in my direction.

Husband fed. One more box ticked off for the morning. I was fixing myself something to eat - before going for my shower - when Jack finally appeared. His chance of making school on time, most likely now gone. Not that this was novel by any means. Jack, being a fourteen year old boy, by this point of his life had already began making the mistake of thinking that he was smarter than the adults. Feels that because he can see that he himself has developed from the wee laddie that he once was that he is now operating on the same level as his elders and sadly, for him, he has a lot of years to go before he appreciates that he is going to be one step behind his dad and mum. Whatever he thinks of or makes up, chances are me or Joe will have done or said it.

As such, he didn't know that I could see right through this being late for school caper. Seemed to hold some fantasy filled thought that because he was going to miss the start of school, that will then automatically mean that he cannot now put in an appearance for the rest of the day. Which he does. Apart from the days where he doesn't and we find out about it via a letter or a phone call from Craigroyston High.

When it came to our son, it had been a difficult year and by that I mean he had become a right pain in the fucking arse. He'd started going around with a new group of boys. I was on to a couple of them from day one, so was Joe. You know how it can be though with teenagers. If they get a whiff of you trying to insert some kind of control over them they'll go off in the opposite direction and you'll only have yourself to blame for their rebellion as a result.

In the past couple of months alone we'd had the incident in Home Economics where he'd been accused of putting Hash into the cake mix that his class had been making that afternoon. His actions only becoming known a few hours later once everyone had went home for the day. The only way that we managed to get him off the hook from being both thrown out of school *and* charged by the police was the fact that there had been no 'actual' evidence that our Jack had done it. As far as proof? Well everyone *ate* it.

I was so proud of Joe that day at the school. They were sat there, already having made up their minds that Jack had done it. Joe was like that Rumpole of the Bailey off the telly. Walking around the head teacher's office while he was making Jack's case.

'End of the day, if you've not got any proof that my son did what you say he did and you go ahead and expel him I hope you've got deep pockets for when we meet in court because I'm going to take you to the fucking cleaners. Human rights, aye? Wonder what that court will make out of a community school trying to stop an innocent kid from learning. It's shameful stuff, really. You're preventing the two of us from making a living by dragging us in here and for what? Where's your evidence? If everyone who said they ate a cake from Jack felt spaced afterwards maybe you should be looking in *their* direction? Could be that your school might have a bit of a drug problem in it. Not for me to say, though, eh.'

He said to the head and her assistant. He was a little in danger of going too far and bringing a bit of ham into his performance but other than that he had them stuttering, stammering and back tracking all over the place. By the time we left the office they couldn't have been nicer.

'I thought it would be a laugh' Jack *eventually* admitting to us after an extensive amount of *interrogation* from Joe.

Grounded and X-box taken off him for two weeks as a result of that and made to help out around the house. Made not one bit of difference. He was only back out two days and had put a fitba through old Mr and Mrs Henderson's front room window. One of those big tall ones that can't open. Of course, who had to pay for it? Wasn't Jack, anyway. As is the case with most things. When I look at the things that I *do* see that he's up to it does worry me about the things that I *don't* know about.

'There he is.' Joe said, looking up from his plate and the back page of the paper which had the headline 'Heartbroken' with a picture underneath of players in bright orange - I'm not sure which team - and maroon of Hearts. One of the players in maroon looking like he was furiously protesting something while the other team's players celebrated behind him.

'Morning, dad.' He replied. The body language to him, looking anything *but* someone who was running late.

'Emmm, mum. I think I've left it a wee bit late to make my first period. It's no ma fault though. It took ages for the hot water to come on.'

While Jack may have felt that this was a suitable excuse for being late down the stairs. The fact was that the boiler was not exactly something that could have been classed as *reliable.* This in itself was hardly a concept new to the family. The cheeky little bastard knew that when he'd went to bed the night before in as far as how long the water was going to take to kick in for him the next morning.

'Well you'll just have to get yourself there as fast as you can. Run don't walk. It's your own fault you're late. Not the boiler's or anyone else' I was in no mood for any of his nonsense.

'I cannae though, mum. I've got PE second period this morning. If I run to school I'll be knackered before I've even put my kit on.'

'I swear, Jack, I'm not in the mood for this. I've still got to get myself out the door and have a double shift at the Co-Op today because Elsa's got her sister's funeral and I said I'd cover.' I replied taking a swig of tea and cramming a piece of toast into my mouth quickly before - no doubt - I'd have to say something in response again to my smart arse of a son.

'It's alright, Han.' Joe interrupted.

'Your uncle Benji should already be on his way over to get me now. We'll drop you off on the way.' Joe nodded to me with a subtle as a brick wink that indicated that for at least today. We both knew that he was going to be in school.

'Why do you continue to call him my uncle? Like, even though you know and I know that he's *not* my uncle?' Jack asked while quickly buttering himself a bit of toast, knowing that - whether he liked it or not - he was going to be leaving the house in a matter of minutes.

'Just one of those things, son. You say it enough times you can't stop yourself after that. Take Easter Road for example. Just say one day they change its name to, I don't know, The Burger King Arena. What are you going to call it from then on? Certainly isn't going to be the fucking Burger King Arena, anyway.'

Jack seemed to ponder over such a possibility as he ate his piece of toast.

'Be well barry if we could get a Burger King at half time though, like' He eventually replied, missing his dad's point completely.

It was when I had just left the living room to go upstairs and get changed that Benji knocked on the door. I stopped to let him in.

'Is Strings ready, Han?' He asked looking a whole lot more awake and alive than I could have said for my husband through in the other room.

'Aye, Benji. He's just finishing up his breakfast, go through.' I answered pointing him in a direction that he - out of any of Joe's friends - did not need any assistance with.

Before I went upstairs I stopped and had a few words with him. Asking where him and Joe were working as they tended to work all over the country at times and weren't back until all hours.

'Saltcoats, not exactly next door but we've been a lot further too as well, though.' 'Did Strings tell you about what happened with Sunny yesterday?' He asked while still moving in the direction of the door.

'I was already in bed last night by the time Joe got home so I've only just found out there because it's in The Daily Record.' I answered. Meeting his moving towards the door attitude towards the conversation by taking my first few steps up the stairs.

'The fucking *Record?*' This piece of news seemed to do the job of stopping him in his tracks.

'Go through and you'll see for yourself. I need to get myself ready for my shift. I'm standing there lecturing wee Jack about being late and I'm going to be late myself. You take good care anyway, Benj, and have a safe trip to Saltcoats and back again. Oh and and keep that man of mines out of trouble.' I said as I continued up the stairs.

'Aye, you too, hen' I heard him replying back.

Chapter 3

Jack

'Told you he would fucking shite out.' Dynamo stood there at the back of the science lab at dinner time when the four of us were getting a quick fag in before all heading off in our separate ways for the afternoon. I didn't exactly care for the way that he was smugly referring to me - almost looking down at - while he stood lapping up the other two's reaction.

- Dynamo, named as such after an unfortunate incident when he was still at primary school when he set fire to his kitchen trying to cook mini kievs when his mum and dad were out. -

It was obvious what he was doing. I'm sure that - if he'd had the time - I would've been treated to his impression of what a chicken sounds like. Pathetic stuff from a so called 'mate.' If you think that someone resorting to the most basic forms of peer pressure like that to get me to do something - that up to that point - I hadn't actually wanted to do would work then you'd be absolutely correcto, amundo.

'I never fucking said I wasn't *going* to do it.' I responded, feeling a wee bit wounded by being made the figure of everyone's amusement.

'Aye, but you never fucking said you would either, Jackie boy, and the look that you've got on your puss right now isn't exactly the look of someone who's *that* full of enthusiasm. Obviously I made some kind of a miscalculation and thought that you were a lot more cooler than you actually are. Easy mistake to make, I suppose.'

Every word that came out of his mouth he knew what he was doing with them. I fucking hated Dynamo when he was like that. He was a couple of years older than the rest of our group and even if he wasn't, he was the hardest. That, obviously, had him as our self elected leader and fine well he fucking knew it too. It was almost a form of bullying. You think that it's as basic as you would get bullied by your enemies but sometimes it can be your mates, too.

'What look?' I tried to protest but even I knew that I wasn't the best at hiding what was on my mind. 'Never play poker, son.' My dad once told me when I'd been caught out stealing all of that OAP's strawberries and pea-pods out of his greenhouse that time. There was also the case of - forgetting my lack of poker face game for a second - I genuinely didn't *want* to do it. What Dynamo was suggesting.

Knew it was a case of going too far. You grow up fast in Muirhoose and end up wiser beyond your years that would show up on your birth certificate. Even at fourteen and in third year I knew the difference between a couple of weeks without an X-Box and seeing my mates and something a *lot* more serious, if caught.

'The same fucking look you had on you that Friday night when Scooter told you that that Meghan Pratt was sitting around the park benches with a bottle of Merrydown and had said that she was going to let you finger her if you went over to meet her.' Dynamo pissed himself laughing as he looked like he was replaying the whole incident over again in his head.

'Mon, Jackie, it'll be a laugh, like, probably, eh?' Scooter tried to convince me. He meant well. Trying to be some kind of gateway between myself and Dynamo to reach some satisfactory conclusion.

'You won't be saying that if we get caught, though' I replied straight back to Scooter. Choosing to let Dynamo's latest dig fly over me without the need to reply.

'Who's getting caught like?' Dynamo butted in. It'll go smoother than the hairs on your chinny chin chin, Jackie.

More laughter.

If this is what it's like to have mates fuck knows what having enemies must be like. A rare occurrence, I'll admit but stood there with the other three of them laughing - well, I say *three* but Flav had been glued to his phone most of dinner time - I was actually looking forward to the break ending and getting away from them all and back to class.

'Well, you know what the score is. If you're there, you're there.' Dynamo sneered again. 'If you're not, then we'll *all* know what a fucking wee shitebag you are.'

'I'll be there,' I said back without even looking at him. Choosing to look out over the school playing fields and fixing my gaze on two pupils who were too far away to make out exactly who they were but with the way that their bodies seemed to be joined from the waist up, you could tell that they were getting fired into each other.

The bell going straight after I answered Dynamo. I was glad it did.

Chapter 4

Strings

'Get one for yourself too, darling, no point making one up for me and him and you not having one, is there, eh? Only if you want one though, like. Share the wealth when it's there because you don't ever know how long it's there for.' Benji said to the old wifie behind the counter. Well, counters, plural.

It was the same old dear who was sat behind the change counter as it was the one who had to go and make your cup of tea and bacon rolls up inside the quaint 'Caledonian Amusements' arcade.

It reminded me of a different time where Scots didn't fly abroad for their holidays and, instead, stayed in their own country. Swapping a week in Benidorm for a week in Burntisland, and so on. Seems fucking mental if you ask me. To stay in a cold coastal town mere hours away from your own house when you could be lapping up the sun's rays by the pool sinking a cold pint of San Miguel. It was what it was at the time though, I suppose.

Apart from the fact that some of the fruit machines and video games had obviously been upgraded. The decor looked like it must've been last renovated back in the sixties. Judging by the age of the old woman she'd probably had one of the paint rollers in her hand, herself.

Apart from myself and Benjamin. There was only around another half dozen punters inside there. A dad and his son who were over playing air hockey where, from some of the reactions that I was seeing from the table, the father looked like he was getting a wee bit more into it than he should've been. More than the son was, anyway, going by the body language of him. Proper competitive dad stuff. I seen him score a goal and celebrate like fucking Bjorn Borg bagging a championship point at Wimbledon. Talk about a red neck, like. Everyone else in there were just lone wolfs. Sat staring hypnotically at their own puggy.

Sinking coin after coin in, robotically, without getting much in the way back of a return.

There wasn't enough inside the place for my liking but crowd control was always something that in my line of work was *out* of my control. Aye, the busier the better. The more bodies to fill the place. The more noise colour and distraction - the alarms bells and sirens and flashing lights - the more of that stuff, the better.

Aye, like I said. The place was quaint and with a staff count of one, who looked like she could've starred in The fucking Golden Girls. The intel that I'd been given was bang on.

'Oh thank you very much, nobody offers me a cup when they're buying one. I could murder one.' She smiled back at Benji. Genuinely appearing to be flattered. Visibly appreciative that he had thought to include her in our order.

'Well no need for any murders, darling. Let's keep you out of Polmont, eh?' Benji joked. She, obviously, didn't know this but all she was seeing was Benji now in full character. Aye, he's a sound boy and always has been but when him and I are 'working' we've both got our roles to play - our business heads, like - and, to be fair to the cunt, he plays his to a fucking tee.

All these old wifies who are working in these type of places are generally bored out of their tits. No one speaks to them apart from the bare minimum - and with most losing, aren't in the best of moods - so to find someone being nice and having a chat works fucking wonders when it comes to walking into a place of business and buttering up the staff before you then proceed to rob the place blind.

'Now we're fixed for a cup of tea and a bacon roll. When you're back in your box again I'll get twenty's worth of pound coins from you please, don't rush yourself though' I said to her before I took my first bite out of the roll.

'Coming up in a jiffy, doll' She replied, moving from the counter and back into her secure little box that she sat in holding all of the money.

'Teddy bears, the both of you, aye?' She said as she gathered the pound coins. Looking at both of our apparel that we had on. Myself with an old Diadora Glasgow Rangers NTL sponsored training top.

While Benj was unleashing his inner staunchness with a - more updated - two piece Umbro shell suit in red white and blue panels.

'Aye, more of a die hard than Bruce Willis. Never miss a game.' I replied, feeling a little bit of my soul saying farewell from me as the words came out. 'I'm not as bad as this one here.' I said turning around to Benji. 'Missed his own father's funeral because it clashed with an away game in Bucharest in the Champions League.'

Benji stood there holding his hands up in a 'busted' gesture.

'Hey, it's what he would've wanted. My dad would've been with me over there in Romania as well had he not already passed away himself,' He laughed while coming across as scary convincing considering he'd had no fucking idea whatsoever that I was about to have him ad libbing on a story that, technically, never happened.

'Oooohhh that's terrible, son, you'll go to hell you know.' She laughed back before going on to tell us about how 'her Jim' had been going since the late Forties.

'Oh well, time to go and make some money' I said to her as I scooped up the coins while handing her the Twenty spot in return.

'You'll be lucky, son.' She said without any hint of humour to it.

'HEY! We've got all the luck in the world. We are the people, after all.' Benji jumped in, laughing while tapping the side of his nose. Going by the confused and non committal look on her face. It didn't look like she was too familiar with the phrase.

While we had been sorting out some scran for ourselves and having the brief chat with the old dear. I'd been constantly scoping out the room. What was my best option. What puggies were the most popular with the punters - and by definition - the ones that likely had more funds sitting *in* them.

This was my art and the arena where I performed my theatre, as such. It did not matter one single flying fuck whether I had visited an establishment before or not. Pub, Amusement arcade or fun fair. Was like the fucking terminator with extra assisted vision when I looked at a puggy. It was as if I knew them, personally. Knew their deepest darkest secrets and what was sitting inside their souls. All I was interested in though, of course, was if they had a suitable amount of money sitting inside them. Which I generally tended to do. Fuck, I swear at times I could be drawn to a certain machine as if I could *smell* the money inside them.

As we had been engaging with the woman who worked there. I had become fixed on one guy in particular. Playing a fruit machine called 'Fantasy Island.' The display and theme on the front looking pretty close to the inside of that car dealership cunt's office in Scarface. Palm trees, sunsets, that kind of stuff. I'd played it before on one of my other 'working trips.' Match up three coconuts, surfboards, ice creams. That kind of deal. The only drawback to it was that when you actually *did* hit the jackpot it played that fucking old eighties tune 'Fantasy Island' at an outrageous level of noise. Proper every cunt stand back and take a look at the person who has just emptied out a puggy material. Fucking surprised balloons didn't fall from the roof to go along with the fanfare, that first time I'd taken its jackpot.

Not an ideal machine to be using when you're trying to keep your wins on the down low. Vegas, where you win a million on a slot machine and the casino management bring out a bottle of congratulatory Cristal to you and a blow job from any of the dancers you choose, this was not.

Just as we'd been leaving the woman to pick a weapon of choice. Through the boy's body language, I could see that he was moments away from jacking the machine in. I'd seen enough people putting their last pound coin into a puggy than I've had rides in my life, and the body language that they display while doing it. They're clearly already beaten by that point, anyway. They know themselves that even if luck shines their way with that one last spin, they're only going to put it all back in again anyway. Way too late for them to go back now. Not when you started with a couple of hundred pounds and are now down to just one, it isn't.

I've seen those types over the years to the point that I almost feel like I know what it's like to go through that pain. I haven't though. My dad taught me otherwise. Showed me a *different* way to success from those things. Fruit machines? My old man Frankie used to call them banks, for fuck's sake. Thing is, he wasn't wrong, there.

'Hang back a second, Benji, and take a few more bites out of your roll. That cunt over there looks like he's about to go in a minute and he's got 'sat there and pished away all of his wages all morning on it' written all over his face.'

'We've found our puggy'

This, being all routine to him, he just shrugged his shoulders as if to say ok and done as told. Getting torn into his bacon roll.

Once I saw the coat going on we were on the move over to take up the hot seat. Benji grabbing one of the other seats that were sat in front of a vacant machine. Strategically positioning himself between me and the woman at the change counter to semi obscure her view.

Of course, the place had cameras inside it. Most did, especially then. I was also a professional, though. Operating at the highest level in my chosen field. It would've taken more than someone watching my every step to stop me from getting paid.

'So what's the strategy today then? What you going with?' Benji asked eagerly.

'Wellllll, Benjamin. If you look to the side of this machine where the company logo is stamped in the top corner.' I pointed in the general direction of where he needed to be looking at.

'Ok, see it.' I replied.

'Aye and what does it say?' I said, coming across as condescending while meaning in no way to actually do so.

'Emmm AMPRO Electrical Company,' He said back. Looking unsure of himself over why this company might have been ringing a bell to him, which it should've done by then, if he'd paid any fucking attention to my tutorials, that was.

'And what are the rules when it comes to *any* games machines that are made by our friends at AMPRO Electricals? This time, the condescending tone most definitely intended due to my frustration that he clearly didn't know what the fucking answer was and that after all this time as my assistant. He appeared not to have learned a single thing about the game that we were in.

After getting a blank look back from him and then looking discreetly around to ensure no one was within ear shot of me.

'These versions accept shaved coins.' I winked back at him. The concept of shaved coins now being something that he was familiar with. The concept itself having helped fill his pockets for longer than he could've probably remembered.

Now for the uninformed who are not familiar with the concept of coin shaving.

Coin shaving is the art of relieving a fruit machine of its internal funds without the participant *ever* being relieved of their own. This involves the careful practice of shaving 0.040" off the diameter of a coin. The reason for this is that puggy machines contain a series of sensors built inside of them where the coins pass through. Almost like a fruit machine form of passport control, if you will.

The coins must first pass through these sensors to register a credit for having a spin on the machine itself. But here is the rub. The *altered* coin passes through the first sensor like a knife through fucking butter. The only thing is though that the second sensor must be a wee bit more screwed on than the first one because *that one* picks up the fact that there's something not quite on the level with the coin and it's *that* sensor which rejects the money and throws it back out of the bottom of the machine at you again.

The beautiful part though being. Once the coin is through the first sensor, the credit to play has already been registered to the machine. Spitting the coin back out does not change that. The even more beautiful part of it is that because of it being such a minute alteration to the coin, itself. You would not even be able to *see* the cut to it unless you had a microscope so it, of course, made it a lot more difficult for someone to stand there and accuse you of ripping off a puggy when they don't have any cast iron proof. That along with 'stringing' a puggy - stringing I'll come to later - is, if you're good at it, can provide a welcome and steady stream of income. It is also - if you are ever caught in the act - a fast tracked way to getting yourself on the wrong side of the underworld.

I learned from the very best, though. Joseph Strings Carson is a professional. He doesn't *get* caught.

Now that day in Saltcoats I was lucky enough to be presented with an AMPRO Electricals machine to play with but on any other day I might well not have and that is where the 'art of the string' comes into play. Once again. For the uninitiated.

The process of 'stringing' fruit machines is much like the one of using a shaved coin. The main aim being to fraudulently take as much money you can out of one *without* actually putting any money *into* one. It is also a lot like the shaved coin route in that - if caught - it is going to be an expedited way to Accident & Emergency. Stringing, however, requires the skill of a top level illusionist where someone will sit there at the puggy creating the facade that they are sat there pumping money into the machine when, in fact, they are doing nothing of the sort. Sat there and armed with, well, whatever discreet implement of their choosing that is the correct shape and size enough to slide into a coin slot and just far enough in there to fool the all important first sensor before being yanked back OUT again with the 'credit' now having registered on the machine.

When my dad first took me out stringing. It was pretty much just that, stringing. The shaved coins came after that. To begin with though. Stringing was the bread and the butter. I was in awe of the way that he did it. Made me think of the magician that was at a birthday party I'd been at a couple of years before. The cunt that made the fifty pence piece appear from out of my ear and then wouldn't fucking give it to me when I made the case that if it had come from me then technically it was my sheriff's badge, not his. Cunt just ruffled my head and told me that I was a character. Might try that approach robbing a bank or something. Just ruffle the teller's head when I'm walking out with the bag of money.

My dad was a wizard though. He'd told me that my job was to be as a look out. Keep an eye around the room just in case anyone was looking in his direction but it was always hard to do that when he was displaying his craft right there in front of me. Had you not known that he had a coin with a wee hole bored into it, enough for a wee piece of fishing gut to be hooked through, and was consistently sinking it in and out the coin slot. You'd definitely have taken him as just another punter, like the rest of them.

Aye he was the teacher and I the pupil. Didn't mean to say that I didn't add to the operation despite my 'inexperience.' Take that time, for instance, where we'd driven three and a bit hours - one way - to The

Highlands because he had heard about a vulnerable wee arcade in the middle of nowhere but somewhere that loads of tourists would stop off - on their way from Loch Lomond up to the Isle of Skye - for a cup of tea and restroom breaks. This puggy was - according to my dad - a complete gold mine. Every cunt passing would have a crack at it but never stop and invest enough time to get anything back out of it. Those fucking Shermans thinking that they're in Vegas and that they can win a million dollars through one pull of a bandit types. Fucking maniacs.

Anyway, we travelled all that fucking way only for the coin to snag inside the first sensor. My dad never admitted it, like, but I felt that he'd put the coin in a wee bit further than he should've done, something had registered inside the machine as a result and the first slot had said 'you're claimed ya fucking radge.' Of course, dad then tried to pull it back out and it wouldn't come. It belonged to the puggy from there. Then the struggle ensued with him completely wasting his time by getting progressively more bammed up at the machine until the gut snapped completely and we both heard the natural sound of coin tumbling into machine.

Over three hours drive for the ball to be burst before he'd had a fucking chance to neither hold and or nudge. Waste of fucking time. Wasn't the easiest of car journeys home, especially considering the amount of petrol we'd had in the car driving there had been based on the amount of money my dad was going to have for us driving *back again*. Got home on fumes in the end.

During the journey home though, which when wasn't filled with Tourettes levels of swearing was complete silence. I decided to speak up and offer a solution to what had just happened, and something that would prevent another scenario where we waste a whole fucking day, without making actually a penny.

'I think I've got an idea, dad.' I said, courageously, not knowing what his reaction was going to be. Sometimes when he was in a zone like that he was best left alone. I decided to take a chance.

'Oh aye, and what would that be?' He said, not taking his eyes off the road ahead and the Eddie Stobart lorry that he had already been flashing his lights at and giving him some grief that the driver was never going to hear anyway.

'Well, see what just happened today, I think I know a way that could, like, avoid that from happening again in the future.' I said it, hesitantly, though. You know when you decide to come out with an idea and you're not sure if you're going to get the piss ripped out of you because it's a stupid one? Only, the mood that dad was in. There was always the danger that instead of derision you'd get a slap for wasting his time and be told not to be so fucking stupid.

'How about, instead of going back and getting another hole put into another coin. You get a *pretend* coin of the exact same dimensions but made of plastic and the 'string' that it's attached to is made of the *same* material. I saw Uncle Stewart fixing the bumper on his car and there was a wee hole in it and he popped this round plug into it which also had a wee bit attached to it that you pulled on. Surely some plastic works would be able to make something like that up. You could say that you needed it for a car or something.' Everything I was saying was part guesswork part entrepreneur. I had no idea what the car part was that Uncle Stewart had been mucking about with that day. Didn't even fucking know what a "plastic works" was *or* if it even existed but it sounded good in my head.

'A fucking car part? Is that your grand idea? For fuck's sake, Jack. Have you actually been *watching* me since I've been taking you out showing you the ropes? I'm trying to sit there like David fucking Copperfield pulling off magic in attempts at fooling the general public over the criminal act that I'm pulling off in plain sight and you're saying I should be strutting in there swinging parts for cars about? Hardly incog - fucking - nito, son, eh?'

I was put in my place, squarely. Still, didn't fucking mean that around a few weeks later when we were out on a 'field trip' for him to discreetly produce - not a coin fixed to gut but - a bespoke made piece of apparatus that resembled *exactly* as I'd suggested coming down the road from The Highlands. I knew better than to come out with any 'I told you so's' to him. Wouldn't have got me very fucking far had I been looking for any medals, anyway. Just knowing that he had thought my idea as one worth looking into had been enough validation for me and showed that I was actually contributing to this father and son operation that we had going on together.

So happy he was with the new device that he ditched the coin on the gut method, completely. Having me one made up, just like his. When he passed though and mum gave me his original one. I made the switch to using his. I know something with a sentimental value like that is generally the kind of thing that you put under lock and key so that it doesn't get lost or anything but every single time I would use it - following his passing - each and every coin that would drop out of it. I would think of him looking down on me smiling and telling me to give them hell.

That said. I would much rather *not* have to be even using said invention (Copyright pending) when it comes to clearing out an amusement arcade. So aye, to see that Fantasy Island machine being the accommodating kind that took a shaved coin. I was able to keep my dad's stringer in my pocket and get myself to work.

I had my wee rules that I would follow to the letter of the law every time I went out to work. Without fail.

A.   **Never string alone**. I mean, due to the ban it wasn't even like I could fucking drive myself to work anyway but that's not the point. Benji was required for more than just chauffeuring me from A to B. My oldest and dearest friend was as needed for his eyes and ears inside the arcades and pubs as he was for driving me to my destination and back again.

B.   **Be friendly with the staff but not 'over' friendly.** Without exception. All of my work is carried out outside my own immediate area. This is used to an advantage while engaging in general friendly chit chat while obtaining the change from the obligatory twenty that - on the whole - is never going to see the inside of the machine.

C.   **Do not draw attention to yourself when inside there.** While Fruit machines can be wonderful things and lavish you with coin after coin if you know what you're doing. They are also noisy attention grabbers. Most of this you cannot do anything about however it *is* possible to limit this through small tricks of the trade. Nothing gets people's attention more inside an amusement arcade than the sound of coins hitting the plastic tray when someone is receiving a payout. The sound of victory will draw the attention. Mostly through jealousy. A carefully placed scarf, for instance, inside the tray ready to catch the coins and suppress the noise of the coins, however, is but one trick that can be employed to help blend into the surroundings.

D.   **Unleash your inner thespian.** Aye, you have been taking the puggies to the cleaners but no one has to know that, do they? Despite the fact that you have already pocketed a few hundred pounds out of the machines since the moment you walked in. Take the occasional walk back up to the exchange desk to swap another Twenty while cursing the luck that you're having.

E. **Know when to say when.** Don't get greedy and push your luck. Know when to recognise that you've had a good day. One that had you been in a day job you'd have had to work a full twenty four hour shift to be reimbursed to the same amount. Know that this specific machine you're playing is *not* the only puggy in the world and that when you choose to go to work again there will be others waiting on you.

F. **Be prepared to leave in a hurry.** And this is where I go back to point A. If you string alone you are not seeing what's going on behind and around you. You are not able to spot the danger until it's too late to do anything about it. No matter how 'lucky' a streak you're on or how the machine you've been working away at is now ready to pay out. The moment that there is *any* sign of danger. Staff appearing to be looking in your direction while talking about you or pretending that they're out cleaning the place while they try and grab a sly look at what you're doing. Or the even more extreme moments where you know that you're going to need to cut and run. When the owner of the joint appears. These, generally tending not to be the cuddly types.

They were rules that had kept me out of jail - as well as hospital - since becoming a stringer so why fuck with the classics, eh?

I turned around just to have a quick look at the old wifie who was engrossed in her copy of TV Quik or whatever the fuck it was. With that I got Benji to position himself where he was obscuring the camera and I swiftly shoved my sweater inside the plastic tray of the puggy - so as to minimise that beautiful sound of my winnings that were inevitably going to be falling in due course - and got on with things.

I mentioned acting abilities? For effect, and I mean every single time. I will take some of those coins freshly exchanged and shove them into the machine. If you win you win, fair enough. Puggies being puggies though, you generally lose. *Then* it's time to introduce the shaved coins into the mix. I normally have around half a dozen of them on me. Once again so as not to draw any suspicion over the highly dubious act of someone putting a coin into a machine and repeatedly reaching down to pick it out of the slot, while weirdly still managing to play the machine. Half a dozen gives you the continuity that a con man like myself so sorely needs in such a - at times - closed and confined environment.

In the scheme of things. Losing two or three pounds of your own money while getting hundreds back is a small price to pay.

I lost my own nuggets within a couple of minutes. Not even coming close to anything. It only took three out of the six shaved coins though to get me a bite. Sometimes that's all you need. A wee nudge - pun intended - in the right direction and then your day all goes the way of a stack of dominoes.

By the end of the machine's spin I was left with a beach ball on two out of the three rows and a sun on the other. The screen lighting up indicating that I had a nudge opportunity. Leaving me with the simple job of nudging on that right hand row on one to bring the third beach ball down and into the line with the other two. Aye, it was only for a Fiver but as my dad used to say - every single trip without fail - 'better in my pocket than it is in theirs.'

My luck turned after that and there was no looking back. Well, I'm not really sure if you've got the right to talk about *luck* when it comes to gambling if you're not actually risking any of your own wedge but you know what I mean?

Best part of an hour later and I'd emptied around two hundred from it before moving on to a different machine. In between time I'd kept up my standard charade by occasionally going up for more change to give off the appearance that I was anything but a winner.

'Ch ch ch changes. Time to change ma score ch ch change i i it'

I sang to the old dear as I thrust the twenty through the small opening at the bottom of the perspex front towards her.

'You know? I don't normally see people so cheery in here when they're losing. Winning, aye? Not when they're losing, though.'

She said as she took the note from me and pushed two rows of ten coins back to me.

'Ach, money comes and money goes, doesn't it? And besides. The law of averages says that my luck's going to turn soon and I'll get back all of what I've put in since I've been in here' I shrugged my shoulders in response.

'Ohhhhh, son.' She said shaking her head at me, almost in a kind of pity. 'Have you *any* idea how many times I've heard that same sad song? There's no such thing as luck in here. Well, not for the punters, anyway.'

Bless her, she was actually trying to be helpful and in a way that had her boss been given access to what was being said. I can't imagine that they'd have been too chuffed about her (too) honest assessment over how things worked in the amusement arcade business.

'Nah, that machine must be ready to pay out. There was a boy on it before me and I've sat at it for a while myself. Only a matter of time, like.' I said, safe in the knowledge that I had already pocketed enough to feed the whole family for the next couple of weeks.

'Listen, son.' She kind of looked to both sides before cautiously leaning in towards the perspex before she next spoke. 'I'm not meant to tell anyone this but the bandits don't work like that. You think you're the first person to come up with the idea of playing a single machine long enough to ensure that it pays out for them? And you think the crafty bastards who make the machines don't *know* that people are going to think that way too, either?'

Every thing that she'd said was absolutely true. None of it was news to me but for the purposes of continuing on with my act of the clueless cunt who popped into an amusement arcade only to - on appearances - lose all of his money. I continued on.

'Aye but, those machines have got a percentage rate of paying out, have they not? Otherwise why would anyone stick their money into them?' It was a valid enough question, I felt, for someone who looked like they knew something about an area that they, in fact, knew fuck all about.

Of course, I already knew the answer before I asked the question.

'Aye that's true, son, but they work on a longer term percentage pay out rate. Trust me, they'll make you wait all day if that's what they've decided. Listen, I'm only telling you this because you and your pal seem decent boys. I wouldn't want you to go back to Edinburgh with nothing in your pocket for one of your 'salt and sauce' suppers.' She cackled at the regional reference that is add odds with the West Coasters.

'Okay, mum, I promise that if I don't get a payout in the next ten, make it fifteen, actually, minutes I'll move on to another machine.' I joked with her while already having decided that I was going to push Fantasy Island as far as I could *before* moving to another puggy - and in the process - slotting smoothly into what I'd just stood there and said to her.

All about appearances in those places. Look and or act dodgy and you shall be looked upon as such and there will be an eye on you from minute one until minute none.

I'd been impressed by the wifie's product knowledge, as such, because what she'd told me was gospel. My dad had explained to me at an early age that while all puggies had an official percentage pay out rate - legally they had to - it was based across a long term amount of time and absolutely in no fucking way pre wired that the daft cunts who play them think that they are. IE. *If I play this one machine for a straight hour I will stumbled upon the thirteen percent chance that lies of winning the jackpot.*

And even then, cunt's probably don't even know that it *is* thirteen percent. Which, with most machines, is the *exact* chance that the machine is giving them.

I mean, it's not like I had ever been known as a mathematical genius, fractions and equations and all of that stuff, but even I could see that when my dad was telling me that a puggy has odds stacked in their favour, to that level, that there's something not quite right … with the heads of those that play them.

'So why would someone play a machine that over three quarters of the time it's going to just take your money?' 'You wouldn't put money on a horse that was seventy five to one.'

I admit, the second part was not something that I was categorically sure was a direct comparison to the odds of a puggy paying out but *did* sound good.

'Well the daft bastards dinnae fucking know that the odds are that or they wouldn't play them, would they? They're drawn in by the flashing lights, the sounds, the prospect that maybe it's going to be their day and at the end of the day, son, never discount how stupid people can be when greed gets the better of them. All I *do* know though is that the more those doss cunts put their money into the machines the more there's going to be for us.'

Aye, he said 'us' but it was hardly like we were fucking splitting the pot back then. I was more on the equivalent of YTS wages.

'It's not about the money for you, Joe' He told me in those early days.

'This is your university and I am your fucking tutor' He said looking around the arcade in Kilmarnock that day with arms outstretched like I was in Willie Wonka's factory and I'd just been handed the deeds to it. Didn't agree with him at the time but - as he generally was - the old man was right. The knowledge that I picked up which left me with the skills that I ended up with. *All* down to him.

Just doesn't feel as fair though when you're being chucked thirty quid a week while you watch him take out hundreds over the course of it while safe in the knowledge that despite the imbalance in 'wage structure' it wasn't going to make a difference when it came to receiving broken limbs from a West Coast gangster.

Fucking knew his stuff though and as far as homework goes he left all of those fucking nerdy cunts at school trailing in his wake. Like the whole spin of a puggy the second that you've pressed the button? Nothing more than a fucking show designed only to build your suspense while you wait to see if you've won or lost. Told me that inside a puggy is something called an RNG which is short for *random number generator* and that is like the fucking god of the puggy because it's *that* which is deciding what is going to show up on your screen. It's the RNG that is the cunt that's taking your money, not the machine itself.

Of course though, showing *any* knowledge of that sort while inside an arcade would be - to anyone with a brain - an instant red flag and would not lead to a profitable visit to that specific joint. Playing dumb is the only way to string. It's not enough just to be able to string at a decent level. There's more to the game than that and having been taught by the best. I - without any hint of cockiness or arrogance -

considered *myself* to be the best, having taken over the throne from the king himself when he passed.

'Okay, I don't want to see you back up here for more change again, now.' She said tapping her nose and speaking in a pretend nagging voice as I made to go back to rejoin Benji at the puggy.

'I'll try to try' I said laughing as I turned and made my way across the carpet to take my seat and finish off what I'd started with my golden goose of a fruit machine.

Once I'd decided that I had taken it as far as I could. I felt that before we re adjusted ourselves and found a new target it would be a good idea to stop for a wee bite and had the old wifie knock up a couple of cheese and ham toasties for us before going back to rinse her place of business, once more.

You know the one thing that I haven't and am *never* going to fucking get used to, Strings? Benji asked before sinking his teeth into his toastie.

Already having a huge piece in my own mouth I wasn't even given a chance to answer before he continued.

'This wearing the currant buns gear, caper.' He pulled on his shell suit top for emphasis to ram home his point. 'It's not right, mate. Feel fucking dirty every time I put it on to go out with you.'

All the potential dangers and pitfalls of coming out stringing with me and the part that he's fucking worried about the *most* is having to wear apparel that is linked to Glasgow Rangers Football Club.

'Aye, but I fucking explained to you *why* we're wearing it. Not like we're fucking parading about Muirhouse in it. Going into The Gunner and sitting in the pub for a few scoops like Barry Ferguson and Gazza after a game, like.' I said, a wee bit put out that this was even a topic of discussion. It was all part of the game and was another one of those rules that were designed to keep me as far away from Saughton, Barlinnie or any hospital in the immediate area of West Coast Scotland.

'Look, Benji. We've been through this before, you fucking know the rules.' I enforced upon the cunt.

'Aye, I know but ..'

I wasn't for letting him get past that last word before jumping in again.

'No fucking buts here to be found, Benji Boy. You know that we're professionals here. More professional than Bodie and fucking Doyle, us.'

A smile crept onto his face as he then started to hum the theme tune to The Professionals.

'No shut it for a second, name that fucking tune, and listen to me. We're professionals and professionalism is what professionalism does. Now your role in our wee organisation is 'key' to keeping us from being pinched. To date you have done it to a - fucking - plomb. *That*, however, is only but part of what I regard as our 'security.' This Rangers gear that we're decked out in? When I was a bairn and was worried about something. Know what my nana always used to say to me? That I was frightened for the day that I'd never see. And you know what? She was maybe right, there.'

I could see by the glaiket look on his face that he had absolutely no fucking clue as to what I was talking about.

'So my thoughts on that are that if I *am* frightened for a day that I'll never see. I may as well be fucking *prepared* for it as well. There's not an amusement arcade in the country that doesn't have cameras installed these days. You not think that when the cunts that own these places go to empty out their machines and finding a few of them seriously lacking in funds that they're not going to ask questions about it? First of all, suspecting the poor cunt that is working in there all day for a pittance before then moving on to examining the cameras from that same day. It's what *I'd* be fucking doing if I'd been robbed, anyway. So when they *do* look at the cameras, what are they going to be seeing?'

'Couple of cunts in Rangers gear stood around the machines that have been taken to the cleaners,' he replied, back on track.

'EXACTLY. By jove he's got it.' I laughed back at him.

'So lets just say that suspicion was ever to fall on you and I from either the hornies or some of the types that we're robbing from - and that's a big fucking if considering we're going to work on the other side of the country where no one knows us - before returning back to the East victorious with full pockets. Well all we start doing is digging out our season tickets for Easter Road, don't we? Fuck's sake. I've got a charge on my record from the Blackley's Baby Crew days. Fucking police would take one look at my record and *know* I wasn't a bluenose. And anyway? The police get a crime reported to them and are told that the culprits were wearing Rangers clobber? The fucking filth would just stand there and laugh considering half the cunts kicking around through in the West own, and undoubtedly wear, similar gear. Where the fuck would they even start looking? Not a couple of cunts from Edinburgh and if they did they'd get laughed out our houses with our Hibs season tickets rammed down their throats.'

'Hey, you think I enjoy wearing it either, by the way?' I said to him after a pause to finish the last piece of the toastie.

'Aye, ok. Point taken. Anyway, lets take another one of these wee bastards to the cleaners before we head back, eh.' He replied nodding his head in the direction of the selection of machines that were all sitting available.

'Sooner we do that the sooner we can get back to the car and out of this fucking shell suit,' he joked as he polished off the last crumbs of his snack.

To the cleaners we indeed took said puggy. Ended up playing one that had a space theme to it. Rockets and planets all over the front of it and a massive NASA symbol employed as part of the design that I'd have been astonished if the space agency had been paid any royalties over.

Now this one, though, did *not* provide the previous fortune that Fantasy Island had brought in terms of accepting the shaved coins. Just spat the things back out as if I'd tried to shove a Two Pence piece into it. This, obviously, meant that I was going to put the 'Strings' into Strings. I was comfortable about it. The position of the machine was more suitable when it came to the CCTV cameras, especially with my 'buffer' beside me.

Aye it was a hassle to go down the more riskier route of using my stringer to wrack up the credits but well, perils of the job and all that, eh? What I'd been put out in having to use my 'device' I was paid back in rewards in pay outs, though. Not sure if someone had pished away their hard earned hours before we'd got there or if they just hadn't emptied it the night before but I ended up losing count of what it had spat out and then discreetly filtered into the pockets of Benji's white shell suit bottoms. It wasn't until I got home and counted it all out that it came to near on Five Hundred.

Thing is. When you're on a streak, the tendency is to push things as far as possible, and I would have. The pair of them walking in and beside us *right* when I had taken the Twenty Pound jackpot to the sound of the 2001 Space Odyssey soundtrack. That altered things, though.

'Winner winner fish supper' One of them stopped and said to us making me turn round to see who had spoken.

I was instantly looking at, what could best be described as a pair of human bulldogs. You could fucking smell the danger from them never mind what their general appearance was doing for the impression that they would give someone.

'Bout fucking time, pal. Kind of feeling like I should've just come in here today and handed the owners the keys to my house and be done with it,' I said, self depreciatingly. Very much still in my act. A man who wouldn't ever come out of character until he was in the car and on his way back to the capital city.

'Aye well, maybe your luck's being saved up for Wednesday night in the cup replay against Motherwell for the boys, pal.' He said, with what looked like a sincere smile on his face.

'You a bear, yourself?' I asked with the air and confidence of - apparently - being one too.

'Aye, we both are.' The other one out of the two broke his silence.

The pair of them actually dressed peculiarly similar. Bad leather jackets with woollen sweaters underneath. More sovereign between them than Buckingham Palace. Both in Air Max and matching Nike tracky bottoms. The boy, telling us that they were both fans, standing there with both hands down the front of his trackies. A comfort thing? Itchy baws? Danger wank, even. Not sure but he stood and held the conversation without me ever having witnessed his hands at any point.

'Aye, pair of us have got season tickets.' Benji added which in the scheme of things didn't seem required. I'd seen cunts like this before a million times. They weren't in there to have a few 'lucky spins' to pass their day. Aye, they were in there for either one of two reasons. They were either there to shake the poor old cunt down for money or the worse out of the scenarios. They owned the place.

All I wanted to do was clean a wee bit more money out of the puggy and we would've been getting our arses back to Muirhouse. Instead I was thrown into a conversation that found me having to multitask between trying to suss this pair out while also try to feign my way out of appearing a genuine bonafide Rangers fan. It also didn't help that - unlike the old dear on the change desk - these two *were* huns. Cunts who would've known what they were talking about.

'Oh aye? Where about do yous sit? The first one asked us.'

This, I immediately worried was going to be a problem. This whole 'let's fake being fans of other teams to help avoid capture' thing had evidently been driven by me. Did Benji even know the names of any of the stands inside Ibrox Stadium? Well. *That* was what I feared.

Aye, we all go to away grounds following our teams but how many of us *really* give that much of a fuck about what the stands are called? It's quarter to three and you're firing out the pub to the game. The name of the stands, apart from the one where you're sitting in yourself, aren't even a consideration for your average fitba fan.

I wasn't taking a chance on whether Benji was going to wing it or not because if a Rangers 'fan' cannot name at least one stand inside their own stadium then it's going to look questionable at the least.

'We've only just switched stands this season, mate,' I jumped in leaving no room at all for anything that was going to come close to resembling an awkward pause. We'd sat in the Broomloan for years but have just moved to the top tier of the Copeland Road to sit beside a couple of the others that we travel through with.'

Whilst I fucking hated myself for all of the words that was spilling out of my mouth because, make no mistake about it. In that moment speaking to them I *was* a fucking teddy bear. While I hated myself I couldn't help but hold a wee bit of pride over just how realistic I was making it.

'Aye, we're bottom tier of the Copeland. We'll look out for you the next home game outside Ibrox,' the second one added before looking towards his mate and with the slightest of nods to each other they carried back on with their journey up the hall of the arcade.

There had just been something menacing about them, though. Almost like the air changed when they walked through the door. I'd noticed a couple of others nearby who were stood playing their own puggies who looked like they were wanting to look in any direction *other* than where the two guys talking to us were stood.

'Don't make it obvious or anything, B, but try and get a wee look at what them two are up to, will you.' I asked him while I turned back around to the ten credits that were still waiting to be used. Changing tact, completely. I was left with the impression that I'd taken in quite a hefty sum for a few hours work and that perhaps I shouldn't push it any further.

D. Know when to say when.

Use up those ten rolls and then we'll call it a day, 'I thought.

Instead, I only used five.

Roll number one out of the ten brought nothing on screen other than the random combination of an alien, a space ship and the planet Saturn.

'They're talking to the old wifie at the desk.' Benji said while I stayed focussed on the fruit machine. Speaking to the woman at the desk wasn't exactly much to be worried about. Frankly, had they been then seen taking change from her then officially I'd have removed them from the person of interest list that they'd all of a sudden found themselves placed on by me.

Roll number two brought the option of holding the two aliens that had occupied the left and middle slots while taking a spin to see if I could get a third and then go onto the chance of the jackpot. The spin brought nothing other than the news that the two boys had now been let inside the change booth by the old dear.

Before taking my next spin I had a casual glance around to see the three of them standing having a laugh with each other. Calmed by that I turned around again and had another spin which was a dead duck.

I had another casual look to the side in the direction of the change booth again and what I witnessed - the second time around - was my signal to get out of the premises. As soon as possible.

On the face of it. The sight of an old lady in a place of business standing talking to two men while pointing at certain machines spread across an arcade isn't exactly what you would exactly describe as the work of horror. It is, however, *not* a good sign for a bandit stringer.

As far as I was reading the room. They weren't there to shake her down for protection. No, they owned the place or at the least worked for someone who owned it and as far as I could see - potential paranoia over committing criminal acts, excepted - she was pointing out what machines had been used, for whatever reasons.

If *one* of those reasons was that they were ripe for emptying. Then Benji and I had a problem.

'Right, mate. We're leaving and we're leaving now. We leave cool and calm. The way we walked in.' I whispered to Benji out the side of my mouth.

'Why? What's happening?' He said with a panicked expression on his face.

'I'll tell you on the way back to the car but for now, trust me, we need to go.'

Of course, there was time for one last 'more front than Santa Monica' episode before we vacated the place. Once we'd grabbed all of our stuff. The hundreds of pounds worth of coins all tucked up nicely in the special pouches that I'd use to avoid the noise of coins when the pair of us would walk back out of an arcade while claiming to be penniless. Instead of making right for the door which was practically right next to us I walked in the *opposite* direction, straight up to the change booth to say bye to the old dear.

'You've had enough of my money for one day but I'll be back so don't go spending your winnings on wine, men and song, eh?' I joked with her.

'Win some lose some, pal.' One of the heavies said with a wee smirk that suggested that the money I'd just spoken of 'losing' was going directly to him in return.

Aye, and just wait until you open the puggies that I 'lost' all my money in ya smarmy cunt, I thought to myself.

'Well I'll take the wine and the song, men are too much trouble, and I've only got the one.' She cackled back at me while I was - by then - too busy being consumed with a rising dislike for the guy behind the counter.

'Maybe see the pair of you at Ibrox for the cup game, boys?' The other one then said to me with a bit more warmth.

'Aye, might well do, mate,' I replied back before motioning to Benji that we were ready for the off.

'No surrender.' One of them said when I already had my back turned on them. For effect though I turned around and gave a cursory one back to neither of them in particular.

'Aye, might well do, mate?' Benji joked, repeating my words back to me, as we approached the door and well out of anyone's earshot.

'More chance of me getting a backie off King Billy on his horse back to Muirhouse, Benji,' I laughed back as I walked through the door he was holding open for me.

That really is what it's all about though. Know when to say when. Recognise that you've made enough for the day. See the signs of greed creeping in. And in the more extreme cases. Be aware of the danger - whatever that might be - and get yourself to fuck.

That, my friend, is how you don't caught. That is why I don't get caught.

Chapter 5

Strings

'Now it's the fucking big one today, lads.'

Jock Hunter paced back and forward across the cold and dirty away dressing room. Punching a fist into an open hand with quite a bit behind it.

'We'd be wasting our breath if we were to ask these bastards for a quarter - not that we would anyway, you understand? - and none shall be given in their direction either.'

'Monk? Remember what I was saying to you in training through the week now? Montana? You better not have been fucking out last night to all hours, by fuck you look it. And Rossi? You need to watch out for that dirty bastard of a number five they've got at the back. That Dove McCallister. Knows every trick in the book behind a referee's back and you're going to find out about each and every one of them over the next ninety minutes so mind and don't play his game and go taking the fucking bait.'

Hunter was going through his usual pre match routine. Singling everyone out with their own bit of personal advice for the battle that lay ahead. And a battle it was going to be, no mistaking that.

The "big one" that Jock Hunter was proclaiming it to be though? Two piss poor teams sitting mid table consisting of a couple of sets of players whose main aspirations from the match would be to avoid ending up in hospital first and to win the game second. Was hardly El fucking Clasico with hundreds of countries around the world all dropping what they were doing to catch the action.

I suppose it all depends on what you class as *big* though.

It would not have been a stretch to say that if there was *one* team out of the whole league that we would never, ever, want to lose a game of fitba against, it would be The Paddock out of Niddrie.

There was 'history' between the two sides. Only really recent, mind. Over the previous couple of seasons it had festered to the point that the fucking Lothian and Borders should've been classifying it as one of those 'Category A' matches like they do for the derby or when the Old Firm come to town.

Of course though, at the level of where teams like The Violet or The Paddock ply their trade, nothing is ever simple. It was all Terry's fault, really. He'd been caught playing away and when I say that I'm not meaning while visiting a rival Sunday league team with a Muirhouse Violet top on his back.

He'd been cheating on his breadknife with this other woman. None of us had known about it until the shagger had got himself busted and it all came out. Was literally on the job when the woman's man came back from work. Something about his construction site not passing a government workplace safety spot check which led to everyone all being told to go home for the day.

Tel's over at her house thinking that he's got the whole day with her to get up to fuck knows what only for to find the husband back before dinner time. According to him. He was banging away at her from behind - back to the bedroom door - Was so much into giving her the message, they both were, that no one had heard the husband come in.

First Terry knew about it was when he felt the right hook from the side that almost knocked him off the bed and someone going fucking tonto at him.

I can't even begin to imagine how messy it all must have been. Imagine going from doggy style to getting your cunt kicked in within a matter of seconds? Too fucking mad to even think about, that. Standing there naked - with a root on - in a strange bedroom while trying to defend yourself from some big bricklayer who - understandably - isn't best pleased that he's just found out that you're riding his wife. Messy, man. Very fucking messy.

Wasn't near as fucking messy though as the *next* time we played The Paddock at Muirhouse Park. Tel and myself were standing outside the pavilion having a reek before heading inside to get changed for the game when a few car loads of The Paddock boys arrived.

'You have got to be fucking kidding me.' Tel said as he took a final draw on his John Player before flicking it out and into the air.

'What's that, mate?' I asked. Distracted, myself, by all of the players getting out of the cars.

It was right about the time that he was following up by telling me that he had just spied the very same boy that had caught him with his dick in his missus that I guess the same cunt had clocked Terry.

'YOU YA FUCKING BAAASSSTTTAAARRRD.'

A guy in a Londsdale tracksuit shouted over in our direction. Instantly a few of his team mates lunged and grabbed hold of him while trying to work out why he had just exploded in such a way. There was a bit of scuffles between them which was just as well because had he been left to it he'd have been right over to Terry. And it's not like Terry would've shirked the conflict.

'BUT HE FUCKING SHAGGED MA FUCKING WIFE, LOGAN. MA FUCKING WIFE, MATE.'

Wisely I got Tel out of there and into the safety of our dressing room where the rest of the squad were already there, in place.

I'd went straight to Jock Hunter to let him know that we might've had a bit of a problem and that maybe he should think about dropping Tel from the starting eleven. 'Nonsense,' I was told by Hunter. Not even an option to drop - who the gaffer looked upon as - one of the team's star players.

'If ye cannae deal with off pitch / on pitch vendettas then you shouldn't be playing at this level of fitba in the first place.' He said, in dismissal, waving me away. Not even thinking to pull Tel over and at least enquire *why* I was suddenly pleading that for the good of Terry, Muirhouse Violet - and The Paddock, for that matter - that he didn't put Tel in the team that morning.

Hey, at least I tried, I thought to myself as I walked over to my peg to get myself changed for warming up.

Ninety hyper violent filled minutes later - and miraculously it *was* 'ninety minutes' - there had been seven players sent off. Two arrested along with another four - off pitch - not so innocent bystanders. It took the association the best part of a year to deal with the fall out from the match and all the individual bans and fines that were, eventually, dished out.

Understandably, a bit of a rivalry developed from that match forward. The boy - whose wife Tel had shagged - didn't even play for The Paddock anymore and, in fact, once the bans started getting dished out that was his time with the Niddrie pub side over. As far as I had heard he was now on the inside after having knocked his wife about.

Even with him nothing to do with the team anymore. Stuff can still run deep. Memories can be longer than fucking elephants, at times. You can stick Muirhouse Violet and The Paddock into that category.

Aye, it wasn't going to be a particularly enjoyable Sunday morning, especially with the match being in their neck of the woods.

Looking around the dressing room though, at all of my team mates. Aye, they might well have been a group chancers, cheaters, con men, psychos and reprobates. No mights about it, either. They *were*. But you know what? There wasn't a group of men ever assembled that I would've rather had beside me going into battle than them. Delta Force, S.A.S, fucking Russian Spetznaz? None of those cunts came close by comparison to the Muirhouse boys.

1.   **Sepp** - Our cat between the sticks who only got the gig as keeper on account of him being a lanky bastard. While not exactly the type that you would ever put your house on saving a shot from an opponent, he *was* capable. Named Sepp due to the fact that not only was he our goalkeeper but he freakishly looked the double of the old German goalie, Sepp Maier. Should've been fucking nicknamed 'push up' due to the amount of times in a match you'd hear him screaming 'PUSH UP, VIOLET.'

2.   **Bungalow** - The kind of cunt that you'd send for some tartan paint and he'd ask you how much of it you were looking for. Name awarded specifically because of that … Fuck all up top. Claim to fame is that when he was a kid he appeared on 'Jim'll Fix It' where he got to re-enact the scene from Empire Strikes Back with Dave Prowse and Bungalow as Luke Skywalker.

Apparently Prowse didn't even have his fucking Darth Vader suit on which, in my own honest opinion, would've kind of defeated the whole purpose. As a player? You'd shove him in the dependable category. Daft as a brush off and on the pitch but knew when to fucking row Z it and when to take a touch. What else are you looking for from a centre half?

3. **The Monk** - Was he religious? I'd have been surprised - if outside of a wedding setting - he'd have ever been inside a church. Did he have a 'Zidane cut' or was ever seen strolling around Muirhouse in a robe? Negative there, again. Did he consume enough Buckfast over a week that would probably be able to keep Airdrie going for a week. Yes, yes he did. Just because he was tanning enough alcohol a week that would've had Oliver Reed putting an arm around your shoulder and saying 'come on, mate, enough's enough, eh?' though, it didn't mean to say that he couldn't kick a ball, like. If Bungalow was the brainless no nonsense centre half. The Monk was more your cool calm and composed Franco Baresi or Davey Narey type. Never one to be phased by what was going on the pitch no matter who it was we were playing and - guaranteed - the only way you ever saw the cunt breaking sweat during a game was alcohol related rather than feeling any pressure from the opposition. Claims that his uncle invented the Burberry checked pattern. No cunt believes it.

4. **Daz** - Young Daz had only got his chance at the start of the season due to Mikey Harris being banged up in Belgium after getting lifted at the Anderlecht Hearts pre season friendly and not making it back to Scotland in time for pre season training. When word came over just how bad a paggering it was that he'd given one of the Belgians and that he wasn't coming back any time soon Daz got the nod from Jock. Not that Jock was too chuffed about losing Mikey. Good left back, like. Dangerous as fuck going forward. That's probably what the Anderlecht ultra would say too, I suppose. Since he got his chance though, young Benny - called Daz by us because as a newcomer into the team we managed to convince him that it was his responsibility to wash the strips every week - was seen as undroppable. His play out from the back deserves to be seen at a higher level than he was playing at. I wasn't sure if he was going to have the mentality to mix it with some of the brutes that he was going to be facing each week but fair play. Duck to water, like. Maybe a bit too much though as he's a cocky wee cunt who knows he's a

decent player and is a bit mouthy on the pitch with it. You want to watch what you say and who to at our level. Because of his youthful arrogance he's been the sole reason for a fair few battles on a Sunday morning but then again. Let he who hasn't instigated a mass brawl on a council fitba pitch on a Sunday morning cast the first stone, eh?

5. **Wullie** - Nicknamed after 'Oor Wullie' on account of the fact that he moved to Muirhouse from Dundee after meeting that Hayley Patterson from Gunnet Court on one of those dating websites. Must've hit it off anyway because he moved from there to Edinburgh to stay with her. Brought his fucking stupid Dundonian accent with him as well with all his 'ehhhs' and 'pehhhs' and that. Something that he repeatedly gets rinsed about from the rest of the lads. Actually, he's a really sound cunt, Cawsey, though, and someone that would do anything for the team or any of the boys in it. One of those utility type of players that if some cunt doesn't turn up on a Sunday morning you can be sure that Wullie will slot right in as if he played there every week. Good man to have in the side, like. Normal service and everyone reporting for duty though, his place as right back writes itself onto the team sheet. A good lad though and someone that I've always had a lot of time for. Even if he's an Arab.

6. **Terry** - As previously already stated. A shagger. Owns a semi successful window cleaning firm that has a few lucrative contracts across the city although it's always been something seen as questionable over *how* he managed to secure the contracts in the first place. The fact that he's six four, about twenty stone and looks like he did two tours of Nam just because he enjoyed the first one so much *may* have played a part somewhere. Nicknamed Terry after that guy who got kidnapped in Lebanon, Terry Waite. Any fucking time you ask him for a help with something he always says that he can't because his hands are tied. As a football player? *Extremely* limited, I'm not going to be the one that tells him that, though. Logically Jock decided to deploy him in a kind of holding midfield position. The reason, I assumed, was that he would be a big imposing lump in the middle of the pitch that you wouldn't fancy trying to play through. Someone simply there to try and disrupt things rather than influence or put a stamp on the game. Breaking up play, breaking legs. Whatever comes first. Despite the lack of any kind of technical skill to the man, whatsoever, he's undeniably a

valuable commodity to have out on the pitch for when it all kicks off. Which it invariably does.

7. **Coffee** - The legend in Edinburgh circles known as the kid who was caught on Sportscene giving John Robertson the wanker signal after he missed that open goal at Easter Road in the Edinburgh Derby. He was only around ten years old or something. Camera caught him perfectly though. Right at the front of the stand behind the goal. Giving it the old Gareth Hunt hand signal to the Hearts striker like the actor did in the Nescafe advert. It's moments like that, though, which can shape a cunt's nickname for the rest of their life. His was well earned. As was his place in the side. Some engine on the boy. A real box to box player and played every match as if his life depended on it. Weighs in with a few goals here and there which always takes a welcome bit off the load of our boys up front. One of the more quieter ones in the side - despite how his image was portrayed across the whole of Scotland at an early age - although make no mistake. When the time comes for him to mix it out on the field he doesn't go MIA. then again, he wouldn't be getting in the fucking team in the first place if that *wasn't* the case.

8. **Me, Strings** - Well, you already know about me but what you *don't* know is that with over fifteen years service I was Violet's longest serving player. In with the fucking bricks, me. Still waiting on my testimonial though, mind. Initially I'd started off as a full back but Hunter had seen something in me that the previous gaffers hadn't. That being that I was absolutely shite at defending but would give the opposition a torrid time when going in the other direction. You always hear that about full backs where they're described as 'good going forward but can't defend' but every cunt shrugs their shoulders about it as if what can you do about it? Well maybe don't fucking play them as a full back then? Doesn't take Fabio Capello to work that one out, eh? Anyway, big Jock made the switch. Moved me further up the pitch and told me to stay there. That I done more damage inside my own box than anything else so to keep myself out on the wing. Dragging the other players out of position simply by my own movements and positioning. It's always hard when you're talking about yourself but as an honest assessment of myself, as a player. There's no denying that at thirty seven you're always going to lose a yard of pace. The good players gain one up top though, don't they? As time went on and I found myself not as

fast as I used to be. Hunter brought me in from out on the wing to a more central role along with Coffee and Tel.

9. **Rossi** - Our goal scoring extraordinaire and prodigal son who returned back to the side after a three year absence. Not through playing for another side over those years or anything like that. Was more of an 'enforced break' from the league handed down to him from the suits after a match fixing scandal that had rocked the league. It was total nonsense, like. How could a striker be in any position to affect a game of fitba? Maybe miss a pen or something like that but, trust me. Getting a penalty on a Sunday morning in that kind of an environment is not an easy thing to do. I remember joking with one referee during a game - after him knocking back a good three or four stonewallers by then - that one of the other team could've chopped one of our boys legs off with a machete and he would've whistled for it being just outside the box. Three years - Rossi got - just because he'd been spotted talking in a bar with Davie McKenna. McKenna a well known underworld figure whose name continually kept cropping up when the whispers about the attempted match fixing started to surface and the CID got involved. Nothing was ever proved but there's always going to be scapegoats with stuff like that. We only started calling Jordan, 'Rossi' once he'd came back from his ban, after Paolo Rossi. Jordan took it in the right way. Actually embraced it, in fact, and told me that he thought it was a brilliant 'fuck you' to the league that he was back playing and had been given a nickname linked to a known match fixer. Capable fox in the box striker as well with a sharp eye for goal. I thought the three years out scooping in the pub would've maybe dulled his predatory instinct to sniff out a chance but he slotted back into the team as if he'd never been away. The only boy in the team that - at the start of the season - you would put your life on ending the season with over twenty goals. And we all need one of those whether you're Muirhouse Violet or Manchester United.

10. **Montana** - If there was ever a fitba player that you'd pray was to avoid being drug tested. Montana would definitely be up there alongside Diego Armando. I knocked all the drugs on the head back in the days when we all used to go to the Rez and Streetrave so at least - unlike most of the team - understood the drug part to him. Didn't fucking understand how he could be up all night and then go straight to Muirhouse Park and play ninety minutes out of his tree, though. Aye, I ken that it's easy to just

say get a line up your beak and yourself out onto the pitch and you'll be ready to go but it would generally be someone who hasn't *taken* a drug in their life that would also say that. I remember one match. - The Royal Arms, I think - where he'd been at a rave at Ingliston then a few hours at an afters before turning up to play. He'd been saying that he was suffering from double vision. Depth awareness was all away to fuck. Hunter was having none of it, though. Told Montana to get his boots on and get on the pitch. Soon regretted his decision though when Montana missed that injury time chance to snatch the points when he completely fresh aired it when thinking he was kicking a ball that actually wasn't there. When he's not in a demented state of mind, though, he's a tidy wee striker and has a decent understanding with Rossi even if Rossi takes all of the glory through goals per game average. Montana would score more on the pitch if he scored less *off* it. Something that I've told the boy to his face.

11.   **Mr Benn** - Given the name by the lads after the cartoon character one day when Bungalow noticed that he never had the same rig oot on twice when you'd see him in the boozer. Proper posing cunt, like. Stone Island this - Gucci that. Goes to one of those fancy hairdressers in the city centre to get his hair cut and pays three times the price of any of the rest us. Hardly the type that you're going to depend on to stick his head in where it hurts if he's scared it's going to mess up his hair, eh? Someone who buys white Adidas Predators to play Sunday league and complains when people take turns at booting him up into the air over it. He was only in the side because of Sunny's previous and recent indiscretions, and subsequent immediate ban. At least Mr Benn had a bit of pace that Sunny lacked, when he could be actually arsed using it. We didn't exactly have an infinity pool of talent waiting in the wings for their chance when or if it came around with Violet so when Sunny's position became suddenly up for grabs. Benn got it more by default than anything else. As far as any long term future in the side. His report card most definitely - for me, anyway - had 'must do better' stamped on it.

And the man behind the starting eleven of Muirhouse Violet? Big Jock Hunter. A man who lived and breathed The Violet and - in some way or other - had been involved with the side since its creation. Various extended league bans given out to him, excepted.

Getting on for late sixties but still pacing up and down the side of the pitch like he was half his age. Giving his own players, the opposing ones *and* the match officials the worst kind of abuse every week. He kept being told - by anyone who cared about him - that he needed to calm himself and not go that radge at his age but he was beyond listening to anyone. *You* listened to Jock, not the other way around. Well in his own mind, anyway, because that was the thing with the gaffer. Obsessively read all the autobiographies of the great fitba managers and this seemed to leave him thinking that just by reading about their practices *that* automatically meant that he was like them with how he ran The Violet.

Like when he found out about the tactics Sir Alex Ferguson employed with his young Man United players by having spies inside all of the main pubs and clubs that would grass up anyone like a Giggs or a Beckham going out for a scoop the night before the match? With Jock staying in Pilton he'd - completely under the radar from the players - agreed with Maisie behind the bar at The Gunner that if she was to see any of the team in there drinking on a Saturday night she was to call him immediately.

First we found out about it was one night when we were all having a pint and a couple of games of pool when Jock came storming in. Still in his slippers, such the rush he'd come out of his house to drive over that he'd been in. None of us were even pished. Not even close. Didn't matter to the gaffer, though. Near enough emptied the fucking pub that night with how many bodies that had been ordered to vacate the premises.

Obviously, once he'd blown his cover with that we would simply use alternative pubs on a Saturday night if any of us fancied a few refreshments. You couldn't help but respect the man's passion and love for the team though and it was something that we all appreciated and - as a result - we all, to a man, humoured and put up with his theatrics.

'Right boys, get up here and gather round,' Hunter ordered the lot of us up into our traditional pre match dressing room huddle, having noticed that we were all ready to go. Forming a perfect circle with the gaffer in the middle of us he gave us one last piece of managerial advice before leaving and heading out onto the pitch.

'How many of you like the taste of liquorice?'

It wasn't a question or if it was, he had already assumed to know the answer from everyone.

'That's right. No cunt.' He quickly then followed up.

'That's what losing is like. The taste that licorice leaves in your mouth. You can't get fucking rid of it all day no matter what you fucking do. Don't be coming back off the pitch today with that same taste in your mouth. Now go out and get stuck right into those bastards!'

I'd heard that liquorice analogy from him more times than I'd been on a winning Violet side. It never got old, though, and would always send me out of the dressing room with a smile on my face.

Well, until the whistle would go.

Sunday league - and especially away trips to Niddrie - had a tendency to wipe the smile off you, pretty quick.

Chapter 6

Han

'NO WAY' Janie Mathieson screamed out before quickly looking around, suddenly aware again of her surroundings. Forgetting, momentarily, where she was.

'I'm telling you, it's true. I didn't know where to even put myself when my Chantelle came back from her shift and sat down and told me. My face went bright red. Near enough spat my tea out, so I did.' Heather said while leaving me - behind the counter along with her - bent over double with laughter.

Janie, who had only popped in for to get a few things for her man's lunch the next day ended up stopping for a natter with us. The shop was quiet by that point of the night anyway so we didn't exactly have much in the way of customers coming in to contend with.

Janie, being one of those types that nothing goes on without them having some kind of knowledge of, was standing there dishing out the gossip. Keep going, hen, and that corned beef will be out of date by the time you get back home to make your man's sandwiches, I thought to myself.

I was though, I have to admit, enjoying all of the goss that she was sharing with us. Aggie Johnson had apparently been caught trying to cheat at the bingo and almost caused a riot inside The Rio. You know what the old biddies can be like with their bingo, though? Even to *legit* winners. Me and the girls decided to go one night when we were having a night out. Chose to go to the bingo in a kind of ironic sense. Well my mate, Caroline Donaldson? Only went and scooped the two grand jackpot for the night. Should've heard some of the nasty comments flying around just because it wasn't a 'regular' who took the cash. I'm not quite sure some people understand the concept of 'chance,' though.

Apart from the uproar at the bingo. Frank 'the wank' Benson had fallen from the top of his ladder while doing his window cleaning round in Pilton. 'Lucky to be alive, by all accounts,' Janie had told us.

'Aye and he'll be lucky to get any sick pay from Terry, too,' I joked. The thought of big Terry being the warm and compassionate employer type, the stuff of fantasy that only Walt Disney on Acid could come up with.

Billy Halliday and Patricia Lilley had apparently been caught in a doorway after throwing out time on the Saturday night with Pat's knickers at her ankles and Billy fingering her and now Deek Lilley is on the warpath looking for Billy who's went into hiding. Even Anne, his wife, doesn't know where he is. Billy's probably the last person Annie want's to see, anyway.

Lloyd's chemist had been broken into, again.

'They bloody junkies.' Janie said almost as if it was now an accepted fact of life that addicts will break into pharmacies and that there was nothing you could do about it.

The biggest news she had, though, was of that weird looking man that had moved into Inchmickery Court only six months before. I'd never known his name but had seen him about, at the shops and that, but we were reliably informed was called Jared Reece Johnson. Well a mob of police turned up last week at his flat and took him away, along with his computer. Old Harry Pearson couldn't get up to his flat in the lift because of all of the commotion and about had a heart attack trying to walk the stairs.

'We'll not see that paedo back in Muirhouse again, that's for sure.'

Janie announced triumphantly, doing away with hundreds of years of Scottish law in one short sentence.

Not to judge a book by their cover or anything but, he *did* look the type. Really tall and obscenely thin with that greasy hair in a side comb style. Glasses that looked like they were twenty years old. Even though he would smile at you and say hello you could still see that there was an element of insincerity to it. It's easy to say these things about someone after the police have marched out of their house with their computers, though, I guess.

It was while Janie was filling the two of us in on all of the Muirhouse goings on - and helping brighten up an otherwise slow and quiet second half of the shift - that Heather decided to chip in with something her daughter had shared with her when she'd got back from her shift at Accident and Emergency at the Royal Infirmary.

'I'd made us a cup of tea, like I normally do when she gets home, and asked her what her shift had been like. I normally cringe when I ask her because she has to deal with some horrific things in a day. Can't stop myself from asking, though. You know what people are like with car crashes. Don't want to see it but not a chance they're going to look in the opposite direction, either. I think she protects me with some of the stuff that goes on and just doesn't bother telling me about them but some of the other ones she shares and I'm not sure how I'd be able to sleep at night if it was me.' Heather said, having a quick look around the shop to make sure that it was just the three of us inside.

'Oh, mum. You'll not believe what happened today.' Heather said, quoting Chantelle, smiling to herself before even telling the story.

'There was this really bad crash on the city bypass involving a few cars and a motorbike. Well, the biker was in a bad way by the time he got to the Infirmary but was at least alive and conscious. As always, when you're in such a messed up state, the doctors need to get you out of your clothes and into a hospital robe. The biker could barely move due to all that was broken so wasn't in any position to take his own leathers off so, as nurses do in such cases, they'll help the patient out. Only the biker didn't want them to take his clothes off. Farcically was in no position to stop them because of the pain he was in but had been very vocal about how 'no one was taking his fucking trousers off.' It was explained to him that he possibly wasn't aware of how serious his injuries actually were and that it was vital that he have his leather trousers removed.'

'Small penis syndrome, aye?' Janie interjected. Must admit, I was thinking the same. Why else would a man be so in fear of having his trousers removed, especially during one of those moments where your health is concerned.

'You're nowhere near.' Heather dismissed Janie. Clearly chuffed with herself that she still had the punchline of the story still to come.

'Well, when Chantelle and her colleague grabbed hold of the man's tight biker leathers to pull them down. He wasn't *wearing* any underwear underneath them.'

'Ewwwwwwwwwww' I said, instantly thinking of how horribly smelly and sweaty it must've been down there inside the leather trousers.

'Oh, that's nasty.' Janie said, making a show of pretending to be sick right there at the counter. 'Doesn't make it any the less disgusting but maybe it's a biker thing when they're wearing their leathers? I've never been with anyone with a motorbike in my life so wouldn't know.'

'Aye, I'm not too sure that was the case *this time*, though, Janie.' Heather continued.

'Mum, when we pulled off his trousers his, well, you know? Crown jewels, they were, like, inside this silver cage with a wee padlock attached to it. The second we both seen it the man's face turned like one of those Ribena men.' Heather said - repeating her daughter's words - while trying to keep a straight face.

Well I just went at that point, followed by Janie. I don't know what images she had in her mind of this man and his 'contraption' and she didn't know mines but it really was a case of laughing before crying.

Heather then went on to tell us how this whole padlock presented a problem. The man had suffered from multiple fractures all over his body. *Seriously* needed an x ray. Needed about *ten* x-rays, by the sounds of things. Only, metallic objects seriously mess with the results of an x-ray. And there lay the rub. He didn't have the key to the padlock. Apparently it was some kinky BDSM thing where he had a keeper who *owned* the key to the padlock. As Heather spoke about it there was so many questions I had. *Lots* of questions.

'I'd never heard of such a thing in my life. I mean, I know those perverts get up to all kinds of stuff but my Andy would send me to Carstairs if I suggested locking his meat and two veg up in a cage.' Heather laughed while Janie stood there agog. Holding her hands to her face that made her resemble that Scream painting.

Once I'd stopped laughing uncontrollably I was straight on to google on my phone to seek some of the answers to the questions I'd been left with.

'Ok, and this is according to Wikipedia, **"Cock and Ball torture"** Which already sounds sore for a start.' I said before looking back to the phone screen.

'So is falling of a motorbike at a hundred miles per hour on the city bypass.' Heather laughed.

'Ok' I said trying to keep a straight face, already having inadvertently managed to take in some key words that had managed to jump out of the screen at me.

'Ok. Cock and ball torture (CBT) Penis torture or dick torture is a sexual activity involving application of pain or constriction to the penis or testicles. This may involve directly painful activities, such as genital piercing, wax play, genital spanking. squeezing, ball - busting, genital flogging, urethral play, tickle torture, erotic electro-stimulation, kneeing or kicking. The recipient of such activities may receive direct physical pleasure through erotic humiliation or knowledge that the play is pleasing to a sadistic dominant. Many of these practices carry significant health risks.'

'Aye, getting kneed and kicked generally does present significant health risks, eh?!' Janie giggled, taking us along with her.

'But, but why, though?' I said rhetorically, having read the Wiki explanation so now understanding the whats of things. I just didn't see the why part.

'So how did they get the cage off him then?' Janie and I, freakishly, asked at the same time once we'd both had the required enough time to process all of it.

'They didn't, well not while Chantelle was still working. Obviously *everyone* in the A and E staff were talking about it so apparently he was having to get the person who was holding the key to come to the hospital with it to 'uncage him.' He'd be bloody lucky if it was me that was holding the key because I'd be too mortified to go to the hospital with it. Imagine all the looks you'd be getting? I'd be calling a taxi and telling the driver to take the key and drop it off to A and E saying they'd know what it was for. Then again, I wouldn't be in possession of a key to a man's genitals in the first place.'

More laughter over the thought of this man - still lying there in a hospital bed hours after a serious injury and in extreme pain - unable to be fully diagnosed and all because his privates were caged.

As we stood laughing. Heather finally made an attempt of starting to scan Janie's items. I noticed the big silver Lexus driving into the disabled spot right in front of the shop. Probably isn't anyone with a badge, I quickly thought to myself on account of how many times I'd see someone pull into that same spot over a shift and how many of them dance out of their cars like they're Fred Astaire and Ginger Rogers.

It was only when the woman got out the drivers door and started to make her way towards the front door of the shop that I realised that I recognised her. It was an old friend of mines, Kelly Cooper. Hadn't seen her in a few years since she "levelled up" and married that banker from Silverknowes and moved away from Muirhouse. The closer she got the same old Kelly she looked … Just richer. Chanel bag with matching velour Gucci tracksuit and trainers to go with.

Seeing her decked out like that - and I'd like to think that it wasn't through some pang of subconscious form of jealousy from myself - I couldn't help but think that for a former friend she hadn't exactly kept in touch with anyone the moment that she got herself out of Muirhouse.

'*Hannah*, how great to see you. I didn't know you worked here.' She said with a combination of surprise and - for some reason - what looked like embarrassment.

One thing that she *should've* been embarrassed over was that she had spoken with an accent that she certainly didn't speak with when she lived around Muirhouse. Moves a few miles across the city and she's getting elocution lessons?!

Well since you haven't been around here for years and I only started helping out at the Co-Op six months ago how were you meant to know? I sarcastically thought to myself while sticking a smile on my face to greet her with.

'Oh, you know, Kelly? Just for a wee bit of pin money plus if I was to stay in that house with my Strings and Jack I'd end up going up the walls.' I smiled back. 'How are you?' I asked.

'Well, I wouldn't know about the need for pin money, that's one thing, not nowadays.'

She really didn't need to say it, the way that she did. It was uncalled for and, quite sad how someone can think that just by having money - where they didn't have before - they think that they are then instantly somehow better.

Ooooh well done you, opening your legs to the right person that then got you out of the squalor of Muirhouse, eh? I thought while trying to stifle all of the potential insults that were at risk of spilling from my mouth.

'And what about Strings? Is he still, working?' She asked.

The way that she had emphasised and inferred the last word of the sentence. That she knew what my man did - on occasion - to earn money and her trying to be smart about it by classing it as 'work.'

Hypocritical bitch, I thought, yeah my husband's a petty crook but if your one's a banker then chances are he's even worse. Only he's got the law on his side and instead of a broken leg or arm he gets a slap on the wrist if caught.

It wasn't as if she had come into the shop seeking any argument or confrontation. She'd only came in for two twenty packs of Regal King Size. The way she was speaking wasn't in any way trying to antagonise me, even if practically every second word that she spoke did.

No, she was simply someone who had - by the looks - lost touch with who she now was. Wasn't the upper class socialite that she seemed to think she was just because she had a Chanel bag over her shoulder but neither was she the girl from the scheme that had left years before. The way she was in the shop, though. The one thing for certain would've been that had she hung around for long enough talking in such a way it wouldn't have been long before someone smacked the schemie back into her again.

'I was just visiting my mum and when I was passing the shop I remembered I needed some King Size' Kelly said, looking behind me towards the cigarettes, trying to eye up the Regal that she was looking for.

'Aye, we all need a bit king size though, don't we?!' Janie butted in with a dirty laugh while waiting on her change back from Heather. Kelly laughed back but after the story I had just stood and listened to. 'Peak funny' had already been for the day. *Nothing* was topping that.

'Actually, it's a bit of a coincidence seeing you here, Han, because I was thinking of you just the other day, you know?' She said as she pulled out her purse - Fendi, of course - out of her bag to pay for the cigarettes.

Aye, of course you were, I mouthed with my back to her as I reached to get the two packets of ciggies. That's, of course, what lots of people say to someone when they've been doing the *exact* opposite. Especially Lady Muck hyphen Toff from Silverknowes and the residents of the Naughty North of Edinburgh.

'Oh aye? Why was that then?' I said, unable to feign any kind of interest whatsoever as I passed her the two packets of cigarettes.

'I seen Jack the other night, with some pals, walking past my house. You could hardly not notice them, the noise that they were all making. It's quite a quiet street, you see. You don't normally hear gangs of boys roaming around outside shouting, swearing and laughing.'

She caught me between not wanting to show myself up as in not knowing what my own son was up to and wanting to probe her for further information. Pride got the better of me, however. Instead of asking her more about it I chose to go down the route that reasoned that it couldn't have been him she had seen and besides, she hadn't seen our Jack in years and that he'd grown up a fair bit since then.

'Yeah, possibly.' Kelly answered with a look on her face that showed that -internally- she wasn't quite convinced with what she'd just said.

Even though I'd just learned this from her. As she had bid farewell and was getting back into her Lexus - without any fake arrangements about catching up sometimes, which I was glad to have not gone through - part of me knew that she was right and that she had, in fact, seen my son walking the more unfamiliar streets of Silverknowes. But why though? What reason could he have ever had to be in such part of the city?

Chapter 7

Jack

Bit of a head fuck, all of it, honestly. Wished I hadn't done it the moment I'd actually went through with it. Instant remorse. Didn't even get a chance to *enjoy* the moment. Endorphins, Miss Jones called it. Like when you really enjoy something and the feeling that you get from it. Weirdly, the same week that she told us about it in class, my dad used the same word when we were walking back from Easter Road to get the bus home after the Dundee United match. The one when we got the penalty in the ninety sixth minute to win the game. One that dad had said the ref should never have given us. Telling me that you can always tell by the reactions from the other team. The United players, that day, going fucking mental at the ref. Took an age before we even got to take it.

'Fuck all like an injury time winner to get the old endorphins flowing, Jackie, eh?' He said triumphantly as we marched towards the bus stop. I just nodded in agreement to him, like, not knowing enough on the subject to really contribute.

Anyway, there was no endorphins to be found the night we went to Silverknowes. Just worry. Worry before we went. Worry while we were there and worry *after* the event.

Of course, as always, it was Dynamo's idea.

He'd overheard his mum and dad talking about a job that his dad had been on. Replacing a cracked window at this big house for the glazing company that he worked for.

From what Dynamo had picked up. It was a house over in Silverknowes, this big mansion. Saying that. Compared to our flat. EVERYWHERE in Silverknowes looked like a mansion.

'Some people are just plain daft, you've got these that needed their window replaced today. Only, they'd given us specific instructions for when we got there to carry out the repair as nobody was going to be home for us. Something about them having to catch a flight to Tenerife earlier that morning and didn't want to be out the country with a broken window in their place so they supplied Bernice in the office with the key code to the gate at the front of their drive and then the security code to get into the house. Couldn't believe it when I looked at my paperwork and saw that their security codes for both the gate and front door was *one two three four five six!* Massive mansion worth fuck knows what, but would cost a pretty penny, and they've got a security code that is probably the *first* one that a robber would try. Well, they would if they didn't think that anyone would be so fucking stupid in the first place as to set that for a code.'

Dynamo told us the story the next day at school with that usual scheming look on his face. Even so, I didn't think that it was going to lead to us actually breaking into someone's house. Well, if you can call it housebreaking when you don't actually have to 'break' anything to gain entry into somewhere?

'I'm no estate agent, lads, or have ever claimed to be but I'm going to take an educated guess here that if you've got a security gate stopping any cunt from even getting to your front door, then you've got to have a few bob kicking around inside the place in some way or other. And that's the beauty of it. We *know* that no cunt is going to be there. You don't go to someplace like Tenerife for a day trip do you, eh? Week minimum or what's the fucking point of going, eh?'

Not only was he schooled in the ways of how real estate works but he also was knowledgable about the patterns and habits of how the average holiday maker plans their trip, Dynamo.

He's always coming out with radge ideas and statements, though. Half never coming to anything so I didn't immediately think that he was actually serious about doing it. Thought that by the next time we all met up it would've been forgotten about again. Only it hadn't.

Next time we all saw each other, at the end of the last period. It had went in the opposite direction of being forgotten about. Dynamo had spent the afternoon planning out the job while pretending that he was reading the Gordon Strachan autobiography that he'd had to bring in with him as part of his project involving reading a book on a famous person from history. You could hardly say that Strachan ranked up there alongside some of the great world figures like Gandhi or Nelson Mandela but I think it was the only autobiography that his dad had to give him and - due to being banned after being caught stealing from Muirhouse Library - other than that. His options were severely limited.

Walking back from school he told us how he had it all worked out and that we'd do it the next again day. This, he estimated, would give us three days (at the minimum) before the owners returned back from Spain.

I could tell straight away that the others weren't exactly enthusiastic about the idea but were too scared to say it. I *definitely* wasn't up for it. Wanted nothing to do with it at all. Bottled out on saying it too though, didn't I?

It wasn't like we were junkies and that was something that we did through necessity to feed our habits or anything. Didn't *need* to do it, at all. If I'd asked Dynamo 'why' he'd have only said that it was going to be a laugh. That's what he always said about that kind of stuff. You know? The stuff that isn't actually a laugh in any way, at all.

I know that teenagers do stupid stuff. They're wired to do it. I think that they're designed that way so as when they make mistakes they're meant to learn from them which then will have them ready for being a proper adult. Robbing a house isn't 'stupid stuff.' You've never seen Dennis the Menace doing a bit of breaking and entering before as part of his mischievous pranks, have you?

Sometimes you just know when something is wrong, though. Like, you get *that* feeling. The whole Silverknowes thing left me in a constant state of that feeling. I couldn't think about anything else that night. Just stayed in my room and watched telly without ever really taking it in. Kept thinking how I could get out of it without actually having to physically say the words to Dynamo.

A day off school sick would've been magic and a brilliant cover story for not being able to go out at night but if you think I can bag myself a sick day from school with the mum and dad that I have then you're off your nut. I could literally be sick right in front of my mum while standing there in my school uniform in the morning before school and she'd still send me out the door with a couple of empty Tesco bags so that I wasn't sick over my desk.

Heart proper sank the next morning, upon meeting up with the other three, when the first subject that came up was what we were doing *after* school. Dynamo starting off with what time we were all getting the bus to Silverknowes. Felt like I'd been given a sly dig in the gut the moment that I realised that it was still happening.

I just wish that I'd been brave enough to say what I was holding back from Dynamo and the rest of the boys. That this was all fucking insane. It wasn't required and why put yourself to a risk, like breaking into a house, if you didn't need to? From the moment it was brought up the very first thing that popped into my head was that there could've been an untold amount of riches lying in wait inside the house and it would've been of absolutely no fucking use to me.

When you're fourteen year old - and with no personal source of income apart from the occasional hand out from your mum and dad or your birthday and Christmas - *anything* that you're spotted with that hasn't come from them is then, obviously, put right under the microscope.

Which pretty much meant that no matter what I was going to make from the job. I wasn't going to be able to spend pretty much any of it. Know how those drug dealers feel with their dirty cash that they have but can't spend, eh? What's the fucking point? Aye, I could've probably sneaked a Playstation game under my mum's radar and even if she'd noticed that it wasn't one her and dad bought me (not much chance of that, like) I would've been able to say that I'd got a shot of it off Flav or something but *that* would've been about it.

What's the fucking point of having money and not being able to spend it? Can't think of anything more pointless than that.

Whether the others were thinking that far ahead, I didn't know. They were down for it. That's all that was important to Dynamo. And if you weren't down for it? Well none of us were going to break rank and say anything to that effect.

'Mind and not turn up wearing anything eye-catching, too.' The last thing Dynamo said before breaking off from the three of us and heading down the pen to his house.

It made me think of my dad's Rangers gear. His 'props' as he called them the day that I asked him why he had a Rangers top when he actually supported Hibs.

'Son, sometimes you've got to hide in plain sight,' he told me. I didn't exactly understand what he meant at the time. I'd played enough games of hide and seek to know that you're not going to last very long if you don't possess the ability to hide yourself from one's vision.

It took me to getting ready after school - and my choice of clothing - for me to actually 'get' what my pops had been getting at. Wear a Hibs top when he's outside Hibs territory and he's not going to blend in. All about blending in to your surroundings.

I'm not too sure that when Dynamo warned us to wear something that didn't catch the eye he had actually considered that four teenage boys walking around a posh area of Edinburgh were *never* going to fully be able to go unnoticed by the locals.

Nifty light footed moving through the night like ghosts, cat burglars, we hardly could have been likened to.

For what it was worth. I put on a pair of black Adidas tracky bottoms and my dark blue Berghaus fleece. Had never had to think from the point of view of a house breaker before but from what TV and films had taught me, it was that *all* burglars wore dark wooly hats, without exception. The only hats I had were green and white and hardly what you'd have classed as covert. I remembered that my dad had that Scotland hat. The reversible one that he wore the day we went to the San Marino match. While the red tartan pattern was of absolutely no use to me, the dark blue with the SFA badge on the front *did*.

I knew he wouldn't miss it for the night. He wasn't going to any Scotland matches any time soon, for one thing. Not after that whole rant he went on about the 'suits at the SFA' when Deek Riordan got his three match ban upheld. *Was* an outrage, though. Three match ban for calling the linesman a 'fucking wanker' for sticking his flag up for offside. Cheating us out of a draw at Ibrox. Fucking Sportscene even proved that he was *onside*, just to rub salt into the wounds.

'They're getting fuck all more of my money. Got to starve cunts like that out and you'll never do that by putting money into their coffers.'

It was a shame, like, because I loved going to the Scotland matches with my dad. The whole day out was brilliant. The noise, colour and general party vibe to the day. Sometimes the only shite part was the actual fitba itself.

Dad had told me though that it was important to be a man of your principles 'unlike all of those politicians who have two sets to choose from where required' and because of that I had written off ever going back to Hampden unless Hibs were there in a semi or cup final. The fact that to attend one of those games would be directly funding the Scottish Fitba Association seemingly something that my dad wasn't making a connection to but also something that I, obviously, wasn't going to be drawing to his attention, either.

Along with his Scotland hat I pinched a pair of my mum's brown leather gloves. The pair that she only wears when she's dressed up and going out. Once again, something that I figured no one was going to need inside the time that I was going to be outside and back.

I'd already decided that I was only going to be putting the gloves on at the very last minute when we were there. No good can ever come out of a fourteen year old boy's mates seeing him in his mum's gloves. Still, I had the whole fingerprint thing on my mind because if there was one guarantee. It was that whenever the family returned back from Tenerife to discover they'd been broken into … the police would be getting phoned.

Not like they had my prints on record anyway but the way I saw it. It was probably a good idea to make sure that it *stayed* that way.

Could barely touch my tea, I was that nervous. Absolutely hated having to straight up lie to mum and dad and tell them that I was going round to Flav's to play FIFA when they'd asked me what my plans had been for after tea. Hated lying to them full stop but - knowing what I was *actually* about to go and do and how much it would break their hearts if they were to know - to lie to them in such a serious way. I felt ashamed of myself that I was letting them down, even if they didn't directly know about it. *I* knew about it. That was enough.

'I'm amazed your fingers haven't dropped off the amount of time you play that fitba video game,' mum laughed, looking at dad for back up and getting a wee nod of approval.

'She's got a point, Jackie.' He joined in.

'Quite the opposite, dad. Just think in ten years time when it's FIFA 20, or whatever they're calling it. My fingers are going to be supremely trained and fit as a fiddle. Fingers of an athlete, like.'

I tried to give them both a standard wide answer. The kind that they were used to and would expect from me. In truth though, while I was replying to my mum I was, inside my head, seeing images of blue flashing lights, detention centres with cunts asking me where my tool was and my life, in general, being flushed down the pan in conjunction.

'If it keeps you off the streets and getting up to no good then god bless EA Sports 'it's in the game,' dad replied, making note to put on that funny wee American accent to go along with it.

He just had to say something like that, didn't he? As if my conscience wasn't struggling enough with things.

Once I'd managed to knock back enough food - that I knew was going to be classed as acceptable by mum and dad and would spare me the 'There's kids going hungry across the world and you're not even finishing half of what you get served up' stuff that I'd been no stranger to in the past. Until I had gotten either sick off it, or wise to. I couldn't tell you which, myself, but knew how to avoid it. - I headed up to my room to get myself ready to go and meet the rest of them at the bus stop.

First time I heard it, my mum, specifically, had said about starving kids in Africa and I thought I'd be the smart cunt by telling her to send my leftovers to them, then. Wasn't feeling so smart when dad told me that if I said that ever again he'd send me to Africa myself on a one way ticket to deliver it to them, though.

With the assortment of breaking in clobber assembled from both mum and dad shoved safely into the pockets of my Berghaus. I popped my head around the living room door to say bye to them when my dad got up from his chair.

'Hang on, Jackie, I'm going the same way as you to Archie's to pick something up. Wait there and I'll grab my coat.'

This was definitely not part of my plan and if I knew anything about omens other than it being something to do with superstition, I'd have probably looked on it as not being too good a one for how the night was going to go.

'Aye, no worries, dad.' I replied. Fuck all else I really could have done without outing myself.

It, I was already assuming, meant that I was going to miss the bus and, as a result, completely ruin my life. Dynamo would've been un-fucking-bearable had I not made it on time. It would've went without saying that he would've made sure that I, automatically, was out of the group. It's not just that, though. When you're finding yourself going off on a housebreaking spree with your pals it's maybe time to get yourself *other* pals. It's not as easy as that. I didn't want to experience things from the point of view of someone who *was* mates with Dynamo ... and then wasn't. School wouldn't have been pleasant and outside at nights around Muirhouse, even that would've been a wee bit dicey. That was pretty much *the* reason that I was even going along with it. Not because I wanted or needed anything. All I was doing was trying to safeguard my future from any grief coming my way. Lot of good that was going to do me, as it would turn out.

Flav's house was in the opposite direction to where I was meeting up with everyone else. Aye, technically I was going *towards* where the bus would've been coming from so if I seen the number thirty seven coming down the road and was near one of the other bus stops I could've jumped on it and been sat there waiting on the rest of them getting on. *Not* when I was walking along the road with my dad under the cover story that I was going to my mate's house to play FIFA I couldn't, though.

'How was school today, then?'

He asked me as we both tried to get ourselves used to the transition from our nice warm flat to the bitter cold that was waiting for us outside. Thank fuck I went with the Berghaus, I thought to myself.

'Shite. Same as the day before and no doubt the same as what the next day is going to be like.' I said, truthfully, and then straight away cursing myself for not offering the standard reply any other kid would give like 'not bad' or 'aye, was good.' Dad, as he's known to do, didn't hit me with the standard reply, either.

'Well look, Jackie. I'm not going to lie to you, I never do. You've heard that saying 'schooldays are the best days of your life' aye?'

I nodded, having heard it a hundred times but, funnily enough, never from any cunt who was actually still *at* school.

'Well that's a lot of pish, that. When you're an adult, the world opens itself up to you in ways you can't even imagine at school age but, well, that's the thing, isn't it? You're fourteen so you're none the wiser about it. But I'm *telling* you that there's better stuff waiting for you *after* school. Here's the thing though. You've got to put the work in NOW so that the world opens up for you *when* you leave. The less work you put in now. the smaller the world's going to be for you when you try to get out into it.'

I never knew how my dad's exams went when he was at school but considering I'd never seen him with a real job. I'd take an educated guess on him not being educated. That was *definitely* not something I was about to bring up while he life coached me.

'Life's all about getting out what you put in, son,' he said with a serious look to his face.

'A bit like you with the puggies eh, dad. Only you don't actually put in much but you get plenty back out.' I joked which, for a split second, had me thinking I'd maybe overstepped the mark but he just pished himself laughing at the irony of his words biting him on the arse. In a deeply personal way, like.

'Aye, always an exception to the rule as well,' he winked back at me.

I was trying my best to hold a conversation with him but all I could think of was Dynamo stood there at the bus stop mouthing off to the other two about how he knew that I wasn't going to show. How I was a wee shitebag. All of that predictable patter.

The closer that we got to Flav's house the closer it was going to also be before I was going to have to go through this whole act of me going up to his front door and knocking on it while, hopefully, my dad continued on down the street. I'd already decided that if he'd clocked me not actually going into Flav's house - which I was never going to be doing - I was going to tell him that I must've got my nights mixed up.

We were only something like half a dozen doors down from Flav's when my luck turned back around again. The noise of the car peeping its horn almost made me shite myself as it was completely out the blue when we were talking about 'The Violet.' Doesn't matter what the conversation's about. Dad will *always* find a way to bring it around to Muirhouse Violet. He was telling me about how things were dying down again after the whole Sunny and the van incident. Thing is, even I knew that it was always only a matter of time before something else radge happened again during one of their games. Not sure how one of the team literally trying to run the referee over in his Transit can ever be topped but I'm sure the team - and the assortment of complete nutjobs it boasts - will have a right good go at it.

Because of how passionately he was into what he was telling me. My dad didn't expect the car to surprise us in the way that it did, either. Two of us almost jumped out of our skins, like.

We both wheeled around at the same time to see the familiar face of uncle Benji smiling back at us.

'Alright, shaggers?' He said as he pulled up alongside us and stopped.

'Where you two off to, then?' He asked before any of us could even reply back.

'The wee man's away to play the Playstation at his pal's. I'm on my way to see Archie about that thing we were talking about the other day.'

My dad replied, confirming that he was up to something dodgy without even having to say it.

Like father like son.

'Jump in then, I'm going that direction, anyway.' Uncle Benji said leaning over and opening the passengers side door for my dad.

'No point me getting in then, is there? Considering Flav's house is right there.' I pointed.

'Aye, you're right enough.' My dad said without a passing thought as he jumped at the chance to be in a warm car and back out of the cold.

'Have a good night then, Jackie and I'll see you back at the house later.'
He said looking back out the car by this point and sticking his seat belt
on.

'Aye you too, dad. See you later uncle Benji.' I said before carrying on
what was left of the journey.

He pulled off peeping the horn in the same way that he'd appeared on
the scene to begin with. Like a maniac. I made a show of still walking -
slowly - towards Flav's. Just enough until I saw the car disappear from
view.

Once out of sight I did a speedy one eighty turn and tore off down the
road in the direction of the bus stop that the other three were waiting
on me. As I ran down the road I noticed some of the glances that some
were giving me.

Kid running down the street in Muirhouse, at speed. Well obviously
it's because he's committed some kind of a crime and is now departing
the scene of it. *Or* running for their life from someone else.

I didn't even have the time to dignify such accusatory looks in my
direction with any kind of a response. I was too busy trying to
maintain the speed I was going at while navigating myself along the
pavement, in and out from others who were on the same side.

Old jakey with his carry out and on his way home to tan it. Mum
pushing her kid in its push chair. Mrs Stephens from a few flights
above us out in her electric mobility car which is so wide it pushes you
out onto the street if you want to get past her. They all had to be
negotiated with if I was to maintain the speed I was going at down the
road while avoiding ending up in the hossie.

The old pisshead went absolutely fucking radge when my knee
knocked into his offie bag when I ran past him. Jakeys generally do
though when they feel that their alcohol is under any kind of threat.
Protect the booze at all costs.

I was on such a mission to get to the bus stop before the bus arrived I
didn't even notice the three of them already standing there. Heard
them - no doubt due to Scooter's uncanny vision. Cunt's like a sniper
rifle without the rifle - before I saw them. All ironically cheering on

seeing me coming down the road. No doubt based on Dynamo already giving it all of the 'Jackie's bottled out' shite to the rest of them.

I was still trying to catch my breath - listening to the digs they were giving me without any way of being able to give them any comebacks, as I stood beside them - when the bus started coming down the road towards us.

'Didn't think we were going to be seeing you tonight.' Flav said, turning to me as he took the free seat beside me, second row from the back.

I then went into telling them my whole story and how I'd had to make a show of going to Flav's to play the Playstation which was the reason for me arriving as late as I did.

'Not sure why you had to hide it from your dad.' Dynamo interrupted, what was a mini conversation between myself and Flav. 'Ah, wait a minute, I know why. You didn't want him wanting in on the action and taking away some of your share. Strings would be right in there like a rat up a drainpipe if you'd given him a sniff of our plans.' He continued, taunting me. As always, looking for a reaction.

I decided to give him one.

The thought of him trying to link what we were about to do and what my dad did to bring money into the house was a bit of a leap. I'd always saw my dad as a kind of Robin Hood, of sorts. Robbing from the rich > Amusement arcade owners and giving to the poor > Us, the Carson family. My dad had told me at an early age just what pain and misery puggies caused families through the addiction the machines themselves caused people. I'm not sure how much of what dad had said had been because of him self justifying for his actions though but it had worked on me as - despite the fact he was breaking the law and didn't have an occupation that I could tell my pals mums and dads about when meeting them - I'd always looked upon his line of work as almost carrying out a noble act. Not something I would have looked on as a housebreaker.

'Hardly the same, is it?' I said back to him. 'Victimless crime, Dynamo.'

'I'm not sure the cunts that own the puggies would agree with you there.' Dynamo laughed back with the rest of them joining in. Me too as I whipped out an invisible violin and started playing it for the benefit of the arcade owners across Scotland that had suffered at the hands of Joe Carson.

We were no sooner on the bus when we were back off it again. Was hardly the journey length that would've turned the head of Phileas Fogg and I'd even mentioned as much when Dynamo had been making such a big thing about us getting a bus there to Silverknowes. Especially when we could easily have just walked it.

'Think how many houses we'll pass on the way there and back? How many people out an about on the street. Cunts driving past us in their cars and so on and so on. Lots of eyes and lots of people that will see us on our merry way only to *remember* seeing us if and when cunts start asking questions about any houses being broken into. We get the bus there and back and it drastically reduces any witnesses.'

He'd had a point with what he was saying, even if it did show the hallmarks of someone who had been thinking way too much about something like this job of his.

Once we'd all got off the number Thirty Seven, never mind all eyes being on 'us,' all eyes were on Dynamo, the man with the plan.

'So what now then?'

'Where we headed from here?'

'What's the plan, Uzbekistan?'

Dynamo had three questions fired at him from Scooter, Flav and myself, all at once.

'Give me a fucking second, for fuck's sake.' He said, irritably, as he looked around to see where he was. Trying to make it look like he knew what was happening next but his face giving the opposite impression in that he looked as lost as the rest of us.

The difference between Silverknowes and Muirhouse always blew me away a bit in the sense of, to me, it always felt like someone had decided that they'd put all of the rich people in one bit of Edinburgh and the less rich somewhere else *but* to take the absolute piss, they then put both parts beside each other.

You just knew that it would've done their heads right in - the Silverknowes cunts - being so close to us in Muirhouse and powerless to prevent us from just strolling right in if we so desired. I always took a wee bit of enjoyment out of that when I was walking through the place. Curtains and blinds twitching. Cunts pretending to be looking at stuff in their gardens when it's completely obvious that they're actually looking at you instead. Neighbourhood watch nonces.

That *protective* side to how the other half live wasn't going to be much good to the four of us when it came to getting in and out of there without any grass getting on the phone to the police, though.

'Right, this way.' Dynamo finally decided on which direction to take. Something I'd already presumed to be through guesswork and nothing else.

'So where about's the house, then?' Scooter - never the brightest - decided to ask Dynamo as we followed on behind.

'Can't fucking miss it, Scoots. Security gate at the entrance, drive that leads up to a massive mock Tudor mansion. Can't fucking miss it.' Dynamo replied without turning around.

'What's a mock Tudor mansion, like?' Scooter responded and *that* was the sixty four thousand dollar question. Mainly because Dynamo, clearly, didn't know. For being the brains of the operation it looked like he didn't even *know* what he didn't know.

'What? You mean you don't know what a fucking mock Tudor mansion looks like?' Dynamo sneered in the way that only some cunt who doesn't know what a mock Tudor mansion looks like and are trying to bluff that they do.

'The fuck do I know about mansions, Dynamo?' Scooter replied a wee bit wounded over the piss apparently being taken out of him because he didn't know his bedsits from his semi detatcheds.

It's mad, the wee nuggets of useless information that you pick up, though. I actually *did* know what a mock Tudor house looked like but *only* because the Wimpy that mum and dad used to take me to in

Magaluf was sat underneath what my mum had called a mock Tudor and how she thought it had been bizarre to see one in Mallorca never mind sitting on top of a fucking burger bar. Don't get me wrong. I wouldn't have been able to go on Mastermind on the subject. Just knew it was a fucking black and white house. Which was more than Dynamo. They made me think of the Juventus strip, anytime I saw one.

It didn't exactly fill me full of all kinds of confidence and hope that we were being led by someone as blind as that they had came to rob a house but didn't know *which* house they were there to rob.

'Not being funny, D, but I don't know what a mock Tudor is either. Like you said yourself, I'm no estate agent.' I lied. Well, not the estate agent part, obviously.

'Trust me, mate, you'll know it when you see it.' came the reply.

After all of his big man talk. All of the instructions like taking buses to limit the amount of people who would see us. The advice to wear dark clothing. All of this coming from what, or who, would've liked you to have believed that they were some kind of seasoned professional. The reality of it now, though, that they were now down to blagging it to the point of 'I don't know what house I'm looking for but I'll know it when I see it.'

In that moment I started to get pissed off at myself - and was doing a good job of hiding it - that I was willingly placing my future in the hands of a fucking moron, but that I was too scared to tell them so.

When I thought about it, like that. Who really *was* the moron? Me or him?

Well, I'm not going to be the one to give him any assistance, I thought to myself as we followed behind. Maybe this was going to be *the* thing that would stop us from actually going through with the job. Finding the actual house that you want to break into during a job would be pretty key to things all going to plan. You don't find it? Then you go home and admit that it wasn't meant for you. I'd have taken that end result at the *start* of the night if it had been offered my way.

Conversation was minimal between the four of us. Dynamo looked to be too much into his zone as he desperately looked for the sign of a house that fitted his own imagination as to what property his dad had described to his mum. He seemed to be focussed on nothing other than finding what he needed to show to the rest of his mates that he had known what he had been talking about all along. The longer we went without finding it though the more he *did* seem to be as lost at the rest of us.

Scooter, Flav and me followed behind but barely breaking breath to each other. I can only speak for myself but I had way too much nerves running through me to even pretend that I was relaxed enough to hold a normal conversation. Scooter and Flav - whatever was going through their heads - weren't for talking either.

I never said it but as we walked along the street I had started to notice that the houses were starting to get a wee bit bigger and the cars parked outside in the drives more expensive. And it wasn't exactly like it was slum village when we'd got off the bus and started walking, either.

'How much longer? It's fucking baltic, man' Flav broke his own silence and in doing so sounding like your average wee bairn in the back of the car going somewhere asking if they're there yet.

'Not long now,' all that he got back from Dynamo. Weirdly spoken exactly like a dad would do to placate his kid.

The fact that Dynamo didn't know where the fuck he was going and that had just been all mouth was as unexpected as it was ideal. He'd have to admit defeat and we'd all go home with face completely saved. We'd showed up for the play, so to speak. Isn't the actors fault if the stage isn't provided for them, eh?

That was what made it all the more gutting when I saw the black and white house a wee bit ahead on the other side of the road. Massive drive leading up to it. Well, massive if you'd class about the approx length of twelve cars - nose to tail - from front door to main road, anyway. If I could see it - and you couldn't fucking miss it - then so would Dynamo.

'Here we fucking go,' he shouted out - louder than required in a quiet leafy suburb like Silverknowes while there on the rob - clapping his hands. 'Mon,' he motioned with his head as he started to cross the road.

'You sure this is the place, aye?' Scooter whispered, looking around to see if anyone was watching us from their houses. Despite how serious the moment was I smiled to myself over the irony of him wearing the exact same Berghaus as me. We'd got them at the same time the year before when my dad had come by a load of stuff. Hiking boots. Waterproofs, fleeces, hats. Everything but the fucking tent. Growing up he kept telling me about things falling off the back of lorries. Whose job is it to secure the back of lorries before they head out onto the roads because clearly they're not up to the task.

Scooter and me had made a pact that we wouldn't wear them on the same day so as not to appear like a couple of dicks but it got too much hard work in the end and I told the cunt to just wear it whenever he wanted as I was ditching it. Almost got to the shared parenting stage where I would wear it three days a week and so would he. Fuck that. Over a Berghaus?

It wasn't just Scooter and me, either. The other two were also dressed like they were ready for a walk up the Munro's. Was a bit mad that without any of us actually discussing it beforehand we'd all came out that night to do a bit of housebreaking while dressed like ramblers.

For one night only, though, the fact that we were 'clashing' didn't matter one single fuck. No one had their mum's gloves on, at least I'd have had that in terms of the originality factor.

'Do you see any other houses with gates to stop you from getting to the front door?' Dynamo replied with that trademark sarcastic tone. This, reinforced by his regained confidence over finding the house we were looking for after initially being left looking like he had no idea of its location.

'Ready, boys?' He said turning around to the three of us as he put his hood up over his head and having a quick look behind us to the houses across the street to look for any signs of movement.

Turning back again he took his hand towards the electronic keypad that was fixed to the wall to the side of the gate and was just about to press the first number before I lunged towards him and grabbed his arm.

'Fuck you doing, eh?' His whole tone instantly changing and - for the first time since we'd became mates - looked like he was ready to go for me.

'Fuck *you* doing, you mean? You going to just type out the passcode on that keypad with your fingers, like?' I thought that would've been a clear way of putting it across.

'What else am I meant to type the numbers out with? My fucking cock?' He laughed. I thought I'd been clear. I was wrong.

'So you're not bothered about leaving fingerprints or nothing, no?' I said, already tired about being the one who least wanted to be there but apparently the one who *knew* what he was doing the most out of everyone.

'Fuck aye, good thinking, lad.' Dynamo's face lit up as if it was - and worryingly - the very first time he had thought of such a tactic.

'Right, Flav, Scooter, keep an eye out for any nosey neighbours while I get us in.' Dynamo dished out the instructions while I stood closely behind him, watching him tap out the numbers. One to Six followed by tapping on the little green thumbs up button that was glowing along with all the other buttons on the keypad.

It *was* fucking madness to set your passcode for such an expensive house, though. Then again, maybe it was a double bluff from the owners knowing that no one in their right mind would set such an easy password. People are idiots in general though. Mr Daly, my Computing Studies teacher tried to tell me that a tenth of the world's passwords for the websites they use is, 'password.' Wasn't sure if he was at it there or not though. How does anyone know that when no one tells anyone what their password is to begin with? Probably a lot of pish from Daly.

Watching Dynamo press that final green tick. Bringing the sound of the electric gate clicking and then slowly opening left the ground below me spinning. I knew it was the house. Dynamo didn't, he'd just taken the chance of typing out the passcode and seeing if it worked. I knew it was going to work because I 'knew' it was the Mock Tudor. A massive part of me wanted the code not to work though. Once it did and the gate started to open. There was no going back after that.

'Mon,' Dynamo grabbed hold of my sleeve and pulled me with him as he slipped through the opening of the gate. Scooter and Flav, noticing this, abandoned their posts to join us as the four of us got ourselves inside.

Having seen how Dynamo had used the pad to get us in, I went straight for the one on the inside of the gate and repeated the same steps as him to close it again.

This enough to stop Dynamo who was already getting set to storm up to the front door.

'Come on, Jackie, fuck's sake, man, what are you fucking about with the gate for?' He said with a look that he'd had just about enough of me when - as far as I'd been concerned - I'd been fuck all other than an invaluable asset to him.

'Fucking hell, D, you've said that the owners of this place are away on holiday, aye?' I tried to put my point across in a calm way that wasn't going to have us arguing while we were meant to be under the radar of everyone.

'Well, obviously, why else would we be breaking in right now?' he continued with the tone.

'Aye, so if you're away on your holidays to Spain why would your fucking gate be lying open? Especially when it has already been closed after you've left for the airport? You know what all these kind of neighbours are like, eh?'

'Trust me, D, anything I do from now until we go our separate ways tonight is going to be through the motivation of keeping myself from being lifted.

I didn't even bother waiting on a response from him. Choosing to go back to closing the gate and then heading up to the house. I hadn't noticed but Dynamo must've told the others to hang back for me because I expected to turn around and see the three of them fucking about outside the front door of the house. Instead, when I turned around, the three of them were standing there still waiting on me. Almost fucking shat myself, finding them there. You know? When you're not expecting something like another person beside you in that way, like.

'Right, boys, now that we're out of the way of the street lights. We just need to keep things quiet and on the down low and we'll be sorted for slipping in.' Dynamo said, putting a finger up to his lips.

It was probably the most sensible thing he'd said all night and would've been sage advice were it not for the fact that the four of us only managed to take around three more steps before the blinding security lights came on. Fucking prisoner of war camp stuff. Colditz or wherever that German place was called.

We were rabbits caught in the headlights when both of them - on either side of the front of the house - came on. Was like Hampden Park on a World Cup qualifier night, for fuck's sake.

'Hide,' I loudly whispered - if that's actually possible? - while running towards one of the big bushes that sat beside the rockery in the massive garden. The bushes so big that the four of us were easily concealed behind them while we all crouched there in panic mode. Trying to remain as statuesque as possible.

Literally fucking *felt* like I was trying to escape a prisoner of war camp in that moment. Crouching there listening out for any kind of noise that was going to follow a couple of security lights going on that - if noticed - would, without a doubt, grab the attention.

There was nothing, though. No voices, dogs barking or foot steps getting closer to try and investigate.

'What do we do now, Dynamo?' Flav asked, genuinely appearing to be bricking it and looking for D to be the voice of calm. Some hope, there. 'Fuck all we can do other than wait until the lights go off and we try again.' He said, like it was the most obvious thing to do. The *only* thing to do.

That was about the point where I felt that I'd had enough of the clueless cunt. Learned a lot about Dynamo that night and one was that he was even more of a moron than I'd already given him credit for. It was only his unhinged and - at times - psychotic personality that masked it and held things together for him, preventing cunts from calling him out on stuff. Bunched up beside him while we were trapped by the security lights and hearing him offer the suggestion that all we could do was to sit there and wait until the lights went off before we attempted to try again.

'Look, I'm not saying that's a bad idea or fuck all but the moment those security lights go off and we move again. You not think that the first thing that's going to happen is that they're going to go *on* again, no?'

I tried to say it with as much of a sugar coat to it as I could but there was no getting away from the fact that *however* it was said it was going to expose just what a fucking stupid idea it had been of Dynamo's to stay there trapped by the lights. We'd have been there until daylight, going by his reasoning.

'You wanting to lead this fucking job or what?' He spat back at me. I think, by then, getting a bit pissed off at me using my head and exposing him to be doing the opposite.

'No, course I don't. I'm just saying that,' I didn't even get a chance to finish my sentence before he cut me off.

'Right, it doesn't look like anyone's coming to check the place out and, with the gates being closed, they'll not get any further than that anyway. Looks like if we can get ourselves up to the side of the house we'll be out of the line of sight of the security lights. Soon as they go out again we just slip in the front door.'

'Let's go' Dynamo said as he slipped out from behind the bush and sprinted over to the side of the house as he'd just told us. It was probably only a couple of minutes before the lights went out again but it felt easily like ten times that amount. Just standing there in plain view of anyone who might have been looking towards the house. It was complete bait behaviour. Had a police car rolled up any moment I, for one, would not have been surprised.

The second the lights went out we carefully, sticking to the walls to avoid detection by the light sensors, made our way around to the front door, Dynamo stooping down to collect the front door key from under the small statue of an owl, exactly as his dad had said to his mum where it had been.

My heart was racing faster than it had ever done in my life. Faster than seeing my first Edinburgh derby win. Faster than the Waltzers at the Links Market in Kirkcaldy that mum and dad used to take me to when I was younger. Faster than the moment I knew I'd been rumbled over the hash cakes I'd made at school. When Dynamo turned the key to let us in and the alarm, as expected, went off. There was, without any debate, the fastest I'd ever felt my heart going. I could fucking hear it vibrating and thumping through my ears.

'Dynamo?' Flav said, bouncing up and down without his feet leaving the ground, almost like he was desperate for a shite. He seemed to be needing Dynamo to be the person to take away all of the anxiety that the alarm was bringing.

'Shut yer pus, the now.' Dynamo replied as he made straight for the keypad to switch the alarm off. Even then, it was still not too late, I felt. Aye, we'd broken into a place, technically. We hadn't stolen anything, yet. The last hope I had was that Dynamo had misheard the part about the house alarm and that when he tapped in the code it wasn't going to work and we were going to be left standing there in a house with its alarm going off and no way of switching it off. That scenario would have left us with no option other than to get ourselves to fuck and back to Muirhouse and say no more about it.

The alarm code worked, though.

'See, Ned fucking Flanders, what's all the panic about?' He turned around to Flav with a cocky smile on his face.

'Ok then, lets go shopping. I trust you all brought your torches with you?' Dynamo pulled out a small flashlight, twisting the end of it to switch it on.

'Damn right,' Scooter said, fishing into his North Face jacket and whipping out one of those torches completely surrounded in rubber. Frank's Army and Navy store, stuff.

'Fuck, I forgot.' Flav said, with it only then appearing to hit him of the importance of a torch in such a delicately discreet situation. Dynamo, in there and out for only one person, didn't look to be giving a fuck one way or another if anyone *else* had a torch with them. He had his and off he went to search for the treasure that he'd confidently - and without any factual basis - told us would be lying in wait.

'And Dynamo goes straight off in search of the bedrooms of the house. Bedroom's in rich households being a veritable goldmine of jewels and valuables. Today he has gold, silver, watches and money on his shopping list. Let's see how much he can accumulate before he runs out of time.'

Dynamo went off up the stairs, putting on an English accent that, I think, was meant to be the voiceover man from that Supermarket Sweep show on the telly. It rung a bell though. Not that I get much chance to watch that in the morning having a mum and dad that would only let you off school if you were dead and even then they'd probably demand to see a death certificate.

Scooter followed him which left Flav and me still down the stairs. Two cunts without a torch to see where we were going, or what we were doing.

'Where should we look then?' Flav asked me, genuinely looking like he needed direction.

'Fuck knows,' I shrugged my shoulders although it was probably too dark in there for him to have noticed either the movements of my shoulders or the blank look on my face. 'We don't have a fucking torch between us for starters so how the fuck are we meant to find anything?'

In the dark of the house I'd quietly slipped my mums gloves on. I had no intention of stealing anything but neither was I going to be having my finger prints on anything - even if just by accident - once the inquest started after the owners got back from Spain.

'Surely it wouldn't hurt to just stick the lights on for a couple of minutes while we have a wee deek around, eh?' Flav said, only now, things beginning to dawn on him that he was literally wasting his time being inside there with the way that he was now finding himself.

'Flav, you're my best mate and I love you but I swear. If you switch any lights on inside here I'll break your fucking fingers.' I replied mainly through wanting to avoid any neighbours tippling that someone was in the house but definitely with an element of not wanting any cunt to see me wearing my mum's gloves, too.

'It's the whole point of why us doss cunts were meant to bring torches, man.' There's no one *meant* to be *in* here so why the fuck would there be lights on? Be as well calling nine nine nine on ourselves, fuck's sake.'

'Aye, you're right enough, Jackie. I'm not thinking straight. Bit heavy all of this housebreaking stuff, eh?'

I couldn't disagree with him there, like.

'CHECK *ME* OOT, EH? BET YOU'D FUCKING GIVE ME ONE LIKE THIS, SCOOTER, DIDNAE KEN YOU WERE THAT WAY, EH?'

We heard Dynamo shouting from upstairs and the sound of Scooter absolutely ending himself laughing. I had no idea what all of it was about and wasn't sure that I wanted to, either.

'You look like that Versace woman with the Jimmy Calderwood tan.' We then heard Scooter saying in amongst laughing. The mind boggled at that and - considering I was hardly busy downstairs looting the place - I decided to head upstairs to see what was going on.

'Best someone keeps an eye out down here in case anyone appears outside. You alright to stay down here for a few minutes, man?' I asked Flav who, himself, had been standing around like a spare prick anyway, not sure what he was doing with himself.

I headed towards the noise which was coming from one of what looked like four bedrooms. I'd be lying though if I said that I'd expected to walk in and see Dynamo ransacking his way through lots of drawers and trinket boxes while wearing a woman's dress and wig. Scooter doing the same, only without any female clothing on.

'What the fuck's going on here?' I laughed. The two of them surprised by my sudden appearance.

'Not bad, eh?' Dynamo said, standing up and, momentarily, forgetting about the drawer he was searching through.

'I think this dress really brings out the colour in my eyes.' He said, giving me a three sixty turn that I could barely see because of the torch being left sitting in the opposite direction.

'Aye, nice pair of heels to go with and you're set, eh?' I joked back.

'Anything worth taking, downstairs?' Dynamo asked me once he'd turned back around to finish going through the drawer.

'Nah, it's all big stuff that we're not going to get back to Muirhouse from here either by walking or the bus. Us carrying a plasma screen is hardly going to be what you'd call under the radar, D.'

I lied to him. If I'd had said that I hadn't looked that would've only meant that *he* would've then wanted to have a scan for himself once he'd come back down which would've only meant us in there for even longer. From the second I'd entered the place all I wanted was to be leaving again and if *that* meant lying to a friend then I was fully on board with such a strategy.

'Aye, we're going to go through the other bedrooms but we've hit the mother load in this one, like. Obviously the maw and da. The others are probably going to be the kids rooms.

I guess there's no respect when it comes breaking into a stranger's house but the way Dynamo treated the owner's possessions was a bit much. Every drawer - once rifled through - thrown up into the air and across the room with all of its contents scattering everywhere. Anything of value shoved into the small black rucksack that he'd had round his shoulders since he'd got off the bus in Silverknowes.

When I watched him rip the dress from off of him, as opposed to taking a few seconds to just slide it back off, I'd seen enough.

'Fucking hell. That was a Dolce and Gabbana, mate!' Scooter said, picking up the ripped threads and inspecting the inside label with his torch.

'Aye, 'was' being the operative word, there' Dynamo laughed as he began to rifle through one of the three wardrobes full of clothes.

I headed back downstairs to find Flav no further forward than he was when I'd left him to go upstairs.

'What are they up to?' He asked, still standing there in the darkness of the hall leading to the kitchen and living room.

'Cosplay, mate.'

'Have you found anything worth taking?' I asked, already assuming it to being the square route of nada.

'Nah, haven't looked. Not exactly the best prepared. No torch, no gloves. Fucking hell, even the coat I've worn here you'd do well to get an apple in each pocket even if I *was* able to find anything.' He said, with a feeling sorry for himself tone while confirming that he was definitely up there in terms of being one of the world's shittest burglars.

'Look, man, it's for the best anyway. This is total nonsense, this. We've went too far and now it's going to be a case of damage recovery and hope we get out of it trouble free. Best just keep your hands in your pockets until we get out of here again.'

I said as much as I could without directly blaming Dynamo for all of it.

There was more laughing and shouting from upstairs again which could've only meant that the pair of them had stumbled across something else of note. I shuddered to think of the mess that they were going to have left by the time they were done. I wasn't going back up there again. What I didn't see I wouldn't be able to tell anyone about if put under severe pressure.

We stayed downstairs while Dynamo and Scooter worked their way through the rooms upstairs. Occasionally myself or Flav would go and have a wee look outside through the living room window just to make sure there was no activity outside.

Eventually the two of them came walking down the stairs singing The Clash's 'Daddy was a bank robber.' It was only when they got up close to me that I noticed that Dynamo was wearing one of those orange sashes that those men in the bowler hats wear on those marches with the flutes and drums.

'Wee look down here and we'll get ourselves back to the motherland, eh?' Dynamo said as he walked across the room. Putting on the funny walk that those guys in the sashes do when you see them marching down the road.

'Told you, we've already had a look down here. You got everything that's worth anything up the stairs.' I said, trying to speed things up.

'I'll be the judge of that,' he said in dismissal. Almost as if he'd pegged on to me actually having never *wanted* to find anything in there.

'Aye no worries, shove that three piece settee in your rucksack for me if you can.' I said back, sarcastically.

If the night had showed me just what a moron Dynamo truly was it also gave me a chance to see the extra layers of what an absolute cunt he could be too. As anticipated, there wasn't anything worth stealing inside the living room but - unlike other people who would've just accepted that and then proceeded to leave the house - Dynamo decided to leave a little calling card, of sorts.

I wouldn't have believed it had it been a second hand story told to me at school about someone but Dynamo went round all of the pictures that were in frames. Some of them really old pictures, by the looks. Gran and grandad on their wedding day and all of those kind of precious memories. Dynamo, decided that it would be a laugh to remove some of them from their frames and rip them up into tiny pieces and throwing them up like ticker tape like what you see the Boca and River Plate fans doing at games.

Some of the pictures, themselves, looked like the kind that people would literally risk their life to grab if their house was on fire and they had to leave in a hurry, and there was Dynamo. Taking the liberty of ripping them up because he thought it was 'funny.' It was sick as fuck and one of the final nails in the coffin as far as us being mates. Most of the other nails being hammered in over the course of that one night.

'We about done, aye?' I said after seeing one too many picture frames smashed and picture inside ripped up while coming around to the fact that we'd been inside there for around an hour and were probably pushing our luck by then.

'Aye, two shakes, man, just need to go to the toilet before I go.' Dynamo replied.

'They say a lot of burglars need to go to the toilet when on a job, eh' Scooter chipped in while having a last sniff around the place with his torch. Before I could even think of giving him some kind of wideo reply that he deserved. I was distracted by Dynamo taking off the orange and blue sash and putting it on the floor.

'Scooter, shine your light on the sash,' he barked before then undoing his belt and then pulling his jeans down.

'Need to make sure I hit the target, eh?' Dynamo said in justification as he squatted above the floor and squeezed. I couldn't look anymore so chose to look out of the living room window, making sure there was no nasty surprises lying in wait outside on us exiting the building. Even though I didn't see, - how could you ever stand there and watch a friend doing a shite with a spotlight on him? - the sounds and smell were horrendous. We left with a warning for me to watch where I stepped. Dynamo wanting it to be all in one piece sat there waiting on the owner of the sash coming back to the house after their holidays.

I didn't even bother asking what the point of that one last gesture was for. What really *was* the point?

It's. A. Laugh. Isn't. It?

Definitely not for the owner of the sash it wouldn't have been. Guaranteed, that.

Getting ourselves back to Muirhouse was a piece of piss. Only saw one person between the house we'd been in and us getting on the bus. Just some woman who was taking out her bin. We kind of locked eyes when we were passing her at the bin and she gave me a smile. It felt a wee bit strange. Almost like a look as if she knew me or something. Anyway, I gave her a smile back just to be friendly, like. It's nice to be nice as mum tells me.

I was in for a few nervy days to follow, though. Aye, technically I hadn't stolen anything - the only ones out of the four of us who *did* was Dynamo and Scooter. Dynamo, the majority. Rolex watches, the lot. - but I'd still been part of the break in and that was as bad.

Even Dynamo appeared to respect the seriousness of what we'd done. Most unlike the boy, he'd been a bit cagey when it came to the subject of what he'd taken from all of those upstairs rooms, rather than be boasting about it to us all. While he was showing us the Rolexes and the diamonds and gold. It looked like he had other stuff still inside the rucksack that he wasn't showing us.

The next day at school. I barely spoke to the other three of them - Dynamo, especially, I wanted to avoid as much as I could - but on the times that we were all in the same spot, the very *last* thing that we wanted to speak about had been what we'd been up to the night before.

I didn't think it was possible to worry even more *after* we'd carried it out but it was impossible to escape from. From the night I got home from Silverknowes - and found it near on impossible to get to sleep through the fear of a knock on the door from Lothian and Borders finest - it only got worse, no matter how many days had passed since we'd done it.

Chapter 8

Strings

'See that's where you're wrong though, Strings' Benji said, shaking his head while making sure he kept his eyes on the large multi traffic light operated roundabout we were approaching.

'Pigeons *aren't* cunts. They're nothing other than harmless flying rats. Seagulls on the other hand are flying CUNTS. The cunt's cunt when it comes to birds, if you will.'

I stood corrected.

We were on our way back to Edinburgh from a wee trip to Perthshire after some intelligence had come my way over a mark just waiting to be exploited at a tea room up that neck of the woods. We were heading back home via Pilton to visit Glenn Jones to pick up Five Thousand Lambert and Butlers and a couple of cases of Smirnoff that was part of his weekly haul he'd brought back from his trip to France. He'd started off just bringing stuff back for himself but the minute that he mentioned it to me when we were sat in The Gunner having a scoop. I had pound signs flashing in front of my eyes at the opportunity of the money that was there to be made.

Didn't take long for him to get a bit pissed off at my constant orders but at the end of the day, he was making out of it as well. Wasn't exactly one way. He'd started saying how worried he was of getting caught with all of the reeks and booze he was bringing back across but, - like anyone else - he got used to the money so despite the fact he was making out that he didn't want to do it, it never exactly stopped him from *actually* following through with anything. And besides, like Benji had told him that day in The Gunner when he was trying to withdraw his 'courier services.'

'The more full your lorry is of Lambert and Butler the less space there'll be for any asylum seekers to sneak in and hide. I'd rather be fined for transporting fags that I *knew* about than getting fucked for illegally transporting a human being that I didn't even *know* was there in the first place until it was too late.'

Benji, of course, in reality having absolutely zero concern for the well being of Glenn but basically just telling him what he wanted to hear to ensure the flow of contraband continued.

'Take the other week,' he continued control of the whole putting me right on my expressing my whole dislike to pigeons. We were in a good mood - having taken a good Two Fifty back with us from The Thistle tea room - and were enjoying a laugh on the journey back to Edinburgh. A pigeon had flown right in front of the car at us, like a fucking kamikaze. Bottling it at the last minute and flying up and above the roof of the car.

'I'd been to McDonalds, through the drive thru, like. Took my scran across the retail park so I could eat it before I got down the road to my house, ye ken how cold it gets before you get yourself home, eh? Fast food my fucking arse. Fast at going cold, ya cunt.'

'So I parked up and opened the bag to get out my Quarter Pounder with cheese and chips and the next thing. This fucking massive seagull comes and lands on the windscreen of the car and is proper staring at me. Like it was trying to psyche me out and put me off my meal so I would give it to it instead. What kind of a cunt would do that? A cunt that finds my windscreen wipers suddenly traveling across the windscreen and almost trapping its webbed feet underneath them. Thing fucking shat itself, wasn't pleased, like.'

'Nah, fuck those seagull, bastards, fuck them all.'

I laughed at the passion of him on the subject. Not like I was a fan of them myself, I thought that I'd be at least afforded the chance of having the opinion that they were both - in their own way - a pair of winged bastards but didn't realise I was in the car with Mr Team Pigeon.

'Hey, you'll get no arguments from me when it comes to the seagulls, Benj. Remember the time those two done that pincer attack on me and stole my Sausage Roll from Baynes? I'm convinced those cunts know what a Baynes bag looks like. Once they see that red and white design they're on alert from then on.'

'Oh fuck, I'd forgotten all about that, Joe.' He laughed while thinking back to that day. He stood there pissing himself, doubled up, like. Meanwhile I'm taking fresh air swings at a pair of seagulls that showed me up like some on his arse boxer who's in the last round and praying to god that the bell will come. Never connected with one of them while they still managed to casually pick up my two bags of freshly cooked pastry based treats before - being seagulls - going on to then fight with *each other* in the middle of the street over who got to keep what was inside.

'Talking about cunts, we've got another one to talk about.' Benji said, changing the subject, as he overtook a caravan that had been boxing us in on the motorway due to the already steady flow of cars coming down the outside lane that had been trapping us in behind this fancy motorhome slash caravan that had a Belgian citizen's sticker on the back.

'Oh aye? You'll need to narrow that one down, mate, we know enough of them to fill a phone book.' I laughed while genuinely intrigued over who Benji wanted to talk about.

'This wee bastard that your Jackie is hanging around with. That Dynamo.'

The face I gave him was enough confirmation for Benji to know that I was already on the same page as him.

'I know more about his big brother, Boney, than I do the younger one but if he ends up even half as bad as his older brother then he's going to be one to avoid. I just don't want Jackie involved in anything, he's a good lad. Bit of a cheeky wee fucker, though. No idea where he gets that from either as well.' He looked to the side for a second and laughed at me.

'Word seems to be that Dynamo is going in the exact same direction as Boney though so, I don't know? Maybe you need to have a wee word in Jackie's ear, like. Not telling you how to parent or fuck all either, Strings. Just looking out for the wee man, eh.'

It wasn't anything to take offence over so none was taken. I'd have said the same thing to Benji if he was in the same position with his kid.

'Well, look, there's no point in me trying to pretend that Jackie's an angel. At the same time though it's always just been a case of boys will be boys with him. Think what the pair of us were like when we were his age and some of the stuff that *we* got up to. Never took things too far though, did we? That's the same with Jackie. Take the hash cakes at school for instance. Don't get me wrong or anything. I was fucking raging at him when I found out. Once the red mist had cleared, though? I was able to see it as a wee bit funny, just a prank where no one got hurt. With this wee fucking Dynamo cunt though? Just seems to be anything that Jackie's been caught involved in the past year. That Dynamo is always right there in the middle of it.'

Benji was half listening and half trying to pay attention to the fact that there was a massive TNT lorry braking up ahead and leaving him to do the same.

'You know what it's like, though, with teenagers, ken?' I continued.

'Tell them not to do something and, at times, you'll drive them in the *opposite* direction. Jackie knows the difference between right and wrong, just the way Han and myself have brought him up. We give him enough rope as a result. Like I told the wee man, 'I trust you so here's the rope of freedom, the *gift* of freedom if you will. Don't come back to me with the fucking thing tied around your neck asking for me to untie it, though. With this rope comes great responsibility not to fucking hang yourself with it' make no mistake though, Benj, if I ever see that Dynamo doing something I'm not happy with or is what you'd consider over and above boys will be boys he'd fucking hear it from me. Not giving a fuck who his big brother is either, he'd fucking hear it from me if he wanted, too.'

'Aye well rather you than me, there.' Benji laughed. 'You seen the size of the cunt? Fairly bulked up when he was on the inside, like. Fuck all boney about him now! I heard that he'd 'acquired' the contracts to half the pubs and clubs in the city centre and that he's 'in negotiations' as to securing the other half. You don't mess with cunts like that.'

Jackie, being fourteen going on eighteen, was at one of those ages that there had to be a bit of give and take with the boy. I'd been there myself so knew what it was like. The pressures of simply being that age and trying to figure out your life in general. School, developing who you are as a person. Girls, peer pressure and all of that stuff.

Confusing time, like, so that was the approach that Han and I took with him. If he stepped out of line then he'd soon wish he hadn't but at the same time allowed to have his own space without us checking up on him all the time.

For years I'd been telling him that, to an extent, it was him that shaped his own destiny. All of that put out into the world what you want back in return stuff. Might be a lot of mumbo fucking jumbo stuff, that, but I think there's something in it. To simplify it. If you're a cunt then the chances are that you're going to experience a lot of people being cunts *back* to you. Act sound and be decent towards others and you'll get it back in kind. To simplify it to Jackie, and as I'd done, more personally.

Bring me trouble and trouble you shall be repaid with, in spades.

'Han can't stand him, either.' I carried on, now that I had Jackie's pal in my head. 'I mean, Han's pretty black and white, eh? If she likes you then she likes you but she won't hide it if she doesn't, either. It was last year, probably the first time he came around to ours to see if Jack was in. Once she'd come back through to the living room she'd even said about this new kid who had been at the door and how she didn't like the look of him. Said he looked a bit shifty and was suspiciously older than Jack's age.'

'Aye well he's definitely one to keep an eye on, Strings, all I'm saying.' Benji said before launching into an instant piece of - over the top - road rage over the car in front whose driver had, clearly, forgotten that his indicator was still on and blissfully unaware about it while driving along the motorway, signaling to go left when there was no left to turn to for miles.

'STICK YER FUCKING INDICATOR OFF YA CUNT'

Benj shouted while flashing his lights to the driver.

'So what do you think this team meeting is about tomorrow night then?' Benji asked, changing the subject, once he'd recovered from his mini episode which had been all for nothing because the driver in the grey Audi was *still* driving along with the indicator on.

I'd received a call from Jock Hunter the night before. Like, I assume, the rest of the squad. Hunter, as always, was brief and to the point. Telling me that he was calling a team meeting and that all of the squad needed to be there in attendance. Only exceptions being any of the lads who worked nights, something he knew most definitely did not apply to me. He was hanging up on me before I even got the chance to ask him why, at two nights notice, he was calling the meeting. It was for The Violet though. Of course I'd be there.

Why he was calling it, though?

Was he announcing that terms had been agreed between Barcelona and us and that Zlatan Ibrahimovic and Rossi were heading in opposite directions?

Had the SFA come calling for him to take the national managers job and that it was simply too big an opportunity to pass up and wanted to say a farewell to us all?

Highly unlikely, I suppose. Definitely likely was that he was going to have some unwelcome news from the authorities regarding some incident that had taken place during a previous match and had only now been reported. With The Violet. I generally liked to give it a full calendar month to pass from one of our games being played before you can safely say that 'whatever' went on before during or after the ninety minutes has been missed out on.

Luckily, for both players and those on the sidelines, the referee and linesmen would need eyes in the back of their heads to take in 'all' that goes on at that level on a Sunday morning. The key to staying under the radar of the authorities is to limit things to a very low level of pettiness on the pitch. It's almost taken as standard that it's going to happen out on the field. Muirhouse Violet, however, never quite managed to nail that whole 'low key' approach to things. Always going for the Hollywood application when it came to radge things happening around or in the game. Why break someone's leg with an ill timed challenge when you can run them over in your sparky's van or shoot them from the side of the pitch with a paintball gun, eh?

Due to that. The league were no strangers to receiving cheques from us. There's been a couple of players over the years for us that we used to joke paid more to the league in fines than they did to the mums of their kids as maintenance. No fucking wonder that Archie Bryson, the president of the association, drives a BMW X5, like.

'Nah, you know Jock. Would've been sat there with his wee phone book going through each player studiously. Probably called us in order starting from big Sepp and worked his way through the team up to the strikers and then the subs.' The two of us laughed as despite me only saying it for effect it was the *exact* thing that you could've seen Jock Hunter doing.

'He was on and off again before I could even get a chance to ask him anything. Soon as he heard me confirm the time we were to meet up he was away again. On to the next player on his list, I imagine. Does your head in though, like when a meeting gets called out of the blue and you're not given the reason for it. Your mind runs away with itself, like.'

'Aye, I know what you mean, Joe.' Benji nodded his head in agreement. 'Like, when I got home last night and the breadknife passed on the message to me from Jock about a team meeting on Thursday night, my mind's been running away with itself over it. Everything from him stepping down to him presenting us with a half year appraisal on the team, proper Don Revie dossier stuff, to us being thrown out the league for something that even I don't know we've done.'

'Well you're there on the sidelines, Benji boy. If you don't notice what's going on then no cunt will.' I said, reminding him that if it wasn't for him I wouldn't even know about half of the shit that goes on out there on the pitch behind my back.

'What was his mood like, you know? When he spoke to you?' Benji said trying to gauge if the meeting was going to be a good meeting or one that would've been better to avoid. Not like any of us was going to have a choice there, anyway.

'He was just Jock. Intensely serious and to the point. Couldn't pick anything out of the call that indicated positive or negative. We'll just have to wait and see tomorrow night when we get there, I suppose.' I replied, trying to take the pragmatic can't do fuck all about things approach but - also like Benji - I hated the unknown when it came to things like that. We were Muirhouse Violet. We done a bit of training, where possible, and turned up on a Sunday and played our matches. We didn't really do team meetings. Any 'meetings' the team did was when they just happened to be in the same pub having an ale.

You can't worry about something that you, personally, cannot change. Something my old grandad had told me in John Menzies when I started crying because they didn't have the Boba Fett Star Wars figure that I had went there specifically to get with my birthday money that time. It was just a toy at the end of the day but the message was one that always stayed with me. Whatever the meeting was about - at least until I was there in attendance - it was nothing I could do about. What I *could* do something about though was see about bringing in some much needed funds into the homestead.

Collecting the cigarettes and alcohol from Jonesy was but part of that operation. From the profit I'd make from the L&B's and the vodka - along with the takings from the puggy up in Perth - it was shaping up to be one for the scrapbook. One that might even have got me some sex out of it from the breadknife.

As we drove into Pilton towards Glen's house we agreed to quickly pick up the stuff from him and then for Benji to take me on a few drops to get rid of half of it straight away. After that a quick visit to The Gunner - to exchange the hundreds of pounds worth of coins I'd been left with from earlier on - and then drop me off back at mines for the night so I could get my tea, put my feet up after a hard days grafting and find out what that wife and kid of mines had been up to.

Chapter 9

Strings

'It's not fucking good enough, that's what it is.' Jock stood there in the corner of the function suite. Gesturing towards the blackboard that he had actually went to the trouble of bringing to the pub with him, along with - what looked like - a freshly purchased packet of chalk.

Violet 0 - Riccarton 3

Oxgangs 2 - Violet 1

Violet 0 - Thornybank 0

Roseburn 1 - Violet 0

When you looked at it written there in big white letters and numbers, he was right. It *wasn't* good enough. Seeing the past month's worth of results spelled it out loud and clear. We'd hit a slump and Jock, it appeared, wasn't about to let things slide any longer.

Benji, while joking, hadn't been too wide of the mark with his comment about Jock having compiled a Don Revie style intelligence filled dossier. Wasn't exactly filled full of intelligence, though. More the examples of *negligence* on the part of the Muirhouse players.

'Look, we've never been known as angels, Muirhouse Violet. Nor will we ever be but I *know* that there's players inside all of you. We all know that we have a bit of a reputation to us and that generally any match that we take part in has elements of 'industrial' to it in some shape or form but, obviously, I know that there's more, much more, to the team than that. I wouldn't dedicate all my blood sweat and tears to the team if I thought that you were all a case of lost causes and you know what? You lot wouldn't turn up rain hail or snow on a Sunday morning if you didn't think there was something worthwhile about it, either. If a job's worth doing it's worth doing right, though, and I will not have my name alongside a team of losers. It's not in my DNA. If the losing gene comes into contact with my own I wither up and die and I'm not letting that happen. If there's any of you sitting in here tonight that *do* have the losing gene then I'm afraid you'll need to leave. I'm literally allergic to you so for the benefit of my, and the team's, health you'll need to go.'

He's some cunt, Jock. I'll always give him that.

'If we could just cut the fucking drama out, *that* would be half the battle. Look at the other week with Sunny. That, for any other fitba team, should've been some kind of earth shattering incident that rocks a fitba team to its core but for us it was just shrugged off as just one of those things. Because, for us, it WAS just one of those things. *Another* one of those things. I want the club, our club, to be known for the results on the park not for the standard incidents that happen to follow the team around from match to match. Take last week for example. How many fucking times did I go round you all and tell you not to fall for the bait of dismantling that Andy Henry for Kingsknowe? Now I fucking know that there's history and that when he stole from the clubs kitty when he played for us that he stole from each and every one of us.'

'Fucking prick done us out of our end of season trip to Magaluf.' Coffee butted in before being stared down by Jock for interrupting him mid flow.

'The *point* I was trying to make to you all was that it was four years ago now that the lad had done it and he'd served his time and that we couldn't go out to break both his legs every single time he played us as if it was yesterday that he'd stolen the money. And what was your response to my instructions?'

Big Tel instantly looked down at the floor.

'Aye might well you stare at the fucking floor, Terry. Two yellow cards inside three minutes? What the fuck were you thinking about? Worst part is you didn't even touch him for the second one but if you had you'd have surgically removed a limb. The boy just stood there laughing at you getting your red card.'

'Aye, he wasn't laughing twenty minutes later when I caught him with my studs when coming out to collect that ball lofted in to me, though.' Sepp said, laughing at the thought of it, a few others joining in with him.

'I don't remember you laughing too much when that big number four banged you straight in the fucking mouth in the resulting melee that you caused with your trailing leg.' Jock said back sharply.

'Look. What I'm saying is that your *own* actions are holding you back. Just focus a bit and the results will follow. Cut out the capers. And it goes without saying. The league are itching for a reason to kick us out. I thought the Sunny incident was going to be enough but we managed to escape a full scale ban by the skin of our teeth. Thank fuck for my masonic connections, that's all I'm saying.' He tapped his nose before looking back at the blackboard and pointing at the horrors of our last four games while tapping his head with a couple of fingers.

He then proceeded to go through every single one of us and did not miss a single player. Some, who had hardly kicked a ball for us, got it as bad as the regulars which wasn't exactly fair but when Jock's in that zone you're best to just let him get on with it. Not to say that every one of the team sat there quietly and took the verbal character assassination that they were being subjected to.

Montana, especially, took exception to the accusation that if he was to 'take the field without having any gear inside of him he'd maybe put in a decent performance now and again.'

'Fucking test me right now then. I'll call your fucking bluff right now. Mon, test me. We'll do it straight away. I'll fucking do you for defamation.' Montana said, making a show for everyone to see, secure in the knowledge that it wouldn't have been as if Jock Hunter would be walking around carrying a drugs piss test on him for such a random moment like that to pop up. The real irony, though, was the fact that when I was in the toilet having a piss before the meeting started. Montana was in there having a fucking line of Ching before coming in to join the rest of the team inside the function sweet.

Rossi was accused, by Jock, of being back attempting to fix matches. The only explanation for the amount of sitters that he had missed the previous four games. Rossi, understandably, wasn't best pleased at such an insinuation.

Not everyone 'got it' but I could see straight away what Jock was doing. No doubt, he'd have been reading some sports psychology book and picked up - from some American who has never managed a team of pissheads who are the furthest you could find from being professional sportsmen - something where being a complete cunt to his team of players would have a reverse effect and they'd all turn into Lionel Messi through sheer will to prove their coach wrong.

It was a classic case of reverse psychology but some in the squad were just too fucking stupid to clock on to it. Bold strategy from Jock, though. Especially with some of the boys in our side.

Big Bungalow, for another example, who would generally be considered one of our more harder players was apoplectic at being called a pussy who goes hiding when some of the more harder players in the league came up against us. It was obviously bollocks from Jock. Bungalow had seen more red over the years than a Spanish bull.

It seemed to be working for Jock, though. Well, when I say that, I mean that he got a reaction from a group of men who - up to that point - had been not exactly losing sleep over the fact their team hadn't won a game in four and only scored one single goal in three hundred and sixty minutes and even then that was a penalty that even we'd admitted to having been fortunate to have been awarded. Coffee, kicking his own foot when trying to take a shot inside the box.

For Jock's sake. I just hoped that the reaction he got was going to be a positive one. We ended up having a proper discussion. After going through the lot of us, Hunter stuck a few quid behind the bar. Enough for us to have a few scoops while we talked about how we could turn things back around.

Things that needed to be said by both players and coaches were said. Those that weren't happy with the position they'd been getting played. Them that weren't happy with the work another team mate was putting in that then, in turn, affected their own game as a result. Cunts that weren't doing enough running, choosing the right pass and losing us the ball every time we got it.

I brought up - and not for the first time - the subject of us needing an injection of new blood. I know it was a case of turkeys voting for Christmas and all that but I was always one for putting the team first and at the end of the day. Muirhouse Violet was going to be there long after I hung up my Copa Mundials. I couldn't have been the only one to feel this way but with such a thin squad there wasn't as much of a hunger from the players to play well enough to keep their place in the starting eleven. Everyone needs a wee bit of healthy competition. Just so that they can stay at the top of their game, like. That was something we didn't really have and, in my opinion, *why* we didn't apply ourselves to the heights that we were capable of.

Wanting players for the team and getting them were two very different things altogether, though.

When you made the choice to put on that Violet shirt and step into that particular arena and level of Association Football you were putting yourself in a position that, at times, would feel anything but like a little bit of recreational sport to help keep you fit. For a comparison. If you stuck a military helmet on with the word 'PRESS' on the front and started running around the Middle East. At least you'd get paid for it. Playing for Violet and all of the heat it brought. You did it for the glory. And there was hardly much of that in supply.

The suggestion of new players, laughably had players in agreement *but* them all suggesting additional players for positions *other* than their own one. I started to whistle Self Preservation Society to myself while we sat debating positions but it went completely over the heads of everyone else.

'Well, look, it's been a good chat we've had tonight, lads. I feel we've ironed out a few problems, cleared some air and I'm looking forward to seeing some of these fresh ideas and attitudes being put into action out there on the pitch. Does anyone else have anything else they needed to speak up about before we wrap things up?' Jock asked as he started to wipe the blackboard clear of what had been, by that point of the night, a badly drawn tactics board attempting to recreate a football pitch but he'd fucked the margins of the lines up to the point you only knew it was a fitba pitch because of the fact that he was a manager and you were a player at a team meeting.

There was a series of head shakes across the room. The free bar had now expired and everyone wanted nothing other than the rest of their night back to themselves.

'Ok, well there's just one last thing then before I let you all get off.'

After his first two words, half the team had already practically began standing up and getting their coats on before reluctantly slumping back into their chairs again.

113

'You've maybe already heard by now on the grapevine but our game on Sunday against Broxburn is off. Two wee bastards apparently tore up the pitch on their scramblers and left the place looking like Armadale Stadium. I offered to switch the match to Muirhouse Park but we've already played them at home this season so the rules said the match would have to be postponed although, you know me? I'm going to be pushing for the points to go to us. Take the points when you can get them. You useless bastards aren't doing anything to bring them in, are you?' He laughed.

I can't say that I wasn't exactly that upset over the news that - for the first time than I could remember - I was going to get a nice long lie in bed on the Sunday morning. The rest of the team was a mixture of those who welcomed a rare Sunday morning to themselves and those that were well miffed about it because to cancel a Violet match would mean that they would then have to spend their Sunday with their wife or girlfriend. Shopping or doing jobs about the house instead of playing ninety minutes and then spending the rest of the day in the pub sinking pints and watching live matches on Sky Sports. Removing a Muirhouse Violet match from the fixture can seriously fuck up a man's weekly plans, like.

'So with us not having a game Sunday I thought that this would be the perfect opportunity for us all to do some team bonding. Especially considering the position we currently find ourselves in. We're in a slump and team morale, obviously, has suffered as a consequence. It's time we got that back on track again, boys, so Saturday night we're having a team night out in the city centre. I don't normally give you all permission to go on a crawl but this is one of those occasions where you'll get plenty recovery time afterwards before the next game. It'll be good for you all to let off a bit of steam other than actually on the pitch. That's part of our problem at the end of the day. So Saturday. We'll start off in Rose Street and see where the day and night takes us. *Everyone* there. No exceptions, mind.'

There wouldn't have been any point in trying to protest otherwise. Saying that you had to stay in Saturday night to wash your mum's feet or anything. When the gaffer said 'no exceptions' that was *exactly* what it meant and whether it was going to be for the better of the team's morale or if it was going to tear the side apart through drunken arguments between a bunch of people who had been drinking for twelve hours. The lads were going to be going to be hitting Edinburgh town centre, en mass.

Chapter 10

Strings

'Here, Wullie, mon over and tell these cunts the story about your wee pet.'

I was sat alongside Benji, Jock, Sepp and Terry in the corner of The Rutland. Now hours into our 'team bonding' session. Aye, it was a session, right enough. The bonding side of things, though? Mixed bag, there, like. I mean, if a sporting organisation such as Muirhouse Violet are going through a bit of a bad spell and are looking to restore its fortunes. I'm not sure that having your defender and midfielder exchanging blows over who the original host of 'This is your Life' was - when the question came up on the pub quiz machine - would be seen as conducive towards the pursuit of group happiness.

'You been getting a wee dug or a cat, Wullie, aye?' Jock Hunter said jovially. It's not like you'd need to drag me kicking and screaming on an all-dayer or a night out by any stretch but for the team day out I'd had the added incentive of seeing old Jock taken out of his natural habitat and inserted into your average city centre boozer alongside all of the tourists, city workers and cunts that have more money than fucking sense. If Jock complained about the price of the liquor in The Gunner - and he did - then some of the prices in the middle of the town were going to be the cause of a fucking implosion on the poor old bastard's head.

Complete fish out of water, like, sitting there in the pub with his Londsdale shell suit on and white vest underneath like an extra from The Sopranos. Sipping on a Guinness while trendy cunts are sticking The Beastie Boys, Beck and Radiohead on the jukebox and ordering Jaegerbombs and all of that stuff.

Fuck it though, eh? Jock was game enough to suggest us all going out in the first place so respect to the old yin for coming along with us. Would've been easy enough for him to have come out with the gesture of us all being allowed a (rare) Saturday out together and then stepped aside and let us get on with it and sat there in The Gunner but instead, he was going with the one for all ethos. Then again, though, if Jock was out with us then he was, by default, going to have a front seat view to be clocking whatever took place on our team bonding exercise so there might well have been an ulterior motive to him coming out with us. The way he was sinking back the Guinness' though? If he was doing it as some act then he was fully throwing himself into his role, methodically, like. I mind sayin that to Rossi after the first hour when we found ourselves in Dirty Dick's in Rose Street to get a quick scran down our necks.

'That old cunt keeps knocking back the black stuff he's going to be in a taxi back to Muirhouse by tea time.'

'You're being a bit optimistic, there, Strings.' He said back to me as he watched Hunter down half a pint in one go like it was the first thing he'd been handed on coming out of the Sahara fucking desert.

'Aye, something like that.' Wullie said, as he tried to get himself from the bar back to the table while carrying a tray with everyone's drinks on it. His face taking on an instant crimson tinge to it the moment I'd brought up the subject.

'Mon, Wullie, get yourself sat down here and tell the rest of the boys.' I pointed to the spare seat that was there for him at the table.

'This will fucking crack you up,' I laughed, looking around everyone else.

'Didn't know you had a pet, either, Wullie. Did you bring it down from Dundee with you when you moved, like?' Terry added.

'Well, no, I only recently got it, like. She wasn't too pleased like but you know, eh? Put the foot down, didn't I?' Wullie said as he started passing all the drinks around the table to everyone.

'Aw, oh right. Staffie or a Rottie or something, like?' Sepp said before taking a big swig out of his fresh pint of Stella.

'Naw, Sepp. A ferret.' The reply.

Everybody, with the exception of poor Wullie, burst into laughter. The kind of levels that has the rest of the public sharing the boozer with you all looking over your way.

'A fucking ferret?' Jock Hunter said, eyes literally full of amazement at this. 'What the fuck do you want with a ferret, for a pet?' He, understandably, asked the question that I reckon anyone Wullie had told the story to would've justifiably asked. I did.

'Well, eh? I just thought it would make a cool wee pet, you know? Just letting it run all over the house. When I'm sat watching the fitba on the telly and having a beer. It could just hang around with me, like. Sit chilling on top of the sofa behind me. Maybe chase a wee ball about the floor. whatever it wants, like. Live and let live, eh?' Wullie replied as if it was the most natural reply you'd ever heard someone give.

'And in terms of what you were looking for in a pet, did it live up to your expectations?' I asked, already knowing the answer to that but in no way able to resist moving his story in the direction that if he wasn't going to I certainly was.

'Well no, not exactly. The fucking thing did nothing but shit all over the place and chew its way through any fucking cables that it could find. Was at Argos twice inside a week for AV and HD cables, like. Major fucking headache from the other half as well. She's watching Emmerdale one night when the telly switches itself off. The wee bastard has chewed its way through the power cable on it. Fuck knows how the fucking thing didn't electrocute itself, like.'

Everyone was in tears by this point, the feeling sorry for himself tone that he was putting it across. Only enhancing things further.

'So what did you do with it? It would've been booted out the back door if it was running about doing that shite in my house.' Terry said, sat on the edge of his seat. Now fully invested in things like every one else.

'Well, aye, that was pretty much Sandra's opinion on things and, if she hadn't been so shite scared of the wee fucker she'd have probably picked it up herself and thrown it out. I managed to talk her around. Spouted some pish to her that I'd take the thing to the vets and have it's teeth de-sharpened so it couldn't gnaw through anything. Not even sure if that's actually possible, like, but she fucking bought it anyway. Of course though, that was all for fucking nothing in the end because the stupid wee cunt ended up fucking it for itself. You try to give cunts the benefit of the doubt and they just spit it back in your face, like.'

'Why, what did it do? Sepp asked, clearly getting himself ready to head outside for a smoke but not a chance he's moving before he hears the end of the story.

'Well later on that night, early hours of the morning or so, Sandra and I are both lying sleeping in bed. I starts to stir, just your usual readjusting your sleeping position, active dream stuff. Only when I do this I started to become aware that my neck was nipping. This searing pain going through it. *That's* when I realised that the fucking thing was sitting on top of my chest and was gnawing at my neck. Fucking look.'

He unzipped the top of the extra long collar to his retro style Adidas tracksuit top - that I guess had been strategically chosen for a night out, given his own circumstances - to reveal a set of teeth marks sunk into his neck.

'JESUS FUCK!' Benji roared. 'Imagine waking and the first thing you see is a fucking rodent gnawing at your neck?!'

'I don't have to imagine, Benji, I know the pain, figuratively *and* literally.' Wullie said, zipping up the tracksuit top neck again to recreate the almost polo neck effect he'd had it sitting at to hide the bite marks from his pet.

'So what did you do?' Sepp asked, taking a cigarette out of his packet of Embassy and sticking it behind his ear ready for sparking up.

'Well it's all a bit of a blur because I acted on pure instinct. I wasn't really awake so it was more a case of nature taking over and me seeing what had happened a few seconds afterwards, when the shock of it all had woken me up. Well, the shock of it and the sound of her screams that would've probably woken my grandad who's still up in Dundee, and been dead for the past fifteen years.'

'So anyway, I've instinctively grabbed the thing. It's then reacted to this by sinking its teeth even further into my neck. Eventually I've managed to free myself from it and threw it as hard as I fucking could against the bedroom wall. I'm not sure if it was through panic or through any real motivation to try and hurt the thing. It was trying to hurt *me* though, mind.'

The whole table sat doubled up laughing but in amongst it Terry managed to ask if Wullie had at least kicked the ferret out after that.

'Well it wasn't in a position to kick its fucking self out after I'd done with it. She's sat up in bed grabbing the duvet up to her chin and screaming her head off while I'm trying to sort my head out enough to pick up the critically injured ferret from the floor and take it outside to the wheely bin. Sad state of affairs, like.'

The fact that he was unable - possibly through some mistaken sense of bond with the animal. Mistaken because the ferret sure as fuck didn't feel the same way about Wullie - to see how funny the story was made it all the funnier. I thought Jock Hunter was going to have a heart attack. Hadn't seen him laugh like that in years. That was Jock, though. Being seen laughing and joking wouldn't have exactly done much good for his hard man manager approach of The Violet.

'That's even worse than my wee brother with the gecko.' Benji laughed as he passed his lighter to Sepp who was now heading outside for a reek. 'Mind of that, Strings?' Benji looked over in my direction as if to jog my memory.

'Daft cunt agreed to take care of this wee gecko, could barely see the fucking thing it was that small, couldn't see the point of even having one, myself. Why have a pet that you can't even see? I'm not fucking talking running after a stick and bringing it back to you or anything. The very basics. Visibility. Apparently it was some woman he worked with at the bank. Her son was some marine biologist or something and had fucked off to Peru or Chile - somewhere like that - on some year long job and had left the gecko with her to watch after while he was there. Only the cunt got a year's extension to the gig so didn't come back to Dalgety Bay again, as planned. Now maybe that should've been the red flag for wee Kyle because mum's will do practically anything for their sons but when she learned that he wasn't coming back she said 'aye, fuck that' and told him that she wasn't looking after the gecko anymore whether he come back from South America or not. And that was when fucking daft works stepped in and said he'd take it. No questions asked. Fuck all in the way of research. Nah, I'll take it from you, Irene, no worries, like. *Plenty* of fucking worries for him though when reality kicked in when the sun rose the very first morning - following the gecko moving in - and it making some kind of screaming noise and wouldn't stop for about half an hour. Obviously, you're not getting back to sleep after that carry on. He thought it was maybe just the thing getting used to its new surroundings and that but naw. Next again morning it did the *exact* same thing again. Turned out it was like a cockerel in the respect that it would make its own wee personal noise when the sun started to come up. According to Kyle, it was on an instant yellow card the first few days after that and then, by the weekend, when he went to clean its tank out and feed it. The thing took a bite out of his finger. Not the wisest thing to do to the cunt that's feeding and taking care of you, eh? Kyle ended up dropping it back off at her house on the Sunday night, not even a week after taking it from her. Caused a bit of bad blood in her office afterwards, like.'

'Well, that's exactly where the saying "don't bite the hand that feeds you" comes from, doesn't it?' Jock said, finishing off a pint that I swear he'd only just started on, unless he'd had another one sat there I hadn't seen.

'What? That originates from someone buying a gecko, aye?' Wullie - not the sharpest knife in the drawer - asked in earnest to the rest of the table's amusement while Jock, evidently a little slower due to the alcohol intake over the day - sat there looking like he was still trying to catch up with the joke.

'So where we off to after this, anyway?' Sepp - back again from his smoke - said as he sat there with his bottle of Corona fixed to his hand. I don't think the boy had put it down on the table once since we'd sat down. Wee piece of lime sat in it as well, obviously. Gimmicky bastard.

'Well, since we seem to be hell bent on pissing away the equivalent of Elton John's weekly flower allowance on city centre prices why do we not head back up to Rose Street again. Maybe put a wee American accent on and lower our jeans and make sure the proprietors give us a proper reaming, eh?' Sepp said, keeping in tune with the attitude he'd had on him. He'd done nothing but moan all day about how expensive the drinks were. There's not one of us who didn't know that in advance though - the price of drinks in the town - so what's the point of moaning about it when you got there? I know it's not easy for some though - with money, like - and you just have to remember that at times.

I could've been the same as Sepp, moaning about the prices of everything had I not had a decent week of stringing as well as a wee bit of buying and selling. Having enjoyed a good week, though, I was just happy to be out with the rest of the team. Getting a pass from Han that I'd be out all day and back when I'd be back and that with no fitba the next morning, a wee lie in requested and expected. Not like I ask the world from anyone, eh? She was happy enough to agree with my demands as long as I was committed to being fit enough to go with her to the circus - that was in town over at Meadowbank - to take our wee nephew, Gary, to. Something she'd promised him a couple of months before and you know what kids are like with memories? Put elephants to fucking shame, those wee bastards, at times.

Can't fucking stand the circus, either. I have my reasons. It's all a game of give and take with your wife, though. She was sound enough for me to be out on the piss - and spending cash that we probably could've done with keeping for the house - so it would've been very much off of me to turn around and say that she'd be going to the circus on her own with the wee man. Until the Sunday, though, I was intent on having as good a time as possible with the rest of the team and getting as royally pished as I could until my last orders came, wherever that would be and whatever time they would arrive.

'Well, how about we get the rest of the team back up at Auld Hundred, *if* they're they're still there, that is.' Said Benji.

'And mind now, Terry. What happened with The Monk earlier on is all in the past. It got straightened out at the time. No afters now, mind.' Jock said fixing a daggers look at big Tel due to the unpleasantness from earlier on in the day and - mostly - why the 'team bonding' day now had half the team in one pub and the other half in a different one.

The day started off in the best of spirits, as well. Went straight downhill soon after, though.

Alfie Anderson, the landlord at The Gunner, even opened the place earlier just for us and had a round of bacon and sausage rolls knocked up to help line the boys' stomachs. Bacon roll and a pint of Tennents to start your day, the fucking berries, man. The absolute berries.

The only absentees out of the playing and backroom staff was wee Mikey Mulraney who was one of our reserves. With him driving a taxi on a Saturday afternoon right through to the next morning. This pretty much excluded him from going on the piss with everyone although - with his chosen line of work - that didn't mean to say that he wasn't going to be *seeing* the Muirhouse Violet players and officials over the course of his Saturday. Mates rates and all that, eh?

We'd had a couple of drinks there in The Gunner before, what could only be described as a motorcade, whisked us into the city centre, dropping us all off on Frederick Street with the short walk to Rose Street where we found ourselves piling into The Amber Rose. The lads were in good spirits in that bright and fresh way you only get at the very start of a sesh where there's only a happy and positive attitude on display and well before alcohol gets a chance to play its part. Everyone was laughing, taking the piss out of each other in the healthy way that a team with good morale *should* be doing.

Terry and The Monk had to go and shatter the relative calm good vibes that were surrounding us, though, the moment they chose to team up on the Who wants to be a Millionaire quiz machine that was sat beside the juke box.

I wasn't exactly paying attention to them as I was standing talking to wee Daz and a very much pinging Montana. Well, I say *I* was talking but Montana was doing enough talking for the three of us put together. It was only when The Monk has went and hooked big Tel square in the coupon and Terry - returning in kind - almost putting The Monk's head through the front of the fucking machine that I'd even known there was a problem.

Once it had all calmed down and, under Jock's instructions, some of the boys had taken The Monk away to another pub so that some calm could be restored that I found out the full story of what had went on.

With them both having their money in the game, I guess, they were equally as invested in it going well as each other. They'd got a wee bit into it and managed to accumulate a bit of cash in the pot. Then came the question about who had been the original host of This is your Life. Apparently The Monk and Terry's opinions had differed on what the correct answer was.

Terry, being the elder out of the two - and therefore of more experience, rather than wiser, as such - shouted Eamonn Andrews. The Monk, however, was the one out of the two of them standing hitting the buttons and, despite having Tel shouting which answer it was, thought that he knew the answer to be Michael Aspel. The Monk, as a result, ignoring Tel's shouts and deciding to hit the button for Aspel, instead. Losing their money in the process.

The Monk, always one to watch when he's had a few drinks inside of him, didn't really take too kindly towards being called a stupid prick from Terry and hooked him one in the face the second the words came from Terry. Well, El Tel was never going to stand by and let that happen and it was only through three of us dragging him off The Monk that he finally stopped slamming the boy's head repeatedly into the front screen of the machine. Put a fucking crack in it that, in the commotion, was - thankfully - missed by the staff inside The Amber Rose.

'I'LL FUCKIN SEE YOU OUTSIDE YA CUNT' The Monk was shouting, blood streaming from a huge cut on his nose, while about half a dozen of the side rushed him out of the place while the rest of us kept Terry in check.

'Anytime ya alkie bastard,' Terry - a whole lot more calm and composed - cockily shouted back as The Monk disappeared out the door.

'Well, you got the fighting spirit that you were asking us for the other night at the meeting, Jock.' I tried to make light out of what had been a nasty wee flare up but Hunter was too busy trying to take care of business when it came to his capacity as a manager of The Violet. Getting first hand accounts from those who were closer to what had transpired. Talking directly with Terry to try and calm him down. Telling him that whatever had happened between him and The Monk that it was going to be nipped in the bud right there and then.

Terry, was stood there, a picture of innocence and one that completely betrayed the face of a man who had just tried to put someone's head through a thick plate of toughened glass.

'Haw, Jock, it's not me that caused it, I'm the innocent party here. If he'd listened to what I'd fucking told him we wouldn't be where we are. Fucking doss cunt's stood there saying that he knew that it wasn't Trevor McDonald as he'd only been doing it for a few years and that Michael Aspel was familiar. Meantime I'm saying, aye but there was some cunt *before* Aspel and to select the option for Eamonn Andrews. Cunt wouldn't listen though and when I lunged over to press the button for Andrews he got all fucking defensive, like he was trying to shield a ball at a corner flag. Blocked me off from pressing it and pressed the one for Michael Aspel and fucking lost us all our dough.'

'Aye, I know, son, I know. You can't be going around shoving people's heads through glass though, Terry. That's not on, is it now?' Old Jock said, kind of - if you were reading between the lines - reminding Tel that he was trying to defend the un-defendable.

Half the team went with The Monk to another boozer and the rest of us weren't that far behind them before we left The Amber Rose too, in search of another establishment. Hoping to press the reset button on the day and start again. We'd had a good few hours of drinking, swapping stories and ripping the complete pish out of each other. Everything that, I'm sure, Jock had imagined when coming up with the idea of a team day out.

Wullie, making the classic mistake of selecting one of the early Saturday kick offs as part of his accumulator and watching Chelsea and Arsenal play out a boring nil nil draw, blowing the rest of his coupon - and getting ripped over it - before the three o clock kick offs even came around. Schoolboy error, that. Selecting an early game as part of your fixed odds. *Always* does you in and leaves you with fuck all to look forward to for the rest of the day, as far as your coupon goes, anyway.

Sooner or later though we were going to have to link up with the rest of the lads. To do otherwise would've pretty much defeated the purpose of going out in a group to instill some new found team morale. If you couldn't have all of them under the same roof for fear of them knocking seven shades of shite out of each other, that was.

'Nah, it'll be fine, Jock,' Terry said, finishing the remains of his Corona, having taken a second to digest the gaffer's advice before we left to join everyone else in The Auld Hundred.

'I'll walk right up to him and apologise for what I did and offer my hand in apology to him. I'll be expecting him to do the same back to me though, Jock, mind. He wasn't exactly an innocent bystander in it all.' Tel said, ominously. There was never going to be any guarantees that The Monk would be in any kind of a mood for extending olive branches.

'Aye, aye, I'm sure the boy will, Terry.' Jock replied with a less than convinced look to his face as he gingerly stood up and straightened out all of the crumples in his shell suit to get himself ready for leaving and heading to the next boozer.

Wisely, I gave Bungalow a wee call to find out the state of play and to give him a wee warning that myself and the rest of the group were heading in their direction.

'How's The Monkey Man, now?' I asked. Figuring if he was still as bammed up - having your face smashed into a gambling machine would tend to do that - as he was when he had been rushed out of The Amber Rose.

Bungalow went on to tell me that the boy - while originally apoplectic with rage - had calmed down, considerably. When they'd went into The Rose Street Brewery. Coffee's cousin was in there on her day shift and when she saw the state of The Monk's face she got the first aid kit out and patched him up. She reckoned that his nose was possibly broken but The Monk was having none of it in terms of going to casualty to get it seen to. Saying that he would go into the Western General to get it looked at if it was still sore the next day. Montana had then knocked him up an extra strength Super Skunk joint which helped chill him out a bit along with some wise words from some of the lads that he should be careful about what he was wishing for because when it came to it, Big Tel would rip his fucking head off. Something The Monk wouldn't have needed any reminding once his red mist cleared.

Aye, as far as Bungalow was concerned. There wasn't going to be any bad blood waiting to be spilled when Terry and The Monk came face to face again for the first time since it had all kicked off between them and that we could all get on with the rest of the day with no underlying atmospheres just waiting to explode and fuck things up again.

I relayed this info back to Jock Hunter whose face lit up like it was *the* most important piece of news he could ever have been given.

'See, Terry, told you it would all be fine. Just you walk right into the boozer and shake the boy's hand and put it all behind you.' He shouted across the room to Terry who was in the middle of rifling through a pile of coats to find his own one before hitting the street.

'Aye, no bother, gaffer.' He shouted without taking his eyes off the coats. Cunt probably heard nothing other than his name being said and went with a safe and non committal reply to appease Jock. Something I, admittedly, had done the same hundreds of times with the gaffer. He gets so into his zone when he's in managerial mode that he doesn't even notice half the time that cunts are barely listening to him.

'Anyone fancy a wee scran before continuing drinking. Needing a wee extra lining to the stomach, myself, especially since this has been nothing more than a wee social Saturday afternoon swally up to this point. Now we're entering into the business end of the day, eh?' Benji said, looking at his watch.

'Aye, I'll probably join you there.' I agreed. Wasn't feeling desperately hungry, like. Was more a case of planning for later on once I'd had a few extra drinks and that all started to dominate things where - until the very end part of the night - food would go on to become nothing more than an afterthought.

We all left The Rutland in the one group. Near on cleared out half the boozer in doing so. The look of relief on the barmaid's face when she noticed us all getting our coats on was not the first look that I'd seen from a bartender up to that point of the day. Little did she know that she'd been let off lightly when it came to putting up with the playing and coaching staff of Muirhouse Violet. By comparison. She'd had the pleasure of having us when we were on our best behaviour.

'Right, back up to Rose Street again, then.' Jock said, pointing in the direction we were headed as if none of us had heard of or been there in our puffs.

Terry passed the reeks around. I was already dealing with that fresh wee buzz you get when you've had a few pints and then leave the pub and hit the fresh air. The first puff I took on the Regal Kingsize that he'd given me almost putting me on my arse.

Starting at the very end of Rose Street. It didn't take long before Benji and myself found a suitable eatery to grab a bite. Letting the others walk on ahead towards Auld Hundred.

'Sure you're not wanting a Doner Kebab, Jock, naw?' I shouted out after the gaffer, on the wind up as Benji and me stopped to go into The

Istanbul. Jock being one of those ' I won't let any of that foreign muck past my lips' old school types.

'I'll be dead in the ground before you see me with a bloody kebab in my hand. You don't know what shite you're eating with those things.' He said, shaking his head as he continued walking along with the rest of the group.

'No worries, gaffer. I'll save you a bit just in case you get hungry later on, eh.' I replied as the two of us ducked in having told the others we'd catch up with them at the pub in a bit.

When you're out in such a big group. Sometimes it's good to take a wee half hour out from everyone else and breathe. Escape the non stop noise and piss taking that wears you down after a while. Aye, take some time out and steady yourself for the second part of the day because if there's one guarantee on an all-dayer. It's that the second half is the messier and more dangerous half of the day. The part where the battle of wills against the booze starts to tip in favour of the alcohol.

The plan had been for us to all end up in The Dome, up on George Street. Well, that was the plan. Didn't take you to go on a door security course though to tell you that Jock Hunter was *never* going to be getting into a nightclub - like The Dome - in a Londsdale shell suit. It had never been a consideration, personally, though that by that time Jock was still going to be out in the town.

It had been a brilliant idea of his to go out as a team and admirable of him to get it all organised but there comes a time where the gaffer has to pull himself back a bit and let the boy's have their fun, eh. Up to that point, though, he'd been enjoying the day every bit as much as the rest of the team. Was good to see, like.

The kebab shop had a couple of tables with parasols above them outside the shop, clearly there for the tourists than they were for the locals. Don't see too many fucking parasols outside kebab shops in Muirhouse or Pilton, eh? Benji sat down at one of them with me grabbing the other chair beside him for us to sit there and shove some food down our necks while watching the tourists and stag / hen parties walking intermittently by.

We had a cheeky wee couple of days lined up in Blackpool for the middle of the week so sat discussing some plans related to the trip. It had become almost a tradition of ours where we would drive down once a year. Take as many amusement arcades to the cleaners as we could while having a couple of good nights out as reward for our day's efforts. Other halves having no idea of how much dough we *made* when we were down there but as long as we came back with some to go towards the housekeeping then they're happy. Win and win.

We were going to be getting on the road early doors on the Wednesday morning for a couple of days before being back up the road in time for the Hibs game on the Saturday - away to Kilmarnock - and then our own match on Sunday away to Drylaw.

Busy week ahead, like, and if it all went to plan - by the end of it - I'd have relieved some arcade owners of hundreds of their English pounds. The cabbages would be coming back from Rugby Park with three points and The Violet would be advancing through to the quarter finals of the Kwik Save Challenge Trophy.

'I hope these two cunts have buried the hatchet.' Benji said as we made our way along Rose Street towards 'Auld Hundred' to rejoin the rest of the squad.

'Can't be doing with the fucking drama, Strings though, like. It's one thing to show that type of aggression to whoever we're up against. We're Muirhouse Violet, it's kind of our thing. A bit counter productive when our nasty streak is used *against* each other, though.'

'Aye, well I just hope that by bury the hatchet, that doesn't mean Big Tel burying The Monk's head into a condom machine in the bogs or something to that effect.' I replied as we made our way past all the smokers who were stood outside the front of the pub having a reek.

Considering the reservations that we both had about the possibility of a full on community spirit waiting there inside the boozer. *Neither* of us could ever have predicted walking in and finding Terry and The Monk doing a duet on the karaoke.

When I walked in, The Monk - two black eyes and a massive strip of Elastoplast spread across his nose - was standing there holding a microphone in one hand and looking lovingly at Terry with an outstretched arm while he sang

'I've been waiting for so long. Now I've finally found someone to stand by me.'

Terry then returning the serenade with

'We saw the writing on the wall. and we felt this magical fantasy.'

Looking at the two of them - and knowing the history between the pair from hours before - it couldn't have been more of a Muirhouse Violet moment.

I looked over towards the team who had completely taken over one section of the pub. All watching the lads with massive grins on their faces. Montana, Rossi and Coffee all with their lighters up in the air.

'Now with passion in our eyes. there's no way we could disguise it secretly.'

They sung in unison. Almost as if they'd rehearsed it rather than being an off the cuff performance from two boys who had been sticking alcohol and - with the case of The Monk - narcotics into them over an afternoon.

'So we take each others hand. Cause we seem to understand the urgency.'

The Monk and Terry holding each others hand and raising them both up into the air like a boxing referee announcing the winner.

From then on the whole of the team, and some randoms in the pub who found themselves swept along with the moment, joined in with the rest of the song.

'Just remember.

You're the one thing I can't get enough of.

So I'll tell you something.

This could be love.

Because, I've had the time of my life.

No I've never felt this way before. Yes I swear it's the truth.

And I owe it all to you.'

Some scenes, like.

I went to get the drinks in for Benj and me but Jock, in his element with this team day out, shouted across to me that there was a kitty on the go and for us both to chip in and then get a drink for ourselves.

By the time the song had finished, Terry and The Monk were putting the microphones down to a round of applause that swept across the whole pub.

'You're next, ya cunt' Terry said, as he walked back to the table. Negotiating his way through a series of backslaps and comments thrown his way.

'Aye, maybe after a few more of these, eh?' I laughed back while raising my pint.

We ended up sitting in there for the best part of the evening and by the end it was very much a case of the men being separated from the boys. You had the ones who - being fair - had had a pretty good fucking stab at the day. Drinking pints and eating bacon rolls before the postie had even fucking been? Long day, to get yourself from that point to ten bells at night and *still* be of any use to anyone. Not all of us would be carrying on with the journey until the DJ at The Dome had played his slow dance last track of the night.

Personally, I should've showed a bit of sense and went along with some the others when it came to who was heading to the club and who was going back to Muirhouse. I had the fucking circus to go to the next day and the longer I stayed out. The more a challenge it was going to be for me the next day.

Fucking Montana, though. Isn't that what they say about dealers, though? That they prey on you when you're at your weakest? The two of us got talking when we were in the toilets. Admittedly, he caught me a wee bit for the worse.

Sunny - who despite now technically being as good as an *ex* Violet player while waiting on the imminent long term ban that was going to be officially handed to him, along with the criminal charges that he was going to have to face up to in court - had turned up later on in the evening. Joining us at Auld Hundred and immediately got me and Benji on the fucking Tequilas which - unless you're Mexican - is never anything other than a recipe for disaster. I was hanging on for grim death when Montana persuaded me to have a line with him.

Hadn't had one in years but I'm not going to deny. It sorted me right out. Completely wiped out the previous couple of hours worth of the peave that I'd been knocking back. He'd seemed genuinely delighted when I accepted the rolled up twenty from him. I know that drugs are that common these days that we all know someone who's doing some or other. As a team though, the only one - openly, at least - out of us who took them was Montana and as a result he took a bit of stick from everyone else. Like he probably gave much of a fuck while turning up on Sunday mornings for our matches in his Escort Cossie and dressed in a Stone Island tracksuit. Just two examples of what the drug game brought his way.

'Awwww fucking barry, man.' He said, passing me the note and nodding down towards the big line sat precariously on top of the toilet roll dispenser.

'It'll sort you right out, Strings mate.'

There really was no need to question such words when they were coming from a man who had been drinking for twelve hours and wasn't looking like he'd touched a fucking sip.

Sort me out it did. Montana never offered me anymore over the night and I never asked for any. Was just a one off thing to put me back on the right track. Which it passed with flying colours. Leaving me raring to go when it came to us making a move from the boozer and along the road to George Street to the club for the final part of the night.

Most of the side went. Some shouldn't have, mind. Absolutely buckled, they were. You try telling some cunt who's pished and having a good time that it's time to call it a night, though. *That's* why we have doormen, after all.

The only number of the group who *didn't* make The Dome you were able to fit inside the one taxi back to Muirhouse. Jock Hunter - which had been no real surprise but the twisted in me had *really* wanted to see him getting a knock back from the doormen because of the shell suit and Jock's (predictable) kick off that would've followed, Daz - who had managed to be sick all down the front of his shirt but despite this arguing that he should be staying out with the rest - There was Sepp who was going down the boring route of having an early night - so he could take advantage of not playing and, instead, was going off fishing for the day - and taking up the last space in the taxi was Rab Stevenson our sometime physio, when he can be arsed getting out of his bed on a Sunday morning, that is.

The city centre, at that time of night, was absolutely heaving. Our own group - were it not for the noise that it was making - could've easily been mistaken for just another stag party due to the numbers that we had walking along the street.

'Are you guys rugby players?' These two girls with Yorkshire accents wearing gangster hats with matching hand drawn pencil mustaches, stopped and asked us as we passed them on George Street.

'Do you see any jeans and shoes here, darling, eh?'

Coffee's - unique - way of telling the girls that no, we were not egg chasers but done so in a way that left them standing there with utter confusion on their faces while a few of the group chuckled away at the joke. Anyone from Edinburgh who had spent even a relatively short amount of time inside city centre boozers during the Six Nations matches would know what Coffee was going on about. Even if the two English girls didn't.

Due to fucking about trying to get my lighter to work. Benj and myself were right at the back of the queue and didn't initially realise that there was some kind of an issue with some of the lads getting past the bouncers. In hindsight. If I'd been a bouncer. The very *last* punter I'd let in would have been The Monk. Two black eyes and very real evidence of someone who has already been up to no good on their night out.

Wasn't just The Monk who had been knocked back, though. Montana, whose eyes were a complete fucking give away, returned to the back of the line - along with The Monk - both grumbling away to themselves.

It looked like it had been a case of everyone for themselves from that point on because after the first two of them being knocked back. The rest of the squad - deemed acceptable for entry by the doormen - all paid their entrance fee and walked on in.

'Hang on though, mate, I'll get us in. Don't worry about it. I've got an idea.' I heard Montana grabbing The Monk, who was in the process of beginning to mouth off at the bouncers.

'Wait up a second, Benj.' I said to Benji as he moved further towards getting himself in. 'I want to see what these two daft cunts are going to do next. Doesn't look like they're taking no for an answer, here.'

I suggested that we stand outside for a wee while and have another smoke before going in. Have to say, I was intrigued by whatever Cocaine fueled plan Montana was going to cook up for the pair of them.

'Right, so what we do is fuck off for a few minutes and swap what we're wearing. No need for trousers and shoes, like. Just our shirts and jackets. The amount of cunts that the bouncers come across over a night they'll *never* make the connection.'

All that money that America have pished up against the wall fighting the war on drugs when all they needed to do was roll out Montana, when he was high, and let him show everyone just how fucking daft a Ching binge can leave you.

'Mate? You not think they're going to remember the cunt they just knocked back with the fucking landing strip slapped right across his nose? No? I mean, I'm not fucking rainman, like, but I reckon I'd probably manage to remember that face twice inside the space of ten *years* never mind the space of ten minutes.' Benji tried to reason with the two of them while he passed his cigarettes around.

'Aye, good point, there, Benji boy.' Montana said, in a hushed tone while looking warily towards the bouncers to see if they were looking our way.

'The plaster's going to have to come off, mate.' Montana said, seriously, to The Monk.

None of us knew the condition of The Monk's nose and whether Terry had broken it or not but at some point someone had felt that it was bad enough in that it needed to be tightly and securely fixed up with some heavy duty tape. *If* the nose had been broken then it was not going to be pleasant for The Monk when that tape was ripped from him.

The Monk - if he was anything - was committed to carrying on the session and conceded to Montana that, aye, if they were going to have *any* chance of their plan coming off. The plaster, first, would have to come off.

The two of them made their way across to George Square in search of a bit of privacy where they could swap their clothes. Masked by the darkness.

'You believe these cunts?' Benji said, still trying to take on board that - somehow - they had teamed up and thought that this was ever going to achieve anything other than potentially push some bouncers over the edge for the night.

'No, but I'm going fucking nowhere until I've *seen* them try to pull it off.' I laughed, just thinking of the prospect of it as I watched well dressed clubbers of all descriptions walking past and towards the front door while taxis pulled up outside with other groups getting out.

Out of nowhere that was when we heard the scream coming over from George Square. You couldn't have ever not notice it. Nobody could. It literally stopped everyone dead in their tracks. Such was the blood curdling effect to it. Had I not known any better I'd have thought that some poor cunt was being stabbed over in the square.

'Take it The Monk's nose *was* broken after all, then.' I winked at Benji who was standing there with an 'ouch' look to his face.

It wasn't long after that when the pair of them appeared again walking along the street towards us. Looking as ill fitting as the other. The Monk - who you couldn't have said was ever likely to be able to share clothes with the much more hench Montana - was walking along with a Stone Island woolen cardigan that was almost hanging down past his arse while you had Montana basically poured into The Monk's white shirt, complete with the blood stains down the front of it from earlier on in the day.

'We set, then?' Montana said once they got back to where we were standing. Looking like he'd just banged a fresh dose of Ching up his nose for good luck. He was going to fucking need it.

'Aye, you two go first.' I said, making sure Benji and me followed behind them.

Even before the two of them got up to the door I'd already clocked one of the bouncers seeing them coming and nudging the arm of his colleague to the side of him which then drew his attention, also, to them.

'Are YOU taking the fucking piss?' One of them said right out the bat. Looking The Monk and Montana up and down, side to side. It was hard to properly pin down the look that he had on him. Disgust? Offence? Distain? I don't know what it was but it wasn't very fucking welcoming, anyway.

'What's that, mate?' Montana said. Sticking on a face that suggested that he was the person who had been left out of some joke.

'What do you mean what?' The same bouncer. This Polish boy with a relic of a flat top haircut, said back again. Appearing to be getting irritated in the exact same way I'd predicted they would when I was standing with Benji waiting on The Monk and Montana coming back.

'Well, I'm not being funny, mate, but I've just walked up to the door here, only out to have a few drinks and maybe a wee dance, like, and you've asked me if I was taking the piss. Didn't even open my mouth at that point, eh?' Montana said, trying to follow through with the act that he'd decided upon going with. Could've admitted defeat at any point and no one would've judged him over it, especially with it being an absolutely fucking demented thing to try in the first place. Nah, Montana was fully there for it and wasn't for backing down.

It almost looked like this had left the bouncer having to stop himself from reacting and - instead - electing to count to ten. This, however, gave the other bouncer a chance to offer his own input. This other one looked a portion older than the Pole. Probably a bit over the hill when it came to doing the doors but neither did he look like someone I would want to go for a wee roll around with, either.

'Look, pal, dinnae take us for a pair of cunts, here. You're clearly the two that we knocked back ten minutes ago. *You* because you were covered in blood and looked like a panda and *you* because you had eyes like fifty pence pieces. And now *you* look like you've been in a fight covered in blood while your eyes are *still* like fifty pence pieces. Meanwhile your mate here looks like a fucking refugee in that cardigan and *still* a panda. Do yourselves a favour and take the both of yourselves to fuck, please.'

He barked at Montana with a much more local accent to his Eastern European chum.

'Honestly, I don't know where this boy's getting all of this. Some imagination, I'll give him that.' Montana looked around at Benji and me in a show of mock character assassination. The Monk, who appearances aside, was absolutely buckled anyway and barely knew where he was so was in no position to be offering up any counter arguments of his own.

'Ok, time you were *going*. Comprendo, Friendo.' The first one said as he put his hand on Montana's shoulder.

While no expert on Cocaine, by any stretch. One thing I *did* know was that someone laying a hand on another person - one who had taken copious amounts of the drug - was never going to present a situation that would end well. And it didn't, for Montana, like.

Once he had done through with the 'don't touch me' and 'get your hands of me' theatrics he had been sent flying down the few stairs leading up to the front door and left on his back. We were Muirhouse and - if we were anything as a group - we were one for all and all for one but there was no point in starting anything with the two doormen. Montana was already on his Richard Gere, The Monk wouldn't have been able to punch his way out of a wet paper bag while Benji and I were more than twelve hours into a session. Hardly prize fighters, the pair of us.

Instead, we managed to appear like the peace makers to the bouncers by ensuring that the two of them were bundled into a taxi with Muirhouse given as the destination before Benji and I strolled straight in with a little friendly nod exchanged between us and the two bouncers.

Things weren't exactly so cordial for the pair of them at the end of the night - with the rest of the team having been informed of what they'd done to Montana - when we were all leaving, though.

That, though, is something that we'll keep between you and I and away from Jock Hunter, who would go on to claim that the day out in Edinburgh - and the team morale inspiring properties that he had been looking from out of it - had been the turning point in the season of Muirhouse Violet.

That two Edinburgh doormen had happened to come by some kind of a mischief during the *building* of team morale was something that Jock didn't really need to know.

If you fuck with the Muirhouse boys then you need to have some kind of realistic ideas of the response that you're going to receive over your actions. Some in the city already know that while others - like the two bouncers at The Dome - needed to find out the hard way.

C'est la vie, eh?

Chapter 11

Han

I bloody *knew* he was going to be like a half shut knife the next day for going with me to the circus with the wee man. Was around four in the morning that he came home. Knocking all kinds of shite from off the walls through banging against them. Got into bed absolutely reeking of kebabs, even had a bit of onion still stuck to his face with chili sauce. I shouldn't complain, really. Other women are sat there worrying themselves sick about whether their man is cheating on them with someone else when they're out for a drink with their pals. While I'm moaning about my man coming home smelling of kebabs, as opposed to someone's perfume. That's one thing for sure. No women would be going near a man looking (and smelling) like that. Not even his wife.

When Strings surfaced for the morning, *much later* in the morning, I should've just taken the decision to take the wee man to Piqueto's Circus on my own after one look at him, while reserving my right to be a complete moaning arsed bitch about it for days afterwards to him. By the time, though, that Joe was surrounded by three big burly Circus workers with a clown lying crumpled at the bottom of the stairs and our nephew, wee Gary, with tears in his eyes, confused, asking me why Uncle Joe had hit the clown. Well, it was all a bit late for should and could.

'Make us a cup of tea please, Han, I'm fucking hanging here, like.' He said when he finally appeared in the living room. Dressed in just his boxers. Hair going in about half a dozen directions and face still coated in red chili sauce from his late night munch.

'Good day, then?' I laughed as I filled up the kettle.

'Maybe too good going by the nick of me this morning, it *is* morning still, aye?'

'Aye, it was a photo finish but you just made it and no more. Doesn't exactly leave you with much time for getting ready before Gary gets dropped off.'

'You going to be fit for going?'

I asked, as I passed him his cup of tea. While, technically, the words on their own suggested that I had asked him a question. My chosen tone let my other half know - categorically - that there was no option of a reply that was going to go along the lines of 'actually, I'm about the opposite of a fiddle right now, darling, so if you would be as so kind as to exclude me from the trip to the circus today. Instead, I think I'll watch two games of football in a row on Sky Sports.'

'Aye, I'll be fine. Cup of tea and a spot of breakfast and I'll be sound. You were off your fucking head offering to take him to the circus though, Han. What was that all about?' He said, on one hand confirming that - whether he liked it or lumped it - he was going with me but on the other hand making sure that he got a sly dig in that it was 'me' who was responsible for us going in the first place.

'Well he *is* only four and it was months ago I told him that we would take him the next time the circus came to Edinburgh. Didn't think that he'd remember about it when the circus actually *did* come. You know what he's like, though, clown daft.' I said in an attempt to defend myself.

'Aye, and about that, there's something not right with your sister to raise a kid and them being into clowns. That's just proper weird.' He replied taking a sip of his tea and instantly wishing he'd let it cool for a wee bit longer.

'Ah, you're only saying that because of what a wee shitebag you are with them.' I teased him over his unnatural aversion to clowns. I know a lot of people say they don't like clowns but they haven't met my Joe. I mean, he won't even go into McDonalds because of the Ronald McDonald statues you find in there or his face plastered all over the walls.

I thought he was a bit of a drama queen with it all and loved teasing him about it. Hey, he loved to dish it out, my Strings, so he should be prepared to take a bit back. That's the rules of engagement.

'Shitebag? Who's the fucking shitebag? Me or some cunt who hides behind make up and costumes to the point you don't fucking know who they are. Hiding from the world, those cunts. Not right, them. Not just hiding from the world but hiding for a *reason*. I'll fucking shitebag, you.' He wasn't impressed which, of course, made me giggle all the more.

Despite all of our years of marriage - and the years we'd spent together before that - I genuinely thought that he had been making more out of the clown stuff than had been the reality of things. Would I honestly have ever put the man I love through the ordeal of going to the circus if I'd thought that it was going to cause him any kind of distress? Of course not. Obviously, like most spouses, there are times where I want to fucking flay the man over what he's done - or in other cases, what he *hasn't* - but, of course, in reality. I would *never* want to hurt a hair on the man's head.

It wasn't long before my big sister, Senga, was dropping the wee man off. He was like a mini atom bomb. So packed full of energy with excitement over where he was going to. Detonating the moment he reached his auntie and uncle's.

'You excited about the circus, wee man?' Joe asked. Sat there a man transformed from the zombie that had got up earlier. With that old Hibs tracksuit that he'd got a few years before on with Whyte and Mackay across the front it was probably as scrubbed up as Strings was ever going to get for a day out in a cold and muddy circus big top.

'YES UNCLE JOE. AH'M GONNAE SEE THE CLOWNS AND THE TIGERS AND THE TWAPEEZE ARTISTS AND THE MAN THAT DRIVES ROUND AND ROUND IN HIS MOTOR BWIKE.'

He said jumping up and down on the spot with nervous energy.

'He *does* ken it's the circus at Meadowbank we're going to. Not a Las Vegas casino one, eh?' Joe said, looking to me and Senga with a cynical look.

Senga - whose relationship with Joe had never been classed as anything less than frosty - screwed her face up at what she saw as Joe trying to dampen her son's excitement.

140

'Oh don't mind him, he's just moaning because he'd normally be in The Gunner right now watching the fitba.' I assured her. Not that Senga ever needed, or looked for, my assurances when it came to my husband.

'Even got you free tickets so you don't even need to put your hand in your pocket.' She said - ignoring me - directly at Joe. Handing them over to him as if to prove she wasn't lying. Joe instantly taking a look at them and shaking his head before looking back up at her.
'They're not fucking free, at all.' He threw them onto the coffee table in a wee strop.

'What part of the front of the ticket where it says **"FREE TICKET,"** in big letters, is it that you don't understand, then?' Senga said, looking a wee bit insulted over her gesture of trying to save us a few quid being thrown back in her face and was now going to have her say back as a result.

'Well I know that the part of the "free ticket" where it says that you have to buy a programme for the circus along with entry pretty much means that it's not a fucking free ticket.'

Joe could be so effectively sarcastic at times. Sometimes I loved him for it. Other times I hated him for. Senga - having already taken her own stance that the tickets were free - didn't really have anywhere to go other than continue with the hostility.

'Well I guess you'll need to buy a programme then, eh? Still be cheaper than paying to get in, anyway.'

'Don't know the price of them, though. Do you?' Joe said back to her, unable to just leave things at that.

'Ok, Han, I'll pick Gary up around six. Will you be alright to give him his tea? I can pick him up earlier, if not.' Senga said - ignoring Joe now - as she crouched down in front of Gary and asked her to give him a kiss before she went.

'No, its fine. We'll maybe take the wee man to McDonalds.' I replied back to her, and in doing so, more or less confirming that we *would* go there to give wee Gary his tea. You can't go mentioning things like that in front of a bairn and then not follow through with it. Nothing other than cruelty to dangle a potential treat in front of a wee one and put it into their heads and then not give them it.

'YAY, MUMMY, I'M GOING TO GET A HAPPY MEAL AND A TOY.'

Gary looked like the combination of a circus trip and then a Happy Meal was going to send him right over the edge before he'd even got around to either.

Sooner he gets his license back the better, I thought to myself as Joe picked up his phone to give Benji a call to come around and collect us to take us over to Meadowbank. It must've done Benji's head in, being Joe's personal taxi driver, you know? Then again it was almost a deal with the devil pact that he'd entered into. While he'd been given a nice car to drive around in, for free. It was under the 'condition' that when Joe needed driving somewhere. Benji would be there on hand to do the honours.

I saw Senga out while getting our coats ready. Knowing that Benji wouldn't be long, having got his call.

'Ok, lets lead with the fact that YOU are clearly not legal for driving right now.' I said when I opened the door to him, on arrival. Bloodshot eyes, still smelling of all kinds of toxicity and clearly - unlike Joe - hadn't showered or anything close to freshening himself up from the night before.

'Don't be daft, Han.' He laughed as he walked past me and into the living room where Joe was doing that thing with Gary where you get a kid to put their feet on top of yours and you walk them around the room with them.

'Joe, tell him. He's not driving us anywhere. Look at him, for fuck's sake. Makes *you* look like Mr Motivator, by comparison.' I appealed for him to show a bit of sense.

It wouldn't have been unlike Joe to have sided with his best mate in a situation like that but it only took him the one look at Benji to see that there was a hefty bit of validity to my point.

'Fucking hell, check the state of it.' He laughed. 'How the hell did you end up like that? You were in the same taxi back as me.' He said trying to work out how Benji had landed up in such a sad state of affairs compared to him.

'Aye, well I was the last out the taxi. Didn't have all the money on me so had to get the boy to stop at the cashline and just paid him up to there and was going to walk the rest. On the way back, though, I bumped into Wattie Lynch and Henry Wallace at the bottom of Birnies Court. Got talking to them, like. They were at a house party in there but were outside waiting on a delivery arriving. Invited me up when they were heading back up to the flat. Thought I'd just go in for a couple of nightcaps but it didn't work out like that. Only left the place around ten this morning. Not been to bed yet.'

'Evidently you've not been to bed yet. You're still fucking pished.' Joe replied in response to this. 'Well I hate to break it to you, Benji boy, but I'm taking the keys off you. There's no point in you having my car to drive us around in for work if you've fucking wrapped it around a lamp post and even away from that. Driving when you're drunk isn't cool. You know my thoughts on that. How the fuck am I going to feel if I let you drive away from here and you end up running a kid over? Mon, hand the fucking things over.'

Joe stood there with his hand out. Benji wasn't impressed but he didn't have much of a choice.

'Fuck's sake, Strings. It's fucking freezing out there and I never planned for this so don't have any money for a taxi back.' He grumbled while trying to stop his hands from shaking while he tried to take his house key from off of the keyring that had the car key looped onto.

'Are we not going to circus now, auntie Hannah?' Bless wee Gary. While too young to fully appreciate what was going on he was smart enough to pick up on that there was something happening that might be affecting his circus trip.'

'Don't you worry, little man, we're still going. We're just going in a different car. We can drop Benji off on the way.' I said, replying to Gary and in doing so. Letting the two men in the room know what we'd 'now' be doing.

'Costing me enough today, as it is, you should be paying the taxi, ya cunt.' Joe said to Benji while he picked up the phone again to call a cab to come and take us.

Despite the change of plans. We were still dropped off in Meadowbank by Mikey - Strings' team mate - in decent enough time for to be seated before the show started. Due to the week's worth of rain that had led up to the weekend. The short walk from the main road to the entrance to the big top was like that time Joe and I went to T in the Park. Joe - who was already trying to keep a lid on the fact that he didn't want to be there - was moaning his face off that his suede Adidas were covered in mud and - by the looks of them - completely ruined. I chose to ignore any of the moans to keep things positive for wee Gary. Faking my own enthusiasm so as to enhance his own. This, though, was beyond my moaning hungover dick of a husband.

'Ten quid for a fucking programme? It's not U2 we're going to see here, eh?' Joe was less than impressed when the young Spanish girl informed him of the 'add on' to the free tickets we were using. 'Aye, free tickets, indeed.' He said sarcastically while I fished a tenner out of my purse to give to the lassie.

Of course. Once you were in there, the Ten Pound programme (which really was more of a pamphlet) was the least of your worries. Animal balloons made up for you while you waited, face painting, flashing battery operated guns that would light up when you pulled the trigger, rides on ponies and much more are all lying in wait ready to be shoved down the throat of any kid that entered.

'Can I get that. Can I get this. Oh look at that thing, Auntie Hannah and Uncle Joe.'

It was a relief when we got seated and the show started and the wee man was able to concentrate on the one thing, without all of those added distractions.

The outfit themselves - as in who was putting on the circus itself - were marketed as a Spanish company but from having a quick glance through the programme it was more a case of the United Nations who were being represented across the acts. The only actual Spaniards - given credit as part of the show - were the two clowns, Gipetto and Harporito.

There was a girl from Lithuania whose act involved Hula Hoops. A couple of brothers from Moscow who were going to be doing some balancing act involving chairs. A Romanian who did a performance with, ominously, crowd participation. Enough to keep a four year old occupied for the best part of a couple of hours.

It was worth all the hassle *and* putting up with Joe's grumpy arse to see the wide eyed and excited smile on wee Gary's face when the lights went out for the start of the show as the spotlight fell on the ringmaster as he - one by one - introduced the crowd to all of the acts that they were going to be seeing. Each performer giving big three sixty degree waves around the tent to everyone as they all lined up together to the dramatic sounds of Live and let Die from the James Bond film.

Things began with a performance by this man - in a suit that looked like it had the milky way spread across it - who was directing a wee Collie across an assault course. Up ramps and through some tubes that ended with the dog pushing a football with it's nose all the way until it scored a goal into the net at the side of the ring. The sound effect of fans at a football match being played over the actual cheers from the crowd at such cuteness. The dog was *so* adorable, though. Would've loved to have taken it home with us to knock some direction into our Stanton.

'YES' Gary shouted jumping up and own in his seat like he'd just seen Hibs scoring a goal.

'That was a good goal, wasn't it?' I said grabbing his hand.

'Aye it was a good one, auntie Hannah.' He replied, more or less using the same words back I'd given him.

The show moved from act to act. Half the time I looked over to Strings - who was sitting beside the aisle and in between Gary and me - and I swear, despite the noise, he was sitting there sleeping.

Funny how he wasn't sleeping when the young blond girl in the tight spandex was gyrating her hips hypnotically while she kept something like twenty four Hula Hoops spinning around all parts of her body. Eyes were popping out of his skull then, funnily enough. Fresh as a daisy, there. I reached over between Gary and gave Joe a shove to bring him out of his trance like state.

'Hey you.' I said, pointing to my eyes and then him to let him know that he was being clocked. Fucking pervert. She looked eighteen at the oldest. Young enough to probably be his daughter and he's sat there catching flies. He waved me away dismissively but I'd known him long enough to know that he knew he'd been busted. Made a show of *not* looking at what was going on down in the ring after waving me away, which told its own story.

Apart from the fact that the girl was dressed in something that looked like it had been painted on her - and in doing so - only rammed home the fact that she had a *much* better body than me. One that my husband obviously approved of. Her act 'was' amazing. I could barely keep the one Hula Hoop spinning when I was a young girl and she's managing to have them spinning around her neck, waist, legs and arms. It was the kind of behaviour that would've had her burned at the stake centuries ago.

As far as entertainment, the circus didn't disappoint. The only thing that we missed had been the two brothers with the chairs through me having to take the wee man to the toilet.

'WOW LOOK AT THOSE MEN, AUNTIE HANNAH.'

Gary screamed out when we emerged back into the big top to see a mountain of chairs all stacked on top of each other and these two daredevils stood on top of it, one standing on top of the other's shoulders and milking the applause from the crowd.

'I hope they don't fall when they're getting themselves back down again.' I said to the wee man.

'Is that dangerous, Auntie Hannah? Will the men die?' He asked, all of a sudden worried for the pair of them because of my throwaway comment. Me forgetting - for moment - just how literal kids can take things that the adults say.

'Oh no, Gary. These men are really good at it so they don't hurt themselves. If you or me tried to do it though we would probably end up in the hospital.' I cleverly replied and in doing so issuing the wee man with the disclaimer that I hoped I would never need to tell Senga about when she came complaining that her son had been trying to recreate the stuff he'd seen at the circus in their house and went falling into their telly or something daft like that.

The order of performances seen to it that the clowns were left until last on which - when it came to Gary's day out least - ensured that we saw pretty much the whole of the show. *Pretty much.*

The second last performance had been the absolutely brilliant tight rope walker. This attractive looking older woman who was walking back and forward on the rope across the ring as if she was held up there by some magnetic force. Kylie Minogue's 'Spinning Around' was playing and the woman was somehow managing to literally spin around - on top of the rope - in time to the music.

It wasn't just me. Gary and Strings were completely transfixed on her, too. And aye, I'll admit, a portion of something like that is watching because you think there's a chance that they might fall. You can't help it.

She was still up there on the rope doing her thing when out of the corner of my eye I noticed the dark silhouette of - what looked like - a clown starting to walk up the stairs, in the direction of where the three of us were sat. Despite how dark the tent was, with any lighting fixed towards the circus ring. You couldn't mistake the shape of that mass of curls on top and the trademark oversized shoes on its feet.

Strings had clearly noticed it too. Moving over towards me to the point of obscuring Gary's view of the show. 'Where's does this cunt think it's going, like?' He asked before moving back over and adjusting himself in his seat again while fixing his eyes back onto the shadowy figure that was slowly - considering the size twenty five feet - continuing up the stairs.

By then - as far as Joe was concerned - what was going on down inside the ring with the girl on the rope was a poor second best. He wasn't for taking his eyes off the clown. By then, it was close enough for Gary to have seen it.

'A CLOWN, AUNTIE HANNAH, UNCLE JOE, LOOOOOK A CLOWN'

He excitedly bounced in his seat and pointed in its direction. The clown noticing this and giving a wave back to him.

As dimly lit as things were, Joe was close enough to me for me to see that he had begun tensing up. It was that obvious I reckon that I'd have been able to *sense* it if I couldn't actually see it. I too was no longer watching the show. Instead, I was watching Joe watching the clown. It looked like he was trying to control his breathing and, looking him up and down, how stiff he had gone all of a sudden. Looking like he was squeezing imaginary stress balls that weren't actually in his hands. I'd taken a thought to get him to swap seats with me so that I would be the one that was sitting beside the aisle but it was kind of too late by that point.

Of course, the clown chose to stop climbing the stairs *right* as he was side by side to the same row that we were sitting in. Now that he was as close as he was. I could see that he had a saxophone strapped around him. When he got side by side with us, however, he didn't do anything further to that. It had dawned on me that all it was doing was preparing for the start of their own performance. Looking around the big top I then saw the *other* clown out of the two of them. They were *also* up and inside the crowd only, on the other side of the ring. It was hard to see due to the mixture of darkness and the occasional random flash of light in the clowns direction but it also looked like it had a saxophone - or some kind of musical instrument - hanging from its neck.

While the - one on our side - stood innocently in the aisle, patiently waiting on its cue. Joe wasn't faring any better. He was no longer looking at it and, instead, was staring straight forward and not in a natural position for watching the circus ring. I doubted that he was actually looking at *anything* in that moment. Purely just trying to distract himself from 'what' was stood beside him.

I was pretty chilled by the fact that the clown wasn't harming Joe so there would be no need for Joe to harm him in return. Which was completely wrong. All it took was the clown - just as their performance was about to begin, woman on the rope now gone from the ring having departed after a massive round of applause from the appreciative crowd - to playfully reach out his hand and rest it casually on Joe's shoulder as the spotlight fell upon him for Joe to lose the plot.

'GET YERSELF TAE FUCK' He shouted while springing up out of his seat and hooking it square in the face, sending its red nose flying into the crowd. With this being caught on the spotlight and there for all of the crowd to see. There was instantly a series of screams and the sound of kids crying.

'YOU FUCKING BASTARD.' The clown shouted back at Joe in broken English while - scrambling to stay on its feet - trying to hit him on the head with its saxophone. Joe - who had managed to get himself out into the aisle too and onto his feet - was too streetwise for this though and moved out the way of the musical instrument. Kicking the clown in the area that 'should have' represented his balls. You're never really sure with clowns, though. I thought to cover up Gary's eyes with my hands by this point but it really was a case of too little too late and he saw and heard Joe's follow up punch - to the clowns jaw that sent him tumbling down the stairs to a cacophony of further screams and outrage - every bit as much as I did.

That was when the three circus workers all came running up the stairs towards Joe, who was now standing with his hands up trying to show that he was standing there in peace. They didn't really read this though and completely rushed him right up around another dozen stairs, pinning him against the back of the tent.

'HEY, IT WAS YOUR MAN WHO PUT HIS FUCKING HANDS ON *ME* YOU'RE LUCKY I'M NOT TAKING YOU ALL TO COURT' Joe shouted at them while they all bawled at him in some foreign accent. Not a lick of English between them so, for all Joe knew, they might not have been able to understand him, anyway. A couple of them beginning to argue with each other over - by the looks - what they're going to do with my husband.

Wee Gary is starting to bubble up while asking me why his uncle had punched the clown and if the men were going to kill him because of it. Simple innocence of a child with such basic questions but the way that these circus workers were reacting to their mate taking a couple of digs, you weren't quite *sure* of their intentions.

I told Gary to be a good boy for his auntie and sit in his seat while I went and helped Uncle Joe although, I was soon having second thoughts when - just as I was standing up - I saw one of them taking a sly punch at Joe while he argued with one of the others. This sending Joe into a rage where he ended up head butting one of the others who hadn't done anything other than hold him back and keep the situation from escalating any further.

I walked up the stairs to the one that looked the least threatening out of the three and with my phone in my hand started shouting to him that I'd saw the other one punch my husband and that if they didn't let him go I'd be calling the police to report the assault. I couldn't blame him for replying that *everyone* inside the big top had seen *my* husband punching the clown.

'HEY, HAN. YOU'RE MY WITNESS. THAT FUCKING CLOWN TOUCHED ME FIRST. CAUSE AND EFFECT, LIKES.' Joe shouted to me between a couple of the workers who were still pinning him back while arguing with each other.

'Oh, I saw it all. Don't worry about that.' I shouted back at him while making a show of starting to type out numbers on my phone.

'There is no need for that.' A man in a suit - who must've came up the stairs behind me during the commotion - reached out and grabbed my arm to stop me from going any further with the call that - in reality - I was *never* going to be making. He then turned his attention to begin shouting at the three goons who were 'taking care' of Joe. It was in the same language as they'd spoken in so I hadn't a clue what he'd actually said but it had been enough for them to grab him and pull him from back off the tent and start to march him down the stairs and past me.

'I'll get the pair of you outside, Han, alright?' Joe looked quickly to the side while he had the chance as he made his way down towards the edge of the ring. I couldn't help but feel that he was maybe being a touch optimistic with that considering none of us knew what the man in the suit had actually said. Could've been orders to take him outside and break his legs away from the view of all of the families there inside the tent that afternoon for all we knew.

'Where are you taking my man?' I said, returning the favour by grabbing the man in the suit's arm as he made to go down the stairs and follow everyone else. I was already grabbing Gary's arm with my other hand getting him ready to leave because wherever they were taking Joe, I was going to be right on their tail.

'He is no longer welcome inside the tent of Piqueto's Circus. Not now, not next year, not *ever*, again.' He said as if he was breaking some kind of earth shattering news to someone. What a blow to deliver someone, eh? Informing them that they were no longer welcome back to a circus that - chances were - they were never going to see the insides of again anyway.

That they were neither calling the police *or* dishing out some kind of self retribution was really all I wanted to hear. It was already going to be awkward when Senga started hearing about what had went on during the wee man's day out so if the police could've been kept out of the day, if at all possible, that would've been ideal.

One horrible, embarrassingly degrading walk of shame - all eyes inside there on us and all comments and whispers *to do* with us - leaving the big top later. I was reunited with Joe outside. Standing there outside the entrance to the red and white striped tent. Casually smoking a cigarette as if the previous ten minutes hadn't happened. I'd not long given up smoking myself but - there and then - there hadn't been a moment that had tested me enough to actually fold and *want* a smoke than that. Had to near enough count to ten to stop myself from asking him for one.

'I fucking told you about me and the clowns. You can't say that I didn't tell you.' He said, all bammed up over what had just happened but with the smallest of a devilish look to him after living the dream by punching out one of his own worst nightmares.

It had all left me in a bit of a position. My inner self wanted to unleash my displeasure of what he'd just done. Wee Gary, standing there crying over his uncle hitting a clown. Crying over the circus workers hitting his uncle. Crying over not getting to see the clown act because of us having to leave. Crying over - in our rush to get out of there - leaving his ray gun (that lit up when he pressed the trigger) under the seat. Poor wee man was probably going to end up traumatised over his day out.

I wasn't crying but was *severely* pissed off at him for the embarrassment that he'd caused as well as the fact that this had all gone on in front of a wee kid who was only there with us to have a fun day out with his auntie and uncle.

Under any other circumstances I'd have let Joe know - and in great detail - just how angry I was at him. He'd spent years telling me that he didn't like clowns. And after all of that. I'd *still* insisted that he went along with us.

It's quite difficult to put your full weight behind giving your other half an absolute bollocking when - deep down - you can't help but feel that some of it is your own fault.

'Aye, we'll probably laugh about this one day, anyway, Han.' He continued. The long and intense draws that he was taking on the cigarette, it was finished almost as soon as he'd lit it.

'So, wee man. MCDONALDS YAY. Get you a Happy Meal, pal, eh?'

Joe crouched down to something more resembling head height with Gary. Ruffling his hair as if our nephew was just going to forget all about his performance with the clown ten minutes before and that a fast food children's meal and toy would supersede the random act of violence that he'd just seen his uncle subject someone else to. Not just someone else but something that he loved. A clown.

When Senga phoned later on in the night going absolutely radge at me and - in his reluctance to take the phone - Joe and how Gary couldn't get to sleep because he kept seeing his uncle Joe punching the clown. It definitely offered evidence that it was going to have taken Joe a *lot* more than a McDonalds to heal the scars that he'd left his poor wee nephew with after his trip to the circus.

It's a shame the way it ended, though. The circus itself was really good entertainment and I'd enjoyed myself, far more than I'd expected. Until the violence.

They really didn't have to send in the clowns, anyway. With my Husband being sat there in the audience it was a case of them already being here.

Chapter 12

Jack

'Did you hear about Flav?' I couldn't text or phone you as I'd ran out of credit. Haven't seen you all weekend, either.' Scooter looked grey. Ill, almost. Stood there - anxiously looking around himself like a junkie who was entering the itching stage - at the school gates waiting on me appearing for the day. There was no sign of Dynamo and, considering how late I was myself - as per - if he was behind *me* then he was without a doubt going to be late in.

It was true what Scooter had said, though. I hadn't seen him over the weekend. Hadn't seen *anyone*. I'd, in fact, been keeping my head down a bit following our expedition to Silverknowes. I'd thought it for the best if I was to keep my nose clean while waiting on the whole breaking into that house stuff to pass.

'What about him, like?' I replied but, going by the look on Scooter's face, wasn't even sure I wanted to know.

'He's in the hossie, two broken arms,' he said with eyes going off in all directions as if he was worried about who was possibly listening in. Looked well para, like.

The first thing I thought when hearing the news was that Flav was hardly Sport Billy so any thoughts of him sustaining such injuries while playing some recreational sports could've been binned straight from the very off. Biggest bit of exercise that cunt ever gets is having to get up from his chair to go across his room to pick up his Playstation controller after he's lobbed it across the room when losing a goal on FIFA or when he gets killed by a camper on Call of Duty.

And even if he *had* been playing fitba or some other sport. Who the fuck manages to break *both* arms. At once? You'd have to be *incredibly* unlucky to pull that off.

'Who did it?' I asked as we started walking towards the building. I had asked it without thinking about it but once the words had came out I found it a wee bit interesting that I'd asked 'who' rather than - what should've been - 'how?'

'Well that's the thing. I don't know much other than that he's in the hospital. It was my dad that told me. Flav's not been in touch and, when you think about it, he might not even be *able* to fucking text even, if he wants to. I tried to go down and visit him but got told that it was family only and there was already enough visitors in his room, anyway.'

'What's Dynamo saying to it?' I asked, already knowing that he would've been full of all kinds of theories and that - presuming there was someone who had done it to Flav - there was going to be payback being dished out.

'Haven't seen him either and, obviously, couldn't text or phone him. Feel like you're cut off at the legs when you've no credit, eh' It was maybe just a combination of the two things at once. The news about what had happened to Flav mixed with Dynamo not being in that morning but things instantly felt, off.

As we reached the point where our paths were going to go in different directions, for the first couple of periods, at least, Scooter looked like he had something else to say but was a wee bit wary of coming out and saying it.

'Look, man, this stays between the pair of us, aye?'

'Obviously, Scoot. What, like?' I asked, hoping he was going to stop fucking about as time wasn't on our side. I should've already been sat in Modern Studies at my desk with jotter out and open by then.

'Well, it's, it's Dynamo. Is it just me or has he been a wee bit weird, quiet like, after what we did last week? I dunno, just a feeling I've had. Like he's been a wee bit different. Bit more muted, you know?'

Straight away it made me think of how Dynamo had been on the bus journey back from Silverknowes. Like how he was a bit cagey with his rucksack and what he showed us that was inside it. Could've been any reason for that, though. Maybe found a couple of pornos and swiped them along with the Rolexes and jewellry but was too embarrassed to share with the rest of the group so kept them hidden in the bag while flaunting the more 'socially acceptable' items that he'd pinched.

'Know what, mate? And, aye, this stays between us, mind. I think Dynamo, for all the fronting that he was doing, was bricking it as much as the rest of us and *that* was it showing through in the way that he's been since. Not being funny but for the first few nights. I could barely sleep in case the pigs were going to be coming knocking on our front door.' I admitted, while my body language was telling Scooter that this wee pre period chat was now at an end.

'Thank fuck' He said with a wave of relief on his face. 'I thought it was just me. Needed to sneak one of my dad's Vallies to get myself to sleep the night we got back from Silverknowes.'

'You should've sent one over my way. Could've done with one or two, or three.' I laughed as I told him that we'd get a proper blether at dinner time and work out the next step when it came to Flav and also see if there had been any sign of Dynamo.

Whatever had happened to Flav, however the circumstances. It was a sore one for the boy. He wasn't going to be doing any fucking wanking for a while. That was one thing for certain.

I tried to tell myself - when Mr Walker began Modern Studies - that I was going to put it to the back of my mind. No point in worrying about stuff you can't change and all of that stuff, eh? I didn't though. Was a complete passenger during that double period.

Thinking about Flav, sat there in a hospital bed with a stookie on each arm and what had brought him to being there. It was that he'd broken *both* that I couldn't shake. *Everyone* breaks something at some point in their life, I suppose. There's always someone with a stookie or plastic protective guards around them when you're out and about. A lot of clumsy cunts around, like. Still, it's a bit hard to be clumsy enough to break *both* your upper limbs at the same time, though.

As Walker was droning on about the impact the war in Afghanistan - when the Soviets had tried to half inch it - had left on the wider world and, even today, its effects being felt with the further rise of terrorist groups, following Al Qaeda. Themselves, being a product of the end of the war in Afghanistan and it leaving some militants with a taste for keeping going and turning their attention to America. I was barely hanging on listening to him.

Mentioning Al Qaeda, though. My mind took me to *that* day. I was only Nine and didn't understand much of what was going on. Obviously thought it was a Hollywood film at first, seeing the planes crashing into the two towers and exploding into balls of flames. It was all anyone spoke about for days so, while not exactly appreciating what was being said, heard everyone's opinions on it.

I found myself thinking about Flav's two broken arms and the two towers being hit. Hardly comparable, though. Only, to me, it kind of was.

I thought back to tea time that same day on September the eleventh and my dad saying his piece on things - as we sat at the dinner table - and that how when the first plane crashed into the tower it was automatic to assume that it had been some kind of human or machine error that had caused it.

'The moment you saw that *second* plane hitting the other tower, though. *That's* when you knew that it was deliberate and no accident.' Dad's opinion on things.

This was how I was left feeling about Flav. This didn't feel like an accident. Whatever he'd been up to, maybe been lippy with the wrong cunt and was leathered for it? Whatever the story was.

If there was anything I was sure of. It was going to be that I would, eventually, get dragged into it once the dust settled.

Chapter 13

Strings

'Mad thing is? If I was to walk into here wearing a mask there would be three police cars surrounding the place before I could even say 'stick em up' and yet its *you* that should be wearing the mask. Three quid for a Magnum?' Benji stood there moaning his tits off at the boy stood behind the perspex glass in the BP at the services near Carlisle.

'Hey, I don't set the prices, my friend, I just get paid an extremely low wage to sell the stuff.' The BP employee - Carl according to his badge - protested at Benji's rage.

'You know that you don't have to buy it, Benj.' I interrupted. Trying to mediate, already noticing that there was a bit of a line backed up because of the delay caused by us at the front of it. Benji wasn't listening, though.

'Aye, fair enough. Don't shoot the messenger I suppose, eh?' He said, with acceptance, fishing his debit card out of his pocket to give to the boy. Carl, looking relieved that the situation had been defused a wee bit.

'Now would you like any coffee, phone top ups or these half price jam filled donuts before I put the sale through?' He asked Benji.

'Is he fucking taking the piss?' Benj looked at me and asked in some kind of sarcastic faux amazement thumbing his hand - like a hitchhiker - in the direction of the boy behind the counter.

'He's got a bit of a point, though, eh, pal?' I said to 'Carl.' 'I mean, he stopped short of ripping your perspex screen off when you rang up two ninety nine for a plain Magnum. What made you think that he was then going to be in the mood to splurge even more in your airport price based shopping emporium?'

'Look, I'm sorry. I *have* to ask it to everyone. I get in trouble if I don't.' He replied, apologetically.

'Aye, and you'll get in trouble *for* asking it as well.' Benji laughed as he picked up his bank card, Magnum and two litre bottle of Coke from off the counter.

Once we were both outside the garage, again, and on our way back to the car we both broke out into laughter. 'Did you see the look on his face?' Benji said, confirming that he was doing nothing more than busting the teenager's balls and was trying to wind him up.

'Fuck that, no wonder the fucking English think we're tight when we've got you doing your best to perpetuate the myth between inter anglo relations. He'll be fucking telling cunts all day long about the Scot who was that tight he almost wrecked the shop over an uncompetitively priced ice cream.' I said. Just being honest with the boy.

'Hey, I'd expect someone from England to kick off about that, *too*. Like I said to the boy, at least with a robber you know where you stand, eh?' He justified.

You could tell how excited Benji was about our wee trip to Blackpool. Just by his general demeanor. Even turned up twenty minutes early at the house at twenty to six. We'd agreed that we'd get on the road early doors and try and get onto the motorway before cunts in Edinburgh started hitting the roads and heading to work. Leaving us with a smooth passage down the M6 and M55.

I was as excited as Benji Boy, too. What's not to love about a couple of days away from the family. On the piss with your best mate and making a bit of dough at the same time. Technically being *paid* to go out on the piss, depending on which way you looked at it. Sometimes life can reward you in ways when you most need it and after all of that caper at the weekend with that fucking clown - and all the heat that it had brought - I was *more* than happy to accept the chance to get out of dodge for a while.

Had fallen out with Han over it because *she'd* fallen out with - her sister - Senga due to the wee man having gone home with a few mental scars after his day out with his auntie and uncle. The *one* thing that was winding me up was - aye, everyone else was wound up, too - that no cunt was willing to recognise the one person who had suffered the most out of it all, me. Fuck wee Gary. He'll be fine and won't even fucking remember it in years to come, anyway. Seemed like everyone was intent on blaming *me* rather than the clown. You know? Not one single person asked me if *I* was alright? Not one. Not even the fucking wife.

Of course. The more grief she gave me off the back of what she was getting from Senga the more I returned, over, what the fuck she'd even been thinking about taking me along with her in the first place when she knew I didn't like the circus. It wasn't like a husband saying that he didn't want to go shopping to Asda with his other half because he didn't like shopping when - it's the blatantly obvious - he obviously can't be arsed getting up out of his seat and going.

I. Didn't. *Like*. The. Circus.

Getting away from underneath the massive mushroom cloud that had been left hovering over the homestead was a case of impeccable timing. Away from the atmosphere that was going on with Han and me. You had Jackie there but not there at the same time. Just your usual teenager stuff. Quiet one minute. A wee fucking wideo the next before back to a gimpy mute again. If it wasn't for the fact that the house rules dictated that he would sit there and have his tea along with the rest of us we would barely see him.

Han had picked up on that, apart from school, he hadn't been out in a week. Just sitting up there in his room watching the telly or playing that X-Box. She'd asked me if maybe he'd fallen out with his pals or something. 'With a bit of luck, aye' had been my reply back to her.

'Our Jack severing ties with that mob that he runs around with would hardly be the worst news we could receive as a family, Han' I'd said, giving her a non required reminder of what I'd already said about that Dynamo and Scooter. The other one, Flav. He was a decent enough wee lad. Used to play pool with Cammy - his dad - years back, like. Good family, you know?

Anyway, they could have all done what they wanted for the next few days as far as I was concerned, without in any way being selfish, of course. As husband and father to the house I didn't ask for much while gave so much in return, as any head of the house *should* do.

My annual trip to Blackpool, though? It was almost like a wee gift to myself - that was dressed up as a business trip - and something that I would always look forward to the more it got closer to coming around.

We stayed in the same bed and breakfast every year. The Tower Guest House - belonging to old Missus Henderson - just off The Promenade. Had got to the point where each year when we were checking out, the old dear would ask us if we wanted her to book us up for the next again year.

There was probably not going to be too many cosy guest houses in the resort that would have been so *understanding* to having put a roof over the heads of Benji and I when on a two day bender. We found it with old Harriet, though. I knew she was sound the second year in a row that we'd went - remembering us as we walked in - when she, looking around her before speaking, said that there was no need for us to be ashamed this time around and that she had no issues at all in giving us a double bed for our stay.

It was a close run thing in the end - whether her poker face was going to crack and she was going to start laughing or if Benji was going to give her a volley of abuse over the mere suggestion that he was gay - but she managed to give the game away, that she was joking, *just* before Benji was about to let rip. Well she opened up the gates of inu-fucking-endo from then on in.

Despite being in her late sixties she's then got Benji asking her how her arse was for love bites as she's dishing out our fry up in the morning and her making comments about the room not having any pay per view porn but that she was willing to offer some kind of improv to assist the customer. Felt like a fucking carry on film I was starring in with the two of them at times but was all said in the correct way. Never creepy, like.

'Here they come.' She beamed at the sight of us coming through the door and across those familiar black and white chequred tiles to that wee reception.

'And here they go, as well' Benji said, dropping his holdall on the floor, giving the old dear a wee peck on the cheek before saying he was choking on a pint after the drive and for her not to wait up on him.

'He never bloody changes, does he?' She said in that familiar Northern English accent over at me.

'Nah, it's much too late for that. We're stuck with the imbecile now.' I said, shrugging like what else could her or I do about it.

Keeping in mind her age and that she was onto her second hip. I wasn't for just dumping the bags like I'd come home to my house and heading out to The Gunner so asked her if our room was ready as I'd nip both the bags in but - with us arriving a few hours before our official check in time - with someone still in the room she said to leave the bags lying at reception and she'd get her daughter - Karen - to put them up in the room once it had been cleaned.

This leaving the two of us with a clear path to hitting the prom with the only real plans we had of food, alcohol and crime just waiting there ready for the taking.

Chapter 14

Han

'I said *well done*. This steak has more blood dripping from it than Mr Orange. No, no, no apologies needed, darling, it's a fine art - cooking a steak - not even one that all chefs have managed to master. You're alright, don't worry about it. Oh and don't tell the chef what I said, by the way. Not wanting him marinating it in any of his special sauces, eh? No you're alright though, it's fine. Thanks for your assistance. Merci beaucoup.'

Joe had called me - let me say hello to him - before promptly ignoring me to speak to the restaurant waitress. Couldn't help but laugh at the predicament he was in, if I'm being honest, though. I'd been pissed off at him that *he* was the one to call *me* only to then leave me sitting there, missing part of Eastenders. Hearing him go through that same old undercooked steak issue fairly cheered me up though and was enough to keep my attention rather than drift back to what was going on in The Queen Vic.

Off the top of my head I genuinely don't think I could give more than three examples of where we'd been out for a meal and Joe had been brought out a steak to his own personal preference. It's true what he says about restaurants. 'You can tell them however the fuck you want it cooked … they're still going to just go on and do whatever the fuck it was they were going to do with it anyway.'

That time in Prague when we went on a city break for a couple of days for our anniversary where - after them bringing it out to him for a third time and it *still* had blood oozing from it - it ended with Joe demanding to be allowed to go through to the kitchens and cook it himself since - and I quote Joe - the chef 'wasn't up to the task.' We didn't have *anything* to eat in there in the end, funnily enough.

'Aye, sorry, Han, cunts don't know how to cook a sirloin, eh?' He said, coming back to me again.

'Some things never change, do they?' I giggled.

'Doesn't stop me from giving the chefs across the world the benefit of the doubt, though. Not sure why I fucking bother, like. So how's things? Everything up the road alright, aye? Just thought I'd check in with you.' He asked. It's just the little things, I suppose, but the fact that he had actually taken a few minutes out to call when he was in the middle of stringing machines and getting drunk with Benji genuinely made my day.

It had been a shitty shift at the shop. Went so slow and I was on along with Christine Parker where there is absolutely zero conversation between the two of us. You'd find more of a conversation in a Charlie Chaplin film than you would with me and Chrissy when we're working together.

Then home to the equally quiet house with the bare minimum spoken between Jackie and me. Had I not actually asked him any questions when we were having our tea the two of us would've sat there in complete silence.

Strings' call meant a lot, more because he made it when he was otherwise indisposed where he was. Most men wouldn't have even given it a thought to phone their wife like that. That's my Joe though. Never the most conventional of husbands and there would be millions of women out there who wouldn't have the patience, or the people skills, to handle a man like him but you know what?

Aye, so, the man might bring money into the house through less than legal methods and sure he might deck a Spanish clown from time to time but not once since him and I met had he not provided or looked after me. When wee Jackie came along he stepped up even further. Aye, so what if he was a radge from time to time. He was *my* radge.

'Everything's fine, Joe. Just enjoying the peace and quiet and having the remote to myself,' I teased him.

'Aye well, don't get too comfy with it, eh. I'll be back to claim what is rightfully mines soon. How's Jack?'

'Barely said half a dozen words at the dinner table.' I answered.

'So same Jack then.' He said, referring to the fact the wee man had been a wee bit subdued over recent times.

'AWRICHT HANNNN'

I heard Benji shouting in the background.

'You hear that? Benji says to say hi to you.' Joe said without any concept of just how loud it had come over the phone. If it was as loud as that. I can only imagine what the levels must've been like inside whatever restaurant they were sitting in. Not like Benji would've cared about that, anyway.

'Tell him I said hello back and for him to keep my husband out of trouble down there.'

'Be the other way around. It's *me* that needs to keep *him* out of trouble.' Joe replied knowing all too well that you can't kid a kidder and that fine well I knew that they were as bad as each other so there was no point in Joe painting himself as the angelic one out of the two.

'So how's it been down there, anyway? Been worth the drive down?' I asked, primarily through wanting to gauge how much money he had made for us and the house and then balancing that up against how much he had spent on drink.

'Been a good wee day, aye, darling. Might well be able to treat us to an Indian at the weekend if the winning streak continues.' He joked. Well, he fucking better have been because he wouldn't have found much of a welcome home if he returned back from a couple of days in Blackpool with barely enough in his pockets for a couple of Lamb Tikkas and a plain naan bread from The Crown of India.

'We had a wee bit of a lucky escape though, earlier on. Silly cunt across the table from me here made a bit of a schoolboy error and it led to us almost getting rumbled. I'll tell you about it when I get back up the road. Had to ditch my old stringer and everything, absolutely gutted.'

It sounded like things had been eventful. When he said that he'd had to throw away his *old* stringer I knew what he meant and how distraught it would've left him. It had been the *original* one that his dad had first used - back in the day - following Strings coming up with the idea of a pretend coin.

I could hear it in his voice how gutted he was, now that he had mentioned it. It definitely wasn't the time for me to ask him if he'd brought any other of his stringing accessories with him so I left it. To ask him, I felt, would have been to immediately diminish the importance of the one that he had just had to get rid off.

'Awww, babe. That's gutting to hear. I'm really sorry.' It felt like I was sympathising with someone over losing a loved one but, in a way, it was. Strings told me that every time he used it - and won money - he would think of his dad looking down on him with a smile saying 'go on, son. Clean those bastards out.' That battered and cut up piece of plastic meant as much to Joe as the money inside the machines that he used it to win from.

'Aye, just one of those things. I kicked it underneath the puggy at the last second before these Albanians came out from a back room going fucking radge at us. Maybe a chance of retrieving it as I can't see any cleaner getting their fucking Dyson underneath there, or why they'd even bother. Things didn't exactly end smoothly with the cunts in the arcade, though, so I'm not sure how Benj or me are going to be able to go back there without them being on us straight away. If it comes down to it though I'll just have to leave it where it is. We're lucky that the two of us managed to walk out the place, unaided. Maybe just call it quits there, like.' He sounded completely heartbroken as he told me a bit more of what had happened.

I'm sure that I was going to hear all about it when he got back but through the gutted tone about losing something of such sentimental value to him I could also tell that - whatever had taken place inside the amusement arcade - he was a wee bit shaken up by things.

'Fuck's sake, Joe. You take care of yourself down there.' I said, leaving me *also* shaken up without really knowing the exact details of why.

'TRYING TO SAY THAT WE WERE STEALING FROM THEIR MACHINES, THE NERVE, EH?' I heard Benji shouting and then laughing in the background. You're never sure with Benj but he sounded like he'd had a few drinks.

'Anyway, just wanted to give you a wee phone before I had a few more beers and forgot. Looks like that's the girl coming back with my steak so fingers crossed, eh.'

'What are you two doing for the rest of the night then?' I asked before getting ready to get myself comfy on the sofa again and sticking the volume for Eastenders back on again.

'Just staying in here. We're in some club where you get a scran, cheap booze and live entertainment.' He replied while apparently being distracted by the waitress. 'Aye, just stick it down there, thanks.'

'Live entertainment? Like what?' I asked, pondering that - depending on where they *were* - could've been anything from a stripper to a tribute band.

'Jim Davidson.' He laughed back.

'Jim Davidson? What the hell are you doing going to see *him*?' I already knew that Joe detested the man who went under the description of 'comedian' but was about as funny as giving birth.

'He only got to be famous and be given the platform he did because he was around *before* racism used to be bad.' He'd said with sarcasm one night when we were flicking through Sky and came across him on UK Gold.

'Aye, I know, like, but me and Benji thought it would be a good laugh to fire in and have a couple of peaves and heckle the cunt. Give him it tight, like.'

'Joseph? You travel two hundred miles to spend your daytime getting threatened by Albanian heavies and your evening heckling racist comedians. I love you, never change but PLEASE be safe, ok.'

'Aye, love you too, Han. I'll bell you tomorrow, darling.'

And he was off. Leaving me to my soap before I moved on to doing some laundry, tidying up the kitchen after tea before catching up with some pals on Facebook for a natter as well as tending to my wee farm on there. *Especially* my wee Facebook farm.

Chapter 15

Strings

'You can fahk off you pair of Jock twats. Bet you didn't even pay to get in you tight cahnts. Fahking Jocks. Tighter than a gnat's chuff. Security, do something baht these two, will yer?'

It was fair to say that the comedian - and our night's entertainment - hadn't taken too kindly to the heckles. You know what, though? Give the boy his due, he managed to put up with a good half hour of constant jibes from our table - I mean, well, it was why we were there, after all - before he finally snapped.

'When you're shouting for security instead of destroying a heckler with your razor sharp wit. That's when you should probably give up the old comedy circuit, pal.' Benji said, having already clocked the two boys in the matching black polo shirts - with arms that suggested extreme roid usage - rushing over towards our table, as he stood up and waved a dismissive hand towards the stage.

I followed his lead, necking what was left of my pint before taking my coat from off the back of my chair and slinging it on.

'Ooooooohhh kkkkkkkkk, fellas. Time you two were going, don't you think?' One of them said to the pair of us in a Geordie accent.

'That could've been said the minute that cunt walked onto the stage.' I said back to him as I started walking, so as to let them both know that there wasn't going to be any kind of resistance on our part. It was daft of me, though, to have ever presumed that my words and actions were going to be sufficient enough to speak for me *and* Benji.

'I'll be expecting my fucking money back before we *do* leave. Get me the manager.' Benji demanded.

The two security boys both kind of done a wee laugh, looking at each other. As if, initially, they'd assumed that the man - that they were about to throw out for unacceptable behaviour - was having them on. The Geordie. Easily in his early fifties, stud ear ring in one of his lugs, in his black polo shirt that was almost being ripped by his bulging muscles. The type of muscles that would have stopped anyone from ever entertaining the thought of trying to slag him about his stud earring. He then turned to me with a face as if to ask if my friend was being serious.

'Look, unless I'm mistaken, here. You've got a fucking poster outside saying that for twenty nine pounds ninety nine pence - in return - you will provide a three course meal, alcohol to go with and *afterwards*, a comedian.'

For emphasis, Benji looked towards the stage where Jim Davidson was standing patiently. Sipping on a pint while looking over some notes that I assume he was going to be using for the remaining part of the night.

'Do you see any fucking comedian here?' He asked the security while - with an out stretched arm - did a three hundred and sixty degree turn around the room.

'I'm looking at one right now.' The other security guy. There wasn't so much bulk to the other one. He was quite wee for someone in that line of work but you see the size of some of those UFC fighters as well, though, eh? Not much of some of them but would put you to sleep for the night with one punch.

'Mon, Benj. We've had our fun. Think of the daft cunts that have actually came here *specifically* to see the cunt? Let's not spoil their night anymore.' I said, looking at the Geordie and giving him a wee nod and wink to indicate that we were all cool here.

Davidson must've noticed that we were being escorted out because just as we were starting to leave, you heard him going back onto the mic again.

'Hit the road JOCK and don't you come back no more no more no more no more. Hit the road JOCK and don't you come back no more.'

With his free hand he was trying to coax the crowd to join in with him but it was a pitiful amount that actually *did* and the ones who 'had' soon stopped again. In his mind he had probably imagined every single living person inside that club would've all sang their hearts out and provided an intimidating last few moments of us being in there. In reality, it never came remotely close.

Resisting the urge to stop and give a bit back in his direction we, instead, kept going. Leaving the place with absolutely zero fucks given.

After that, I was happy enough to have a couple of quiet pints somewhere - drama free - and then get back to the guest house and have a kip. We'd been up early doors at the start of the day to get ourselves down to England. Had a profitable - if dangerous - day of stringing and then after that. A big three course meal and drinks. It had been a long day. Somewhere that we could sit and have a laugh going over what had just happened would've been just what the doctor ordered.

'When he shouted down that Aids was funnier than us I thought the cunt's head was going to explode, like in that Scanners film.' Benji laughed as we went over things back at the restaurant club.

'I'm surprised that we lasted in there for as long as we did. Good fun while it lasted, though.' I laughed back at the thought of some of the exchanges between us and Davidson as we walked in search of a boozer.

'What do you think you're going to do about your stringer, then?' He asked, as we got sat at the bar in the Pleasure Beach Bar - which had been the first licensed establishment that we stumbled across - for a nightcap or too.

I hadn't even mentioned it since the incident with the Albanians earlier on in the day but, fucking hell, I'd fairly expressed my emotions at the time when we left - more chased, really - the amusement arcade that we'd been working in. Had a proper meltdown once we were outside and the dust had settled and we didn't have some fucking CSKA Moscow Ultras waving a baseball bat in our face. Kicked the fuck out of a metal door shutter to a hairdressers that didn't look like it was open anymore. Proper meltdown, like. Everyone in the street stopped what they were doing and watched on while I lost the plot. I didn't care.

I had to channel the rage and frustration that was overflowing from me somehow and - considering it was fucking Benji's fault - in the scheme of things. It was probably beneficial to make sure that I took it out on an inanimate object instead of him.

There's not too many rules that I ask Benj to follow but one of the *key* instructions is that he fucking stands or sits *exactly* where I tell him to *when* I tell him. I don't need him to be a statue but I *do* need him to be where the situation dictates.

In 'The Beachcomber Amusements' it was a complete dereliction of duty from my assistant. I mean, he only did so through trying to be a sound cunt because some wee kid had been running around in there and tripped up and smashed his face against the corner of an Astroids machine. Screaming the house down, as you would.

Benji, seeing this, abandoning his station to pick the wee boy up from the floor. Now don't go thinking that I'm some cold hearted prick who is against adults helping out another man woman or child when they need it. That is most definitely not the case. Just *don't* go fucking helping someone out when you're meant to be shielding me from other people's line of vision and *especially* don't go doing it while I'm *right* in the fucking process of the art of recreating the act of putting a coin into a fruit machine RIGHT as a street smart arcade worker just happens to be looking.

I didn't know that she'd seen me, of course. Didn't know that the game was up. Sometimes though - when you see things like tooled up cunts in velour Fila tracksuits walking through your average family friendly amusement arcade in a popular tourist destination as Blackpool - you don't really need anyone to bring you full up to speed with how things are.

They were looking, and heading, straight for us. One of them - the boy with the baseball bat - pointing directly at us with it.

'Ok, Benj. I don't know what the fuck has happened but these cunts know what what we're up to.' I whispered to him while hoping that my attempt to drop the stringer and kick it underneath the puggy had been discreet enough for none of - who was heading our way - to have noticed.

'You fucking thieving scumbags.' The boy with the bat said as they got up to us both. The two of us standing up from our high chairs on alert as he pointed the bat so close to us I could make out all of the relative scratches and chunks that had been collected through previous usage and the odd small blood stain.

'Who? Us?' I said. First looking at the pair of them and then back to Benji for back up.

'Who are you fucking calling scumbags?' Benji said, offering a little too much hostility when it came to the back up that I had been hoping for. These two had the jump on us, we'd already had around three or four pints by then and had that nice wee afternoon buzz so weren't the most mobile and, forgetting all of that for a moment, anyway. They were the ones with the baseball bat.

'You, you robbing scumbags.' The guy with the bat and the scruffy nailed down home salon hair cut - cunt looked like he went to the same hairdresser as that fanny, Boris Johnson - replied, turning his attention from me to Benji.

'Oh aye, eh?' I said, slowly moving one hand towards the tray on the front of the puggy where my coins were sitting. 'Just because I'm winning you take the fucking cream puff and start saying that you're getting robbed. Funny how you lot never say that when us mug punters are pumping our nuggets into your machines and getting fuck all back out though, eh? Strangely quiet, then, like.' I went on the defensive and hoped that - whatever it had been that they had seen or been told - I was going to be able to bluff my way out of it.

D. Unleash your inner thespian.

'You think you are the first to try it in here?' The other one, this big guy with what wasn't so much of a tended to beard and more a case of someone who looked like they'd just not been arsed shaving for a couple of months, sneered at me.

'Try what?' I continued with the act.

By this point, the two of the Albanians had maneuvered their way around us to now block the path to the front door.

'Empty your fucking pockets, you fucking bastards.' The one with the bat said, bringing the bat up to my forehead. Gently enough to press it against me and then give it a little push - forcing my head back - to try and hurry me along.

'We don't have to empty our fucking pockets for any cun ...' Benji offered his opinion but I cut him off. As a double act - in a situation like this - we could never be beaten.

'No no no, mate, these two are obviously mistaken about something so let's empty our pockets for them. Don't know what the fuck they're expecting to find, though, like.' I said putting a hand up to stop him while then going through all of my pockets for them. Thank fuck we'd been in a hurry to drop the bags at the guest house and I'd forgotten to lift my fake coins, I thought to myself as I turned out all of my pockets for the two of them like I was going past the security at T in the Park.

Benji did the same and - between us - the Albanians were left looking at fuck all other than the staple ingredients of your average man's pockets. Money, phone and keys.

They were well pissed off, like. Well, you would be if you'd went all out and running around threatening cunts with baseball bats and not come up with the evidence you were looking to justify it. Even so. With no smoking gun found, they *still* weren't convinced and the level of hostility didn't drop even after that, as I'd expected it to.

The one without the bat kept saying that one of the staff had seen with her own eyes when she was going to help the little boy who had fallen. It was hard to fully understand what he was saying due to how animated he was and the broken English - as well as the Albanian that they spoke between each other - but from what I had picked up.

The wee boy had fallen and started screaming. The woman that worked in the arcade who was nearest to the incident went to help. Benji got there first but by *getting* there first he had left a wide open space for her to then see me sliding a coin into the puggy, only to miraculously pull it back out of the machine again.

Fucking Benji.

'Aye well, fuck this. You come steaming over here accusing us of all types of skullduggery without even a fucking shred of evidence. Fucking stood in here for hours and pumped in hundreds into some of your machines with very little coming back my way in return. I think I'll be pishing away the rest of my dough elsewhere, gentleman.'

I said, thinking that it definitely would've been for the best if I could just remove us from this whole situation. Their mood hadn't changed despite finding nothing on us so it would've been daft to try and predict what they were going to do next. They couldn't exactly call the police when there wasn't any evidence. Neither could they have given us a paggering in one of their back rooms without evidence, either. That didn't mean to say that they *wouldn't* have done either, though. *Especially* the second option. They didn't really look like the type that calls the police.

'Don't you put a fucking finger on those coins.' I heard while feeling the bat pressing into my chest and pushing me slightly away from the machine as I discreetly - I'd felt - moved for the pound coins sitting in the tray.

'Oh, Oh, Ohhhh. that's the boy's fucking money. He won it fair and square and you're pulling out that shite?' Benji said, taking one step closer to them and going further than either of us really needed or wanted him to. It was also a bit of an unnecessary piss take on my part to have even attempted to have scooped up the coins that were sitting there - looked to be around Thirty quid or so - when between us we were already holding the best part of Four Hundred that we'd *already* pinched from them.

'You touch those coins and I break your fucking hands.' Babe Ruth said and from the look on his face I could see that it wasn't exactly a veiled threat.

'He'll do it too.' The other one - with the haircut - said. Trying to assure me that this wasn't for show.

'Now fuck you and fuck off and do not come back. Next time you come back here you will be crawling out the front door, if you are lucky' He added. Taking a step towards us along with his mate.

'Fucking disgrace of a place. Only trying to come down from Scotland to have a few days holiday after working hard all year, put a bit into the Blackpool tourism coffers and *this* is how you get treated, eh? Think I'll be going to fucking Skegness next year, instead' Benji continued but was saying this to them while he walked slowly backwards in the direction of the door. We *had* to, though. How hyped up the pair of them were you'd have been off your fucking nut if you had turned your back on them.

I took one last look at the puggy that we'd been playing, and what was now masking a piece of stringing history underneath it. Kings and Queens, it was called. I looked back at it as they shoved us backwards towards the exit. All the memories of me and dad flooding through my mind. The feeling that even though it was only a stupid wee piece of plastic. It felt like I was leaving a part of me behind, lying underneath that puggy.

Took me a few hours of the day before I even started to get over it. It's funny how a certain thing - no matter how small it might appear to be - can become so important to you like that. Alcohol always helps in those cases though and with the amount that Benji and me put down our necks. By the time we got to Jim Davidson I was pretty much at the 'acceptance level' when it came to the old stages of grief.

In actual fact, though. I'd got the fucking thing back *before* Benji had even opened his eyes for day two. I'd woken up needing a piss around seven in the morning and it was when I was standing there - trying to concentrate through my half shut eyes enough to hit the pan - when I had the lightbulb moment. Sometimes it can be such an easy connection to make for someone, like there.

Now while Benji and I were no longer welcome back at the amusement arcade. Neither was it going to provide a scenario where I could've asked someone else to go in and retrieve the stringer for me. You can only imagine how it would go if you were to ask a complete stranger if they would like to do you a favour. Oh aye? What kind of favour, the stranger would, rightfully, ask. If they even allowed you enough time as to give you a reply.

'Well, I need you to pop into that amusement arcade right? Then head to a certain fruit machine, get down on your hands and knees - in front of all of the staff and cameras - and try to squeeze your hand underneath to grab my very much illegal implement that is used to steal money from amusement arcades. We cool, aye?'

It was never an option. It had to be either me or Benj. Technically it *should've* been fucking Benji considering he was the one who caused it all but him being the liability that he was. There was no guarantees that he wouldn't have made things even worse and ended up giving them the proof that they'd been looking for the day before.

Nah, it would have to be me, if any of us.

I'd tried to put it behind me but, considering the very first waking thought I'd had had been about it. I obviously *hadn't* shrugged it off, though, when I'm standing there doing a pee and it's the first thing that is in my head.

Looking at my watch and seeing how early it was. It occurred to me that it would've been too early for the arcade to be open, not that I was welcome there anyway, obviously. Then the cleaners popped into my head. Chances are that they'd probably have been in and blitzed the place after it had closed for the night like you see with the cleaners at the bookies after they've closed but - and it was only an extremely outside but - with how late some of those Blackpool arcades actually closed for the night. There was always the chances that - instead - the cleaners would do the place before it opened for the morning and - if that being the case - there was practically no fucking chance that the owners or staff of the place would be there at that time. They'd probably still be in their beds at that point.

With Benji still lying sleeping, half of him hanging off the bed from his moving around in the night. I shoved on some clothes and decided to take a walk in the direction of the arcade. When I got there - as anticipated - it was in darkness with no sign of anyone inside. It was still early, though. About eight-ish. There was a cafe that was two doors down though that *was* open. Looked to be quite busy in what was an otherwise quiet street at that time of morning.

'Hi, love, what can I get you?' The woman with the smokers dirty blonde hair asked me when I walked in. Taking a look around there was only one spare table so it wasn't going to be much of a case of where I was going to choose to sit down.

'Cup of tea and a bacon roll would be an absolute joy, darling.' I replied before telling her that I was going to take a seat over at the free table.

I was struggling a little from the night before so the sit down was as welcome as the prospect of a cuppa and a bacon roll. That, though, had been ordered more as so I could buy myself time to work out a plan while sitting inside there. Once I'd ordered it I realised just how much I could've done with it, though.

'There you are, hun, is there anything else that I can get you?' She said having come from behind the counter to bring my tea and roll over to me.

'Actually, there maybe *is* one more thing you can do for me.' I said stopping her from walking away.

'Anything, my love.' She smiled back in the flirty way that women in their fifties tend to do - when they're not getting any sex but would love for that situation to change - with literally anyone from the opposite sex that they come across in a day.

'Well, it's more information rather than anything else, you see? I'm down for a couple of days with my mate, from Scotland, like. We come down every year. Anyway, yesterday I've only ended up losing my wedding ring.'

Absolutely no fucking idea where I plucked that one from but I was hardly going to tell her what I *had* lost, was I?

'Aye aye, *lost* your wedding ring, did you? Bad boy.' She winked at me while trying to insinuate that while she had bought the story of me having a wedding ring she wasn't for purchasing the side story of me 'losing' it.

'No, no, it's nothing like that.' I protested but, despite my actual innocence, only made myself look like I *had* taken it off, on purpose.

'Oh I believe you, thousands wouldn't.' She cackled the dirty of laughs before asking how I thought that she'd be able to help me.

'Well, I go home soon so don't have much time to find it. It's probably gone now but can you imagine the earache I'm going to get when I go back home to my wife in Edinburgh, missing it from my finger?' I said before she cut me off from finishing.

'Well if she kicks you out of bed you're more than welcome to fall back into my one, hun.' She winked again.

'I might well need to take you up on that.' I humoured her.

'So anyway, the arcade, couple of doors down from here? Me and my mate were in there for hours yesterday and, I know it's a long shot, like, but I thought that it had possibly fallen off my finger when I was sat at one of the machines. You know, the repetitiveness of putting coin after coin in? And by the way, whether I go home with my wedding ring or not I'm already in the shit with how much money I stuck into those machines yesterday.'

D. Unleash your inner thespian.

She was smiling but I wasn't sure whether it was because I'd said that I'd maybe need to sleep in her bed or if there was something a bit more beneficial towards me about to come out of it.

'Ooooooh I *can* help you there, love, well, hopefully.' She replied before telling me that with the arcade not opening until eleven in the morning the cleaners went in there in the mornings before it opened up. The two cleaners themselves, Holly and Jen, coming into the cafe every morning around half eight for a cup of tea before they started their shift.

'You might have to hang around for a while until after nine and they go in there to get started but I'm sure they'll let you have a quick look.' She said, filling me with hope. The absolute *best* kind. The kind that follows what you'd initially thought of as a lost cause.

'Oh you are a LIFESAVER!' I said back to her.' Putting my hand on my heart. 'We're heading home to Scotland before the arcade actually opens so this is going to work out better than I thought. I'll let you get back, looks like you've got a few hungry punters waiting.' I went with the lie to ensure that - providing these cleaners appeared - there would be no talk of me being told to come back when the place opened at eleven.

'Pleasure, love, I'll let you know when the girls come in. Give me a shout if you'd like another tea.'

Talk about a fucking stroke or what, though.

It was around twenty minutes later when the two women walked in, chatting away to each other. I'd guessed who they were before the wifie from the cafe started to talk to them. When she did, though, it had them turning around to look over in my direction.

While one stood chatting at the counter, the other one came over to my table and started speaking to me. She kind of reminded me of Aunt Sally from the Worzel Gummidge programmes, because of the round and rosy red cheeks that she had.

She told me that 'Katie' had told her about my predicament with my wedding ring and that if I was able to hang on while they both had a cup of tea and their breakfast they'd let me have a quick look before they got started with the vacuuming and cleaning.

When they were finished. The same woman, Holly, told me to sit tight for five minutes as they'd need to go through the alarm set up to get in and she'd pop back in and give me a shout. Which she duly did. Soon finding myself - improbably - inside the same premises that I was face to face with a baseball bat less than twenty four hours before.

Being as good as one hundred percent sure that I was going to find it. I made a show of looking under a couple of other machines first before crouching down at the Kings and Queens machine. With the smoothest of slight of hands. I managed to take a pound coin and insert it underneath the puggy while scooping up the plastic stringer and sliding it up into my sleeve.

'Any luck, honey?' The other one, Jen, asked while she unravelled the flex of a Henry Hoover.

'Nah, sadly no, I'm afraid. I *did* though find a pound coin, so, you know? Every cloud, eh. Here, take it for your next cup of tea next door.' I said flicking the coin up into the air and her catching it first time. 'Thanks for at least trying to help. Can you let me out again, please.' I asked.

I departed with a despondent look on my face or, well, the look of the face that I *thought* someone who had lost their wedding ring would have on them.

Benji was still lying crashed out when I returned, victorious.

With luck like what the early morning had provided. It would've been mad not to try and attempt to tap into that, in a gambling sense. Eventually we'd taken over seven hundred pounds over the course of the late morning and early afternoon. And with absolutely zero in the way of 'issues' in us doing so. No weapons, police or goons to contend with. Just how we like it.

You know though that sometimes you're best not to push things to far. When things are going, well, if there's one prediction that you could stick you fucking house on it's that they won't stay that way forever.

Because of that. We ended up leaving Blackpool to come up the road a bit earlier than we'd planned. We'd came down. Had a good time, made a pile of money and had even been blessed with the opportunity of ripping the pish out of Jim Davidson.

It was probably a good idea that we got out of town before the luck began to turn again.

E. Know when to say when.

Chapter 16

Strings

'Do you think these cunts do this on purpose? Trying to be like Wimbledon when the big teams would come to play them, like?' Bungalow asked in reference to the one temperature system that the taps and showers in the changing rooms seemed to have in operation. Cold, obviously.

'Aye, we're a big club right enough, Bungalow.' Coffee turned around and said. Any cunt could see that from us stepping off our Muirhouse Violet branded private coach all carrying our Louis Vuitton and Chanel shower bags how big time we are, mate.' He said this while letting his tracky bottoms drop to the floor and stepping out of them while holding his shorts in his hand.

'Aye, you know what I'm saying, though? Anything to put the opposition off, like.' Bungalow reasoned.

'Well its going to take a whole lot more than a cold fucking tap to knock Muirhouse Violet out the cup this morning, my brainless friend.' Jock Hunter interrupted.

'I popped my head into their dressing room ten minutes ago to grab a wee word with Patty Pearson, their gaffer, and I could see it written all over their faces. They're fucking bricking it in there, boys. You need to go for the jugular from the very start. None of this feeling the game out to start with because you're on away turf. Take the game to *them*. Don't give them a chance to breed any confidence. You score in the first ten minutes today I'll be dishing out your cigars and slippers during the second half. I guarantee you.'

As always, Jock was talking complete pish and trying to give it some mind games. Drylaw had beaten us four scud the last time we'd played them in the league - there at the same pitch - so there was no fucking reason *whatsoever* for any of their players to be sitting in their dressing room. Knees knocking together with a pool of urine there on the floor sat underneath them between their legs.

Cup games are different, though. Anything can - and at our level of fitba, generally 'does' - happen over ninety minutes and if you don't believe that then what's your point in even sticking on a pair of boots and going out onto the pitch? Then again, it's a little hard not to be too cynical about that when you turn up and find half of your team are still healthy inebriated from the night before and are more capable of passing wind - violently - than they are to pass a football.

There was quite a decent wee crowd out there to watch. A few car loads had come over from Muirhouse to cheer on the boys to join what was an already decent turnout from the locals.

When we did the exact *opposite* of what Jock Hunter had instructed to us and *didn't* score an early goal (instead gifting them the easiest of goals after an attempt at playing them offside went horribly wrong) and in turn letting them breed the confidence that Jock had specifically told us to prevent. It didn't look good. Good team, Drylaw. The number eight that they had. This young kid was skinning Wullie for fun, time and time again. I was surprised that it took The Monk as long as it did for him to take matters into his own hands and dish out some 'correction' on the boy, taking his customary yellow card in the process. The young kid was barely seen again for the rest of the match. Aye, one of 'those' players.

After conceding the stupid early goal we had started to come back into the game again and had had a few close chances that - on another day - would've went in. Same for them, though, mind. One of their midfielders - from fucking miles out - decided to have a dig. I was running behind him and - seeing how far he was away from goal - seconds before he hit it I even thought to myself, aye hit it, mate, hit it from there all day long if you fucking like. Well he obliged. Aiming a shot that looked like it was going miles over the bar *only* to dip at the last second. You could see by the panic on Sepp's face when it began to dawn on him that he was in the shit. Which he was, due to how far out he was stood.

Like the rest of us. All he could do was stand there and watch the ball dip over his head. Smacking against the crossbar with Bungalow being the first player on the spot and alert enough to knock the ball out for a corner.

The ref was about to blow for half time right as we grabbed an equaliser. What a time to score as well. That it was my good self who scored his first of the season only sweetened things further. Now while it was never going to rank up there as goals scored through sheer technical ability like a van Basten at Euro Eighty Eight or Maradona in Eighty Six … it still meant the same in mathematical terms.

Having not made it back to midfield from one of our attacks. I was still loitering around - without intent - when one of their defenders passed the ball back to their keeper. I felt it was a little short so decided to chase after it. Even if it was enough to give the keeper something to think about and potentially cause him to make a mistake then it would've been worth exerting the energy, I thought, as I chased it down. The keeper seeing this, injecting an extra small burst of energy into running towards the ball.

The distance between myself and the ball and him told me that he was going to reach it before me but I figured that the closer I was going to be to him when he connected, the less options he was going to be left with. Make the target smaller, so to speak. My thoughts were that he would be left with no choice other than to kick it to either side of me and end up giving us a throw in.

When he *did* go to boot the ball I had reduced his options of where to kick it dramatically and - instead of do the sensible thing and kick it to the side and give us a throw in - I think he just panicked by booting it straight against me. Preparing for a full on goalkeeper's kick, - through his general body shape as he went to kick the ball - at the very last second I jumped up into the air and twisted myself round with my back to him.

First I felt the ball slamming against my back and then, looking back up the other end of the park, I could see some of the Violet players standing there with their arms raised, expectedly, in the air.

I turned around just in time to see the ball rolling - slowly - across the goal line with the Drylaw keeper flailing desperately at it, trundling just out of reach and into the net.

While not one of my better goals in my time with The Violet. I celebrated more than Diego and Marco combined. Running with my finger pointing at some of the crowd standing there watching on and 'shuuuushhhhiing' them all. Receiving a nice piece of sweet sweet abuse back from them.

'Get it right fucking up yous' I screamed before being mobbed by the rest of the team. After the added time that the ref had put on from the treatment the young kid needed after The Monk's challenge, as well as our over exuberant celebrations from the goal. It gave us time to get back into the changing room, get a cup of tea and a chance to regroup. With a second half to go, the lads were very much in contention.

'Bungalow, Monk? What the fuck was that offside business all about? You're not fucking Adams and Bould, for fuck's sake. Other than that. Faultless. That's the only way these cunts are going to fucking score against us today. If we let them. It's down to you boys. You shape your own destiny when you walk onto that pitch, mind.'

He went through us all. Offering us his own observations on what he had seen in the first forty five minutes and where we needed some improvement.

'REMEMBER NOW, LIQUORICE.'

I laughed as he dished out his own last piece of advice after the ref had popped his head around the dressing room door to tell us that we were late in coming out for the second half.

The start of the second half couldn't have been more different to the start of the first. As opposed to the open way that the teams had began the match. The second half started with a lot more caginess to it. As if both teams didn't want to risk going behind to the other, which led to each other cancelling the other team out. We even got a penalty each and had managed to cancel each other out by contriving to missing them both. Rossi's attempt so bad I thought that it was going to go out for a throw in to Drylaw.

I think there was about twenty minutes to go when the ball had went out for a throw to us. Coffee who was nearest to the side of the pitch went to try and get it from one of the crowd standing around the pitch.

'Here, mate.' He said with outstretched hands to this man who was standing holding tightly onto the ball. I thought he was just trying to be a prick for the sake of it by hanging onto the ball. You see that all the time when you're playing away on a Sunday morning, like. *Especially* if you're getting beat at the time.

'I fucking know you. Been trying to work it out since the start of the match but I remember now.' He said, holding the ball protectively to his chest with his arm while pointing towards Coffee.

'Don't be fucking daft, pal. Gies the ball.' Coffee urged, wanting to get the game going again as we were in a good place on the pitch at the time and wanted to keep the momentum going.

'Nah, you're one of the cunts that did my conservatory last year. Fucking cowboys. Thing came down after two months and then when I tried to call about it the company had ceased to be in existence. Even called Rogue Traders on you and *they* cunts couldn't even fucking find you.'

By this point one of the Drylaw players had come over and wrestled the ball of off him to throw to us to try and get the game started again.

'Don't talk pish. You've got me mixed up with someone else.' Coffee said, shrugging this off before taking a quick throw in and getting the match restarted again.

'Aye, you'll see what pish I'm talking about, ya prick.' The man shouted but Coffee chose to ignore and get on with the game.

Despite Coffee pleading ignorance. I knew that there was something in it. The man looked absolutely *sure* he'd seen Coffee before and, beside that. Coffee *had* done some off the books work for Brian McLeod for a few years before his company had folded, practically overnight.

I snapped out of it, myself, when I was forced to 'intervene' and break up play when one of their midfielders had got himself into a dangerous position. It was one of those yellow cards that you're left with no choice other than to take for the good of the team. And one I'd take another hundred times in - what was left of - my career, if need be.

As time drew in the chances became scarcer and scarcer for each team. The prospect of extra time - with the general fitness we had, collectively - scared the fuck out of me. I didn't see where a goal was coming from. We were barely getting over the half way line but without ever really being troubled by them, either.

It was always going to take another penalty to be awarded if we were going to score a winner. Even when we were awarded it though, it was with the height of contention. Personally, I seen it up close and knew that the ball hadn't hit their players hand. It was clear as day that it hit him on the hip but with his hand being hanging down there too, it muddied the waters a bit. I was hardly going to step in and tell the referee that he'd got it wrong though, was I?

Rossi had given the ref something to think about with his instant cry of 'PENALTY REF' when he'd taken the shot from inside the box. He seemed to hesitate. Taking a second to make sure he got the decision correct. Which, to our advantage, he didn't. 'IT'S A FUCKING STONEWALLER.' Rossi continued, while the Drylaw defender started his protest. Now in fear that Rossi's screams were going to possibly have an effect.

'NAW, NAW NAW, REF. IT HIT THE SIDE OF ME. NEVER TOUCHED MY HAND. NOWHERE FUCKING NEAR, EH?' He shouted while wagging his index finger back and forwards.

Once he'd awarded the penalty. That was when the arguments started over *who* would take it. As soon as the whistle went and the ref pointed to the spot Rossi had instantly scooped the ball up.

'Aye, like fuck you're taking it after your last attempt.' Coffee said as he tried to grab the ball out of Rossi's hands. This resulting in a mini scuffle between the two which only ended when a yellow card was brandished at both of them.

In between time. Jock Hunter had ran onto the pitch himself - taking a novel yellow card himself for his troubles - and given Terry the instructions that *none* of them would be taking the penalty since neither of them were in the frame of mind to go and win us the match.

'Just fucking melt it, Terry.' Jock shouted while he was being escorted back off the pitch. 'No fancy Dan stuff, mind.'

Melt it, he did. The speed and determination that he ran towards the ball seemed to completely psyche out their keeper who hadn't even bothered to move by the time the ball had hit the net.

The subs, traveling support, even Jock risking another yellow, were on the pitch celebrating in the corner along with the rest of us all on top of Terry. It was when we were all getting back off of him and regaining our composure - as well as getting a much needed breather - that I saw the boy from earlier who had been mouthing off at Coffee. On the pitch and right behind him with some kind of ninja samurai sword in his hand.

'COFFEE, RUN FOR FUCK'S SAKE'

The only thing that I could really do with such a short time space available to play with.

It didn't take his confused look to change to one of extreme panic when he looked behind him and saw the glint of the morning sun bouncing back off the sword.

'What do you say about my fucking pish now, eh?' He said. Walking with a swagger towards Coffee with a confident, yet manic, look in his eyes.

It was one of those scenarios where everyone *wants* to do something about what's going on but no cunt wants to be the one to tackle the person holding the sword that could, most likely, decapitate you.

Something about the way the guy spoke, the look in his eyes and the purpose filled way he held and swung the sword told me that he very much intended on using it. This was a man who had spunked fuck knows how many thousands of pounds worth on home improvement that wasn't quite what the brochure had promised and had been desperately searching for someone to take it out on and now had found them.

Coffee, to his credit, sensed this as well - and of course, would've known himself that he *had* seen this man before - and rather than try and talk his way out of things. Ran off the pitch with the guy chasing after him. Obviously, someone in a long Arsene Wenger style manager's coat, jeans and a pair of Caterpillar boots - holding and swinging a samurai sword - was never going to catch up to someone in fitba boots and kit.

A few of the boys from Muirhouse who had came over to watch us went off in chase after the boy with the sword, just to make sure that nothing happened to Coffee. It was hard to see as they were that far away but by the time the referee had got us all back in our own halves and blown for the restart. I could've sworn that I'd seen the figure of Coffee getting into a car by the main road and it pulling away with the others all still running in its direction.

Now that wee interruption in play might have been enough to affect lesser men but we took that as inspiration to - get a subbie on - see out the match and move through to the next round of the Kwik Save Challenge Trophy.

Takes more than some cunt with a samurai sword to put the Muirhouse boys off their game and if that Drylaw mob didn't know it before then they certainly knew it that morning.

Chapter 17

Jack

'Fuck fuck fucking fucking fucking FUCK. Like, fuuuuuuck. This is bad, Jackie, like *bad* bad.' Dynamo danced apprehensively around me as we walked in the direction of school. He was stating the very fucking obvious, though, and all of his hyperactivity was the main case of me not being able to think straight while I did my best to stop my whole world from spinning and me being sucked away like the flush of a toilet.

One of those times in life where all you really want to do is speak to a parent. You've always relied on an elder to make it all better for you. Only with *this?* Bring it to their attention and it's not going to make it better. Only worse.

He wouldn't stop talking, though. For even just one second. As if he'd thought that if he was to stop talking he was going to have the gift of speech removed from him so was now too scared to.

'We're fucking next, by the way. You know that, Jack, eh? Fucking obvious, that, like.'

I didn't need reminding of this from him, either. There was a lot of jumbled up scrambled thinking going on but *that much* was now pretty much spelled out.

Walking towards school, thinking of Scooter in hospital with a broken jaw, cheekbone caved in and most of his fingers snapped. Probably having his breakfast through a straw right now. It was clearly obvious that - by now - with two out of our group having been hospitalised within days of each other. Logic would dictate that there was definitely now a connection.

There was a *lot* of reasons for me to be frightened of - that morning - but it had been the *level* of brutality that had been dished out to both of my mates that scared me the most and that - unless Dynamo and me managed to figure things out - I was going to end up on the receiving end of the same form of punishment.

This wasn't like some differences with someone where you'd have whatever kind of a straightener with. Even if it was only a two minute scuffle with very little in the way of punches or kicks thrown. Generally no cunt ended up in hospital, though.

Things had been still shrouded in mystery when it came to Flav, even before Scooter had been given his face readjusted to him. All attempts to visit - or get in touch with - him were given the knock back by his parents. Both Scooter and myself tried to go to the Western General (and then his house when we'd heard that he'd got out) but were told that he wasn't up to visits.

Dynamo - knowing that all of our parents can't stand the cunt - didn't bother and, instead, relied on us for any update. Naturally we'd both asked them what had happened to Flav but - and maybe it was just me - they kind of like, clammed up at the mention of it and said that they'd have to go. Tried to call him and text - when he got back from the hospital - but hadn't been able to get an answer.

I'd kind of put it down to his mum and dad getting a bit of a shock over what had happened to their son so were putting a protective ring around him. Understandable, really.

While I'd been suspicious over what had happened to him. I knew that me and Flav were cool with each other. Had been pals from well before Dynamo came on the scene and started hanging around us and that he'd contact me when he wanted to, or could.

Finding out about what had happened to Scooter changed the whole thought process on things, though. Dynamo getting up extra early so he could be waiting at the bottom of my flats for me leaving in the morning to tell me, since I'd completely blanked any attempt that he'd made to get in touch with me the night before.

'Why the fuck did you not call me back last night?' His alternative version of a good morning he had to greet me with.

'Aye, sorry, D, was sitting playing GTA online and the battery ran out on my phone. Only saw your missed calls this morning when I'd got a wee bit charge in it.' I lied before - over the course of the walk from Martello Court to Craigroyston High School - he went on to tell me about how around ten o clock his big brother, Boney, was in The Golden Triangle waiting on his takeaway when Scooter stumbled into the place. Boney had thought, at first, that Scooter was hammered because of the fact he wasn't walking too steady and then when he tried to speak he didn't make any sense.

It was only then that Boney sussed out that it was *because* he'd had a doing. Jaw completely smashed in. Scooter attempting to hold it as if it's going to drop from his face if he didn't. Only with fingers on his hand going in different directions due to being broken.

'Ma brother would've taken him to the hospital himself but he'd had a few drinks in The Gunner, eh, but he grabbed one of the taxis from the rank and sorted the driver out with some cash for the fare. Told him to go via Scooter's house to pick up his mum and dad. Only way I know about it myself is because of Boney.'

'Who the fuck you think did it?' I asked. In terms of any remote kind of prime suspects, I had zero.

'Well, same cunt that put Flav in the hospital. Has to be.' Dynamo stated the obvious.

'Aye, which is?'

Dynamo, a boy with an opinion on everything and everyone - mostly the wrong one - was conspicuously silent.

'Well whoever the fuck it is we're either going to have to find out who they are or just let them come to us.' He said taking on a defiant tone, once he found his voice again.

I didn't particularly relish the prospect of either. Whoever it was that had been carrying out the attacks. They didn't really look like being a person who was the talking type. Definitely more an 'actions' person, by the looks. Why would you want to go *looking* for someone like that? Neither would you want to be just going about your business in the knowledge that a person - with pretty obvious violent tendencies - has you on some kind of a hit list and that - at some point - you're going to be getting a visit from them. Almost makes you want to go with the first option and get your hospital visit over and done with.

'You know it's because of that Silverknowes house, though?' I just came out with it. Something about the two broken arms for Flav had nagged away at me that it hadn't been an accident but I'd tried to tell myself that I was just being overly paranoid due to having broken into someone's home for the first time in my life. As soon as I heard what had happened to Scooter, though. What more evidence did I need to sooth my paranoid mind?

'Nah, can't be.' Dynamo shook his head as if it was completely out of the question.

'Police would've visited us by now if we were getting caught for that. We got away from that clean as a fucking whistle.' He said with such confidence that it almost tempted and pulled myself into thinking the same way.

'What about some of the stuff you took? Who exactly have you sold it to? Things like someone wearing a five thousand pound Rolex watch while having a pair of Air Max on their feet can stick out a bit.' I wasn't sure which way he was going to take that as it definitely came across like I was suggesting that only a complete moron would try to sell an expensive Rolex to someone in the street.

There had been a lot of things that had worried the fuck out of me with breaking into someone's house but - when I'd seen what kind of things Dynamo had stolen - where he would sell on his gear was one of the things that I worried would have got him - and by the most likely of extensions - and me caught.

'Nah, you're alright there. My brother is taking care of the gear. He knows a fence through in Glasgow but for now it's all still in my room. Better to sell it away from Edinburgh than in it, just in case, like. Small world, smaller city.' He said, to my relief.

Dynamo surprised me with such a sensible side. I'd already assumed that he'd have started selling it all the moment he got a chance and to *whoever* had money on them first. I thought it a guarantee that he was going to end up selling the Rolexes for the tiniest of fractions of their true worth. Not the case.

If he hadn't sold anything. It could only have been Scooter who had sold any of the stuff that had been taken. Flav and myself pocketing absolutely fuck all in the way of any of the swag. That didn't make sense though because why did Flav take the two broken arms first if that was the case?

Approaching the school gates and with Dynamo in the middle of talking through his strategy that he thought we should enforce - him and I practically being joined at the hip for as much of twenty four hours as we could so that when one of us was attacked the other would be there to assist. Joined at the hip with him, not a fucking option - when I spied Scooter's dad hanging around outside the front.

Before I could even cut Dynamo off to warn him. His dad appeared to clock us too and started walking, pacing actually, towards us. The look on his face not exactly one of warmth and friendship.

'I want a word with you two,' he said. Body language already spelling out that he wasn't in the best of moods.

'Alright, Mr Cox how's ...' Dynamo's attempt to speak was instantly ignored.

'What the fuck have you been getting my son into? Eh?' He said, more concentrating on Dynamo than he was on me. Well, Dynamo was the one getting the personal space invaded and the finger poked into his chest, anyway.

Mr Cox, Scooter's dad, looked like shit. Drained and with red eyes, obviously from crying and most likely up all night through everything.

'I, I, don't know what you're going on about,' Dynamo said, taking a step back to get Scooter's dads finger back out of his chest. Other pupils, on their way into school, all either stopping to watch or record on their phone.

'That son of mine has been lying in a hospital bed, unable to even speak, but you know what, though? He can still write.' He left this hanging for us to try and digest. Possibly to try and flush out anything from us that we might not have been so forthcoming about, beforehand.

I, and most likely Dynamo too, cringed at what Mr Cox was going to say next. What kind of a confession had Scooter written down for his dad? What did it say about who had taken him? Did it give any hints as to what was going to happen to us next? More than anything though I cringed - and prayed to god wouldn't be the case - that Scooter was going to have admitted to breaking into the house because once someone did. It was out there then and not ever going back in again.

'Aye, he can just about write. Looks like someone has been playing baseball with his head as the fucking ball, though. And you know what he wrote?' He said, like he was teasing us with the reveal. Like how the TV presenters tell you that you're going to have to wait until after the break before you get to see the *exact* thing that you're watching the show for.

'Nothing. Absolutely nothing and you know why? The boy is lying there petrified. Whoever done it to him have really done a number on him because, never mind the fucking police, he won't even tell his own dad who did it to him, or why. And *that's* why I'm here. Figured that if he won't tell me then you will.'

'Honestly, Mr Cox.' I attempted to try and say my own piece.

'Me and Dynamo have just spent the whole walk here to school trying to work out who would do that to him and that once we find out they're going to be sorry they even looked at Scooter.'

It made me feel well guilty. To stand there and put on such an act in front of a man who was stressed to the fucking max and was just looking for answers - as a father - over why someone would put his son in hospital in such a brutal way.

'Naw, naw, Jackie. That's not going to solve anything, that. I'm not wanting retaliation but I *do* want to know what the fuck has been going on here. I'm not a cunt so don't take me for one. First your pal with the broken arms and then days later my son is lying with a smashed in face and half his fingers broken. A broken jaw that the doctors reckon won't be able to set one hundred percent properly again and that Scott will speak a wee bit different to before. Doesn't take fucking Taggart, here, lads.'

You could tell which one was the adult out of the three of us. Whether he bought our lies or not. It still didn't stop him from completely controlling things. He wasn't *my* dad but it sure fucking felt like he was with the way I stood there and listened to him.

'The slightest mention to him over who did it to him or what the reason was near enough sends him into a panic so we've had to just stop mentioning it. He wouldn't tell the police that came and spoke to him at his bed. I'm not fucking letting it lie though. You better get me answers or it'll be *your* dads that I'm speaking to next, alright?'

Having said what he needed to say he stormed off in the same way that he'd came up to us. I could already hear the giggles and whispers around me from some who had watched it all take place. Shit, though. There was a *lot* more to be worried about than being the subject of school gossip.

Scooter and his dad were tight. Like going fishing at the weekends and building Airfix models when he was younger, tight. While you would never have expected Scooter to be shouting any names or descriptions of who had done him in to the police. You'd have *automatically* expected him to have shared any intel with his dad. Scooter's dad being someone who - around Muirhouse - it was said that he'd served with the S.A.S although he never admitted that he had, just that he served in the army, was definitely a handy reinforcement to be able to call on when you're a kid getting into scrapes, like Scooter did.

That he hadn't told his dad what had happened. And that he was too *scared* to do so. It only helped to add to all of the stress and worry that I'd found myself taking in at a crazy rate since I'd stepped out onto the street from Martello Court that morning.

What a way to start your school day, though. Walking through the gates with your head, complete mince. Whatever classes I had ahead of me were going to be a complete waste of time. All I had to think about was that - for someone out there - it was a case of two down and two to go.

And I was one of the 'ones to go.'

'We need to come up with a plan, you and me.' Dynamo said, clearly shaken by the surprise ambush from Mr Cox, in amongst the obvious.

'Up the woods, after tea time, six o clock, at the spot, alright?' He said before starting to drift right, in the direction of the PE hall.

'Aye, see you up there.' I replied, less than thrilled at the prospect of a full day at school - where I would be left with my thoughts and fears while wondering what it would take for me to get back out of this shite I was in - and then, after all of that. Having to share what I had of my free time with Dynamo in the middle of the woods. Given the circumstances, though. Back of beyond and the middle of the woods was far preferable to hanging around Muirhouse shops in plain sight with him.

Not when - by then - I was starting to feel like there was some kind of a target on my back.

Chapter 18

McKenna

Fucking liberty taking BASTARDS.

I knew something was up when I heard Marge's screams from the house when I was bringing the suitcases and my golf clubs in from the Range Rover.

'OH, DAVEY, COME QUICK.'

In all the years we'd been with each other I'd never heard that tone of voice from her. That level of hysterics. Size of our house? I shouldn't have been able to *hear* her as loud as that from the drive outside. I dropped my Mizunos straight away and quickly followed her into the house.

Bloody carnage, so it was. Inside waiting on me. I could see why the wife was so upset. I was upset too. For a while. Then angry. Angry, though, was probably a word that didn't even come close to *how* I was left feeling.

The place had been bloody ransacked. Some filthy rat bastard had broken in - when we were sunning it up in at our villa in Costa Adeje - and wrecked the place.

The liberty that some cunt takes by deciding to break into your house? Well that speaks for itself. What they had *done* to the house though? Pure vindictiveness from one very sick fucking mind. It clearly hadn't been a professional as most of the rooms looked like they'd been turned over, just for the sake of it.

Valuables? Aye, all gone. Well, the ones that the cunt had been able to find, that was. Was there any fucking need though to rip up some of Marge's clothes, break ornaments, add stupid fucking faces with marker pen to the paintings on our walls and rip up priceless family photos. That alone - what they did with the pictures of my mum and dad and gran and grandad, all four no longer with us - showed the level of lowlife who had dared to cross my threshold uninvited.

And when I say 'dared' it had already been assumed that 'whoever' it had been. They hadn't actually *known* whose house it was they had broken into. Had they known they'd never have even dreamed about it. Still, what's done is done, though. Whether they did or they didn't know. All academic now, I thought to myself. As I consoled the wife, who was in complete pieces at the sight of the photo of her along with her mum and dad on their golden wedding anniversary. Her dad, Harold, passing away three days after it.

'Why would someone do such a thing, Davey? Why? I don't understand it.' She asked, as I stood there rubbing her back while she tried to figure out how another human being could be so capable of such twisted behaviour. I - on the other hand - had *plenty* of understanding on such matters.

It was only then, amongst the mess that was strewn across the floor and everything that had been competing for your attention wherever you looked, that I spied my sash. Lying there on the floor with - what looked like - a piece of shite sitting on top of it. Leaving Marjory alone for a second, I walked across the room to have a closer inspection.

It *was* a piece of shite sitting - strategically placed - on top of my lodge sash.

'THE FUCKING DIRTY LITTLE BASTARD SHAT ON MY SASH. SOME CUNT IS GOING TO FUCKING **DIE**.'

It's fair to say that I didn't take it well and - looking back at things - it probably wasn't too good a look that I'd been more upset over my accessory for the Masonic Lodge than I'd been about anything else but hey, we all react in our own personal and individual ways in these testing times.

Fucking last thing you need after flying back from holiday is to walk into *that*, either. All you want is a cup of tea and put your feet up. Instead you walk into an immediate clean up job that looks like would take a good twelve hours for a team of workers.

'Fuck this, Marge. We'll tackle it tomorrow. It's too late to do anything about it now. Given the fact that our bedroom, right now, looks like the fucking council tip. I'm booking us into The Scotsman for the night and we'll sort things out tomorrow, ok? Grab some stuff while I go make a couple of calls.'

The Marge that I knew and had been married to for thirty years would've wanted to have just dropped things and got to work cleaning the house up. Working all through the night if she'd had to. I wasn't going to let her, though.

'Wha, what about the police? Shouldn't we call them, Davey?' She asked hesitantly, and naively. Hesitantly because she probably knew what the answer to that was going to be but this was no regular situation, either. Who was daft enough ever to have broken into *our* house? Straight away I thought of the glazing company that had replaced our window but that would've been a little *too* obvious. A company, trusted with the security details to our home and then it gets turned over? They, themselves, would've known how obvious that would've looked, and besides. Me and Gus Campbell - the owner of Pilton Panes - went back a good while so it's not like him or his employees didn't know 'whose' house they were working on.

I made a quick call to The Scotsman - where I'd usually check into if staying overnight in the city centre for any reason - to make sure that they had a spare room. Me putting in a call personally generally *always* meaning that there's a spare room. After that, I put a quick call into Budsy - one of my security team - to explain the situation and to instruct him to get over to mines and to go over the security tapes from the week that we'd been out of the country.

'I FUCKING WANT YOU TO FIND ME THE BASTARD THAT DID THIS AND BRING THEIR HEAD TO ME ON A PLATE. YOU CLEAR, BUDSY?'

It probably wasn't the return to the country that my security team had anticipated but, then again. If they're going to be on my team then they *should* be prepared for just about anything. That's what I pay the cunts for.

'I'll get right on it, boss.' Budsy, said.

Fucking right you will, I thought to myself.

'The place is like a fucking bomb has gone off it in but don't be worrying about that. You know where the tapes and the monitor is so get cracking. Stupid cunts obviously didn't find the monitor or see the hidden cameras otherwise they'd have been half inched along with whatever else has been taken. Schoolboy error, that, and one they're going to regret.'

I knew that the level of home security that we had at the house. If whatever dense cunt had decided to rob the home of Davey McKenna, and had chosen not to wear a mask when doing so. Then the bastard was about to be made famous. I didn't pay all those thousands online to that tech company in California for that FBI endorsed pinhole night vision camera technology for the sake of it.

I'd only had a quick glimpse over where the watches and jewellry had been kept and they were all gone. Not the end of the world. They were insured for even more on the house policy so would all be replaced in any case. The robbing bastard - in the scheme of things - was going to make me richer, ironically.

It would've only been fair to pay it forward so to speak and give them their own wee personal 'reward,' wouldn't it?

I suppose all of that was all besides the point. I'd only be able to claim on the insurance *if* I was to file a police report and well, you see? Me and the police? Not exactly the best of pals, us. Those cunts wouldn't be getting a call. Couldn't catch a cold anyway, them, and would hardly be the most motivated once they knew *whose* house it was that had been tanned.

The intention, however, was to *very much* still issue that 'reward,' though.

By the next day - and us checking out of the hotel - we'd arranged for a cleaning firm to come around to the house and help restore the house back to something semi resembling what it had been like before we'd left for Tenerife. Marge - understandably - had wanted to be there for during the clean up operation due to it involving our personal belongings in addition to her wanting to see the extent of what had been done.

We'd both popped back from the city centre in advance of the cleaners coming round to make sure that anything that was considered more on the personal or - more importantly - incriminating side of things could be shored away in advance of them arriving.

Once I was comfortable that there was nothing lying around that I didn't want to be found. I headed off to the scrapyard and left Marge to it. Reminding her that all of the stuff that had been broken could be replaced. Her dresses that had been ripped apart could be replaced. Fuck, she could have a new wardrobe to herself if she wanted.

Even on the short drive to the scrapyard I'd had to take and make enough phone calls to see me from the front of our drive all the way up to the entrance of my porto-cabin. It was enough to remind a man that he was no longer on holiday. That, would be to suggest that I had disappeared to the Canary Islands and had switched my phone off from the world. Any-fucking-thing but. There's no such thing as a day off in my world but Costa Adeje had been as good as.

It was like the switch had been flicked back on though, that morning.

One person saying they had money for me. Another saying that they needed a couple of extra days. Someone else telling me that they were on their way to collect some from another who had it ready. A contact asking if I was still ready for the drop that, we'd agreed on prior to Tenerife, in a few days time. And the last call that came through, just as I was approaching my yard, from Piotr, one of my other security boys.

Piotr, one of the main reasons that a man like myself can sleep soundly at night. The type of person that would haunt your dreams. I know a lot of Scots moaned their faces off when Poland became part of the European Union and loads of the Poles moved here. Typical cunts that sit there and moan about a foreigner coming and 'taking their jobs' when the reality is that they'd never do that fucking job in the first place. I on the other hand was more than happy to welcome the ex Polish special forces straight out of the GROM division in Warsaw, Piotr into the fold.

'Boss, your house. Budsy and I. We have the people who did it.'

Fucking hell, I thought to myself, that was quick. Generally these things tended to take - at least - a couple of days before tracking down whoever it is that you're looking for. Sterling work from my guys. I smiled, impressed.

'Nice work, indeed, Piotr. Well now that you have them, and anyway? Them? How many was there? I'd like you to bring them down to the scrapyard where we are all going to put them, one by one, into the car compactor.'

I said it as if I was simply asking him to pop by Baynes and bring me a sausage roll and cup of tea down to the scrapyard for me but - at that point and the way the whole thing had left me feeling - I would've *easily* followed up on those words.

What, whoever it was, had chosen to do. Fuck me, it was a line and a half for someone to cross. You'd be pissed off and seeking revenge if it happened to your house. Anyone would. Me on the other hand? I did too, with a passion. It wasn't just that though. I had to be *seen* to be doing something about it. The optics of Davey McKenna's house getting broken into and the culprits getting away with it would send out a very dangerous signal and as far as precedents go, no telling what something like *that* would set.

'No, boss. We don't *have* them.' He replied back in his limited version of English.

'Wait a fucking minute, did you not just call me a second ago. As in, *you* called *me* and your reason was to say that you and Budsy had the people responsible for breaking into the house?'

'Yes.' He replied.

'Aye, but then the next thing you said was that you *didn't* have them. Can you see why I might be a little confused here, Piotr, and WHY I'M NOT IN THE FUCKING MOOD FOR ANY INCOMPETENCE OR FUCKING ABOUT FROM ANYONE TODAY' My patience - after all I'd had to put up with since flying back - had now reached an end.

'No, we have them on video, boss. I show you. You won't be pleased when you see some things.' He replied. Finally coming through with something that was now making a bit more sense.

'Well I'm not exactly on top of the fucking world as things stand right now so we may as well keep the streak going for the morning, eh? Right get the tape down here to the office and we'll watch it down here, bring Budsy.' I hung up without letting him answer.

The heating had barely been given a chance to dent the cold air of the unused (in a week) and unopened porto-cabin before Budsy and Piotr pulled up outside in Piotr's black BMW and the both of them charging in.

'Little. Fucking. Bastards.' Budsy said, throwing the tape down onto my desk. 'I've left it at just before they come in the house. It was a few days after you and Marge left for Tenerife.'

I took the tape out of its sleeve and slotted it into my office security tape player.

I'd been talking about which bastard had done it but within a few minutes of watching, I could see that it was a case of plural. Very much bastards with a fucking 's.' Four of the filthy cunts, in total.

I'd never needed a reason to actually ever properly look through the security cameras but, fuck me, it was some quality technology, mind. You could - unfortunately for them - see their faces up clear due to the night vision cameras. Only time you couldn't see anything was when they shone their torches at the camera but even then that was an unconscious thing of their doing more than anything else.

For the best part of an hour, the three of us sat in silence while I diverted my eyes across the multi room set up that was on screen. It was made easier by the fact that two out of the four mainly stayed downstairs but - compared to the two upstairs - weren't going through the stuff on their level of the house.

What was going on *up* the stairs, though? I sat there, silent but with that trademark rage of mines slowly catching fire inside of me like a piece of kindling. The more I watched, the more the flames started to grow.

One of them, in particular, the biggest one out of them, had been the particular focal point of my rage. This little cunt in a crewcut, prancing around in one of Marge's dress while ripping out drawers and throwing them all over the place. I wanted to throw the monitor across the room at the part where he ripped the dress from him and threw it away like a filthy rag rather than it - a dress whose worth would've fed him and his scummy fucking family for a year - being what it was.

By the time I saw the same one wearing my sash and then taking a shite on it just before they all left, I was Mount fucking Vesuvius.

'THAT CUNT FUCKING DIES, THEY ALL FUCKING DIE BUT THAT CUNT, THAT SHITEING CUNT, ESPECIALLY. I WANT HIM FUCKING KILLED, BURIED, THEN DUG UP AND FUCKING KILLED AGAIN. REPEAT TO FUCKING FADE.'

I pointed at the screen for the benefit of Budsy and Piotr.

'THAT CUNT, THERE. Fucking FIND HIM'

I'd paused the video right at the moment where he was crouching over my sash. Big stupid smile on his face and one that I was already looking forward to wiping from him.

'You get screenshots printed off for them all and hit the streets. Some cunt is going to know one of them and then after that we'll get them all. I'm going to stick in a couple of calls to see if I can get ahead of things in the meantime.' I said as I rewound the tape back to where there was opportunities to get some clear close ups of them to print out.

The very first thing I did while I left Budsy to try and work out how to print the pictures off was to call one of my contacts at the lodge who was high up with Lothians and Borders Police.

Knowing that we had security cameras dotted around Silverknowes. I'd figured that four kids - and having now seen the video, that's all that they were - walking around the area would've been something that the cameras would've picked up.

Putting in a wee discreet call to him and letting him know the night of the week and rough time to check over. He asked me to leave it with him while he contacted the correct department. As is always the case with my fellow brothers. He was back within the hour to tell me that there were four boys seen getting off a bus coming from the Muirhouse direction before the time of the break in and the same four getting on a bus *after* the time of the crime.

Didn't mean that they were *from* Muirhouse, obviously, but at least it was a start. If you don't have a lead you don't get taken anywhere. As any dug will tell you.

Thanking him, while assuring my brother that I would not forget the favour and saying I'd see him at the next lodge meeting. I put the phone down and told Budsy and Piotr that they were off up to the Naughty North.

Despite being the capital city. Edinburgh really isn't that big at all and if I wanted to find you. I would. It would really all be a matter of 'when.'

Still, you get what you pay for and with a security team like mines it is not exactly considered over ambitious to expect near to instant results. Information is not hard to extract from people.You've just got to know *how* to get it out of a certain person. Pablo Escobar - one of my own personal heroes - called it 'plata o plomo' as in do you want the silver option or do you want the lead option? Not like things had ever gotten so binary in Edinburgh but those same values held true in our capital city.

You didn't need much in the way of silver, in Muirhouse. Like anywhere else in Edinburgh, all you needed to do was go find some junkies waving a tenner bag of smack around above you and you'll have them singing like canaries.

My boys, actually, managed to find and grab one of the fab fucking four by the end of the next day day. Once I'd had a chance to calm down after having watched the video and the violation that these little pricks had done to what was mines and my wife's property. I'd given Piotr and Budsy strict instructions that the two who had been downstairs most of the time were to be given a lesson and reminded of 'who' it was that they had robbed but the two of them who had been *up* the stairs. I wanted something a bit more extreme but that - explicitly - I wanted to deal with the taller one with the crewcut - and who had ripped Marge's dress apart - directly myself.

After they'd dealt with the first of the four. That was where - as I'd imagined - the information then started to flow. The kid had told them that he was fourteen. Imagine a fourteen year old kid being taken to a scrapyard and having both his arms laid out and broken and *then* being made to watch a demonstration of the capabilities of the car compactor while being reminded that he's going in there next if he doesn't tell Piotr and Budsy the names of the other three who were there with him in the house.

A scenario where you categorically KNOW that whatever they tell you it's the truth, the whole truth and absolutely fuck all but the truth.

Before being dropped off back in Muirhouse he'd been issued with the warning that if he went telling anyone *who* had broken his arms *or* that he'd been to the scrapyard. *Or* warn off any of his other three mates. We'd grab him as easily as we had the first time around. Only, the next time he really *would* be going into the compactor.

Sensibly he had heeded the advice as there had been no visits from the police in connection of any claims from a kid that they had been brought to the yard by two of my men. This confirmed by how easy the *second* out of them had been found and grabbed. Hanging around Muirhouse shops as if he hadn't a care in the world. Which I guess he maybe didn't. Until it had been brought to their attention 'whose' house it had been that they'd broken into. And by then, of course, it was too late for them.

It had been one of the two who had been up the stairs going through our stuff but not *the* one. The one who had - through his own actions - made himself very much a person of interest to me and who I wanted a 'personal meeting' with. The boys were as kind as to carry out my instructions to the letter of the law. I'd suggested something related with their hands to show them that they shouldn't steal from people. Piotr deciding to randomly break half of his fingers, an act that would definitely be preventing the young man from stealing anything for a long while. A deterrent that stopped just short of the Middle Eastern tactic of the removing of a hand to scare people off robbing again. A move that earned Piotr a gold star on his report card when I was filled in on things afterwards.

Two out of the four taken care of within a matter of days. It had been, by no means, a magic wand waved that erased all of the shit that had been caused but to know that a couple of them were now lying in hospital having belated second thoughts about what they'd done *was* a small crumb of comfort to me.

I wasn't going to be happy though until I'd got a full card. Calling out fucking bingo on the bastards. Especially the one that - through my boy's enquiries - was called Dynamo. Some wee Muirhouse rat. His big brother had a bit of a rep but if you want to play the reputation game with any cunt from Edinburgh then, come ahead. While - through our investigations - I'd found out about his big brother his big brother would've *already* known about me. It was only going to be a matter of time now before we picked him up. Even taking into account the possibility that the wee bastard would go to ground, having seen two of his pals hospitalised in quick succession. If he had a fucking brain cell to call upon - and that was very much in doubt - then that's *exactly* what he should've been doing.

As it was to turn out. The boys rounded him up soon after the second one.

'Got him, gaffer.' Budsy said. The way he said it, I didn't feel that I needed to ask 'who' it was that he had.

'Good work.' I replied.

'Wanting us to bring him down to Leith to the scrapyard?' Budsy - not without foundation - asked.

'No, keep him in Muirhouse. I'll come to you. Take the wee prick up to the top of Martello Court. I'll see the three of you up there.'

I was out of my seat before the call ended and sticking my shoes back on. Telling Marge that I needed to go out on business but would be back soon. She knew better than to ask why a 'scrapyard owner' would need to go out on business at nine o clock at night so didn't bother doing so.

When I joined them at the top of Martello. Professional - as has always been of my demands, as an employer - they had a thick black tammy pulled down over his head and his hands duct taped behind him.

'YOU'VE GOT THE WRONG FUCKING PERSON. I HAVEN'T DONE FUCK ALL. YOU'VE GOT IT WRONG.' His voice was hoarse from - no doubt - having repeated something to that effect from the point Piotr and Budsy had snatched him as he was walking down the street towards his house.

I hadn't spoken yet but motioned for them to march the kid closer towards the edge of the tower block, looking out over the city, *my* city.

'Oh but you fucking well *did* do something. You did *lots* of things. Didn't you, Dynamo fucking Kiev?'

I broke my silence and made for Piotr to lift the tammy from off his head. The noise that he made upon seeing 'where' he was and how high up was unlike something I'd ever heard a human being make in my life. Fear, surprise and a sudden realisation that he really *was* in a lot of trouble. When you find yourself snatched by a couple of men twice your size and, more or less, kidnapped. You should already be feeling that you are in a bit of a sticky situation. To then move that on a little and find yourself with these same mystery men who are standing holding you while you teeter over the edge of Edinburgh's tallest residential building. Aye, *that's* when you know, categorically, that your day has taken a most unfortunate turn for the worse.

'IT, IT, IT WISNAE ME. IT WAS SC SC SCCOOOOTER, AND FLAV. JACKIE CARSON ANAW. I WAS JUST THERE WITH THEM, LIKE, BUT AH NEVER STOLE ANYTHING. I SWEAR. DID THEY BASTARDS GRASS ME UP TO YOU BECAUSE I SWEAR I DIDN'T DO FUCK ALL. THEY'RE FUCKING LYING TO YOU.'

I hadn't even mentioned the break in and he had folded like a fucking deck chair. Then again, though. If you threaten to throw someone from a building as tall as Martello Court they'd probably admit to both being Bible John *and* stealing Shergar if they thought it would avoid them being thrown off the edge.

'Take that lying little bastard another step further. Actually, Dynamo, you're still a kid, what are you? sixteen, seventeen? You'll like games, won't you. You like the Playstation, aye? Well this game isn't as good as any of those video games but it should hold your interest, regardless. Everytime you tell me something that's not true. You know? A lie. My men are going to take you another step towards the edge of the top of here. Obviously, we're not exactly five hundred miles from the edge, as things stand. If a Proclaimer was to start any of his pish up here it wouldn't be long before he would be a man that had walked a hundred yards to fall down flights before being scraped from the pavement, or what would be left of him.'

So, we're clear and to test this theory to see how much you were paying attention because, I can see that the whole of Edinburgh that's in front of you is kind of distracting you. Trust me, my friend. This is not a time for distraction.'

He was shaking, physically shaking, uncontrollably. Like he was cold. This wasn't through anything in relation to the temperature up there.

We were at the top of a tall building. It was cold, anyway. He was shaking through something else, though. Fear in its extremities.

'So, lets start, shall we? Who took all of the jewellry and watches from up the stairs in the bedroom?' I asked. They say that if the FBI ask you a question they already know the answer to it. It would've served this kid correct to have known, *what* I'd known.

'We all took it between us when we were going through the house. I took a wee bit but so did everyone else.'

'WRONG!' I said, like a game show host to a contestant.

'Boys' I nodded to Budsy and Piotr to take yet another step closer.

'NO NO NO NO, PLEASE. OK, OK.' He pleaded, shouting out.

'And.' I prompted him, impatiently. It *was* cold and the less I needed to be standing up there in that wind, the better.

'OK, IT *WAS* ME THAT GOT ALL OF THAT STUFF. SCOOTER AS FAR AS I SAW JUST THE MONEY THAT YOU HAD IN THE BEDSIDE DRAWER AND THE CAIRDS THAT WERE LYING. I DON'T KNOW ABOUT THEM TWO DOWNSTAIRS. AH NEVER SEEN THEM.'

'CORRECT!

I kept the game show theme going. So much so I amended the game to include the three of them taking a step *back* to reward a correct answer.'

The young man, seeming to take a sigh of relief at this. Very much mistakenly taking this as a sign that things were looking up for him. In reality. From the moment my security got their hands on him things were *never* going to be looking up for him. There's not really much to see, regardless, when you look up from the top of Martello Court.

'So, lets discuss the fact that you and your friends didn't just steal from me. You went out your way to destroy everything and anything you came across. Wife's dresses. Family photos. Why the fuck would you want to do something like that? Is there something fucking wrong with you? Anyway, those photos were priceless. Hardly like we can dig up the family members now so that we can all recreate the pictures again. And you lot ripped them up the point that they're beyond repair. Fucking thought I'd come back to the aftermath of the Argentina Seventy Eight final in my living room with all the bits of ripped up photos. I want to know who fucking did it. What sick bastard would do such a thing?'

'WELL, IT WISNAE ME. IT WAS THE OTHERS, IT WAS JACKIE CARSON. HE LIVES IN THESE SAME FLATS. GO DOWN AND GET HIM AND ASK HIM.

He screamed. Now at the point where he was willing to lie and attempt to pass the blame for his despicable - and soon to be punished over - actions even though knowing what that would've led to, had we believed him.

It hadn't been the first time that the name 'Jack Carson' had come up during these little interrogations so - by now - it had appeared that he was the remaining one out of the four. We'd matched the first two to their pictures. I'd already had Dynamo's face embedded into my brain from the moment that I'd witnessed him taking a shite over my sash so it was obvious that the final one from the video was - who they had said was Jack, or Jackie, Carson.

I'd also recognised the name, though. Carson. Especially from Muirhouse. *That* would be looked into in due course. Once fool number three had been dealt with.

Following his latest reply, and it being yet another lie. I issued another nod for Piotr and Budsy to take one step forward again.

'NO NO, NO, OK. IT WAS ME. I DID IT TO THE PHOTOS.' He finally copped.

I told them to turn him around so that he was facing me. His heels now slightly hanging over the edge of the roof. Not exactly advisable for such a moment with his legs not looking too strong and steady.

'Now why would you want to go and do a thing like that? The pictures of me when I was a boy with my mum and dad. The ones of me and *my* kids when they were younger. The vintage black and white ones that one look at would've told you how precious they would've been. What kind of a sick small minded fucked in the head prick would do something like that? Why would they even *want* to?'

'Ma, ma, ma dad reckons that it's something like ADD or ADHD or something with some letters in it.' He stammered.

It wasn't really a time for laughing but I had the briefest of thoughts of what it must've been like to *be* someone like 'that's' dad and the grief that it must've brought, daily. Of course, though. At that point of proceedings. I hadn't been made aware of the young man's own dad's loose lips and that - as a result - *he* was going to be receiving a visit of his own.

'Aye, he's maybe got a point.' I chuckled. 'You definitely look like you need a check up.'

I was the only one stood up there who was chill enough to muster a laugh. The kid - quite naturally - was completely shitting himself and not in the mood for much smiles. Piotr and Budsy standing either side of him - close to the edge of a tall building like Martello - were looking towards me for any kind of a hint in terms of next moves.

'So then, Dynamo. You've done well. You made it to the final round and through to the bonus game which is titled *"Thrown off a tall building or torn from limb to limb."* YOU READY?' I didn't mean my continued impersonation of a game show host, when discussing such grave matters, to come across as sociopathic as it did but, anyway. In scenarios like this. The more sociopathic you come across. The *more* it tends to help smooth things along.

That was the moment though when he realised that whatever happened now. He wasn't being let off with all of what he'd done.

'Ok, contestant. To find out if you get thrown from the top of here tonight before the end of the show OR my two men dish out some - by comparison - more agreeable recompense of punishment. Did you or did you not take a Masonic Lodge orange coloured sash and defecate onto it?'

I could see that he'd been left in a conflicting position. Every time he'd lied he'd been taken further to the edge of the building. He'd ran out of space now, though. Any further step would be to take one right off the edge BUT this was his issue. I had never said which answer from him would result in which action would follow from me. But was this a truth that he actually *wanted* to own up to in such a precarious position.

Piotr and Budsy both looked at me. Just waiting on the nod or the word and they were going to let him go. They were prepared. They would've been prepared for where we now were from the moment that I had told them to go to the top of Martello.

He took a second to decide on an answer that would *then* decide his fate.

'Aye, aye I did. Look, don't ask me why I did it. Same as the pictures. Just a case of doing radge stuff for a laugh.' He said. Now crying, beginning to fear the worst.

'A FUCKING LAUGH? LAUGH? YOU SEE ME, DAVEY FUCKING MCKENNA, LAUGHING HERE YA WEE FUCKING SLIMY CUNT' I let rip at him. Resisting the urge to just lunge forward and push him over the edge myself. 'IT MIGHT SOUND LIKE A FUCKING CLICHE BUT THAT WAS THE SASH THAT MY FATHER WORE, AND HIS FATHER BEFORE ... AND YOU GO AND TAKE A SHITE ON IT?'

I let things fall silent for a moment while I stared at him. I'd seen a lot in my time while building the empire but I doubt I'd seen such fear in a person's eyes like there was in the teenager.

'PLEASE DON'T THROW ME OFF MR MCKENNA. I'M BEGGING YOU.' He pleaded. Tears in his eyes, snot running from his nose and spit flying out along with his frantic screams.

I stayed silent. The longer I did the more crazy it drove him.

'BUT CONGRATULATIONS, YOUNG MAN, YOU MADE IT THROUGH TONIGHT'S BONUS GAME AND HAVE WON THE MOST BRUTAL OF BEATINGS TO WITHIN AN INCH OF YOUR LIFE.'

I said, changing tone dramatically and back to that sociopathic side.

'No, please, Mr McKenna, I didn't know it was your ...' He said, trembling.

'You want to go with the other option instead, aye?' I cut him off, tired with him. There was absolutely *nothing* that he was going to be able to say or do that was going to get him off the hook.

I hadn't exactly shouted it from the rooftops that my house had been tanned. It was just common sense. Keeping something like that under wraps because, on the face of it. *No cunt* should be attempting to break into the house of Davey McKenna. You know how things get out, eventually? With three out of the four now taken care of, so far. If word was to slip out about the break in it would go hand in hand with the additional information over what happened to *those* that were stupid enough to do it.

'Right, I want a proper job done on him. The deluxe package, mind.'

I said to my the boys while I puled the collar up on my coat around me as the wind kicked up around us.

'And it goes without saying, young man. You'll be returning *all* of the watches, jewellery and everything else that you took from me. Don't panic, though. I'm not going anywhere so don't rush to get them to me. I'm not sure you're going to be that mobile in around ten minutes time. I'll let you sort out the details with my two boys, here. And, obviously, it goes without saying. If you don't get my Rolexes and the wife's diamonds back. We'll be back up here again for your first - and last - flying lesson.

'Ah promise I'll give you it all back.' He whimpered and sniffed while not really telling me anything that I didn't already know. None of the stuff had been fenced in Edinburgh, anyway, otherwise I'd have known about it so in that respect. I was sure that he still had all of our stuff and if any of it had been sold it wouldn't have taken much to retrieve it.

'What about this Carson boy, the other one? He said that he stays underneath here? Want to take care of that while we're here?' Budsy, ever the eager and enterprising one out of the two of my security, suggested.

'Nah, we'll leave that until tomorrow. It's fucking baltic up here and I've got the next episode of The Sopranos to watch. Season four on the box set, likes. You've put in a good enough shift tonight and you've still got a wee bit left yet so I'll let you get on with things and you can call it a night after that. Come by the yard tomorrow morning and see me.'

'Will do boss. Good job.' Piotr replied as I made my way towards the service door at the top of the flats leading to the stairs.

'Aye, mind now. Platinum service carried out on the boy. No expense spared. He took a shite on my sash, need I remind any cunt?' I replied continuing on with my back to them. I was already hearing him scream out in pain by the time I had made my way through the service door at the top of the tower block to make my way down the stairs.

Chapter 19

Jack

It was around midnight when the loud knocking on the front door woke us all up. Can't even describe the scare I got when I heard my dad shouting from bed, down to mum, asking who was at the door 'at this time of night' and her shouting back up to him that it was the police. This piece of information enough for dad to have him getting out of bed to go down and speak to them. I lay in bed like a statue, hoping that no one had noticed me stirring in my room over the noise at the door.

While I heard the squeak from mum and dad's bed - as he got himself out of it - and then the footsteps going downstairs to join mum I felt that, unless I had the situation forced on me, I would just keep upstairs and hope that I would be able to pick up what they were all talking about.

From the sounds of things, the police hadn't actually come into the house because nobody's voices were getting any louder. Was maybe only a total of two or three minutes before I heard the door closing and mum and dad's voices getting more louder as they walked upstairs to go back to bed.

I timed this with a 'coincidental' bump into them outside the bathroom.

'Who was that at the door, mum?' I asked her as she got to the top of the stairs.

'None of your business, get your arse back to sleep. You've got school in the morning, Mister fucking twenty four hour party people, there.' Dad butted in.

'Hey, I was happily sleeping away until the door went.' I replied back and - in doing so - completely setting dad up for his standard reply.

'Hay is for horses, now get to your fucking bed!' He said with a lot more finality to it this time.

Grumbling under my breath I did as told but - considering I'd been spending almost every waking hour shitting it that the police were going to come knocking on our door, and now they *had* - couldn't resist asking one more time. Knowing that it was probably going to keep me awake all night thinking about it. The only encouraging signs were - that with the police gone - there were no further questions being asked in my direction from mum and dad.

'Who was at the door though, mum?' I knew to ask dad would've been a case of sailing too close to the wind but that mum would tell me. Even if it was just so that I would go back to bed.

'Don't worry about it, Jack. It was just a routine chap at the door. They're going to everyone's. There's been an assault here in the flats and they're looking to see if any of us has seen or heard anything suspicious. Nothing for you to worry about, son. Mon, lets all get ourselves back to sleep.' She motioned for me to get into my room.

Fucking phew, she was right. It *wasn't* anything for me to be worried about. It didn't involve the pigs asking my whereabouts on such and such a night so *that's* all that mattered. The fact that there had been an assault in Muirhouse was hardly going to be headline news across the area. Any day that ends in a 'Y.' I think it was possibly the relief from having the police at the door only to find it all a false alarm but I got myself back to sleep quite soon after getting back into bed.

Police and an ambulance unit were called to Martello Court in the Muirhouse area of the city late last night where a violent assault had taken place. One man is believed to have been found badly beaten towards half past ten. Police made door to door enquiries in the block of flats and are continuing with their enquiries but are said to be treating it as attempted murder.

Today, Nicolas Sarkozy, the French president, will visit Holyrood to meet with ...

Dad turned the radio down.

'Sounds like someone took a bad one last night'

I was in the middle of trying to shove a bit breakfast inside me, trying to make sure - and with the greatest of respect to whoever had taken a doing the night before - that I wasn't going to be late for school. We all have our own problems, eh?

'Well, I thought it *was* a murder, Joe. They don't normally go knocking on doors at that time of night unless there's something serious been going on.' Mum said, taking her polo shirt for work up off the radiator where it had been drying overnight.

'No smoke without fire, no doubt there'll be a story behind it and whoever it was got what was coming to them. Apologies if I don't spend the rest of the day moping around the house in sympathy.'

It really was that easy for my dad. If someone has been battered then - through his own basic reasoning - they'd have deserved it.

'I'll see if I can find out anything today on my shift.' My mum said, looking actually excited at the prospect of getting to work and potentially finding out what gossip there was about what had happened because there's one thing you'd guarantee. If Radio Forth were talking about it 'their' intel was going to be at a much lower level clearance to your average Muirhouse nosey bastard.

When I left the house there was no sign of Dynamo but that was always a hit and miss in the morning anyway. If I seen him on the way then I did but if I never I wouldn't exactly go looking for him, either. Some mornings, though. You'd see the full four of us walking to school, all meeting up on various parts of the journey. Now? With two of us either in hospital or having just been released - and both dropping from the face of the earth, apparently - and Dynamo nowhere to be seen. It was a case of walking there to school alone with the thoughts that I'd rather not have had to entertain. At least when you're talking to someone it helps you blank out all of the bad stuff that you don't want to be thinking about. Any distraction, you'll take. When you're stuck with yourself, though. It's not that easy to distract yourself.

When it came to dinner time. Dynamo wasn't to be seen around our usual area of the school that we'd hang around, behind the science lab. I wasn't even really sure why I *went* there after I'd eaten my dinner in the hall. Went there more out of routine than anything else. Knew I wasn't going to find the other three standing joking around and taking the piss out of each other. I don't think I knew where *else* to go and spend what was left of my free time of the break before going back in for my period of geography.

With no Dynamo to stand and talk to. I ended up just sitting down on the grass and watching some boys from the year below who were playing a quick dinner time game. I reckoned that there must've been some shady goings on when it came to which players had gone on each side because it was all one way traffic. Every time one side would score a goal it was just a matter of time before the other team took centre, gave the ball away again and then conceded *another* goal. Didn't look like there had been a fair pick going on when the teams were being sorted out, anyway.

I'd seen Dynamo the night before when the pair of us had went up the woods. The two of us being a wee bit on the paranoid side to be hanging around Muirhouse, after what had happened to Flav and Scooter.

We had a nice wee secluded spot that the four of us would go up to that we knew we wouldn't be bothered by anyone. Go up there and smoke a joint or swig a bottle of Buckie or Thunderbird between us.

'Fucking heavy stressed with all this shite, Jackie, lad.' Dynamo said while crouching down in front of one of the big trees - that was one of the reasons why we were given such privacy in our spot - and reaching into the big opening at the bottom of it, stretching and stretching until he made contact with the bag.

'This will sort things out, though.' He pulled his arm back out from inside the tree, clutching the old discoloured and faded Morrison's plastic bag. Putting it down on the ground, reaching into it and bringing out a portable camping cooker (basically one ring out of a set of four that sits on top of your gas cooker that you can carry around with you and use) and a couple of silver knives, the top half of them well burnt and at complete odds with the shiny silver handles.

'I mean, it could be a case of you or me not even seeing the end of tonight before we get a bit of what the other two have had already.' He said as he took out his piece of hash and started biting tiny pieces off the block. Putting them down while spacing them out on a flat stone that was lying beside him.

'You know, you're not exactly helping things with that kind of talk, though.' I said, wishing he would stop talking about the whole subject but - with us specifically meeting up to try and form a plan - knowing that it was going to be *all* that he was going to talk about.

'Stick your head in the sand if you want, Jackie but you know I'm talking facts, here.' He gave the travel cooker a small shake beside his ear, so as to make sure that there was enough gas inside it, before putting it back down on the ground in front of him and lighting it up.

'No, I'm not denying it or fuck all, D. It's just that it's *all* I've thought about for days now and I reckon that if I think about it any more my head's going to burst.' I replied back to him. It was all a case of well little well late but - following the break in - I'd been a lot more forthcoming during my interactions with Dynamo than I'd ever been and was doing so without really caring what he would think, feel or say in return. Something I couldn't have said the same about myself, previously.

'Well patience, my friend, I'm just preparing your medication right now.' He laughed as he took the two knives and held them over the open flame that was shooting up from out of the metal ring.

He'd actually walked around with that same travel cooker in a rucksack - around Muirhouse - boasting that he didn't need someone's flat to have hot knives and that he - which meant, we - could have them 'on the go.' Once there was a few cases of the filth stopping and searching people around our way, though. Once all of that started, he stashed it up the woods. I did find it funny, though, that an activity - such as hot knives - that, vitally, needed the use of someone's cooker and (and by that I mean house) for it to be carried out could be re-wired in such a way by him. Changed the game, completely.

We then went on to spend the next couple of hours sitting there in the woods getting baked while talking about our current predicament but *without* actually coming up with anything that even resembled a 'plan.'

Other than Dynamo's promise that whoever laid a hand on us would then have his big brother, Boney, on their case - which was not exactly the most reassuring of plans considering it involved me having a hand laid on me *before* anything else - we were no further forward.

How could we be any further forward though when we didn't even know *who* it was we were meant to be on alert over? It was proper weird but we'd still not been able to get any contact with either Flav or Scooter so were none the wiser over 'what' had happened to the pair of them. Scooter had - from Boney's detailed description - taken the kind of hiding that made Flav's broken arms seem like getting an Indian burn off someone.

Normally, something like that happened to a mate, you'd hear all about it. Every gory detail, like. It hadn't been like that with the pair of them, though. It felt, 'off.' No one could say that I hadn't tried to see either of them so my conscience was clear, there. Was still weird as fuck, though, that I hadn't been allowed to visit my pals following them going through a bit of a bad time. Normally a mum and dad would be doing all they could to help cheer their son up by letting his pals in to visit him. Well, that's what *I* would do if I was a parent, anyway.

We walked back from the woods together. Through all of the hot knives that he'd taken, Dynamo wasn't so animated on the journey back to civilisation. I was glad that I'd not taken too many of them myself as knew I'd still have to face mum and dad and wouldn't have been able to do that if I was too baked. You get all paranoid that they know what you've been doing when - in reality - you're just acting normally *but* through your own paranoia you end up acting differently which *then* fucking draws attention to yourself. Fuck that. Too much hassle. Far too much.

With him not being around at dinner time at school - apart from the short text I sent him which was (selfishly) more to put my mind at ease that he was alright than it was through actually sincerely being someone always on the look out for his health and wellbeing - I just went back and put the head down to get me to half three and back home.

Checking my phone on the way home from school. I'd not received any reply back from Dynamo. That, though, wasn't much of a biggie smalls because half the fucking time one of us was always out of credit on our phones so getting each other by that mode of contact was never, ever, sitting at a one hundred percent success rate if you were to check the monthly stats.

Eventually I had to wait until the back of ten that night and my dad coming back from a few drinks with some of his team mates from The Gunner. Shouting me down from my bedroom when he got through the front door and I'm talking he was 'shouting me' down before he was even closing the front door shut behind him.

My nerves had been put through the shredder so much I'd been left paranoid about everything and *anything* but even so, something like my dad shouting for me to come down in such an urgent way didn't seem like 'nothing.' I thought the game was up.

'You didn't tell me about your pal, tonight when we were all sat having our tea?' He hadn't taken his coat off yet but I could tell from the look on his face that whatever he was on about wasn't good.

My main problem was that with the ambiguous 'your pal.' I didn't know *who* he was talking about. I'd kept what had happened to Flav and Scooter on the down low and hoped that mum and dad didn't hear about it. Too many why's that would've been fired at me that I couldn't or wouldn't have wanted to have been able to answer. Plus, if *I* had been able to put two and two together and realise that by Scooter there was more to it all then so would two grown adults.

'Which pal?' I tried to play it safe.

'That Boyd boy, Dynamo.'

'What about him?' I asked, at least genuinely able to look like I didn't know what he was talking about.

'You mean, you don't know?' He said, the fact that he was now considering this as an option, enough to kind of put the brakes on him.

'I've not seen him since last night and he wasn't at school today.' I said, literally telling him how it was.

'Go through and take a seat, Jack.' He said, now taking off his coat. Mum always had the place like a sauna - or so I've been told that's what a sauna is, anyway - and it wouldn't have taken him long to start having the breath sucked from him in that big puff jacket of his.

'It was your pal, last night, and on the news this morning. It was him that was found up the top of the block. He's in Intensive Care at The Royal Infirmary. Lucky to be alive, they're saying.'

Mum sat there with a shocked look on her face. Well, what you could make out of her face minus the hand that was covering her mouth while dad spoke. I was sitting there in the uncomfortable position of being given some 'shocking' news while not in any way being really that shocked. Dynamo said it himself the night before that him or I could be grabbed at any point. Hours later his prophecy came true.

'You sure it was him, dad? How do you know?' I said, trying to make up for my poor attempt at appearing shocked and surprised by - instead - trying to make a show of denial that this had actually happened to my friend. I didn't need any further information from my dad to confirm that it had been Dynamo. It was practically expected. It was probably just a natural reaction that everyone has to something like that but I was just glad that it wasn't me. I didn't beat myself up for thinking that. There looked to be someone - out there - who was edging their way closer to taking care of 'that' part of things, anyway.

'His big brother, Boney, came into The Gunner tonight. A man on a mission, like. Stood up on one of the tables and shouted for silence while he told everyone in there what had happened to his wee brother. You know what Boney's like, bit of a radge, eh? Anyway, he's shouting about that Dynamo was left for dead last night and that he was looking for any information and that he would be willing to pay for it. Got a pen and pad from behind the bar and wrote out his mobile number and put one sheet of paper on every table and then one behind the bar and left as soon as he had came in.'

I fell silent. I didn't know *what* to say even if I had wanted to say anything, which I didn't.

'Now I know that this probably isn't the right time to be saying this.' Dad said which - as an indicator - meant that whatever he was going to say he *definitely* shouldn't have been saying it.

'But it's not like I've not said how I feel about the boy Boyd. I can spot bad news a mile away, son, and I saw him coming a couple of miles even *further* down the road. Was only a matter of time before some of his carry ons caught up with him.'

'Aye, it maybe isn't the right time to be saying something like that, Joe.' Mum interrupted, looking disapprovingly at him. 'The poor boy's lying there with god knows what tubes sticking out of him in a hospital bed and you're standing there bad mouthing him. How would you like it?'

'Aye, fair enough, Han, like I said, myself. Maybe not the right time to be saying it. Doesn't make it any less true, though. You know me, darling? I don't want to be the one that says I told you so, eh?'

Attempted murder, they'd said on the news on the radio before I'd went to school. *Attempted murder.* What did that mean? Did whoever *try* to kill Dynamo but were disturbed and had to leave it? Attempt is one of 'those' words, eh? I 'attempted' to get Jayne McPherson to go to the UCI to see Fast and Furious with me but never quite managed to achieve my objective. Someone had 'attempted' to kill Dynamo, by that same use of the word.

'I'll go and see him tomorrow.' I said. It's what a pal would do, anyway.

'No you won't, son. Best leave it to close family for now. It'll be a difficult time for them. I know I wouldn't want any old Tom Dick or Harry shoving their beaks in if *you* were lying in the hospital like that.' Mum said, and in doing so giving me a little bit of clarity over how Flav and Scooter's parents had possibly been feeling.

'Aye, don't get yourself involved, Jackie. Steer well clear, there.' Dad backed mum up.

'If you hear anything, about who did it, like. You'll tell me who it was, dad, aye?' I asked as I got myself back up from the chair. I needed to be anywhere but sat with mum and dad following this news. I wanted to be somewhere that I could let my face rest at the natural position that it so desperately needed to. I couldn't be doing with putting on the other one for the benefit of throwing mum and dad off the scent.

'What? You going to go all fucking Charlie Bronson on them, like.' Dad laughed.

'Well wouldn't *you* want to know if something like that happened to one of your mates from the team?' It was a fair enough question and one that my dad couldn't argue over.

'Aye, I'm sure it'll all come out. Who done it and why. That stuff *always* comes out in the end.' Dad replied, almost sending a shiver right down my back at the prospect of all of what had been going on. It 'all' - as dad said - coming out.

I left the living room. Telling mum and dad that I needed to let Flav and Scooter know what had happened to our mate. Which I did. Whether they were even reading my messages or not by then, I wasn't sure. I felt that it was something that they were going to want to know about.

And that left one. Jack Sprat who could eat no fat.

Once again, it had looked like even after having been hospitalised, one of my mates had clammed up. The police were literally at our door making a general enquiry while inside our flat was someone who - for all I knew - had been the last person to see Dynamo before it had happened. Technically they'd have been around *specifically* to visit me and ask questions, if they'd known that we'd been together that night. That they hadn't, by then, made me think that they weren't going to, either.

That was just one potential problem that looked like being not as much of one as it could have been, though. The *main* one was still there alive and kicking. Clearly it was now going to be a case of 'when' it happened. The chance of any if's now long gone. I thought of everything that night lying there with eyes wide open and sleep nothing but a pipe dream.

'How' were we being tracked down like this? Hunted, almost. I'd convinced myself that it *had* been Dynamo who had brought the heat onto us and that he'd lied over what he had done with some of the gear he'd stolen and that something had fallen into the wrong pair of hands, or pawn shop. It was the only explanation for it.

I suppose it doesn't really matter how, now, I thought to myself. Not with Dynamo - whose fault I had decided it all was - lying in a hospital after having had someone try to murder him. The only objective that really mattered didn't involve playing any blame game with anyone. It really was as simple as seeing if I could keep myself out of The Royal Infirmary or The Western General. Unlike everyone else.

I didn't want to admit it to myself but the seriousness of what had happened to Dynamo - AT - TEMP - TED - MUR - DER - had shaken me. I'd been trying to convince (fool, rather) myself that it was all going to blow over and that I was going to be cool, personally. Hearing about Dynamo, though, was the final alarm clock going off. The one *after* your first two snooze presses.

It was the absolute nuclear option but, as the night went on and turned to the small hours of the morning and then into day. I was starting to think that I might have now reached the point where I was going to have to tell mum and dad.

Chapter 20

Strings

That move? You know the one? Where someone carrying a gun pulls their jacket to the side *just* enough for to show what's strapped to the inside of them? Gets you every time, so it does. Not that I've seen that signature move too many times in my life, thankfully. Not an absolute stranger to it either, though. It's like the check mate move for cunts to make. Where are you going to move yourself to when that move comes out? Absolutely fucking nowhere, that's where.

Me and Benji were meant to be away to Troon for the day but we'd had to reschedule for the week, once he'd got the call from the docs to say that he was to go into the hospital for the appointment he'd been waiting on word back on. Health before wealth - every time - so, of course, I had no issues with my compadre taking the day off from ferrying me around and, generally, being my buffer inside my chosen place of business. Just don't let him know I called him that though, eh?

With Han away to do her shift and Jackie off to school although, he'd tried to get out of going, of course. Said his head had been left messed up over what had happened to his pal and that he didn't want to go. Fucking told the wee chancer that school was *exactly* where he needed to be going to. Stay at home, what's he going to do but sit there thinking about the very *last* thing that he should be tormenting himself with. Told him that school would be a welcome distraction even if he didn't realise it. The king had the castle entirely to himself.

Didn't have much in the way of plans, like. Maybe stick on a couple of lines at Ladbrokes. Couple of pints in The Gunner in the afternoon. Resisting the temptation of smoothly transitioning myself from bed to sofa and having a see what was on Sky. I threw on some joggers and trainers and a hoody to take the dog out for a walk. If I was to get myself settled then there wouldn't have been a fucking chance I'd be taking Stanton out for the rest of the morning. Dogs shouldn't have to pay the price for their masters laziness, though. I've always said that. Those things fucking rely on us types for what quality of life they get and when you're a Heinz fifty seven variety dog who stays on the fourteenth floor of a high rise you're already in arrears when it comes to 'quality of life.'

Fucking hell, how excited wee Stan gets though when he catches wind that there's a walk on the cards. White men can't jump? Aye well tri - coloured fucking dogs *can*. Wee bastard almost reaches fucking head height with the springs in those legs when he sees me getting out the chair and saying 'mon then, we going for a walk?' That simple four letter word that sends a K-Nine into fucking orbit. I've said it before to anyone that would listen that if you could convert the feeling that the word 'walk' does to a dog, into some kind of drug, like. You'd be fucking Roman Abramovich rich. *Every* cunt would take it.

When we got out the bottom of the lift and out onto Pennywell Gardens - on account of him being an out and out radge who can't be trusted, I did once and never again - I stuck his lead on and headed towards the stretch of grass. It was baltic, again, and I'd soon found that the hoody I'd shoved on was not in fact as sufficient as I'd believed it to be when heading out.

While Stanton went through his routine of sniff - piss - sniff - sniff - piss - sniff - piss - piss - sniff - sniff - shit and so on, I reached for my Embassy. Instantly getting the worried pang of advance regret that I couldn't remember lifting my clipper. I was past that, I could still *see* the fucking lighter lying there on the coffee table, up in the flat.

A walk with Stanton is no good without a fucking reek, I thought to myself, taking it out on the head of a kid's toy baby that had been randomly lying there decapitaded. Booting it as hard as I could. Stanton, obviously, noticing this, his natural instinct kicking in with him trying to fire after it, only to find the lead stopping him. Daft wee bastard.

A wee bit down the path - while he was obsessively sniffing away at a bush - I thought I saw an opportunity to cadge a light off someone when I saw a jogger coming running in my direction. This blonde woman, probably about ages with me, with a pony tail bouncing up and down behind her while she ran. Decked out in a two piece black and fluorescent pink outfit and Diadoras that looked like the Italian sportswear company had given John Squire a gig as a designer for them. Random splashes of coloured paint, all over them.

'Oh, hen' I put my hand up in a friendly manner to get her to stop. She had white earphones in her ear. One of those ipods, I think. So I already thought that she wasn't going to hear me at first. Which she didn't. She'd read enough fo my body language, though, to come to a stop. Taking one of the earbuds out of her ear as she did. She must've had it blaring in her ears because even from the tiny wee earbud she was holding. I could hear The Rolling Stones' 'She's A Rainbow' coming from it. Barry tune, like. Not sure it's a running one, though. Then again, what do I fucking know about running?

'Oh, hen. I was wondering if you had a light? Come out the house without mines, eh.' I said with a friendly smile, appreciative that she'd stopped for me when it could've been easy as fuck to just keep running and pretend that she hadn't heard me because of her music.

'Are you joking?' She said, visibly unimpressed. I could tell from her posh accent that she wasn't from around our part. Maybe strayed from Silverknowes. Felt the burn that much on her morning jog that she'd just kept on running into the Naughty North.

'What part of 'have you got a lighter,' while I'm stood here with a packet of Embassy in my hand came, across as a joke?' The way that she had replied - to what had been nothing more than a sincere question from one human being to another - back to me immediately brought out the not so nice side of me.

Life isn't as difficult as some cunts try to make out. Be nice to me and I'll be nice to you back. Cunts have you believe that it's more difficult than performing brain surgery, in a rocket science lab.

'Well, do I look like a smoker?' She replied back in some kind of justification. While she spoke she kept herself moving on the spot. Lightly bouncing on her feet while loosening and swinging her arms back and forward, side to side.

'Oh right, so because you have a tracksuit on and a pair of Diadoras, that - as a result - completely exempts you from smoking cigarettes, probably any vices at all. Feel a bit daft in asking you, now. Obviously no one who wears trainers like that and decks themselves out in Spandex would ever take a snout to their mouth.' I pulled on Stanton's lead to move him on. The only thing I was looking for out of her was flame. And besides, it was too early for an argument, as well as too cold.

'Sarcastic prick' She said as she broke into a light jog again and ran on in the direction of Martello. *'Obviously never fucking heard of Doctor Socrates then, eh? Cunt puffs more than a Three Pigs story, him.'* I shouted back at her.

'Aye she's got me fucking well pegged though, eh Stanton?' I said to the wee man who was doing what seemed like his fortieth pish against a lamp post. Hearing his name spoken, his ears pricked up and looked towards me. Part Welsh Terrier, Irish, Fox Wire and fuck knows what else on top of that. He really was one of a kind. I suppose we all say that about our pets, though?

Stanton, with his wee tuft of hair that sprung up and looked like a mohawk. Punk dog! His old man scruffy beard that put ten years on his actual age but with no fucks given by the wee man whatsoever.

As we continued along the path. I clocked another jogger, only this time they were behind me and going in the same direction. Appearing that they were maybe a bit tired as - instead of running - they were walking slowly at the back of me. I got a wee look at the guy every now and again when Stanton stopped for a sniff at something.

When he'd managed to catch up a little with me - due to the constant stoppages on my side - I couldn't help but feel that he wasn't so prepared for a jog than the posh bird had been. Tracksuit was zipped half way up and exposing a white t shirt underneath but I could see a hefty amount of bling around the boy's neck as well. Looked like he also had a pair of white Nike Cortez on, hardly what you would class as running trainers. The clue is in the fucking name for starters, like.

Now *that* was how a Muirhouse jogger should look like, I laughed to myself.

Carrying on, my plan was to reach the end at Pennywell Medway and then turn around and walk back down the other side and give the wee man some extra things to have a sniff at. As I was reaching the end of the grass I spied a guy standing outside his car. Nice Three Series, like. Figured that I'd at least try my luck and see if *he* could give me a light.

I thought that if he was a sound cunt, even if he didn't smoke he'd give me a light from the car lighter if it had one in it.

There was something about the smile on his face, though. Like, when I was walking towards him. He didn't know me. I didn't know him. Absolutely fuck all reason for there to be a smile like that on his face.

'Any chance of a light, buddy?' I said shaking my packet in the air? 'Help yourself to one too, eh.' Whether he was a smoker or not I just wanted him to know that the offer was there.

'Yes, friend. I smoke with you. It is very cold today though, yes.' He replied in the most basic of broken English. Fucking barry, I thought to myself. Was well ganting on a reek.

'Let us smoke inside, warm, nice. Good yes?'

As I'd approached the end of the path and saw him parked. He had been leaning against the passengers side front door with his arms folded just looking ahead of him. Now that I was beside him he was opening the passengers side door for me to get in. That - having only asked him for a fag - wasn't the most normal of reactions. Spent all of Jackie's life telling him not to get into strangers' cars and I've got one asking me to do the same.

'No, you're alright pal. I appreciate the offer though, fucking brass monkeys just now and no mistake, eh. Plus, I've got the dog, eh?' I stated the obvious. Nodding down towards Stanton, that he'd obviously seen me walking with.

'I did not ask you question.' He said, smile completely dropping from his face as he opened up his leather jacket to show what was inside, strapped to him.

'Tie the fucking dog up. It does not come in car.' He pointed to the railing that was by the main road.

He looked a serious character in *every* way. Now that I was close to him he absolutely reeked of gangland. The car, the clothes and the menacing aura that he seemed to be smothered in. What the fuck was he on *my* case for, though? When you lead a completely guilt and crime free life it would be far easier to get some clarity with a question like that, though.

Instead. Some scary fucker like that 'approaches' me and it leads to me scrambling for who - out of a long, *long*, list - I may have burned that is now coming back to bite me on the arse over.

'What's this all about, like, eh?' I pleaded, without tying the dog up on the railings as he'd told me to do. Something that even him having a gun wasn't enough to have me doing, yet.

'Our boss wants a word with you about something, Strings.' The voice come from behind me. I'd, understandably, been distracted by the boy with the gun and had forgotten all about the jogger that had been behind me. He hadn't been a jogger at all, though. Fuck all other than someone who had been watching me from one side with his mate covering the other.

'It *is* Strings, isn't it? Joseph Carson, Martello Court?' Considering one - or the other of them - had probably seen me fucking *leaving* Martello taking a dog for a walk. There was no point even trying to pretend I was some cunt else. They had the right man and everything about them showed me that.

'You got my date of birth, mother's maiden name and first pet's name as well, aye?' I said. Trying to be the brave cunt, fronting things, but was feeling anything *but* brave.

The boy in the tracksuit and the bling impatiently sighed at this.

'IN THE FUCKING CAR, NOW, CUNT' He said, ditching the cocky passive aggressiveness in favour of just simple and uncomplicated aggression.

'Look, what's this all about, like.' I tried to stall things.

'You will find soon.' The foreign boy said.

'Well I'm not fucking going anywhere without Stanton. You can fucking gun me down right her in Muirhouse if you think I'm leaving my dog.' Obviously, I wasn't exactly egging them on or fuck all and hoped to fuck that I wasn't going to be provoking them into anything hasty. I wasn't leaving the fucking dog, though.

'He's right.' The Scottish one said. 'Can't just leave the dug here.' He looked towards his mate with the BMW.

'NOT. IN. FUCKING. CAR.' He stared the other one out. 'SHIT, PISS, NO.'

'Hey, if you're worried about that, you shouldn't. The dog's done about fifty pishes in the past fifteen minutes. Your car's safe, like.' I tried to assure him. Not like I wanted to be dipping a toe into the unknown of wherever the car was going to be whisking me off to but it was the better option of leaving poor wee Stanton on his own with Han and Jack most of the day still away from getting back home. As for me? Well only fuck knew if I was coming back home, at all.

The subject of the dog ended up creating a bit of a heated debate between the two of them. They got so much into it that there was a moment where I almost felt like I could've just walked off with Stanton and neither of them would've even have noticed.

I think it all came down to the boy in the tracksuit being a dog lover and the other, with the beamer, not being so much of a fan. No cunt would leave a dog there like that, if they did otherwise. German luxury car or not.

'It's only fifteen minutes drive, hardly John o' Groats to Lands End, eh.' He shook his head at his associate.

The foreign boy, reluctantly, eventually agreed that the dog could ride in the car in the front of the car with me, sat at my feet, while the tracksuit sat behind me and made sure I didn't try anything.

'So can I get that light now or what?' I said, with nothing really to lose. Fucking bricking it over what or who was waiting at the other end of the car journey and figured a smoke would've at least helped calm my nerves.

'Ah, yes. Smoke.' The driver said, as if he'd forgotten the whole initial way that we'd come by each other. 'Yes.' He pulled out a Zippo while I pulled out my packet of Embassy. Fucking hate those Zippos. Can't trust myself with them for fear of setting fire to myself so let him - while driving - reach over and light it for me.

'You wanting one yourself, aye?' I asked and he nodded his head while I took another cigarette and lit it for him.

'What about you, big man?' I turned around and asked the boy in the back who took a few seconds to decide whether he wanted one or not.

'Fuck it, aye, go on. Normally can't have one until I've had my breakfast but, aye, I'll join you, cheers,' he finally said, accepting the Embassy that I passed back to him.

Had I not already been ushered inside the car under the threat of - at least - one of them being strapped. This passing out of the cigarettes could've been just a standard conversation between mates on their journey somewhere.

'So where are we off to, anyway?' I asked, still very much feeling intimidated but - having already been reminded more than once that their boss had called for me and they'd been given the job to find and deliver - comfortable enough to ask them questions while we all sat there having a cigarette.

'Not far.' The driver said in the bare minimum.

'Aye, just across the town, like, not be long, ten minutes.' The voice said from the back.

I knew asking them what this was all about was going to be a waste of time. I'd tried several times since coming across them and the stock answer had been that I'd find out when they delivered me to their boss.

I sat in the car, having my reek, looking out the passengers window while trying to have a think to myself over who - if they'd been telling the truth to me - in the city that I could've done something to that would've had him sending his goons out to pick me up over. As a rule, and this came from how my dad taught me. You never, *ever*, took a shit where you slept or ate. Ever.

As a result of that upbringing. As a rule, I would never intentionally go anywhere near a puggy within the Lothian and Borders area. And as for any of the other wee business ventures I'd sometimes dabble in like the reeks, drink and fake gear like the Stone Island and Hilfiger jerseys? Well none of that was really stepping on anyone's toes as far as I could see. We all need to eat, eh? You just need to make sure that you're not taking your food from some cunt else's table.

With the beamer making it's way all along West Granton Road until we reached the water and then took the right onto Lower Granton Road I'd started to get the feeling that we were heading to Leith. Stanton was as good as gold, sitting curled up at my feet, enjoying the heat that was flowing in from the floor vents.

With me giving up on conversation it only then highlighted that if it hadn't been for me there wouldn't have been *any*. The driver choosing to just, well, drive, while the other one sat in the back smoking and singing away to the Billy Joel song that was playing on the radio.

Five minutes later and we were pulling into Alba Scrap and Metal in Salamander Street down in Leith. Had never been there. Never the need. Had passed it a few times when down in that neck of the woods, though. Didn't know fuck all about it or *who* was the owner of it but it was looking like the end of the journey so it would've been a good shout to suggest that I was possibly about to find out.

I was told to get out and take myself into the filthy looking porto-cabin that we'd parked up beside. The only sign on the outside of it, a white and blue '24 hour CCTV' warning for any would be wrong uns. Nothing in the way of any indication of it being a place of business.

We went through the same charade as we did back in Muirhouse, when it came to Stanton.

'Leave dog here. Outside.' The driver, and the one who hundred percent, I knew had a gun, spat at me. I just ignored him, like. I wasn't leaving Stan to run around a fucking scrapyard. I'd never see the wee bastard again.

'HEY.' He shouted as I just turned the handle to let myself in, taking Stanton in along with me.

'Leave him, Peter.' I heard the Scottish boy say to him behind me.

When I walked in there was already someone up on their up feet. They wheeled around at the sound of me coming in. Done this kind of wee double take at the sight of me. What looked like a pretend squint of his eyes as he took a theatrical couple of staggered steps towards me.

'Joseph 'Strings' Carson, as I live and fucking breathe.' He said with a huge smile written all over his his face. Taking another two steps forward to meet me. Hand outstretched to shake mines.

'Jesus fucking H, long time, Davey, eh?' I shook his hand gratefully.

He was a familiar face but not what I would ever have classed as a 'friend' and because of this, I didn't feel the massive sense of relief that you'd maybe think that I'd have been left with after being picked up from off of the street by a couple of goons - without any reason being given to me - only to walk in to that porto-cabin and be greeted with a warm smile and a handshake.

I'd done some work for Davey McKenna years back in a him asking me to do something for him kind of way and - because of the reputation and clout that the man carried - I'd not really been in much of a position to say no to him. He wasn't really a person who heard the word 'no' too often, McKenna. He'd been engaged in some war against someone from the West Coast who had bought up a chain of pubs in the city. He had been informed all about my obscure 'talent' and put me to work. Cleaning out as many puggies in pubs belonging to the cunt from Glasgow as possible, as part of a much more bigger scale assault on the guy's businesses.

It was bizarre. McKenna fucking *paid* me to string the cunt's puggies across the city centre. So I got the money from the puggies that I strung *and* was paid a token payment from Davey for services rendered. I didn't *want* to do it, though. Stringing city centre fruit machines is fuck all other than bait. Be that for getting lifted or leaving the pub in a body bag. Every single pub I ripped off for McKenna I was literally taking my life in my hands when I took my place at that puggy.

Eventually, the Weegie had to admit defeat and sold up and went back along the M8 with his tail between his legs and McKenna didn't need to use me any more. It was *easily* the most profitable time I'd ever experienced as a stringer due to the sheer volume of pubs I was hitting each day, along with the contributions that McKenna was throwing my way. Still, though. I was relieved when it came to an end. It had been starting to affect my health and what good is money if you've not got health first?

Fucking hair started to fall out with the stress of it all and everything. I'm a stringer - and a fucking good one, at that - but it has to be on *my* terms and in my own natural chosen habitat. For me to do it under any other circumstances *that's* when you leave yourself open to mistakes being made and it's mistakes that can be the difference between finding yourself in Sunny Saughton or the Western General.

'So, you keeping well, Joe? I'm not going to show you the disrespect of trying to pretend that I know if you have a wife or kids. But you *do* have the most beautiful of dogs, though. C,mere, boy.' He crouched down and put his hand out to Stanton. The dog, being the daft friendly type, took to him straight away and was like putty in McKenna's hands.

'What's its name?' He asked, as he - still crouching - patted him on the head. Stanton lapping it up.

'Stanton,' I replied. Reaching down to let him off his collar.

'Haw, Budsy. Look. Pat Stanton. *Pat* Stanton, get it?' McKenna said, while making a show of patting the dog.

'Very droll,' I said, really just wanting him to get to the elephant in the room of 'why' he had instructed his men to come and bring me there. I was already fearful at the prospect of McKenna personally seeking me out to 'employ' me again for my specialised services.

'I love dogs. So loyal, they'll never do you dirty. They don't have the emotions to deal with such chicanery. Would be nice if human beings could all be the same, eh, Strings?'

As far as talking about people doing dirty deeds. Davey McKenna offering an opinion on such a subject was like Chic Charnley hitting out about fitba players picking up up too many regular red cards. I didn't like the tone he'd chosen to say it, though. While it had appeared that all he was doing was thinking and reacting to Stanton being beside him and showing him, love despite having never met him before. Why did it feel that he was being a bit more 'personal' with the words that he was choosing and the way that he was putting them across to me?

'They're also daft as fucking brushes and drive you up the wall, too, well this one does, anyway. Wouldn't change the wee bastard for the world, though.' I replied, giving him a pat on his coat while McKenna was still running his hand over Stanton's face and playing with him.

'Aye well, so are humans, Joe.' McKenna replied, a bit more colder and definitely confirming that I hadn't been just paranoid with how I'd felt he'd delivered the last sentence my way.

'Mon, take a seat. I need to talk to you about something. Wanting a tea or coffee?' He took control of things now that the dog had stopped distracting him.

'Aye, a cup of tea would be rare, please.' I answered before reaching for my packet of cigs and asking McKenna if it would be cool for me to spark up before then remembering that I didn't even have a lighter in the first place and having to ask if anyone had a light. The Scottish boy - who was still standing behind me along with the other one - producing a clipper out of nowhere to give me one.

'Peter, two cups, pal.' McKenna clicked his fingers towards the driver of the BMW.

'How do you take it?' McKenna asked.

'One sugar, some coo and a dip and a squeeze.' I replied, looking around at 'Peter' to see if he'd got that. Could've drawn a question mark on his forehead to go with the look on his face.

'What the esteemed gentleman means is one sugar, a dash of milk and dip the tea bag in. Give it a squeeze with the spoon on the inside of the cup and then bring the tea bag right out again, that right, Strings?'

'Bingo, mate.' I confirmed.

'So you're probably wondering why I've brought you in here today?' McKenna said, like some boss who has - completely out of the blue - brought one of his employees into his office for an impromptu chat.

'Well, aye, You could say that.' I laughed - nervously - while trying to take a sip of my tea and almost burning my lips in the process.

I knew whatever it was that he had to say. *None* of it was going to be of any good. Well, to me, anyway.

'Well, first of all. I want to say that I had you brought down here out of respect for the good work that you did with that Halligan cunt that thought he could just move across from the Weeg and run this fine capital city of ours. They weegie cunts would be best served at times to remember that *we're* the capital city, not them. Anyway, I digress. Don't think that work you did for me went unnoticed, Joe, and *that's* why you're sat here.' He said this as he reached into one of his office drawers and pulled out an A4 sized brown envelope.

It sounded a *lot* like one of those moments where all some cunt is doing is lubing you up before they fuck you with something big and bad. A lot like when someone leads with 'with the greatest of respect' and then goes on to say something that is completely lacking in *any*.

'I've just got one question for you, pal. If the answer is no then my boys here will take you and that adorable wee Stanton of yours back up the road to Muirhouse and leave you exactly as you were before they rudely interrupted your morning. If you say yes, though? Well, then we're going to have a bit of a problem, us.'

I didn't have a fucking clue where he was going with this but the *one* thing I knew for a nailed down fact was that me and Davey McKenna didn't need any problems with each other. A better way of putting it, and a much more exact method, would've been to say that *I* didn't need a problem with *Davey McKenna*. No one in their right mind would.

'But lets not get away with ourselves here, eh?' He smiled as he shoved the envelope across the table to me. 'Take a wee look, pal.'

I was filled with the worst kind of trepidation as I opened it up. Kind of knew that what was inside I wasn't going to like but with the three of them all looking on, it wasn't like I had much of a choice.

When I pulled the photos out I saw one of Jackie's pals, Flav, on the top of the pile, standing in a living room. Taking that photo and putting it to the bottom of the pile, the next photo was of Dynamo, the one who had been found the night before up the top of our flats. *That* was when I fully made the connection. After seeing the picture of Dynamo - someone else was in the background but you couldn't make out their face - I looked back up at McKenna.

'Aye.' He said, raising an eyebrow. Saying a lot more than just the one word he'd chosen to speak. 'Keep going.' He pushed.

The next photo was of Dynamo again - in a woman's dress - but with Jackie's other pal, Scooter, more closer to the camera. The one after that. Dynamo wearing a Mason's sash with a stupid fucking grin on his face. One that he was guaranteed to have now wiped from his face. When I eventually came around to the picture that I feared - but deep down knew was coming - I was going to find my facial reaction to it did all of McKenna's work for him.

'Well I *was* going to ask you if you recognised the kid in that picture there but you've pretty much just confirmed that for me. Broke into my house, the four of them. You should've seen the fucking state of the place.' He said with a tone that I found difficult to read. Maybe this was because I was going through a bit of a moment where I felt a battle of emotions over killing my son or protecting him. Anything else - while I sat staring at that picture of him - was just distraction. McKenna, included.

It was a black and white grainy picture but only the most delusional of parents would've sat there and tried to deny that it was their son. It was him. The wee cunt even had my fucking Scotland Supporters Club beanie hat that I got as part of my membership. Was a reversible one, like. Tartan on one side and if you turned it inside out it was blue but with the SFA badge on the front. He was standing there with that SFA badge right above his stupid fucking face.

'I'm going to fucking kill the little bastard.' My response to McKenna when I managed to come up with some kind of words for him.

He laughed at this.

'Well, that was pretty much *my* feelings towards him, too. Funny, that.' He said while his couple of goons behind me laughed along.

'Excuse me if I don't laugh along, Davey. I've just found out that my son is a fucking thief. A fucking housebreaker?! That's NOT how he's been raised.'

I felt instantly ashamed. What had Han and I done bringing him up that was wrong? Aye, Jackie was no angel but who *was* around Muirhouse? He wasn't a housebreaker. Whether I liked it or not, though. There would have to be another time to reflect and search the soul for how Jackie had ended up down such a path. The more pressing issue of the day, and it would've served me well to not forget this vital part, was over *whose* house my son had broken 'into.'

I sat in silence as McKenna went on to tell me all about it. That he had come back from holiday to find his mansion ransacked and thousands of pounds worth of valuables pinched or damaged. How he had tracked down the culprits and through 'interrogation' carried out on those that had been grabbed. He had managed to piece it all together. And by now it had resulted in three kids being hospitalised. And Dynamo's dad - I was informed - pencilled in for a visit over his own loose lips that had caused it all in the first place.

It had been 'lucky' for Jackie that he hadn't been one of the first few that had been grabbed and before the name 'Carson' had started being given up by the others - as McKenna had told me - because it was only *due to* him knowing he was dealing with kids from Muirhouse and that one of them had a second name of Carson that had stopped him from taking care of the last of the faces from the pictures.

He'd obviously held my work for him years before a lot higher than he'd, personally, regarded to me because it had been *this* which had prompted him calling for me to be brought to him. Almost as a show of respect in that he wanted to make sure if this kid - that he was about to do fuck knows what examples of medieval stuff on - was linked to me or not before he went on with doing his thing.

'Well, like I said, Joe, if you were going to answer yes to my question. That was going to leave us with a problem. Fortunately, you're already up to speed with things as in you already know that I'm not someone that you really want to be having issues with so that'll save us a bit of time, there.'

While he'd held my work for him in high enough regard to stop him from snapping my son into pieces. It hadn't been quite enough regard to prevent him from issuing threats my way, either.

'I'm not wanting any problem with you, Mr McKenna.' I subconsciously slipped into calling him by a more formal name when I hadn't done so earlier on. And I felt instantly all the weaker for it.

'You and me have always been cool with each other. Done a lot of work for you, back in the day, eh?' I appealed to his sense of fairness. One that I didn't know was there and - generally speaking - you don't end up with a reputation across Edinburgh (and to a lesser extent, Scotland) like Davey McKenna does by displaying 'fairness.'

'Well, aye. True, true and that's *exactly* why you're sitting here, Stringsy, instead of by your son's hospital bed right now.' He replied. I guess that was as *fair* as things were going to get.

'Whatever he stole, I'll pay back. With interest, obviously, like.' I offered straight away. *That* was the bare minimum to try and make up for Jackie's part in it.

'Well, that's the thing. He didn't actually *take* anything. Took us to study the video carefully and then interrogate the first three before we worked out only two out the four actually stole anything from me.'

Inside I breathed a massive sigh of relief. Whatever shite was now going to follow. I still took comfort in the fact that Jack hadn't stolen anything. You don't break into a house only to not steal anything - while your mates *are* - if you didn't want to be inside there in the first place.

'Well thank fuck for that, at least.' I said to him, nervously pretending to wipe a bead sweat from my forehead.

'That's not the fucking point, though. He stepped over my threshold, uninvited. An example has to be made, Joe. You know that? If I didn't set examples I'd be as well putting a full page advert in the Evening Times with my address - along with key code numbers - inviting any cunt to come over and help themselves to my things.'

He stood up, banging his fist on the table. So hard it made the two tea cups move.

I felt the best policy would be to just keep silent. The chances of saying the wrong thing - especially to someone as unpredictable as Davey McKenna - was much too high.

'So how do you suggest that this 'debt' is repaid, then, Joseph?' He asked, sitting down again having regained his composure after the mini explosion had subsided.

Well when a debt has absolutely no figure on it - like with Jackie stealing nothing from McKenna - how the fuck are you meant to set the repayment terms? I thought to myself but chose wisely not to share it out loud.

'First up, I just want to say that I appreciate the respect that you've shown. My Jack's not a bad lad, just fallen in with the wrong crowd, eh. That Dynamo? It's him that's been the worst out of them all.'

'You think there was a coincidence that he got the worst going over out of the three, there either?' McKenna cut me off.

'If I can respectfully continue, I just wanted to say that I appreciate the gesture that you didn't lay a finger on him and that you came to me first and whatever I can do to pay you back - that you need - then you only need to ask.'

I regretted the all encompassing way that I'd put it out there to him. A man like Davey McKenna could find *many* ways to call upon your help. None of them you'd ever want to do. He pounced on this, as you'd expect a gangster to do on someone who was vulnerable and ready for taking advantage of and manipulating for their own financial gains. Straight away mentioning that he would have Jackie sell drugs for him around Muirhouse. Saying that my son was the perfect age to be punting gear to others, around his same group.

Regardless of the fact that I was right under his thumb. I still found enough cojones to stand up to him. Showing the loving and protective father side to me. The side that you'd rather *die* than see your kid a drug dealer.

'Well, in terms of making a real impact on the debt of not being put in hospital. Other than selling gear for me, your son's not of much use to me.' He said, shrugging his shoulders and bringing both hands up - like they were a scales - as if to say he'd tried to keep Jackie out of hospital but what could he do in the end.

'Aye, b b but, *I* could be of use to you, though? You already know *that.*' I was completely scrambling and it was the first thing that I could think of.

'Aye, there is that.' He said, sitting back in his chair and stroking his chin with a wee smile creeping on his face that - and call me paranoid -

made me think that this was 'exactly' where he had seen the conversation ending up.

'So, a favour for a favour, eh Strings?' McKenna said, as if for confirmation of what I was saying to him. 'Be a pretty fucking big favour, mind.' He assured me. Being due someone like this man 'a favour' you really don't need to be getting bogged down with the *levels* that exist. Not when you're fighting for your life. Or in my case, my son's.

'Hmmm that might work, you know.' He said, appearing deep in thought. I just sat there tensely waiting on some kind of an outcome. Stanton seemed to sense this from me and had got up from off the floor - where he had been lying before contently - and came over to nestle his head into my legs.

'Right, give me your phone.' He said, arm out with open hand expectedly waiting on me handing my N95 over. After getting my passcode out of me he then went on to call his phone from mines and then save my name and number onto his from the 'missed call' that he had engineered.

'I'm going to take a wee think what I'm going to do with you. No panic, though, Strings. Not like you're going to be skipping the country or anything, eh. I'll know where to find you, when I need to.'

Gutted over the implications of this all I could do was offer a small nod in his direction.

'But it's been good to see you, pal, good to see you're still healthy and above ground.' He stood up and offered me his hand. I then stood up behind him and did the same.

'Wishing it was under a bit better circumstances, like.' I replied, regretfully, as I was shaking his hand. Trying to hide the array of emotions that were bubbling up inside of me. Some only really simmering and which weren't going to fully come to the boil until hours later.

'That's life, that's what all the people say. You're riding high in April, shot down in May, Strings.' He sang back at me as if it was all water off a duck's back.

'Now if you'll excuse me, this housebreaking thing has pretty much dominated my morning and it's really starting to get in the way of the general running of my criminal enterprise so, Budsy, can you make sure Strings here gets back safe and sound to Muirhouse. He's going to be valuable to us. This man, here' McKenna said before picking up his phone and looking up someone to make a call to.

'Aye no worries, boss. We'll both take him.' The Scottish boy replied while McKenna put the phone to his ear. Giving me a small nod to indicate I was on my way before he started speaking to the person who had answered on the other end.

'Aye, I'm interested, about that thing. You got time to give me the details?' He said, as vaguely as you'd expect him to be on a phone line.

The two heavies saw Stanton and myself back out of the porto-cabin. While I'd entered it - unsure of what the fuck was going on but full of worry over what was about to follow - I left it with my world feeling like it had collapsed. I felt sick, everything was spinning while I tried to come to terms with being right back in the pocket of someone that I had worked so hard to get *out* of, all those years before.

'We take you, same place?' The driver asked once we were all in. 'Budsy' in the back, a lot more relaxed now that things had been addressed and I was no longer traveling with them under any kind of threat. He even crashed his packet of cigarettes around the car. I took him up on the offer. Already accepting that it was going to be a day where the smoking of reeks was going to be unusually higher than normal.

'Nah, take me to The Gunner, pal.' I replied as I sparked up the Regal King Size - posh cunt, eh? - that he'd passed over to me in the front.

'I could do with a couple of drinks, like.'

Chapter 21

Han

'RIGHT WHERE IS THAT LITTLE BASTAAAAARD?' Joe came through the door, around tea time, with Stanton behind him. Wagging his tail excitedly on seeing me and itching to get its lead removed.

'He's up in his room. Says he's not feeling too well.' I replied. I hadn't been able to disagree with him - when he'd told me - as he'd been looking a bit grey when I'd seen him after getting back to the flat from my shift.

'Aye well he's going to feel a lot more fucking poorly after I'm done with him.' He said dropping the lead. Allowing Stanton to run around the place with it trailing behind him while he tried to run and jump up on me. With the way that Joe had come in. Acknowledging the dog was the very least of my worries.

Joe made right for the stairs with me chasing up after him. Still none the wiser over what our Jackie had done.

'Joe? What's going on?' I asked - a little scared by then - but was wasting my time. I'm not even sure that he 'heard' me, despite being only two stairs behind him. I think it was primarily through a mother's maternal instinct than anything else but I genuinely feared that Joe was about to tear our wee boy from limb to limb once he got into his room. I'd seen him pissed off at Jack before. I'd been *just* as angry at him in the past. How could we not? It was Jack. That was what he did. It was his brand.

I'd never seen him *this* angry, though. Especially over how all at odds it had been the last time we'd all seen each other which had been the morning after him finding out about what had happened to his pal. Any sympathy over that was long gone by the looks, but why?

What with Jack almost fifteen and that, we'd given him the bit of space and privacy that a teenager needed. Would knock on his bedroom door before entering. Just one example. *That* went out the window on that occasion, however. Joe just storming right in. Lucky he never took the door off it's hinges, the force he went through it. The door, smashing against the side wall.

My heart was beating out of its chest with panic. I'd seen Joe in all kinds of ways over the years. Some complimentary, some not so. He wasn't a violent man, by any means. Might've been a lot of things - and if you owned a series of puggies then chances were, you'd have a few things to say about him - but aggressive? Never. Well not *off* a football pitch. More chance of *me* having a fight with someone than my husband and when I say that I mean, factually. There's been more fights involving me on a night out between the two of us than there has through him, I'm ashamed to say.

So *this* was why it was so out of character to see him behaving like this.

'THERE YOU ARE, YOU WEE FUCKING ROBBING BASTARD.' He shouted. Jack was sitting on the edge of his bed with his X-box controller in his hand and almost fell off, through the fright he got. Joe, grabbing the controller out of his hands and throwing it across the room.

'DAD, I was on a twenty seven kill streak on COD.' He said like the little wideo that he is and - by doing so - completely misreading the seriousness of matters.

'AYE AND I'M ABOUT TO *START* A KILL STREAK OF MY OWN, WITH YOU, YOU LITTLE CUNT.' Joe shouted back as he went for him.

'What do you mean by robbing, Joe?' I asked.

Out of everything, *that* was the one word that had stuck out the most. Had Jack maybe helped himself to a tenner from Joe's bag of change and been caught out or something like that, I thought to myself. If that *had* been the case then Joe's actions - I'd have opinionated - were a bit over the top.

'Our son, here, Han, is a fucking **HOUSEBREAKER!** That's what I'm fucking talking about.' He said looking at me but with one arm outstretched like a fancy maitre d welcoming you into their restaurant.

'Eh?' Jack said, screwing his face up like it had been one of the most stupid things he'd ever heard.

'Don't you even fucking try it, son. Seriously. Trust me when I say that *now* isn't the time for any fucking lies.' Joe said, shutting down Jack's attempt at fobbing this massive accusation off.

'Oh aye, robbing houses in Silverknowes, Han.' Joe said, having now grabbed Jack up from the bed - by his shirt - and pushed him along the room. Pinning him to the wall by the throat.

'JOE, LEAVE THE BOY.' I screamed. Whether any of this was true or not. I wasn't standing by and letting him do that to our son who - by now - at least was treating this as seriously as he should've been doing. The terrified look on his face seeming to confirm as much.

'It's rubbish, dad, I've not been anywhere near Silverknowes. Can't remember the last time I was even there.' He said, frightened and looking at me for some kind of back up.

He found himself looking in the wrong place. There was something about Silverknowes. Where had I heard it before, recently? I thought to myself and then it came to me. That Kelly Cooper coming into the Co-Op and saying that she'd seen our Jack walking around with other boys *in* Silverknowes.

'Don't lie, Jack.' I then got myself involved. Joe loosened his grip around him and kind of looked around at me, almost in amazement that I had - despite him not stopping to share any of what he knew with me in advance - sided with him so easily and was now full on accusing Jack of lying to us.

'I'm not, mum.' He lied.

'A customer in the shop told me that she saw you and your pals walking around Silverknowes last week.' I said and watched his face deflate as a result. God loves a trier though, right?

'Sh shh she must've made a mistake.' He attempted to try and ride it out.

'AND I SUPPOSE *I* MUST'VE MADE A FUCKING MISTAKE WITH THE CCTV PHOTOS THAT I LOOKED AT TODAY WHERE I SAW

YOU IN THEM. OBVIOUSLY YOU'RE JUST MY FUCKING SON
AND NOT SOMEONE THAT RECOGNISABLE. EASY MISTAKE TO
MAKE, EH?'

Joe exploded again. Jack not admitting to it only making things worse,
as cliched as a teenager might well have thought of such a scenario.

'RIGHT, family meeting in ten minutes. I'm going out to get some
cans, going to fucking need them, tonight. You wanting anything,
Han? He asked. Picking up on the vibe that there was a *lot* that Joe
hadn't yet shared. I said for him to get me a bottle of Lambrusco. That
son of mines would drive you to bloody drink, so he would.

Joe returned with the provisions around twenty minutes later and we
got ourselves sat down in the kitchen, where he told us all of what had
went on when we had both been at work and school. How he had
been picked up by a couple of gangsters, driven to Leith and shown
the photos from the break in and how he was now in debt to someone
you could, diplomatically, describe as dangerous.

Jack had well and truly left us - as a family - knee deep in the shite. I
was with Joe before when he had to do those jobs for that Davey
McKenna and it had almost split us up with the stress it had caused
him and, as a result, us.

'I was going to tell you both, I promise. I was thinking about telling
you today but I was scared to. Didn't know how, though.'

Jack said - crying his eyes out - after, finally, taking on board the
consequences of his actions and how serious it now meant for his dad.
'I never slept any of last night when you'd told me about Dynamo.
When you got back from the pub. *That's* when I knew that things had
went too far. I just didn't know *how* to tell you. I didn't steal anything
though, dad, I swear,' he - it was hoped - sat there coming clean about
things.

'Bit late to try and make promises or swear, having done nothing but
lie your wee arse off in our faces since your dad came in the door.' I
said, absolutely furious with him. I would have been just as furious
had it been some random person he'd broken into. Someone who did
not have the same 'reach' of a Davey McKenna. For the family it was
an embarrassment. I felt ashamed. Felt like I had failed, as a mother,
somehow.'

'No, Han, he's actually telling the truth, for once.' Jack found unexpected support in Joe.

'McKenna told me that Jack didn't lift anything. It was only two out the four, and even then, most of it, all the valuables, were scooped up by that Dynamo.'

'I only went because I didn't want to be called a chicken by the others,' Jack pleaded with us. As if that was ever going to make it all ok again.

Nothing, short of a time machine, was going to make it all ok again.

'Well you know what they say, eh? If you fly with the crows, eh?' Joe dished out one of the golden oldies. 'You get fucking SHOT!'

Joe sent Jackie up the stairs, eventually, so that we could talk over things further. Grounded - indefinitely - and X-box sold to Cash Generator first thing the next morning. And that was just for starters.

Joe wasn't fucking about. Jack had completely fucked his father and - as a result of this - Joe was going to make sure that the young man of the house was going to feel the pinch over it.

From the way Joe had put it across to me - when Jack was back up in his room - it was a miracle that he was neither charged with breaking and entering *or* ending up the same way as the three of his - now ex - pals.

The plans that McKenna wanted to enforce, by having Jack selling drugs on the estate for him. Everything connected to the break in and the ripple effect that it had now all caused.

The little pain in the arse - through absolutely nothing other than the sheer luck of whose son that he was - was lucky that *all* he was having taken from him was his freedom and games console.

Chapter 22

Jack

Awww WHIT! Proper fucking heavy, like, but my dad found out about Silverknowes. How ironic is it that I was *thinking* about telling him about it only for him to then find out himself so it *then* looks like when I told him that I was *going* to tell him. It makes it look like I'm just lying to him.

Absolute shan. Total shan, like.

An instant grounding - with no cause for appeal, dad had said - and my X-box Three Sixty taken from me. Not the first time that I'd had the console taken from me, of course.

'You've got to hit people where it hurts.' dad would always say when he was taking the X-box from me. He knew my weak spot. You don't have much when you're a teenager, I suppose, but your parents - out of *anyone* - know exactly where they are.

Was about crying when he took it to Cash Generator the next day and sold it, mind. He *did* say that he was going to take it there and sell it but dad says a lot of things that he doesn't mean or - in the end - won't end up doing.

When I came home from school in the hope that - being grounded - I was at least going to get my X-box back to play and was told that it had been sold, I was well gutted. The receipt for the transaction stuck to the fridge by dad, specifically for my attention.

I'd wanted to say how all unfair it was but knew that it would've brought me close to a smack in the mouth from my dad who was now in trouble because of what I'd done.

I was told that I wasn't getting to hang around with Flav, Scooter and Dynamo again. *That* was another thing, though, that I'd hoped was going to come under the say but not seeing through category. Well, with Flav, at least. It was too early days to offer any kind of protests or arguments over *anything* and it was a position that I could only blame myself for being in. Flav and I had been pals for ever and had never done anything like breaking into houses until Dynamo came along and I was hoping that between my mum and dad and Flav's that they'd maybe recognise that.

For now though it was a case of no getting out (apart from for school) no pals, no X-box and, until further notice, no Hibs matches with dad.

I'd never heard the name Davey McKenna - or of his scary reputation - before but seeing the fallout that had come through breaking into his house, and all the punishment I was getting handed out? It almost felt like the *humane* way to deal with things would've been to leave me for McKenna, himself, to sort out.

Chapter 23

Strings

'The *little fucking bastard*. Not being funny, Benji, but if it wasn't for the fact that it would defeat the fucking purpose of it all. I would disembowel him. Is it not polar bears that once their kids get to something like two years old - or something like that - they just chase the cunts away after that. None of this family pish for them. A case of, right you've had your induction period in how to be a polar bear now take yourself to fuck. Maybe they've got something, there. The polar bears, like.'

I was off on one, as Benji drove down the motorway in the direction of the Scottish borders. I'd had the brainwave when we were coming back up from Blackpool and we'd stopped at Gretna Green. I'd told him to stop there because of the pub that I knew was always busy due to the constant wedding parties that would be in there for a quick pre wedding scoop, or one shortly after the tying of the knot.

Another of those hiding in plain sight, examples. Pub went like a fair the whole time we were in there. Non stop, like. Due to that. Who was clocking the two cunts sitting at the puggie? Aye, exactly. No cunt.

Would *you* be interested in who was pumping their coin into a fruit machine moments before you were about to go through with the ultimate of commitments a human being could ever sign up for? Nah, me neither.

Service stations. *That* had been the brainwave. Busy as fuck and already having a mentality of the public getting fleeced the moment that they get out of their car, so why not capitalise on that and give a little bit back? I loved the idea of being Robin Hood, when it came to the stringing, like. Definitely giving to the poor, anyway, us, The Carsons. Charity begins at home. As they say, eh?

I wasn't exactly in the best of states to go stringing. I'd always looked upon myself as no different from anyone else who had to go out and display their craft. Fitba players, guitarists, hypnotists and that kind of deal. It's not like a light switch at times - your talent - like. Can't just switch it on and off, at will, you know?

'To be fair. There's not a parent out there who would judge you if you were to flay him and then dump what was left of his carcass into the Forth for the seals to nibble on.' Benji said, dryly.

'Nah, catch twenty two, for you, though, Strings. I was no different to you when our Leah was born. Not being dramatic or fuck all but I said to the other half - when she handed our baby to me for the first time - that I would be prepared to throw myself in front of a bus for her. And I'd only just met her. Hadn't even had the chance for her to get to talk and start to tell me things about her for me to feel that, either, too. Just a feeling that's magically there the second that you become a dad. You don't feel it five seconds before they're born but fuck me, you feel it when they're actually *there*. Thing is, though. You'd jump in front of the bus for them but other days you'd happily get behind the fucking wheel and run the cheeky little bastards over.' He said while pointing to indicate that the services near to Carlisle - which had spawned this 'road trip' - were now only ten miles away.

'Aye, you're not wrong, pal. If I didn't love the boy I'd have just lied to McKenna yesterday and said I *didn't* recognise him in the photo. Of course, I didn't even *need* to say any words to him, though, Benji. Fucking face gave the game away straight off. Some things you can't hide, eh?'

The rain started to come on which was the last thing that we needed. Not that we were going to be spending any time outdoors so that, in itself, didn't present too much of a problem. That Benji was a lazy bastard who wouldn't ever listen to advice such as ' those windscreen wipers look like they've seen better days considering there's barely any rubber left on them, probably should change them.' Well, that *was*.

The constant scraping sound - the wipers were making traveling back and forwards across the screen - was leaving me wanting to just switch them off and take our chances with the rain splattered windscreen and what was on the other side of it.

'So what do you think that McKenna is going to have you do to pay off the debt, like?' Benji asked. It made me shudder to even think about it but certain realities had to be faced.

'Ach, he'll be wanting to use me to extract some money from a puggy or two.' I said, passing it off like it wasn't going to be the pain in the arse it, undoubtedly, *was* going to be. Whatever it was he was going to end up using me over, whenever it was. That's *the* thing about being in debt to someone like him. Fucking sword of Damocles dangling over you and no mistake. Just ready to drop whenever Davey McKenna feels like letting go of it.

'When all is said and done, those other three boys are lying in a hospital or recovering in their houses. Jack's at school today fit and healthy. That's all that matters when it comes down to it.' When I put it across to Benji as basic as that. It pretty much said all that needed said.

Benji took on a bit of an awkward look to him. You know? Like he was wanting to say something but wasn't exactly sure how to go about it. On other days - recognising this - I'd have just told the cunt to spit it out but with so much on my mind I couldn't be arsed with the ground work. Eventually he plucked up the courage to say it.

'Look, Joe, you're right. That's the only thing that *really* matters but, well, like, you know what it's like around our way, any other area of Edinburgh, too, I suppose. You know what people are like, eh? Quick to jump conclusions, some.'

For as many words as he'd come out with. He hadn't really said *much* but was obviously trying to put some kind of message across.

'Look, what the fuck are you banging on about, Benji? What some people are like?' Either he wanted to tell me or not but I wasn't in the mood for his fanny patting.

'Well, you know? Like how the other three boys, like you just said, being in hospital and that, and their one remaining mate, out of their group, you know? Like that, the only one out the four of them - who was in on the housebreaking that night - that didn't end up in hospital, you ken? People talk. Make assumptions, Joe. You know that they're going to be putting two and two together and getting five and having wee Jackie down as a grass. I mean, if I didn't know you and know the story *I* would think that there was a bit of grassing going on to save one's neck. You know how things look. All optical illusions and smoke and mirrors with things, though.'

Finally Benji found a way to get his point across. And he was right, as well.

'Fuck.' I said in realisation, and besides, he was starting to ramble and needed to be stopped before he went too far. 'I got that caught up in the whole son being a housebreaker and me having to go deep into the pocket of an infamous East Coast gangster that I'd never even thought about that *other* side of things. It *does* look a little iffy. Four pals all commit a crime - that ends up being settled outside the jurisdiction of Lothian and Borders' finest - and only three of them *appear* to pay the price for it.'

'And the best part, or worst. Is that you - or Jack - can't fucking *tell* anyone about it because it's going to potentially grass yourself up over whatever you end up doing for McKenna to pay back your debt. I mean, you can hardly go about shouting that everything's ok and that your son *isn't* a grass because you've agreed to commit some kind of a - yet to be determined - crime for a well known gangland don to pay back the debt.' Benji laughed, ironically.

'Aye, kind of fucked one way or the other.' I shrugged my shoulders figuring that a cigarette would probably help. I'd been going through the reeks at a much faster rate than that shadowy smoking man in The X-Files, following the unscheduled visit to Leith the day before. He *was* right, though. It absolutely stunk the fucking place out that my Jack was walking around - seemingly - scot free while his 'mates' were going to be walking and talking a bit funny for the foreseeable. You could see why people would point the finger, like. It was something that we'd just need to deal with as and when.

'Have you heard anything about Terry's hamstring? I was hearing that Jock was talking about bringing him back for the cup match at the weekend.' Benji - using a bit of common sense, for a change - decided to change the subject. Something I was all for. Can't escape the situation but at the same time if it's all you talk and think about you'd end up a fucking basket case.

'He's only been out for two weeks, can't bring him back so quick. Every cunt knows that if you do your hammy then you're out for a month minimum. Rushing someone back only causes more problems in the long run. We'll end up losing him for a lot longer than a fucking month in the end.' I replied. I wasn't surprised to hear Benji tell me this, though. This was pure Jock Hunter.

Man's torn his hamstring. Needs a month to six weeks rest and recovery > Jock Hunter 'aye but it's a cup match coming up. The man plays.'

Reminding Hunter that *just* because it's a cup match doesn't mean to say that, as a result, a human being is capable of cheating science would be a waste of breath so no one ever bothers trying.

'Aye, that's what the rest of the boys were saying. Apart from Terry, like. Selfish bastard. He's bound to know himself that he'll last fifteen to twenty minutes tops before he pulls the same hammy and is substituted. And we might well be needing subbies on Sunday, already. Pentland are a right bunch of dirty, nasty, bastards.' That Benji had chosen to call Pentland AFC *'dirty, nasty, bastards' while* on the backroom staff of Muirhouse Violet was a remarkable piece of hypocrisy.

'They'll need every bit as many subs as we'll do. Can't see the full twenty two being on the pitch by the end of the match. Be that through reds getting dished out or the teams running out of players through injuries. If it's anything like the league game near the start of the season at Muirhouse, anyway.' Benji winced at the recollection of that day.

Third match of the season. When Rossi took that deliberate elbow to the face in the first few seconds of the game, the tone had been set. You can't really say that the ref lost the place that day. He never got a chance to get his hands on it in the first place with a start to the game like that.

In a match that *occasionally* saw the odd spell of fitba break out over the ninety minutes. Pentland came close to having the game automatically abandoned due to being on four red cards and one away from having the game ended. With three red cards. We weren't far behind them, mind. It was bizarre. Because they'd taken the complete huff over an offside goal that - admittedly - was miles on. They ceased to play any further 'football' of any kind. Instead, choosing to completely half any of our players who got on the ball.

With fifteen minutes left and with four players already missing, they were actually *trying* to get the match abandoned. The ref seeing through this and - I imagine - he'd looked at his watch and with there only being a quarter of an hour left of the match. Thought there would've been no point abandoning the match by then and having to have the two teams play the match again. After the first seventy five minutes between them. The smart move would have been to keep the two sides apart for as many months as possible.

That had even worked out when we were scheduled to play them back at their pitch - The first game since the match with the seven men sent off - when it was postponed due to a waterlogged pitch following a couple of days worth of heavy rain. Was probably a blessing in disguise, though.

Sometimes fate has to step in and has *its* say and show that you can't keep two things apart, if they're meant to be together. That came through getting them in the quarter finals of the Kwik Save Challenge Trophy. Aye, it was going to be spicy. Habanero pepper levels, like. I just wanted us to rise above all of the capers that was sure to be going on out on the pitch. Get past them and you're into the semis and you've got that whiff of cup final in the air. Some of the bigger sides had either not entered the cup or had put in a weaker side and as a result were no longer kicking around in the competition.

'Could be our year, you know?' I said to Benji as he took the slip road for the Carlisle services that had been the focal point of the journey. A stopping place for all your long distance motorway travelling needs. Ours being a generally sized amusement arcade filed with all singing and dancing puggies with nothing other than a bored looking spotty teenager fucking about with their phone behind the change booth with no actual thoughts to keep a check on who was actually in there or 'what' they were doing.

Come. To. Papa.

Ker - fucking ching.

'Our year? What, like the year where the league finally kick us out?' Benji laughed as he pulled up into the space and turned off the engine.

'I've got the brains, you've got the looks. Lets make lots of money.'

I sang at him as I took off my seat belt, making sure I had everything before we headed inside.

'Aye, time to go to work.' He rubbed his hands together. 'Cause if I've to go back up the road with what's in my pocket right now I may as well not fucking go back home at all.' He replied.

'Preaching to the choir, there, pal.' I answered as I got out the car. Checking that I had my shaved coins in my usual pocket, along with my trusty stringer.

Chapter 24

Han

'They say that they'd broken all of the young lad's fingers and all of his *dad's* teeth. Talk about a message to send out to a family. It's Sarah Boyd, that I feel sorry for. That poor mum and wife having to mop up after all of that. She must be scared shitless.'

Heather said as she appeared with our cups of tea. She'd been talking about the same subject before deciding to go and make us up a cuppa. *Continued* to talk while she'd went into the back room to stick the kettle on - only raising her voice so I could hear and then, without skipping a beat - before returning back with a mug in each hand without having ever skipped a beat.

'And then there's the other two young lads that were given a going over, no doubt by the same people. You and Joe must be worried sick about Jack? What with him being pals with the other three and all of that.'

I *loved* Heather and she was always my preferred colleague to work a shift with but she *did* love to gossip. This normally wasn't too much of a problem as I also enjoyed hearing all of what was going on. Some of the things I swear, left you saying 'only in Muirhouse.' Normally, though, the gossip wasn't ever so closely connected to myself. *That* tends to take the enjoyment out of things. Or so I'd found out.

While Jack's pals Flav and Scooter's parents had chosen to keep their mouths closed over what had happened to their sons. The Boyd family, however, and specifically 'Boney Boyd.' They weren't much for keeping their counsel. Boney, instead, choosing to do everything but stop traffic to tell anyone who would listen what had happened to his little brother and what he was going to be doing about it. I suppose the fact that it had made both Radio Forth and STV news didn't exactly help keep things under wraps, though. Not that it would've mattered to a nutter like Boney who would've been shouting from the rooftops abut the revenge he was going to be carrying out on the attackers. Media exposure, or not.

Not to Davey McKenna - he wasn't - but with no one privy to the information over *who* had been responsible for the beatings. Boney was free to dish out his fake threats and - at least *sound* like he was saying all the right things. You know how these things all start to come to light, though? Once the news had crept out over what had happened to the younger Boyd brother it then ALL started to come out. You had his dad going to visit Dynamo in hospital one day and then joining his son in there the next. Even put them in the same ward and everything. Then we - well, when I say 'we' I obviously mean everyone else in Muirhouse - started to hear other parts emerging as the story took on arms and legs. Me having, unfortunately, already heard about the full story days before everyone else.

Obviously, most folk took the no smoke without fire train of thinking which was of the opinion that saw people generally assuming that the three boys had been up to no good, been caught, and suitably straightened out. Happened all of the time to some unfortunate. That they were all of Jack's friends? *That* was what drew a bit of scrutiny on us, as a family. Because if you're going to go down the smoke and fire way of thinking then you're *also* going to take the leap that our Jack was involved, only, he - unlike the other three - had managed to escape the purge.

'Aye, not as much as you'd have probably thought,' I lied to Heather. 'Our Jack hadn't been going about with the three of them as much as he used to. Been spending a lot of time either in his room or going over to Craig's to play the Playstation. Looks like whatever the other three had been up to was something heavy. Was hardly a slap on the wrist that they all were given.' I hoped that I'd managed to come across as convincing to someone who had seen me at my worst *and* best. Having to work with me in all kinds of moods because of what was going on in my own world at the time.

Having virtual meltdowns there in the shop because we barely had enough money to feed ourselves some weeks. I'd never hid myself or who I was to Heather before and I felt a bit shit in doing so there and then. Wanted to just tell her *exactly* what the 'real' story was but due to what Joe was now roped into, I couldn't. Couldn't speak to anyone, outside of the family home.

'What do you think the story is with the Boyd dad, though? That's a bit of a strange one, isn't it? Aye, his two sons are not exactly something for a parent to be proud of but Shaun. He'd never been anyone that was in trouble around here. He came out to fix my window that time Mary Dick's son kicked his fitba through my kitchen window. Nice man. I made him a cup of tea for his break and we sat and had a wee chat before he finished up. Really friendly and polite. Doesn't make sense for him to be wrapped up in something like that. Just shows you, though. You think you know people.'

That was what was creating the most amount of rumours and conjecture surrounding the whole story. The dad. Well - and if he manages to keep his job after all of it - he'll not be so quick to dish out passcodes to customers' houses in future, I thought to myself as I replied back to Heather that it would all come out eventually as those kind of things always tended to. Plus, with Boney being on the warpath straight from the off because of what had happened to his little brother. Then add what had happened to his dad and he was hardly going to be discreet over how he went about things.

'Boney will be the one where it'll all come from.' Just watch. I assured her while hoping that he'd be keeping as much of what he knew to himself.

If he wanted to, then the rest of Muirhouse would know that Jack broke into a house along with his brother. Figuring, that it would've been counter productive for anyone to go shouting about how their brother had broken into a house, while the police - up until then - had not actually been involved, and weren't looking like doing so.

This was Boney Boyd, though. A man who acted on his emotions and his impulses. Those exact same reasons why he was only just getting *out* of jail. He was unpredictable and - having discussed it at length - Joe and myself had already assumed that none of the other families were going to speak a word over what had happened. Through fear of any reprisals from Davey McKenna, inviting police involvement on their sons *and* the angle that would see great shame passed onto their family. *Nobody* was innocent so it would've made sense to go grab the broom and get it swept under the carpet.

Joe and me had planned for everything and all events, the night before when we'd sat down. Having sent Jack back to his room while we got fired through the alcohol that Joe had brought back before our family meeting.

'Up to this point. The *worst* case scenario is that someone from the Boyds - feeling sorry for themselves over what McKenna has done to them - is going to start mouthing off about Jack being involved in the break in. That's as *much* as they - or anyone - can say because that's all they know. No one knows about my chat with McKenna, where others didn't get that opportunity. No one knows about the deal that I've made with him but I'll tell you what, though? Any cunt with a nosey bone in their body and a decent enough memory on them will remember that I done a bit of work for Davey McKenna years back. *If* it comes out that Jack and the other three broke into the house of Edinburgh's most infamous gangster - leading to this spate of hospitilisations - *that* is going to be the cover story. That it had only been my connection to McKenna that had saved Jack's skin. Which isn't exactly that far from the truth. Fuck, it *is* the truth, apart from the bit about me having to carry out some yet to be determined crime to pay back the debt, obviously. That's definitely the part that you say quietly along with the other parts that you say loud, eh?'

We had our story set out in front of us knowing that the first couple of days were going to be the most intense - where a lot of eyes were going to be on us - and our family name would be the topic of conversation around a few dinner tables that night.

Muirhouse, being what it was. Something else would've come along by the next week and no one would've even remembered the three kids brutally beaten up, apart from them and those close to them.

Whether the residents of the Naughty North were taking about the Carson family, or not, did not solve the real problem that the same family had found itself in, courtesy of that mixed up kid of a son. He had landed us in a world of shite and the best part was that - because of his age - we protected him from the seriousness of being in debt to someone like a Davey McKenna. A gesture like selling his X-box was meant to give him *some* kind of an idea over how we felt but even that had been a tame display from us, considering.

It scared me that Joe was now in this man's pocket, again. Some of those types love the power. Knowing that they hold your life in their hands and that they can do what they want with you as they wish.

Joe had passed it off like it wasn't going to be much of a problem to him, when we sat speaking about it in the living room the night before. Made it out like it wasn't going to cause too much hassle to him but I could see in his eyes that he didn't actually *believe* what he was telling me. I think that's what made me scared. That I'd been able to detect a bit of fear in Joe's eyes. I wasn't used to that.

He was never really one for fighting, Joe. Well, if you want to take away the Muirhouse Violent carry ons, of course. 'All of that stuff is just like ice hockey players.' He'd told me, when justifying the level of thuggery that went on during those Sunday morning matches. 'It's practically encouraged, like' Normally though - and away from a fitba pitch - he wouldn't have hurt a fly. As a man, however, he never shirked a challenge - whatever it was or from whom - and ran from *no one* or *nothing*.

Davey McKenna was his only exception to the rule and - I reckoned - that with him now gatecrashing Strings' life again. It had kind of reminded Joe of those feelings from before.

A text came through from Joe while I was stood there sipping my tea and talking with Heather. This, while someone came into the shop. Heather went to serve the woman - in looking for if we had any 'nieces' birthday cards - while I saw what that man of mines was saying to it from the borders, top of England or wherever he - technically - was.

Still down around the borders. Going to get tea at The Little Chef so won't need anything when we get back. Be back around 8 - 9 x

Before anyone else came in and distracted me I sent him a quick reply.

The Little fucking Chef? You're meant to be down there to "make" us money not spend it all ;) About £10 for a bacon roll in those places FFS! Be safe and I'll see you when you get home x

No sooner had I pressed send but a mini flurry of customers all came in at once. "The bus arriving" as Heather and me would call it when lots of punters would all appear at the same time. It was a welcome break and distraction.

Other than think about the obvious, *anything* was preferable.

Chapter 25

Strings

**Wemberleeee, Wemberleeee, we're the famous Muirhouse Violet
and we're off to Wemberleeee.'**

The whole of the pub was belting out.

Were us, the players of Muirhouse Violet football club going to
Wembley, London in any capacity as fitba players? Were we fuck! Of
course not. But when a catchy chant gets introduced to an already
boisterous and celebratory bunch of men, when the alcohol is flowing.
Just you try and fucking tell them that, factually, their song doesn't
make any sense.

I couldn't really speak for the rest of the players but - sat there in the
pub following what had been every single bit the battle that I had
predicted Pentland would be - I felt almost like a Viking back on home
turf after one of their raids and now it was time for their big
celebration. Big fucking tankards and holding what looks like the leg
of something with enough meat on it to feed the five thousand.

I'd already told Han she wouldn't be seeing me for the rest of the day
when I left the house to go and help get Muirhouse Park ready for the
game. Murhouse versus Pentland in the quarter finals of the Kwik
Save Challenge trophy followed by the 'Super Sunday' derby edition
on Sky Sports with Arsenal against Spurs - the early game - followed
by Man United and Liverpool. Ken that Liverpool and Man U isn't
exactly a derby match but you can't blame Sky for pushing their luck a
bit, though.

Must've been a bit of some weird coincidence because there was a lot
of other derbies across Europe all going on the same day, as well. The
Milan one was on at night but the chances of that being on the big
screen inside The Gunner wasn't exactly high.

'Get that tippy tappy shite aff.' You'd hear someone shout pretty much straight away at the sight of a Serie A team's shirt. 'Fucking one nil scoreline, pish.' And so on.

Out of the whole squad and backroom team. Daz was the only one who wasn't singing. Sitting there staring into his pint with his face completely tripping him.

I managed to jam myself in-between him and Sepp.

'OH? What you doing, eh?' Sepp said, a wee bit put out at finding himself having to move along a bit.

'Shut yer mooth and budge up,' I smiled at him while not leaving the boy with much choice in the matter as I forced my way down beside them. I was squeezing myself in so I could have a wee motivational word with Daz, whether Sepp liked it or not.

'Hay, pal. Don't beat yourself up too much about today.' I slipped an arm around his neck.

He'd got himself sent off, near the end of the match. One of their players had been nipping him all game long and, being human, Daz had taken enough and - when the player wasn't looking - came up behind him and took an intentional kick at the back of the boy's calf. I'm not sure 'what' it was Daz had actually done but the boy for Pentland couldn't even walk on the leg after that. Never mind finish the match.

It was a straight red card for Daz and he was now sat there in the pub with the double fear of whoever replaced him, for the semi final, keeping their place, should we manage to reach the final. On top of that there was the question of what kind of a ban he was going to *get*. Generally, a red card would mean a one game ban from the same competition but with this being - what had appeared as - a premeditated assault on the Pentland player from Daz, rather than a simple late challenge. The ball was up the other end of the park when he did it, to offer some perspective.

Because of the *nature* of what he had done. There was a good chance that they would've handed down a three match ban for violent play and if that was the case then Daz would've been kissing goodbye to *any* chance of a Kwik Save Challenge Trophy cup final appearance, regardless of who came in for him for the semi final, and how well they might've done.

'It was fucking stupid, Strings. Game was almost done and we were two goals ahead. Only a few minutes to go, for fuck's sake. If ever were was a time for a team to just keep things simple. Do the easy things, make the safe passes and just generally keep your nose clean, it was then.'

I just nodded. It *was* stupid. Two goals up, at home, against nine men. There was absolute zero clear and present danger as far as us not going through to the semis.

'He was being a total prick the whole game, mate. Saying really weird shite that was getting to me. Wasn't just the physical side of things and those wee tricks like pulling out my body hair and that. It was more 'psychological, ken?'

'What kind of stuff was he saying, like?' I was genuinely interested. I'd seen a *lot* of tactics used on the pitches of a Sunday morning so was always up for hearing about new ones that some players would employ.

'Well,' Daz, looked a wee bit hesitant to really say. Kind of taking a look around him to see if anyone was listening. Not a chance in amongst all of the singing that the rest were doing.

'He was saying, like, gay stuff to me.'

'Fucking *gay* stuff?' I laughed. 'Like what?'

'Well, he was saying that he couldn't wait until after the game and how he was going to sneak a peak at me in the showers. And how if I 'measured up' he'd give me a post match blow job. Kept calling me 'big boy, and that.' The wounded look on his face as he told me had me in fucking stitches.

'Is *that* why you were fucking dreaming for their goal? He went past you like you weren't there to stick that cross in?' I said, suddenly realising that young Daz had been - uncharacteristically - caught napping in the build up to their equaliser in the first half, and before they began to lose their minds in the second half and start getting players sent off.

'Fucking right it was. The cunt had only jogged by me a few minutes before that and had patted me on the arse as he passed me. Saying that I had a nice pair of buns and turned around and blew me a wee kiss. Still had that in my fucking head when they launched their next attack. Head was all over the place, mate.'

'You could see why I snapped though, eh? Any cunt would've done with that. If the cunt had been doing it to me in the work place I'd probably be on for a quarter of a million payout in compensation by now. Sexual harassment, eh? And you know me, too, Strings mate? Far as I'm concerned. Anyone can shag anyone else if they're all adults and consenting and that. I walk along Princess Street and pat a *woman* on the arse I'd get the fucking JAIL. Gutted about missing the semi, though. And dying inside at the prospect of us getting to the final and me missing it. Never played in a final before, like.' He slipped off into a thought of his own.

'He was pulling your fucking pisser … about, weirdly, pulling your pisser. And you fell for it. That cunt isn't fucking GAY. That was Billy Fitzpatrick. He's not a bufty, Daz. I've seen him with his wife a few times.' I assured Daz that he'd simply been done by a radge with a bit of 'on field experience' in how to get the edge over your opponent.

'Oh aye, two words for you, Strings. Elton John.' Daz countered back at me.

'Weeee arrrraaa champions WEEEE arrraaaa champions. No time for Pentland cause weeee arrrraaa champions of the wurrrrrrld.'

Muirhouse belted out around us.

'Nah, trust me. I know big Billy. Known him for years. He's definitely not gay, pal. The mad bastard would probably suck your cock *because* of what a top fucking radge he is but *not* because of seeking any sexual gratification, or providing you with any. You've got to be more streetwise, young man. You got away with it today because we won but how do you think the rest of the team would've reacted if we'd lost. And all because you'd been spooked out by someone saying they were going to suck your knob? They wouldn't be too chuffed, I can tell you.'

He seemed to stop and take in this advice.

'As far as the semi goes. Well you can't do fuck all about that so there's not point worrying about it. Just pray to fuck that the ban you get goes the right way but you know that Jock will do all he can to make sure it *stays* a one game ban. Just pray that whoever comes in to take your place doesn't have a fucking stellar man of the match performance, though, eh? Nah, you're alright, Daz. You've never dipped beneath a solid seven out of ten in any game you've played this season so far. Cunts don't forget that just because you miss out for one match. Obviously I'm not picking the team but we'll get us to the final and you'll be back in the team again for it. Chill, pal. It'll be fine.'

I extended the arm, that was already around his neck, to then tighten itself into a headlock while I executed the final phase of getting Daz back into the spirit of things with the rest of the troops.

'Now forget all about the red card. You wouldn't be fucking playing for us if you didn't collect the occasional one of those, eh? Now get that pint down you. We win as a team, lose as one and fucking well *drink* as one. Cheers, ya fucker!'

I loosened my grip from around him again and left him to it. Looking back around again in his direction, when I'd got to the bar to get another drink in. Him nodding back to me across the room as if to say that the last five minutes had been appreciated. Doesn't take a Jock Hunter to know that some in life need an arm around the shoulder while others need a boot up the arse and that working out one from the other is the key to management.

'Some fucking win the day though, Strings, eh, ma man.' Mr Benn was standing there in a split new jacket. Fucking goggles, like actual sunglasses, you know? Goggles built into the fucking hood. I've seen some of the CCS wearing the same coats around Easter Road, so they're obviously worth a few bob. Just cause it costs hundreds of pounds and the cool cunts are wearing it doesn't mean to say that sticking sunglasses into a hood isn't just fucking daft, though. Maybe I'm just biased but I reckoned that my Superdry jacket was superior in every way, for about a quarter of the price along with it. Know what it's like with Mr Benn, though. Next time you see him he'll be wearing something else again. Fuck knows where he gets the cash from, like.

Being how he is - with his clothes - I thought I was doing him a favour when me and Benji got that batch of the fake Stone Island gear and I came into the pub and offered him it. *Mr Benn* was the very first person I'd thought about when I'd taken delivery of it. Six hundred pound jacket for only a Ton, I'd told him. Fucking laughed me back out the place when I brought it out the bag to show him, which was shite considering he was the only cunt that I was banking on taking one off me. Him asking me if I was 'seriously' thinking that he was going to wear a Stone Island jacket that - in reality - didn't exist. Tried to tell him that who the fuck would know if Stone Island made a jacket like that or not. Not like there's any cunt going about who knows every single jacket that a clothes brand has ever brought out. He told me that I'd be surprised about that and that there was some 'anoraks about anoraks' out there. He *also* told me that the Stone Island compass badge on the side of the arm was - without doubt - the worst attempt he'd ever seen a counterfeiter send out. He was right. Had to take a massive hit on those coats and in the end you had old jakeys cutting about Pennywell Drive in them, instead of the casuals that I had bought them to punt on to.

'Aye, some performance from you, as well.' I patted him on the shoulder. The feel good factor that was running through the pub was a joy to behold. Even the cunts that hadn't watched a single Violet match in their puff were getting carried away with everyone else. Having a sing song and that. Proper party atmosphere, like. If this is what we're like when we win a quarter final what the fuck are we going to be like when we *win* the thing? I thought to myself looking around at everyone.

'Aww cheers, mate. Good of you to say. Kind of know I'm still on probation, so to speak.' He replied, looking well chuffed with himself.

Make no mistake, though. I wasn't just complimenting him for the sake of it. He'd had - in my own humble and honest opinion - his best game in a Violet strip. Fuck know's where he got the energy from but he was up and down the pitch all game. Wore out their full back by around the hour mark and then he ran riot after that. Helping himself to two goals when - up to that point of the season - he'd never troubled a goalkeeper in any shape or form. Aye, if they did those OPTA stats at our level of fitba they probably wouldn't have been too kind to Benn but none of that mattered, there and then.

'What you wanting? You shouldn't be putting your hand in your pocket today, after that brace you scored.' I said while trying to catch Erika's attention behind the bar.

'You can get me one when I come back, I'm popping out for an hour but I'll be in a bit.' He said, waving away my offer.

'Where you off to, like?' I asked, noting that the teams were coming onto the pitch at White Hart Lane.

'Shagging, mate.' He winked as he downed his vodka and coke and put a thumbs up in the air to acknowledge the taxi driver, who had popped his head round the door a few seconds earlier.

'Who you fucking at half two on a Sunday afternoon, then?' I was well intrigued by this and if he thought he was going to be able to say something like that then just disappear from The Gunner then he was sorely mistaken, taxi or no fucking taxi.

'Ken what, Strings? I've actually *forgotten* her name. Only know her by her screen name 'Hornyvixen69' I'll need to have a quick look on the website and our private messages to see what her name is again. Cheers for that.' He laughed, already taking one of those new fancy Apple phones out.

''Is this some internet thing, like, aye?' I asked, feeling like this was something that I'd been completely left out of. Not that I'd be fucking shagging anyone other than my good lady wife, obviously. If I even dreamed about cheating on Han I'd be waking up to the sensation of her taking a cheese grater to the tip of my fucking cock.

'Aye, mate. this is the third different woman I've met with this week. Fucking loads of them in Edinburgh. *All* ganting on it. Fucking barry, ma man. Life is beautiful, eh.' He patted me on the cheek as he walked out to his taxi. Face down in his phone, no doubt looking up the name of the stranger that he was about to go off and have sex with somewhere across the city.

Blew my mind, a bit. Like how Mr Benn could go off to someone - who you've only exchanged a couple of messages back and forth with - and go straight to fucking RIDING them?

I had so many questions on the subject. *One* of them being answered with him coming *back* to The Gunner before Spurs and Arsenal had even got to the half hour stage. I'd ended up just staying at the bar so - when he walked in all biscuit arsed looking - I hadn't moved since I'd last seen him.

269

'So? How did it go then, shagger?' I was all smiles and ready for some - non contact - probing. 'If you don't mind me saying though, you weren't gone for long.' I laughed at my own joke but he was in no mood for having the piss taken out of him.

'Fucking waste of time, mate. Waste of a good couple of weeks of my time talking back and forward with her. Trying to get her to agree to a meet with me, and that. *Finally* she agrees for today. Taxi took me to the address that she'd given me. When I knocks on the door I thought I'd got the wrong hoose when it opened. Looked like her mum or auntie was maybe home or something - which I wasn't chuffed about for a kick off, why invite me round if there was going to be someone else there, eh? - when she smiled though and said my name. *That's* when I sussed out that she'd been sending me pictures of her, from when she was twenty years younger.'

Just you try and not fucking end yourself when you pictured the whole scene, like I did. Mr Benn, there, in the taxi with a fucking stane on. Imagining all of the filth that he was about to get up to only to find out that he'd been talking to someone more his mum's age group. Fucking class, like.

'FUCKING YASSSSS, GET IT RIGHT UP YOUSSS YA YIDS BASTAAAARDS'

Rossi erupted over by the telly. Looking up I could see Cesc Fabregas with his finger up to his lips at the home support. The replay showing a beautiful chip from the Spaniard that floated majestically into the net. Rossi - for reasons unknown to me - had an unhealthy obsession with Arsenal. Didn't even support any Scottish teams despite having barely left the country since being born there.

'Sit doon, ah cannae see the fucking telly,' someone's voice came from the gallery, directed at Rossi. Our "alleged" match rigging striker in his own wee world for a moment and not giving a single fuck about anyone else inside the place.

'Ended up having a big argument with her, on her doorstep. She wasn't chuffed but no half as not chuffed as yours fucking truly.' He was livid which, obviously, made it all the more funnier. Swaggering out the pub half an hour before like he was cock of the fucking walk only to return a lot sooner than his dirty arse had been intending.

'I'd already told the taxi driver to hang on a second for me. I always do that - just in case - because you never know what's waiting on the other side for you. As today has proved.'

'Aye well, what can I say? Maybe you've scored enough today already, eh? Now what you having to drink, seeing that you're back?'

Fast forward around five hours and everyone was still going strong although - hardly - in as fit a state as had been earlier in the day.

'I'm just glad that you've got a whole week to recover before the next match because there's going to be some sore heads, following this,' Jock Hunter had said to me as we watched the analysis, following a two all draw at Old Trafford.

'Aye, there'll be a few going to work tomorrow like half shut knives.' I cringed at the prospect of having to get up at around seven in the morning - like most of the lads - and head out for a nine to twelve hour shift.

Benji and myself had already taken the decision - by half time of the North London derby - that we would put off any 'business trips' until the Tuesday. Monday's normally being the key day for us going out as the pair of us have generally ended up being broke after the weekend but - to save us travelling hours around the country, hungover - one day extra wouldn't have broken the bank, we'd agreed. The rest of the boys deserved a day *off* from their employers for the effort put in towards the Muirhouse Violet cause the day before, if you'd asked me.

The only sour part of the day was by the time we reached the Milan Derby. Played a wee part in it, myself, though, like. I knew the cunts in there wouldn't have wanted to watch it. Not cultured enough, technically, when it comes to fitba. Stuck in the fucking dark ages, some of them.

'Nah, we're not wanting to watch that fucking negative shite.'

'How can you go from that end to end Man U - Liverpool game to a fucking snore-fest?'

'Fucking BOOOOOOO'

'Serie A is shite. Get it aff.'

Just some of the comments that I'd managed to absorb. There was one in particular that set me off. And don't get me wrong, I'm *always* going to listen to the other side of the story and someone else's opinion but when someone suggests that - instead of watching the Milan Derby - we have the fucking X -Factor on? Well, *that* is just taking the piss.

'So let me get this right? Instead of watching cunts like Ibrahimovic, Pirlo, Snieijder and Sammy Eto'o you want to sit and watch a bunch of fucking fannies that can't sing? Fucking grow up, eh.'

There was a few arguments that came back my way after that but I stood my ground. I was having a good time, wasn't wanting to go home but you can get fucked if you think I'm sitting watching any of that X-Factor pish.

The two Milan clubs completely had my pants down in front of everyone, though. I sat there just *wishing* them both to put on a complete display of fantasy fitba. A four four draw with sending offs and controversy. Shite goals off players arses and worldies from forty yards out.

Final score.

AC Milan - 0 Internazionale - 0

And didn't - who was left inside the boozer by full time - let me know about it, as well.

'You happy now, Euro boy?' Jock shouted over the bar to me to a ripple of laughter.

'You should've been watching and learning how to line up a defence, Jock, and maybe we'd start to move a bit up the table. When you think about it? You're all moaning about a game of fitba and the reason for that is only because two sets of defenders done their jobs given to them.'

It was a bit out of order from me, biting at Jock, like. We'd had a good day but you know what it's like when you've had a few. The Milan Derby had been brutal to watch but I wasn't admitting it to any of the others. Not after making such a song and dance about watching it in the first place.

One thing you have to admit about the Muirhouse boys, its that when they do a job of something, they put their fucking *all* into it. Most of us were still there at throwing out time, despite being in there since just after mid day.

Before leaving we'd made a severely drunken pact that we - as a team - were going to bring the Kwik Save Challenge Trophy back to Muirhouse. We'd be fucking legends. Cunts would point at us in the street when we were walking past them. Our victory still spoken of long after we've gone.

Aye, I'm sure - well seshed by then - we looked like a bunch of fitba players capable of winning such a prestigious piece of silverware, too.

The night ended with a kebab out of The Bosphorus. More of it ending up on the pavement on the walk back to Martello Court than in my mouth as I staggered my way back home.

Barry day though, from start to finish. Milan Derby, aside.

IT'S COMING HOME. IT'S COMING HOME. IT'S COMING, THE KWIK SAVE CHALLENGE TROPHY'S COMING HOME.

UP THE FUCKING VIOLET YAAAASSSSSSSS.

Chapter 26

Strings

Time is a healer, is it not? That's one of those sayings, eh? Kind of true, though, at the same time. Around a month had passed and before you know it you've forgotten all about your whole son having broken into a gangster's house and you then - by proxy - *pulled* into the whole sorry mess, shenanigans.

Not that it had been an easy first couple of weeks, by any means. Far from it. We got through them though and it was because of this which had me saying to Han that we should have a wee night out. A meal and then a few drinks somewhere, after that. About bit my hand off, when I'd asked her. She'd been in that exact same boat though, I suppose. Was probably thinking the same thing as me. We'd *all* been feeling the same pressure, collectively.

She'd had to put up with the whole gossip doing the rounds with all kinds of conspiracy theories shared regarding Jackie, and why he had remained untouched, compared to the rest of his pals. That Jackie had went off on some frenzied revenge fueled mission and killed everyone who had hospitilised his mates - and therefore remaining without so much as a hair out of place - my own personal favourite. I wasn't so bothered about all of that stuff. Just laughed it off, more or less.

It was my phone that was giving *me* the problems. The phone, my Nokia N95, itself was working fine. Nothing wrong with that, like. I kept staring at it though, for those first couple of weeks. Having unexpectedly finding myself visiting the scrapyard in Leith. Obsessively expecting it to ring and McKenna being on the other end. It was driving me up the fucking wall. *Knowing* that he was going to phone me, at some point.

After the first week to ten days, it started to ease off and I soon found myself forgetting all about it for huge chunks of the day. It gave me a huge wave of relief, the first time that I'd found myself realising that I *wasn't* thinking about it because there had been times, at the start, when I thought I would *never* get it out of my head. It was with me twenty four fucking seven.

I'd already arranged with Mikey to come and pick us up from the flat. Benji, himself, already out on the drink himself and exempt from ferrying me about, on that occasion. I don't mind giving Mikey the money though. Seems to fucking *live* in that taxi at times. Eighteen hour shifts and everything which probably can't even be legal but that's the hussle, eh? Hard game to be at.

After initial discussions through the week - when I'd asked Han about us going out - we'd decided on going to that Bay of Bengal in the city centre and then a wee walk around and try a few pubs. Already knew I'd be getting fleeced, drinking down there, but it had been an extremely good week with the puggies so we could afford it, as a wee special occasion. As a couple. No one could've said that we hadn't deserved it.

Mikey - like all self respecting taxi drivers - was there bang on time. Not a minute early and not one too late. Of course, Han wasn't ready when he gave me his usual wee 'prank call' of three rings to let me know he was outside.

'Two minutes,' she said, applying some more make up and then touching up her hair.

Two minutes my arse, I thought to myself knowing, that it was *always* going to be longer than that.

'So, you been busy tonight?' I asked Mikey once we were sitting in the back of his Skoda and on our way into the town centre.

'Fuck off!' Mikey said, laughing back, knowing *why*, specifically, I had asked him that. It hadn't been out of any interest in actually how many customers he'd had. It was due to me knowing that Mikey - having driven literally thousands of people around, as a taxi driver - was way past being tired over the standard Scottish customer to taxi driver patter.

'Awwww come on now, Mr Driver. That's not exactly a friendly tone to take with a customer. Are you not meant to be like some kind of a custodian for the council? Is that not part of you getting your Hackney where you promise not to be rude to the customers, assault them or shag them? That kind of deal?'

Han giggled away at this.

'Aye, doesn't apply when you fucking ken the customers, though' He joked back, reaching over and tapping the Hackney taxi drivers license that was clipped to one of the air vents on the dashboard.

'Aye, I know, mate. I know. So anyway, meant to ask you. What time do you finish?'

BOOM the second question out of the two that every single person setting foot into a Scottish taxi will ALWAYS ask their driver. Even if it's the only words that are uttered by them *over* the journey.

'I'll drop the fucking pair of you off here if there's anymore of your pish.' Mikey jokingly touched the brakes as if he was going to stop the car.

'Aye well, whatever time you get finished at it, better be early enough for you reporting for duty tomorrow morning. Be a tough game, against Oxgangs, like.' I said and instantly felt like I must've sounded like old Jock. Telling the players what to do in their own spare time.

'Aye, I'll be there. Don't know why I fucking bother, though. Hardly ever get any game time, despite being there week in week out.' He replied. Did have a point, though. Very rarely got a chance in the team, the boy.

'Well. Daz is going to be suspended for the semi final so Jock's going to have to have to cut his cloth accordingly and move a few players around to accommodate. You might get your chance because of it. Keep the head down, pal.' As one of the more elder statesmen of the side. I felt a wee bit more responsibility to have one to ones with some of the players, like I'd done with Daz a couple of weeks before after the Pentland match. Works wonders, like.

'Aye, you're probably right. I never thought about Daz.' He said, brightening up as he took the turn onto Victoria Street. The Indians sitting at the bottom of the street at the Grassmarket.

'You wanting picked up again later, aye?' Mikey asked as he pulled up alongside the restaurant and stopped the meter.

'Aye, not sure what time at just now though so will bell you later on. All depends on how quickly I can get Han pissed and then back to bed to have my wicked way with her, eh?' I said, knowing I'd get a bite out of her.

'Well if that's the case, Mikey, you may as well switch your phone off. He wasn't much use to me the 'last time' he was out for a drink - if you know what I mean? - so I'm not holding out much hope this time around' She joked back - unable to resist - burning me so much in return I almost had to cancel the dinner date and get Mikey to take me to A and E and then on to the burns unit. I wouldn't give it out if I couldn't take it back, though.

I paid Mikey, along with a generous 'friends' tip, and - being behind a group of four who were already in the process of entering the small premises - watched him speed off in search of another fare.

Right barry scran, in that Bay of Bengal, though. Never fails, anytime you go. A top meal. Almost needed a fucking wheelbarrow to get me out of the place after I'd squared the waiter up for the bill, though.

A tame Chicken Korma for my good lady and a Chicken Tikka Massander - every time I have it Han asks how they make the chicken green and what that does to the colour of your insides. Like, does it stick and make you green? If you cut me open I'd bleed green *anyway* so no real difference, there - along with us sharing three naan breads which, aye, pretty much meant that I ate two and she had one to herself.

It had been barry as fuck to actually enjoy a meal, like in a relaxed atmosphere, having a laugh and a bit of a chat. All of that had been the opposite of our dinner table experiences of late, back at the flat. Ice with a capital T, so they were. Jackie knowing just how not the flavor of the month he was so keeping as quiet and under everyone's radar as he could. Gone the wideo comments from him that I both equally enjoyed - as it was showing my son was growing up with some patter about him, something absolutely fucking *vital* if he was to survive in Muirhouse as a young male - as much I had to constantly monitor and review to ensure that he didn't overstep the mark.

Aye, he was a shell of the young lad from even the month before. I would bring him out of it too but wasn't in the frame of mind to approach such things, initially. Not when the feelings to *kill* him were still as strong as they were at the time.

Again, though, like I said. Time's a healer and there would be time for me to turn from bad cop to good cop. This was no case where your kid had been cheeky to a next door neighbour scenario. Was far worse than that and - as a result - the wee man was being left to stew for as long as I saw fit.

Han, was on form. *That* was what had attracted me to her - back in the day - her sense of humour. Well, that and her big tits. If I was to say otherwise about that, you'd all call me a liar, anyway. Giving me all of the gossip that she'd heard in the shop throughout the week. Brian Kirk, from Fidra Court had apparently been on that Deal or no Deal, with Noel Edmonds. The one where he's on it hasn't been shown yet, Han says, but sounds like the boy had a mare. Signing up for that type of show. It's not a case of just going down for the day and back home again. There's fucking tonnes of contestants so you've got to be prepared for being down there a while.

So Kirky apparently managed to get a place on the show. Worked it that he'd take a couple of week holiday from work and that - law of averages being taken into account - he'd have been picked to play within that timescale. Out of the twenty two contestants. Didn't work out that way for him, though. He was still there hanging around the studio like a bad smell having *still* to get his turn to come around and was now out of holidays. Boy phones his gaffer at the council and explains the position that he's still down there in England, hasn't been picked yet but whatever happens will be picked within the next week, even if they stretched it right out and made him wait until it would be mathematically impossible to be there one day further.

Gaffer knocks this back, though. Telling him that one of his colleagues already had that week booked to go to Italy so they needed him back in the office. This resulting in Kirky thinking to himself that he'd came that far by then and would be mad to walk away from it now. *Especially* with that two hundred and fifty grand prize money up for grabs. Ended up jacking his job in and staying down in England to appear on the final week, there on the show.

End result? The daft cunt had the one pence in his box, took it all the way and - at one point - was turning down some decent wedge. In the end, though, the poor cunt was left with no job with the council and not even enough money handed to him that would be enough to get him from the TV studio to the train station, never mind his journey back home, which, incidentally he had to fucking pay for.

Very rarely a man of violence, like, but if fucking Edmonds tried to give me a cheque made out for a penny it would be getting rammed right up his crinkly bottom while I ask him if he's trying to take the fucking piss.

Gerry Nicholson had been finally caught out on his disability benefits scam that he'd had on the go for a good few years. He *did* take the complete piss at times, though. Like that time the linesman injured himself that morning at Muirhouse Park and Gerry stepped in to run the line. Fucking claiming disability and he was keeping up with play better than any of the players on the pitch. Anyway, some cunt grassed him up about his false claim. Couple of DHSS undies were sent out on the case to catch him without using his walking stick. Didn't take them long. They'd watched him walking into Han's shop - complete with limp and walking stick - to buy a few things where he preceded to stop and chat with Han for a bit and get so carried away with things he completely *forgot* to lift his walking stick when he was leaving.

Fucking strolled right back out of the Co-Op without a care in the world. It was only when the two officers got out of their car to confront him that he even realised that he wasn't walking with his stick, or limp.

I swear, that's why she works there, to get the gossip first hand. The fact that she gets a wage along with it just an additional perk of the job.

Not *once* did either of us feel the need to bring up - or talk about - the whole cloud that had been hanging over us. It felt natural to be out together - just like any time before - and the easy and relaxed mood that we were left with, down there in the Grassmarket, showed that it had been a piece of 'us' time that we'd been sorely crying out. Coming at a time where it had felt like everything was getting itself into position to turn to shit.

We'd moved onto The Last Drop, just a few yards from Bay of Bengal. It wasn't so much the pub of choice as such and more really down to Han and myself being that stuffed from the Indian that we didn't have much walking in us. Aye so what if we were going to get charged for drinks as if we'd flown in from Wisconsin for a weeks holiday in Scotland and didn't have a clue the value of Scottish notes - as is the case down there in the Grassmarket - but when the money is coming directly from 'The Lucky Chicken Amusement Arcade' sometimes you just have to treat yourself to some overpriced booze.

Han was already a wee bit on the way - drink wise - by the time we left the Indians. She's an ok drunk, though. You know how some can be once they get a a couple of peaves into them? She's quite a daft one out of all the different types of drunks. Depressive one, violent ones, overconfident smart arse ones and so on. Han was more of a daft one although - it has to be said - not *without* her occasional violent flare up, mind. We *all* have our 'moments' with the drink, to be fair. Han, generally, though? Up for a laugh and doing silly things that - due to the lack of inhibitions - you'd never catch her in a decade's worth of Julember the 45ths.

Despite it being a Saturday night and town being on the busy side, we managed to get a nice cosy wee table for two looking back out onto the street. Sitting together just chatting, alongside remarking about some of the 'specimens' that were passing by on the street, in a people watching sense. Some cunts in the city centre of Edinburgh really do make it too easy. I suppose all cities can say the same, though.

Rather than sit in there, and then move on somewhere else, as had been the original plan. We ended up getting cosy where we were and after having a couple of glasses of wine - something I would rather be castrated with a rusty spoon than do in The Gunner - and getting a taste for this nice wee tempting Chilean Cabarnet, we decided just to stop the fucking about and bought a bottle for to stick on the table. By the time we got ourselves half way through *that* it would've been about right to offer an estimation that the pair of us were 'wobbling.'

I was in the middle of telling her the story about Mr Benn turning up to shag a granny when I - remembering that I'd been putting it off for ages - quickly nipped away to the toilets. Could still hear the sound of Han's laughing behind me as I headed towards the gents.

The pokey wee bathroom was empty so I managed to get a quick pee and go to wash my hands, to get back to my good lady wife, when who walks into the toilets but Boney Boyd. I was crouched over the sink washing my hands and just turned to look at who was coming in, natural reaction, eh? From the look on his face, as soon as he walked through the door and set eyes on me. I knew there was going to be a problem.

'Oh aye, it's the father of the wee fucking rat grass.' He said, looking me up and down like I was a piece of shite.

'Fuck's that meant to mean?' I said, taking my wet hands out of the sink and - without taking an eye off of him at any point - moved towards the yellow Dyson hand drier.

'I think you know *exactly* what I mean so don't try to play the ignorant cunt with me, Strings.' He said, confidently, as if there was no debate to be had which - from his perspective and fuck knows what he'd dreamed up - there probably wasn't one.

'Nah, pal, you'll need to enlighten me.' I said as I shoved both hands inside the futuristic style hand drier that sounds louder than a Harrier Jump-Jet when it kicks in but by fuck, fairly does the job of drying your hands. He had attempted to respond to me but as soon as the hand dryer started blasting, he knew there was no point in competing with it. Only one winner, there, and it wasn't going to be him.

'My wee brother, Flav and Scooter. All ending up in hospital, for doing a house. Aye, I *know* about the break in, by the way, and while the other boys have been scared shitless into saying nothing to anyone, including their parents. Wee Dynamo told me all about it, though. Fucking asked me to help fence the gear that he'd stolen. Your Jack, also does the house and yet? Well you can see where I'm going with that. Fucking obvious as fuck that he grassed on the other three to save his own skin. No point even trying to pretend it's not. Fucking obvious, *well* blatant, ya cunt. And as for what happened to my dad? Fucking well out of order.'

Someone else tried to come into the bathrooms but with Boney not having actually taken much in the way of steps further, once he'd seen me, in addition to the hostile stance that he appeared to be taking. The guy turned around and sacked his idea of coming into the mens, altogether.

'You need to watch what you say with talk like that, Boney. Accusations, like, you know? You don't know the fucking half of all of what is going on, and neither does your wee brother. So fucking watch it with the grass talk. The Carsons aren't grasses, alright?' My hands now completely dry. I was now ready to leave and go back and join Han.

'I'll accuse who the fuck I want. Ken what they say about snitches, eh?' He took a couple of steps forward to meet me.

'You fucking threatening my kid?' I shouted. The simplest of thoughts, in that area, sending me off on one. He wasn't someone that I'd have *chosen* to get into things with but when kids get brought into it. That can alter a situation, rapidly.

I was about ready to go for him while he looked like he was ready for it right there in the bogs when the door opened again. This time, the boy coming in.

'OH, OHHHH Boney? What the fuck's going on here?' This cunt - who appeared to be out along with Dynamo's brother - decided to act first *then* ask questions second by grabbing hold of Boney's two arms and pulling him a couple of steps back from me.

'No hassle, here, mate. We were just having a wee blether. My son knows his wee brother.' I said trying to cool things down.

'Aye, tell wee Jackie I was asking for him, Strings, eh. Say to him that that I'll catch up with him soon, my man.' Boney said confidently and with a bit of menace behind it. With two of them there - and me being given a few seconds to breathe again and be in better shape for making rational decisions - I knew that there was no point in reacting and instead, left the two of them standing there.

I wasn't sure if it was just by chance or not but my feelings were that when we left the pub - and with Mikey already on his way to pick us both up - Boney just happened to 'engineer' it that him and his three pals all left at the exact same time as us. Walking right behind Han and me, as if the moment they'd seen us getting our coats on they were then ready to leave as a result.

We'd left a few minutes earlier before Mikey was scheduled to arrive so that I could get a quick smoke before going into the - friends or not - smoke free zone of his Edinburgh City Council approved chariot.

As we stood on the side of the road. Me enjoying the nicotine hit while Han stood there trying to move her legs and arms to keep her from shivering. Having went with the classic move of wearing what looked good and to fuck with practical, only to pay for it at the end of the night. The part where nobody gives a flying fuck *what* you look like by then.

'Grass'

It was really softly said, like. As in it had been an intentional whisper but a whisper intended for to be loud enough for anyone around us to be heard.

It had come from Boney right as his group of four left the pub and were passing us to go back up towards the top of Victoria Street. The 'sensible' thing would have been to just let it go. There was four of them and - when it came to Boney Boyd - one of them would've probably been enough. You can't go letting people call you, or your direct friends and family, a grass, though. Not when it isn't fucking true, anyway.

'No cunt calls my son a fucking grass.' I said, flicking what was left of my cigarette in the direction of the backs of the four of them. The Embassy hitting the heel of Boney's trainer, causing a mini explosion around his foot and the thud of it against him making him turn around.

'What was that? Who said Jack was a grass? Him? One of them?' The second I'd said the word grass. Han's ears pricked up like a dog when you say that W word to them.

'Did you call my son a fucking grass?' She shouted after Boney, who had now stopped walking away - as did his pals - and was standing there looking back at us.

'Hey, not my fault if you and the rest of your family can't look in the mirror and are in denial. I probably would be the same if my brother did that. Bit embarrassing, like. ' He sneered, from a distance.

All the things that I could *but* - in reality - couldn't say to him at that. That 'his' brother had coughed up Jack's name in a second and, in fact, had tried to pin the blame of all the valuables being stolen on. Aye, no honour amongst thieves, eh?

I couldn't say any of that, though. Stuff that would've shut his fucking mouth right up. Not without incriminating myself, anyway. I still had to front things up though. When grass accusations get thrown around if you *don't* react? Well, what does that say, in itself?

'NO, JOEEE,' Han shouted after me when she realised that I was going up to the four of them. You know the score. The four of them - having had a few ales - no doubt Boney sitting there filling their head's full of all kinds of lies, were stood there all ready for anything if it kicked off. I was wanting fuck all to kick off but *still* make my point, as well as showing I wasn't backing down from *any* of the cunts.

This caused a wee bit of a scuffle. A few elbows and headbutts thrown, accidentally on purpose, in amongst it. As is sometimes what's required in a case like that. You need the calming influence of the opposite sex to take care of all that testosterone. We got that, through Han. Although I wouldn't go as far as to say that it was done by deploying a 'calming influence' on us, to put a stop to the handbags.

'RIIIGGGHHHTTT, YOU GET TAE FUCK, JOE.' She grabbed hold of me, in the middle of being right in the face of one of Boney's pals who had given me a sly boot in the shin when I was arguing with Boney.

'Give me your lighter, she demanded while I stood out of reach from the four of them, who were all jeering and laughing at me, on account that my woman was shoving me around and - apparently - taking charge of things.

I'd actually thought of it at the time - that she had given up smoking earlier on in the year - but with all that was going on, right there. I never really thought to ask her *why* she wanted my lighter, until I'd actually handed it over. Even if she was deciding to fall off the wagon. It was hardly a fucking choice time to be sparking one up.

'Can see who wears the fucking trousers in your house, eh.' Boney bounced about the street, pissing himself laughing and pointing at me.

'What you wanting with my lighter, Han?' I asked her, while I saw her reaching into her bag. Had she been packing cigarettes all this time and sneaking a fly one now and again, unable to admit to her hubby that she'd been smoking? No, instead of pulling out a packet of reeks, she produced her tin of hairspray.

'BECAUSE I'M GOING TO SET FIRE TO THIS CUNT'S FUCKING FACE.' She screamed - with such ferocity and her cadence displaying this, near the end of the sentence - at Boney, while holding my clipper and her extra long tin of Insette.

Aye, *that* fucking wiped the smiled from his face and turned him from a jack in a box to a statue.

'Woah woah woah, no wanting any trouble, like,' he said, backing a couple of steps away. The first of him looking in any way diplomatic, throughout any of this.

'WELL TROUBLE'S WHAT YOU FUCKING GET WHEN YOU CALL MY WEE JACKIE A GRASS'

She shouted back at him. Now I'm not sure if she categorically 'knew' that they were far away enough from her or not - my guess is that she doesn't go around using her tins of hairspray as weapons so was less than skilled and not exactly tried and tested - but rather than issue the 'crazy lady' threat of setting fire to them all with her aerosol. She went fully in and clicked the lighter wheel right as she sprayed a blast of Insette (Extra Hold) into the night air and - quite literally - set fire to it.

The blast of yellow flame, ending maybe a metre or so away from the four of them.

'IMMA FIRESTARTAH TWISTED FIRESTARTAH' Han screamed across at them.

'WANT TO FIND OUT JUST HOW MUCH?' She followed up, trying to get her point across. As if the gesture of spraying as much fire into the Edinburgh night sky as she could hadn't already made some kind of a definitive point, already.

'THAT BIRD OF YOURS IS FUCKING MENTAL. YOU NEED TO GET HER FUCKING SECTIONED.'

Boney shouted across in my direction but what she had just done - momentarily at least - had completed out-cunted them. It was enough to buy us time for to get our way out of the situation.

Mikey had actually turned the corner just in time to see Han lighting up The Grassmarket with her hairspray. Telling us that for a split second he'd been fooled into thinking that it was festival time again in the city. That she'd been some street performer, or something. One of those fire breathers, like. Something that wouldn't exactly be out of place during the festival in the middle of the city centre.

'Aye, she's a street performer alright, Mikey. Right wee twisted firestarter' I said looking to her, referring to The Prodigy line she had so manically shouted out as if she'd been Keith Flint himself, and shaking my head in amazement over the theatrics that had came from her.

Now that the moment had passed and the adrenaline had started to dip. I was able to catch the small mischievous smile that was on her face, every time we passed a street light. Intermittently streaming flashes of light into the taxi as we headed back to the Naughty North.

Chapter 27

DCI Galbraith

'Alright, mucker. How's tricks and aw that?' His voice, enough for me to get up out of my chair and go and close my office door, before taking my seat again. In fact, so on edge the voice had actually put me at. I went for a pace around my office floor - while talking to him - *before* I was relatively at calm and enough to sit down again.

'You shouldn't be calling me on this number, *any* number at all. Our business was completed and we went our separate ways, remember.' I urged him but - despite being the one talking from within the walls of a police station - severely lacked in the authority that I should've had behind me.

'Aye, aye, aye, I know Dee See Eye Galbraith but when you've got pictures of one of Strathclyde's most awarded inspectors getting a blow job from a fifteen year old. Sometimes the temptation to exploit that can sometimes prove to be too much to resist. Tell you what, Roy, this'll be the last time, Scout's promise.' I didn't really have much of a choice and his cocky tone let me know that he *knew* it.

'It's just a wee plate check I need you to do for me, Roy. Nothing that you can't do from the comfort of your desk. No need to get that fat arse of yours up on my account. Just need you to check a reg and come up with an address for me.

'It's not as easy as that, though. If I get caught checking a car that is nothing to do with any of my own investigations I'll have the internals all over me. They're already cracking down around the force. One of my colleagues got sacked last week for accepting a couple of pornos from a corner shop in Stepps. We're all having to be on our best, mate. Best behaviour, you know?' I tried to at least put him off. Give him an inside view into that it wasn't just a case of doing as we pleased in the force. Well, not without things catching up with you, eventually.

'*Exactly*, DCI Galbraith.' I always felt that he made a point of always saying my name during any phone calls between us just in case the

at, for absolutely zero fucking pence *including* V.A.T,
ers family or not. Steal from me and I'll treat you like one
mob,' from across the city.

t right for a kick off.' Benzo had said, as he looked at the
as counted out in front of him on the table in our office
ack.

e get from the Fantasy Island machine alone on a daily
than what I've just counted out.' He said, looking up at
going to be the one who was going to be able to give the
r when - obviously - I'd just found out about the very
all of income lying there in front of me.

ur old Auntie through - who very generously volunteers
the change desk three days a week for the fraction of
d to pay anyone else - to ask a few questions as we
wn investigation into where the money had went to.

? That one with the palm trees on the front of it?' She'd
work out which machine we'd asked her about and
ey had come out of it.

barely anything came out of it when I emptied it. I
you had maybe emptied it the day or two before
normally almost puts ma back out when I go to lift
y.'

knew we'd been hit.

ouple of days where the weather was shite and not
y of day trippers around the place. We'd still be
nner upwards out of the machine.

let things lie if someone had nabbed five hunner of
cally?

d kill the dirty thieving bandit robbing, bandit, was
So serious I was, I cancelled my spray tan booking -
Coast of Scotland not exactly what you would call
complexion - that I had arranged for that afternoon
ped it for an afternoon of sifting through hours and

call was being recorded. 'Now just imagine what they'd be like over an inspector shagging a minor, in his work's car, if *that's* their reaction to another officer only borrowing a couple of pornos to watch in his house?' He countered, smug as you like.

'Ok, give me it then.' I sighed, wanting him off the phone and knowing that wasn't going to happen without me either helping him or - not for the first time - issuing me with a threat that the photos of me and the girl in my car would be dropped off at the reception to the station.

'Awww, ma man! Fucking knew you wouldn't let me down. You're a pure toff.' He said cheerily.

Right, you ready? It's **L for Lime - P for Parrot - five - seven - R for Rab - S for Snake and I for Itchy**. You got that?' I had already typed it out onto my keyboard by the time that he was asking the question.

'Ok, give me a second and I'll have it for you.' I told him, putting the phone down on the desk for a moment. In no way wishing to engage in any kind of small talk. He hadn't appeared to have even noticed this as when I picked the phone up and put it to my ear he was saying something about how the police should be happy that men like him took matters into their own hands and - by extension - meant that he was making our job easier.

'Ok, you got a pen?' I asked. There was always the possibility that anyone could have knocked on my door and came in for all sorts of reasons and, because of that, I wanted him off the line again, a-sap.

Preferably, though, he wouldn't call at all.

'Aye, Roy, on ye go.' He affirmed.

'Ok, it's a white Seat Ibiza and is registered to a Joseph Carson in Edinburgh.' I confirmed.

'Annnnnnnd, the address, DCI Galbraith.' He prompted.

'49 Martello Court, Muirhouse, Edinburgh, EH4 4SG'

'See, that wasn't exactly what you would call, taxing, was it?' He laughed.

'Until the next time we speak. It's been an absolute pleasure. Ta ta for now.'

I was in the middle of trying to tell him that there wouldn't *be* a next time when he had already hung up.

I pitied Joesph Carson - whoever he was - over whatever was coming his way.

As cold as it all might've sounded, though. Looking at the man's postcode and area of Scotland he resided. I only gave him a passing thought as, at the end of the day. He was going to be Lothians and Borders mop up to deal with.

Chapter 28

Lloyd 'Hendo' Hende

If there's one thing that I CA - apart from peados, terrori they can come into one of r anything. The kiddy fiddle taking money from my pocl

And I'm not giving a shiny can believe that as well. whether it's a Findus crisp fucking jot. You're going stick.

And you know what the Well you *especially* don' Henderson - Copeland twenty years - with sti sometimes, others have than just a sharp stick to

I *knew* it was those twc my wee brother - were - out of the four we ow look into things.

The pair of them had standing having a tal Normally I'd have p arcades for as long i radar for any thievinf

No doubt, it had be about Rangers that talk with a fellow be all about, eh?

Tell you wh though. Rang of that 'other

'Well this isn money that v through the b

'The money v basis is more me as if I was cunt an answ obvious short!

After getting o to work behin what we'd ne launched our o

'Fantasy Island asked, trying t how much mor

'Oh there was thought one of because that on the sack of mon

That's when we l

Even on a bad much in the w emptying five hu

Would 'you' just your hard earnec

Operation find a swiftly launched. life on the West conducive to one and, instead, swa

hours worth of CCTV tapes from inside the arcade, of the day in question where the dosh went walkabouts.

Now, understandably, any staff member would have had no option other than the finger of suspicion to hover over them. When something like money goes missing. Can almost be like one of those 'whodunnits' you get on the telly. *Not* when it came to our auld auntie, though. Not a chance that she would've stolen from me and Benzo, so that wasn't even considered as a consideration. It helped narrow things down, I suppose.

All I had to do was keep watching the footage from the camera that was facing in the direction of our Fantasy Island machine. See if I could spot any irregularities, so to speak. Fucking hell, was it boring. It had been a struggle to keep awake, at times. Almost hypnotic, to watch someone repeatedly put coins into a machine. Would put anyone to sleep, that kind of a gig.

Couldn't skim over things by fast forwarding through the day's tapes. Doing that would've defeated the whole purpose. It was probably going to be the smallest of tells that I'd pick up, if anything. There could be no skimming.

I have to admit. As abhorrent as someone stealing from me is. You almost have to *admire* the remarkable set of balls of someone to come into one of my places of business and do something like that, and not get caught in the act. Because of that, I knew that whoever the fuck it had been, in sat at the bandit, had been professionals. Professional wankers, at least, that one, a guarantee. I very well might have been wasting hours of my day because they might have been *so* good that there wasn't even going to be a trace of their craftwork left by them.

The second I saw him in the shell suit and the other in the blue home top walking in - and still a wee bit before they actually sat down at Fantasy Island - I fucking *knew* that it was to do with them. You know that feeling that you get in the gut sometimes over something and even without any kind of reasoning you just seem to *know*.

I hadn't seen any of them sitting at the specific fruit machine that I was fixed on when I'd been at the arcade. They were already moved onto a different one when Benzo and me popped in to see Vera that day. I didn't need to. Before I even seen them set up camp around that Fantasy Island - and at least confirm that they'd actually *sat* at the machine - I *knew* they'd sat there.

They hadn't reacted in the way that the Rangers Family normally do whenever they come across each other - wherever that might be, - Larkhall to Lagos, Belfast to Buenos Aires or even Dundee to Hamilton. Normally, despite having never met before, you'll usually find each other greeting fellow bear like some long lost brother. Those two weren't like that and - as a matter of fact - it didn't take me long to remember the quick exit the pair of them had made, soon after Benzo and I had arrived.

When it came to them at the machine and playing. It wasn't really a case of what you could see, more of what you *couldn't*.

At the two machines that they had sat at during their time in there. Both times - before actually starting to play - the one with the home top on had made a point of looking around to see exactly where the CCTV camera was situated and once he clocked it. You seen him looking straight at the camera at the moment where he finds what he's looking for. Once he saw where it was, he then directed his pal - in the shell suit - to adjust his chair and sit beside him. His mate, who never put a single coin in a machine the whole time he was in there, would intermittently look around and scan the arcade while the other one carried on playing.

Textbook stringing tactic.

One does the robbing. The assistant keeps an eye out to ensure the other one doesn't get caught. You can't have one without the other. You can *try* but without a spotter, you won't get very far. Now in a criminal court of law. The tapes, themselves, weren't going to prove a single fucking thing in terms of evidence. The way that they had purposely positioned themselves for the camera? The two of them were pros and had made it impossible to pick out any substantial proof that they had been stealing from the two fruit machines that they'd sat at. Aye and neither had I just sailed up the fucking River Clyde, either. As good as they might have *thought* that they had covered up their tracks? Well it was a case of close but no Castella, ya pair of salt and sauce wanks.

Took a bit of tracking down, the East Coasters, mind. All we had, when it came to footage of the bastards, had been them walking out of the arcade a few minutes after Benzo and me had arrived there. I'd been able to see that when they'd exited they'd went to the left - to go down the street - before going out of view of the camera, covering the doorway.

I should be in the fucking police, I tell you. With them taking a left to go along Harbour Street. I took a wee punt that they were maybe heading off in the direction of the carpark opposite The Harbour Bar. This being through the combination of one of them saying that they were having to head back home and there not exactly being much of the way in parking *apart* from the car park in that area. Was nothing more than a punt but I headed along to the bar to talk with Tam Moffat, the owner.

Obviously, the big man was only too happy to have a wee look at his security cameras which faced out onto the street. Maybe I watch too many of those Hollywood films - police ones where they're always trying to track down the bad guys and have only the smallest of clues to go by - but my own personal thoughts were that if the two East Coasters had headed off in that direction then Tam's cameras would've picked them up. Hardly unnoticeable, the two of them. Wasn't like it was a match day in Govan or fuck all, was it?

Not only did Tam's security camera pick them up but were also able to show them getting into their car. The positioning of the cameras so perfect, in fact, that it was head on with the car as it drove out of the car park and back out onto Harbour Street.

With Tam pausing the video long enough for me to scribble the reggie number down and me taking the most gracious decision to let him off with his weeks 'insurance money' that he was going to be due Benzo and me in a few days time. It was never going to exactly be what you'd class as a challenge to track them down from there on in.

One phone call in to my man on the inside - the always ready to assist, DCI Royston Galbraith - and I had all the information I needed.

Those salt and sauce robbing bastards would be getting a visit soon and the cunts wouldn't be needing much in the way of salt and or fucking sauce.

You don't need condiments when you've already *had* your chips.

Chapter 29

Strings

'Ahhh Joseph, hombre. Como esta?'

McKenna asked, in what was a short - and not so sweet - voicemail he'd left on my phone for me. Let's face it. The call was *always* going to come. As each day passed, though. I started to forget about it. While that was fucking barry for things like my sanity and marriage, to rattle off a couple of things. It didn't actually change the fact that McKenna was always going to be putting in that call to me to say 'Mind that time I didn't put your son into the hossie after breaking into my house? Well it's time to make up for it.'

Or something to that effect.

His, instead, was a very cryptic.

'I want to see you down at the scrapyard 'immediately.' I have a job that I need you to do for me. Don't make me have to send Peter and Budsy out to find you, now.'

The line going dead straight after.

Here we fucking go then, I thought to myself. If anything, it would've been some light relief to get the chance to clean the slate with McKenna, although that's the thing with gangsters and their pockets. Once you go into them, they make it *extremely* hard for you to get back out again. In a way, I was almost relieved that I was finally being given the opportunity of removing the dark cloud that was hanging over not just myself but the rest of the family's heads. Whether we pretended - and had pushed it away into the subconsciousness - that it wasn't there or not.

Then again. I didn't know what *exactly* it was that McKenna had in mind for me.

Chapter 30

Jack

'SOON AS AH CAN FUCKING WALK I'LL BE COMING LOOKING FOR YOU, YA FUCKING GRASSING BASTARD. FUCKING SNAKE'

My visit to see Dynamo hadn't exactly went as I'd imagined that it would go. Unlike Flav and Scooter's mum and dad. Dynamo's had been happy enough to let me in. Or maybe the better way to put it would be that they - well, his mum as the dad wasn't around - had been happy to let me in but not exactly happy to see 'me.' Happier than their son, though. Much happier.

I'd went around to see him with the best of intentions. Obviously, had I thought that he was going to react to my visit in the way that he would then I wouldn't have bothered going in the first place.

The past couple of weeks had been absolute shan as fuck. Take *any* time that your mum and dad have ever been pissed off at you and you can multiply it by any fucking number that you want and you wouldn't have came anywhere near close to rivaling the levels of anger and hostility that mum and dad were bringing. That saying about not crying over spilled milk or something like that? Well the pair of them were *still* crying a long, long, time after the milk had dried. Or, at least, I *thought* it had dried.

I just tried to keep myself to myself and out of the firing line as good as I could but it's not easy. Hardly like we live in a mansion with different wings in it that we could all sit in and avoid each other, is it?

As a kid, there are definitely those times though where you kind of 'get' the sense that you've went too far with something, simply by the reaction you receive from your parents. Just a certain look or a turn of phrase that they'll come out with that lets you know that you messed up.

This was different from any of those other times. It would always make me feel like the worst son in the world, any time that mum or dad would tell me that they weren't angry, just disappointed. Following the break in - of who I would go on to learn to be the house of some gangster - they somehow managed to transfer over the feelings of both anger *and* disappointment. It's not exactly that cool when you're on the other end of it all. Even if I *did* deserve it.

That time my primary school team lost that summer challenge trophy cup final against Tollcross Primary. When I completely fresh aired an attempt at a clearance and it fell right to their player, who scored and won the match for them. Felt well sorry for myself that day because I knew that it had been my fault that we'd lost the game. On the way back home. Dad had told me about that how losing can turn out to be a good thing. Didn't quite see it that way at the time, myself.

'When you lose, don't lose the lesson.' He said, trying to make out that he was coming out with that from his own mind but you could tell that he was just quoting someone famous.

When you've got a whole set of team mates - and their families - all giving you daggers and calling you names under their breath when you're collecting your losers medal, you don't need any reminding on what it felt like to lose.

'What? Don't lose the lesson not to fresh air a football right in front of your own goal? Check, dad. I'll remind myself of that in the future.' I'd replied back to him feeling sorry for myself even though I could see that he was only trying to help me feel better about things.

Well it felt like the same applied with the present day. When you break into some scary bastard that puts all of your mates in hospital, don't lose the lesson. And there were *plenty* of them to be taking on board, no doubt.

If it had been just the case of things being on the iffy side. I might've been able to handle it all a bit better. It wasn't, though. Outside the house wasn't much better, either. While cunts weren't saying it straight to my face I knew they were talking about everyone else landing in hospital - with proper dull ones - while I was walking around without a scratch on me.

It was confusing as fuck. You had people thinking I'm a grass while the reality of it was that I was going through a mini hell, consumed with guilt, *because* I had escaped the same punishment as Flav, Scooter and Dynamo. Obviously, I wasn't much on board with receiving some of what they'd been handed out to them but, at the same time. I kind of felt that I *deserved* it. Didn't seem fair that they all got a slap - well, a wee bit more than that, you'd have to concede - and I never.

Not that I'd been given any choice in any of it. Once dad got involved it was all taken out of my hands and there hadn't been a single day that dad had let me forget it either at some point or other.

Lucky if I don't end up with the doctor giving me some of that Prozac stuff that he'd given to Flav's mum that winter when she'd started to get depressed when the dark nights started to come in, I thought.

Since Dynamo had come up with the idea of doing the Silverknowes house it had been just one long line of worry after worry.

About breaking into the house - being caught afterwards - friends starting to drop like flies in connection to it - dad ending up involved and having to work for a gangster - people thinking I'm a grass. The list went on.

Fourteen year olds should be worried about shite like not having their homework done in time, how to finger a girl properly and what their ranking is on Call of Duty. Not all of the other stuff listed.

School had been a case of arriving - getting through my lessons - and home again, even if I'd have rather went anywhere else at the end of the work day. With Flav, Scooter and Dynamo all off on 'long term sick' I didn't have much in the way of other mates to hang around with there at Craigroyston High. Replacements to speak to? It's funny how those options begin to drop like shite from a shovel when your *existing* pals have all started to fall by fairly seriously looking mischiefs. Cunts will be calling me The Black Scorpion next, I thought to myself when I tried to go up to speak to Stevie Blackley and Luke Wilson at dinner time that day and they looked like they'd come face to face with fucking Hitler.

A completely blackballed black sheep, like. I kind of had fooled myself into thinking that once mum and dad had found out - and we'd dealt with the whole intense as fuck reaction to it that they'd both had - that things would then get better, but it wasn't feeling that way.

They'd been careful about what they were saying in front of me but I'd been able to pick up enough to know that I'd put dad in a bit of a sticky situation. The fact mum was crying about it told me all I needed to because mum hardly ever cried. I've seen her crying more over stuff that's happened on the telly - in her soaps - than in actual real life when it comes to her family, and that. I could see how scared she was over dad having to do a favour for the guy whose house we'd broken into. Even when dad was trying to calm mum down by telling her that it would be fine. I could see that it was one of those 'it'll be fines' where the person saying it doesn't *actually* know that it's going to be or not.

The best policy to take for myself was to act like a dug that's taken a shite on the new carpet then rubbed its dirty smelly arse along the ground to clean it and has now found itself in the bad books of its owners. That being, to just remove yourself from the situation and hope that, eventually, everyone would be ok with the mess that you'd made.

Of course, it would've been far, far, more easier to do had my dad not sold my X-box. He'd been like the boy who cried wolf when it came to selling any of the consoles I'd had, when I'd been acting the fanny.

'Any more of your pish and I'll be selling that video games machine of yours.' He'd say.

Never, ever, sold it, though. So this time around, when I came home from school and found out that he actually HAD sold it. Proudly had the receipt from Cash Generator stuck to the fridge and directed me there to look at it when I'd come running down the stairs after school, asking where my X-box was.

'Fucking telt you, Jackie. Maybe this time you'll actually *take* a telling, son.' He'd said with half an eye on me and the other half on the racing on the telly while I was stood there with the receipt in my hand trying to get my head around this new reality.

Wanted to lose the plot at him but what really could I say? I was hardly in any kind of a bargaining position.

'Now there's one thing you can't say about your dad and that it's that he's not a fair person.' He said, pointing at the receipt in my hand.

When the person who is responsible for selling your games console, without your approval. When they bring up the subject of them being a fair person. Well, you can see how hard it can be to take them at their word?

'The money that I got for your X-box will get put aside and *if* me and Han see an improvement in your behaviour and attitude and that you keep yourself out of trouble, *then* it'll go towards a new one for you a bit down the line but, and it's an awfy big but, here. You're way deep in the middle of the forest with no compass and no way of seeing sunlight to guide yourself back out of it, in terms of you showing us how sorry you are over all of this. And it goes without saying. You go nowhere near any of those pals of yours.'

What twisted sick bastard would dangle the possibility of getting you another X-box, on the *same day* as they'd sold your other one? My dad, that's who. And it worked as well. The thought of no X-box absolutely terrified me so, naturally, the prospect of *any* kind of scenario which would see one sat taking pride of place in my bedroom again was one that I was *always* going to be interested in investigating.

I already knew that I was going to miss winding up the Americans on X-box live. The Arkansas Young Team as Flav had described them as in *any* mouthy American that he came across and ended up having a wee mini personal battle with on Call of Duty multiplayer. Not like me or Flav are grown up adults, like, but some of those Americans that you come across on there, they sound like they're about eight year old while sitting there talking like they're hard as fuck. Meanwhile you've got cunts like Flav and me ripping the absolute shite out of them, with both patter *and* bullets.

Half the time they can't understand what you're talking about though, like. Because of the Scots accent, and that. Couple of weeks before dad had sold it I'd ended up having a carry on with this yank, think it was on the Shipment map, not sure now, like. Anyway this wee bastard was camped up in a spot and kept killing me. Time and time again, without ever having to move. Got personal after that. He kept slagging me and laughing, each time he picked me off.

'I am the greatest. Step to me and I'll whoop your ass, boy.' He said in that daft fucking accent. Eventually I sacked trying to achieve anything else, inside the death match. I just wanted to kill 'him.' Even if it was just the once, to get him re-spawning and out from that wee spot he was hiding in.

'YASSSSS GET IT RIGHT UP YOU, YA LITTLE CAMPING CUNT'

I shouted into my mic, the moment that I 'finally' did stick one in his head. Next thing I heard.

'Excuse me, just who in the hell do you think you are talking to?' This woman's voice - in an American accent - came through the headphones.

Not the wee bastard that was trying to come the cunt with me for the past seven minutes, anyway, I thought to myself. A wee bit surprised by this development.

'The wee camping dick that's never moved a muscle since the game started. There's words for people like that.' I replied, while carrying on with the game. Once again, going looking for the American who had got under my skin so much.

'What accent is that? I can't make out a word that you're saying.'

By this time I'd managed to find him again on the map. Predictably, like most campers, scurrying back to his wee hidey-hole to do it all over again. Putting a round into his back before he even got a chance to set up shop. By now I'd kind of sussed out that this woman was his mum, auntie or something.

'Oh dear, looks like I just killed your kid.' I said, on the wind up, but she was already in the middle of her rant.

'I may not be able to understand you with that weird accent all the way down in Australia but I can still understand when someone is calling my Tyler a cunt and I WON'T STAND FOR IT. I'm going to report you and have you thrown off X-box, Australia boy.'

Fucking Australia?

I admit, an adult losing their shit at me in such a way might not have been as funny if I'd been in the same room as them but from thousands of miles away, it was funny as fuck.

'HEY,' I shouted back at her. 'Your *Tyler* is the one that's sitting there telling me that he's going to do all kinds of stuff to 'my ass.' What is it with you Americans and your insults? Always involving something sexual, eh?'

'NOW LISTEN UP YOU LITTLE KANGAROO COCK SUCKING MOTHERFUCKING LITTLE SHIT. I'LL FLY TO AUSTRALIA AND TRACK YOU DOWN AND MAKE YOU WISH THAT YOU'D NEVER BEEN FUCKING BORN.'

By this time the game had ended and it was going through the scoreboard. I'd ended up second bottom but that was all down to this wee American dick and nothing else. I knew there wasn't going to be much more time before the conversation cut us all off, anyway.

'Aye, well I'll make it nice and easy for you, eh. Ramsey Street in Erinsborough, second name Kennedy, first name, Carl only it's DOCTOR to you. That should narrow it down a bit. I'll throw some shrimp on the barbie for you coming down.'

That was the last of things before we were cut off and I was taken back to the lobby. Can you believe that I, *me*, got reported as well? Thought I was going to get a ban but got mum to word it for Microsoft in a way that let them know that an adult had been giving me abuse and that they should monitor things like that better. That an adult threatening to harm a fourteen year old was well dodgy. How the fuck were they going to ban me after that? Would've been funny if that boy Tyler copped one though. Aye, I was going to miss that stuff and - also being without anyone in the way of pals to hang around with - without an X-box, what was I going to be left with? The TV? Dad had told me that I should read some books instead. As if, dad.

You really don't need telly when you stay in Muirhouse. Better things happening outside your door than there is on Sky, half of the time. Dad sent me to the shop for fags for him last week and inside the short walk there and back to get them. I managed to see a policeman chasing some boy into Birnies Court and then about thirty seconds later the *same* policeman coming running *back* out again. Chased by about half a dozen of the residents. *That* was on the way there to the shop.

Coming back, I could see a crowd, made up of around a dozen or so, all looking up to the top of my own tower block. I thought maybe someone was going to jump off and kill themselves as that had happened a few times before at Martello Court. When I got closer to them, though, I could see that they were all laughing and shouting up at someone at the top who was looking down at everyone.

'What's going on, like?' I asked wee Craigey Simpson who stayed a couple of floors down from us.

'We stole this bag from the back of a car that was parked outside the doctors surgery and when we went through it we found a fucking parachute inside. Mad as fuck, eh? We dared Jim McKeown to jump with it on. Think he's going to bottle it, though. He's been up there on the ledge for ten minutes now.' Craigey said, pointing up at McKeown. Standing on the ledge with what looked like a big rucksack around his back.

'JUMP JUMP JUMP JUMP JUMP JUMP JUMP'

Everyone shouted up with fist pumps in the air. Fuck, even I joined in. Why would you 'not' want to see a scheme radge - with no parachute training whatsoever - jump from the highest tower block that the city of Edinburgh could boast? Still no jump from him though. That's when the chicken noises started to follow.

'AWRIGHT AWRIGHT, AH'M DAEN IT AH'M DAEN IT'

Jim McKeown shouted down to everyone and - without any kind of hesitation - just went for it. There was that one second where once he'd jumped, and the parachute hadn't opened, you thought that he was a goner but around a second later it unfurled up over him. Not that he'd remotely given himself enough distance to get from A to B while using a parachute to break his fall though, obviously.

All the parachute had managed to do was pretty much stop him from, like, dying. Never stopped him from going feet first into the sunroof of some poor bastard's Ford Focus and getting stuck. The alarm going off straight away, sending everyone - me included - running off in all directions. Leaving McKeown floundering inside the car with a massive parachute covering him, the car and the immediate area. Meanwhile, Jim was screaming about how he's broken his legs. I'd have given him a hand - to try and get out before he got caught - but going back late with dad's fags and telling him 'why' I was late was only ever going to result in a whole lot of grief over him not believing me (why would he believe a story like that?) up until he then heard that it *had* actually happened.

Not being worth the hassle. McKeown was left to sort himself out.

All of that stuff is better when you've got pals to hang around and see it with, though.

It had been the guilt which had led to me visiting Dynamo more than it had been as a 'pal.' I really didn't need mum and dad to tell me that I couldn't hang around with him anymore. The break in changed *all* of that, anyway. Even if none of us had been put in hospital or caught over it. My attitude towards being 'mates' with him had shifted, but without there being any kind of a major falling out. When my dad told me though - about Dynamo - that when he'd been snatched by McKenna's men and had tried to say that I had stolen stuff from the house. Proper grass me up to save himself. *That's* when I finally 'got it' that as much of a fanny and big man he liked to play around us. He wasn't *actually* our mate at all.

It's impossible to say what I'd have been like had I been in his position but one thing that I'm pretty sure about is that if I *did* find myself grassing someone, up it would actually be the person that deserved it. Snide as fuck to do that to someone. You look out for your pals and they look out for you. Or that's how it's *meant* to be, at least.

I didn't feel any reason to go and see him to catch up as a pal, or even to cheer him up. It wasn't about 'him.' You always see people taking grapes and Lucozade to someone who has been in the hossie but there was none of that. It was out of me more being selfish than it was to lift his spirits. The guilt had been eating away at me. Not so much with Dynamo but more so with the other two. I couldn't get near Flav and Scooter, though. Both their mum and dads looking like they'd taken the same attitude towards me as much as mines had done with *their* sons. I got the message.

Getting to see Dynamo had been a lot easier.

Seeing him, though. *That* wasn't so easy.

When I walked into his bedroom, where he was lying watching The Empire Strikes Back - a trilogy on the go by the looks with all three DVD cases for the first three Star Wars films lying out - all I could see at first was the multiple stookies, bruises, cuts, scars and stitches. I'd heard the rumours about how bad he was and had already assumed that they'd been well exaggerated and that he was nowhere near as bad as people had been making out.

Seeing him sitting up there in bed. If anything, the rumours had *down*played the state of him. It was only after I'd had a good look at the injuries that I then noticed the look he was giving me. He'd heard me come in but instead of saying anything he was just staring back at me. Almost looked like he was genuinely amazed to see me standing there, which I couldn't really make any sense out of. It was only a five minute walk from one Muirhouse flat to another. Not exactly a journey to the top of Arthur's Seat.

'Ah can't believe the fucking nerve of you, ya wee snake. Actually coming here? You taking the fucking piss?' He sat there in bed, looking me up and down with disgust. I hadn't bothered to take my coat off or sit down. From the welcome I'd got from him, it didn't look like I was going to be staying for long. There were a few names scribbled onto his plasters. Already I could see that I wasn't going to be signing my name onto any of them. Not that Dynamo would've been able to stop me if I'd wanted to, mind.

'How you feeling, D?' I replied, completely ignoring what he'd just said. There would be time for getting to me being a so called snake before I left.

'You honestly fucking think that I believe that you're caring about HOW I'm feeling? Especially since you're the one who fucking put me here.' He made an attempt to point at his bed but didn't get very far through all the broken bones that he'd been left with.

'I'm not sure what you know or what you *think* you know but you're off your head if you think that I had anything to do with you being put in hospital.' I shook my head and looked him right in the eyes.

'Fucking lying wee prick.' He scowled back at me.

'Four of us did that house together. Three of us get grabbed by big scary fuckers asking us questions about the house, who was involved and who stole what before then fucking us up. Funny how it was only the 'three' out of us, though? And how did they know *our* names in the first place? Almost as if someone had *told* them who we were. In return for saving themselves, eh?'

He wasn't saying anything different to what the whispers had been about me but, at least, I was finding out *his* position on things, even if it was entirely predictable how he would be left feeling.

'D? I was *next!*' I tried to tell him. 'I suppose I should thank you, really. You're sat there accusing me of putting you in hospital, which I never, but YOU definitely kept me OUT of it' I continued but without offering any hint of an explanation to this. 'Well played, brother. That's what friends are for, eh?' I sarcastically slow clapped him.

'Fuck you mean by that, like?' He kind of sneered my way.

It was then that I suddenly realised that I wasn't scared of him anymore and it wasn't because he'd been broken into pieces and was incapable of getting out of bed to batter me, even if he wanted to. *Nothing* I said was going to change his mind. I could see that. His big brother would've hardly been helping things with what he was putting into his wee brother's head, either. I wouldn't have believed it had anyone said it to me weeks before but having Dynamo as an enemy or on my case, so to speak, was not something that was going to rank as top of my worry list and this started to come across through the tone of my voice as I stood there talking to him.

'I mean that by you giving those cunts my full name. Their boss managed to put two and two together - with us all being from Muirhouse - and work out that I was my dad's son. My dad and this Davey McKenna going way back. *That* was the only thing that saved me from the same treatment as the rest of you so aye, cheers for namedropping me in the grassing way that you did. Best thing you could've done for me. Aye, I ken, D.'

I hadn't had much wins over recent times so I absolutely soaked in the enjoyment of seeing his face absolutely drop - probably the only part of him that was able to freely move - as I stood there and let him know that *he* was the grass, not me.

'THINK YER A FUCKING BIG MAN, EH? STANDING THERE CALLING ME A FUCKING GRASS CAUSE YE KEN THAT I CAN'T GET OUT OF BED TO LEATHER YOU. IT'S NOT ALWAYS GOING TO BE LIKE THIS, REMEMBER.'

Dynamo was raging. Face had literally went red with anger and frustration. Anger over being called a grass and frustration through not being able to do physically anything about it.

'I'm not standing here calling you a grass because I know that you can't get out of bed, though, D. I'm standing here calling you a grass because you *are* one. The mistake you made was trying to grass me up to a mate of my dad's. That's the kind of stuff that gets back to people, eh?' I said but having moved closer to him, leaning in towards his ear and saying it a bit more quietly.

When the words registered with him. He - the radge bastard - tried to headbutt me with the side of his head but due to how limited his mobility was he may as well have sent me a letter a few days in advance, telling me that he was going to headbutt me.

'SOON AS AH CAN FUCKING WALK. I'LL BE COMING LOOKING FOR YOU, YA FUCKING GRASSING BASTARD.'

He projected, shouting loud enough for the whole of his house to hear. Absolutely apoplectic there in his bed.

'Aye well, D, keep in mind who put you in hospital in the first place, eh? You can shout all you want but we both know that there's only been 'one person' telling the truth so when I say that my dad and Davey McKenna are good mates, you'd probably be better to remember that before you set off on some revenge mission. Well, when you can manage to find the strength to lift up one cheek to fart, that is.' It was a side of me that Dynamo had never seen before. That was the best part though, it was a side *I* hadn't seen myself.

He was full of all sorts of threats, after that. His mum coming running upstairs to find out what was going on before then escorting me from the premises. I could still hear him from down the stairs, when I was walking out the front door. None of what he was shouting down to me, anything that he was actually *going* to carry out.

He didn't know it - simply because I hadn't shared with him *all* of what my dad had told me - but his mask had slipped, for me. I *knew* who he was. Had the measure of him. For all that came out of his mouth and the image that he tried to give himself, he was just a kid like me and he proved it the way he reacted when he was grabbed by the gangsters. What was there to be scared of about him?

'Wee fucking grasses like you *always* get what they deserve in the end.' Dynamo's mum hissed as she was throwing me out.

'I think you better go back up those stairs and have a wee chat with your son, a proper one, eh? Maybe he'll tell you who the REAL grass is. Then again, he wouldn't be much of a grass if he was to grass on himself though, eh? I'm only able to walk *because* I'm connected. Shame the wee man up the stairs wasn't though, eh' I admit, I was milking the connection between dad and McKenna and was likely over-stretching the realities of their 'friendship' but the way I saw it. All she had - as far as facts went - was that I hadn't been harmed, and their son had.

'You take yourself tae fuck ya wee bastard and don't come back here again.You're not welcome.' She shouted while making a lunge out of the front door that I highly doubt that she was never going to follow up with. More to test how much of a shitebag *I* was than anything else.

I left like a man possessed or as much of a man as a fourteen year old could ever have, anyway. Were all the problems now magically fixed? Not a fucking chance they were but for some reason I was left feeling energised. Like that bunny on the adverts. Fully charged up and reborn.

As I'd find out later - and in what would be an improvement to the slanderous rep that I'd been gathering around Muirhouse - it was a stroke of luck that old Mrs Agnew, - the wifie who called the police on Dynamo's brother that time she seen him leaving the house with a machete in his hand - had seen all of it.

Probably *the* biggest gossip in the whole of Inchmickery Court (if not the whole of Muirhouse) had been standing there outside her front door - watering her hanging flower baskets - and witnessed the whole exchange between me and Dynamo's mum.

Something, that could not have been scripted *any* better.

Chapter 31

Strings

'Time to pay back that wee debt of yours, Strings pal.'

McKenna said as he pushed the envelope across the table, inside the porto-cabin. I'd been sat in there on my own. Shivering my fucking arse off while he had been outside talking to someone who had arrived in a white Range Rover, just as we'd been about to begin. When McKenna had noticed the guy pull up he got up in a hurry and left, telling me that he needed to see him about something and that he'd be back in a moment.

I'd ended up having flick through the topless calendar that was hanging up on the wall. Puzzled me a bit, like. It was for some exhaust manufacturer and was going down the old route of topless calendars that you'd find hanging in any back street garage. Sexist as fuck and far from what you'd class as PC but try telling that to a grease monkey of a mechanic. What puzzled me, though, was that despite it being Two Thousand and Ten the actual models there, for each month, looked like they were from the fucking eighties. No cunt has haircuts like that anymore, I thought to myself while looking at some of the styles they had, which could've easily housed a family of starlings inside it. Couldn't help but feel that I was missing the aims of the people who had designed the calendar by looking at the hair on the models other than their bodies. Literally looked like the models from the side of the Tennents Lager cans which might've been considered eye candy back in the eighties but not so much these days.

'CAUGHT YOU, pervert.' McKenna laughed as he burst back in the door to find me with Miss September opened out.

'I've had easier wanks, mate.' I joked, as I hung the calendar back up onto the wall and walked back towards his office desk and sat down.

'Now, I'll be honest. It wasn't the type of work that I'd envisaged me having you do for me, to pay back the debt accumulated by your lad. Use people to their strengths, that's what I always say. *That's* why it would've been logical of me to utilise your, unique abilities - so to speak - and put you out to work on the puggies for me until you'd paid back what was due. Current events have, shall we say, overtaken things, however, and due to one of my men going and getting himself deaded - unfortunate business - I need *you* to step in for him and do the job instead.'

I still hadn't touched the white envelope that was marked '**CARSON**' in black felt tip pen. Instead, choosing to let him carry on. I mean, technically I *was* doing a job for him but as he rambled on in front of me, it almost felt like he was a gaffer at work, delegating out something that needed done. Well, having never really had a job. It was what I'd *imagine* a boss talking to you would've been like.

'So what is it you need me to do then, if I'm not going to be doing any puggy work for you? Puggy work is pretty much all I'm good at, eh.' I decided to ask him as he was all filler and no actual content, the way he was rambling on. Didn't help that he was - on average - getting a couple of sentences out before his phone would go and he'd tell me to hang on, while he took the call.

'Oh, nothing too big, Strings. Just a wee bit of driving.' He said, as if the ins and outs of the job - whatever they were - were going to be nothing at all. Sat there holding an imaginary steering wheel in his hands moving it from side to side.

'Just need you to collect something for me down in Manchester and bring it back up the road with you. Sunday morning.'

It's funny but the first thing that I thought of wasn't the fine details of *what* it was that I was going to be collecting for him - because that in itself *should've* been something to worry about - but that he'd said Sunday morning.

We had the Kwik Save Challenge Trophy final against The Paddock - from Niddrie - early dinner time. With it being the final, it was getting a bit of the showcase final treatment and awarded a later kick off time. Jock Hunter had said that Jim Jeffries was going to be presenting the trophy at full time and everything. What better motivation to win the trophy do you need than the opportunity of collecting a winners medal from Jim Jeffries and then saying 'Cheers for the medal ya beetroot faced fucking yam?'

'Well, look, Davey. I need to be back in Edinburgh for one o clock, at the latest, on Sunday dinner time. Whatever the plans are that you've made. Muirhouse Violet stuff, like.' The first words that I managed to find on the subject.

'You know, normally some cunts *asks* what it is that I'm having them pick up for me first of all.' He laughed across the table at me.

Then it hit me. It wasn't exactly much of a surprise to me that the very first thing I'd thought of - over everything - was The Violet. I hadn't even begun to contemplate that I didn't even have a fucking drivers license.

'Ah shite, Davey. Actually, I can't do it at all, now that I think about it. I'll need to do something else for you to pay back the debt.' It wasn't the easiest of words to choose. Telling a gangster who - if he so desired - could see to it that you never saw the outside of his scrapyard again. Sitting there informing them that you weren't going to be able to do the thing that he is telling you to do never 'is' easy, though.

'Oh aye, is that so, is it?' He asked with a wee smirk on his face. As if what I'd said had been genuinely amusing to him. He hadn't reacted with anger or any kind of hostility - as would have been very possible from a gangster being told 'no' - but the passive aggressive and intimidating smile that he was looking back at me with felt almost just as bad because I knew there was *no* sincerity to it, whatsoever.

'To be fair, it's a decent enough reason, pal. I don't have a fucking drivers license.' I laughed out but found that only I had found this funny. Even then, mines had been a nervous laugh rather than through anything else.

'I'm not understanding your problem though, Strings?' He said, which confused the fuck out of me. He needed me to drive for him while I'm not allowed to drive. Fairly clear cut. No pictures needing drawn to assist.

'Well. I'm banned from driving, Davey. Don't get my license back for a while yet.' I said shrugging my shoulders as if what else could I do to change that.

'Aye, but. You still remember *how* to drive though, don't you? As in when they take away your license the DVLA don't send someone around to remove all of your memories of *how* to drive, do they?' Sarcastic approach aside. I could see what he was getting at.

'Well, no, obviously.' I replied. Knowing that I had to watch my tongue. I was already in the position of sitting there knocking back the favour that I'd already agreed to do to spare wee Jack so it wasn't going to help matters if McKenna detected any kind of lip from me.

'Well where's the fucking problem then? I see no problem.' He brushed this minor piece of information aside as someone who *would* do when not having to drive while under a ban themselves.

'Aye but, Davey? If I get stopped by the police when I'm driving for you while I'm banned I'll go to jail.' I said, trying to show the serious implications that would be impacting on me if I was to be caught. He found this funny though. Laughed right in my face, like.

'Trust me, Joseph, if the police stop you. You're going to the fucking jail anyway.' He said, once he'd stopped laughing at the worries that I was expressing to him.

I was never going to be travelling down to somewhere like Manchester to pick up a set of Royal Doulton crockery for his family home or a job lot of boxes of Golden Wonder Salt and Vinegar. All McKenna did was offer some kind of confirmation that *whatever* it was that I was picking up was going to be less than above board.

'So apart from the fact that you're banned from driving - which we've covered - and that you have the Champions League fin, erm I mean the Kwik Save Trophy final to play on Sunday - which we'll come to in a minute - are there any *other* concerns that you might have?' He said, mocking me while motioning for me to open up the envelope that was still lying untouched in front of me.

'Well, no, nothing else that I can think of right now.' I replied, not even sure what to think anymore. Obviously *whatever* it was that he was going to have me do to pay back the debt was going to be illegal. That much was assumed but to have me committing crime upon crime as part of it was a bit of a headfuck. If the driving while banned doesn't get you slammed up then the illegal transportation of *insert applicable contraband* will.

As I opened the envelope McKenna began to take me through things. Inside was a one way ticket to Piccadilly Station. A print out of the address and directions from the station to a Holiday Inn with a phone number scribbled onto the sheet of paper with the name 'Wesley' written underneath it.

'What time's your kick off on Sunday?' He asked, while I looked at the ticket. Edinburgh to Manchester with a connection in York. Leaving Waverley on the Saturday night.

'Emmm, half one.' I answered him without taking my eyes off the ticket. Well there goes your quiet night in with the feet up to rest before the big game, I thought to myself, when it all started to sink in.

'Easy! You'll be back up the road well in time for it. Don't sweat, pal.'

He explained that I was to get the train down and check into the hotel for a bit where I'd already have the keys to the rental van dropped off at reception. After that I was to wait for a phone call on the burner phone that McKenna had also given to me. I'd get the directions of where I was collecting from, once I got the call.

'Now it's going to be the middle of the night, early morning that you're going to get the call so no fucking sleeping on the job, mind. It's a *very* sensitive time frame for collection so you need to be ready to go at the drop of a hat. A *lot* of money at stake here, Strings, so no fucking about. If you've not had a phone call by six in the morning though you call that number and ask for Wes. *Don't* phone him a minute before that, though.'

'What is it that I'm picking up, Davey?' I asked, knowing that driving a van for four to five hours - on the face of it - did not equate to being enough to pay back the heinous and - much more importantly, - disrespectful act of breaking into a feared gangster's home.

'Do you *really* want to know?' He asked, seriously.

'Well I don't know? When you put it like that. Do *I* really want to know?' I replied.

'Well, that's it, do you really *want* to know?' He said, keeping it going.

'Let's just say that if it goes missing on route from Manchester to Edinburgh then you're going to be wishing that you'd just left things as they were and for your wee man to have taken his beating. One member of the family as opposed to all three of them might well turn out to have looked like the more attractive one.'

I could've done without the menacing threat that he'd thrown in just to offer some additional motivation to me. He was already talking to someone who knew the score, and he already knew that. Which he then proved by following this up with

'And it obviously goes without saying, Strings. You get stopped by the police on the way up the road. You take the hit and the punishment that comes along with it. You're a man of the world so you don't need me to remind you of what would happen to your wife and that ragamuffin of a kid of yours, if my name was to come up.'

'Awww, Davey, there no need for the threats, pal. You and me go back. You know I'll not rip you off. It's only because I'm a decent cunt that I'm even sitting here with you, eh?'

'Aye, ah ken, ah ken but just giving you a wee reminder. You ken how it is, eh?' He replied like he was almost apologising for his actions but it coming across as an apology for the way that he felt he had to act in such circumstances rather than apologising to me, directly.

'Well, if there's no further questions I'll let you get back to things. I'll give you a bell on Saturday night on that phone, once you've got down there and got yourself settled. Just to make sure you made it there alright.' He said to me while - already thinking a few steps ahead - he picked up his phone to make another call. Not even waiting around for any 'further questions.'

I didn't think it possible but I left that porto-cabin with a sickening feeling and spinning head that absolutely pissed all over the one that I'd had when leaving the same place, having just secured a way to saving Jack. This was reality now. I had to assume that it was going to be drugs I was bringing over the border with me. To assume anything other than that would've been just plain naive. A heavy jail term, if caught, for definite. Heavy jail term, heavy full fucking stop.

And yet despite all of the fears and threats in regards to my family or my freedom. Han and Jack being hurt. Me being given even worse of a punishment or, at best, thrown in jail Standing there waiting on the bus to Muirhouse coming. I had all of this flooding through my mind. Competing with each other and all trying their best to be front of the line for me to have to think and stress over.

The weird thing though. As grim as things were looking in terms of my future. The one dominating thought - over everything else vying for attention - was how this was potentially going to impact on Sunday's cup final. McKenna had said that it was going to be a through the night job so I wasn't going to be able to have a kip and *then* after that I was going to have to drive four hours from England to Scotland and stick on a pair of Copa Mundial and play ninety minutes, with the possibility of extra time and penalty kicks. And all of that was *providing* things would go on time and smoothly. If there was *any* kind of delay it would mean that I wouldn't be up the road in time to take my place in the starting eleven.

As I saw the number fourteen coming along the road I managed to clock myself. My wife and kid had just been threatened - minutes before by one of the worst people in the city you could have do so - and I was there fretting about whether I'd get enough rest in before I played a game of amateur fitba.

To be fair, though. It's not every day you get to play in a Kwik Save Challenge Trophy final. Some go their whole life and never have the honour. Whether I was transporting drugs, illegal immigrants, stolen designer gear, or weapons of fucking mass destruction. I wasn't missing the match. End of.

Chapter 32

Han

'Staring at it's not going to make the situation go away, sis.' Senga said, breaking the silence as the two of us sat at the kitchen table, having a cup of tea, while both looking at the letter that was lying there. 'You're going to have to go. I'm pretty sure that they put you in jail if you *don't* turn up. Warrant for your arrest gets put out, and that. It's not something that you take lightly.'

She'd popped in for a visit while Joe had went out down to Leith on some business. The topic of conversation, the letter with the massive 'JURY SUMMONS' stamped at the top in red that you could've read from space.

'Aye, Senga, it says something along those lines on the letter.' I said while picking it up from the table and reading out loud.

'**Warning - You may be committing a criminal offence punishable by a fine of up to One Thousand pound if.**

You do not respond to this summons without a reasonable excuse.

You do not attend for jury service without reasonable cause.

When your name is called, you are not available to be a juror without reasonable cause.

When your name is called, you are not fit to serve because of drink or drugs.'

I let the letter go again and watched it float gracefully back down onto the kitchen table again.

'When do you have to be there for?' Senga asked, as she took a swig of her tea and picked up a Jaffa Cake from the plate.

'Half eleven. Benji's picking me up to take me down to the court. This is just us all going in to see who they're going to select for the court case next week. I'm shiteing it, sis. What if I end up being picked and I get a murder case, or something like that? I'm not sure my nerves would be able to take that. Sen. Having to be part of the decision whether someone goes away for the rest of their lives, or not. I'd rather be steering well clear of that whole stuff. Government, Queen, council, fucking boys in blue and whoever else you want to mention can do one with their civic duty shite, as far as I'm concerned.'

I'd already well discussed things with Strings and he seemed a bit underwhelmed by it all. As if there was nothing to jury duty and that I was worrying myself over nothing.

'Just fake some Tourettes when you turn up and they'll have you on your way out the door again within ten minutes. Fucking telling you.' He'd said. As if it was as simple as to walk into a court of law and start throwing out random swear words at the most inappropriate of times and you'd get out of it. Surely it couldn't have been as easy as that?

'I can't go doing that, Joe.' I'd said to him.

'How come, like? Just swear marginally more than you normally do in a day and you'll be golden. Just marginally, mind.' He'd teased me.

We did a wee bit of role-play in the living room - the same day that the letter had arrived - going over it where he'd pretended to be me and I one of the government officials.

'Right, ask me, Hannah Carson, if there's any reason that I can think of why I should not be a juror on the case.' He said to me.

'So, Mrs Carson. We've called you in today to establish if you are fit to serve as part of jury duty on behalf of Her Majesty, The Queen.' I said to him. *No* idea if this was actually the kind of thing that they would be saying at the court but it sounded pretty official to me.

'No, no reason at - FUCK SHITE CUNT - all that I can - WANKERS - think of.' He replied, throwing in a couple of random nervous facial ticks, following me asking the question to him.

'And there completes your lesson on how to get out of jury duty, darling.' He concluded before standing up and telling me that he was going down to The Gunner for a couple of drinks.

A support system of a husband like no other, my Joseph.

Senga had only come by *because* she'd already texted ahead to check if Joe was in. Since we'd taken the wee man to the circus. Her and Joe hadn't been on speaking terms. Gary, apparently, was still having nightmares over his uncle twatting that clown. The best that you're ever going to get from Strings is an apology. That's at the very best, before he just gets on with things. Senga got her apology - the day of the circus - but had decided to keep going on and on about it so Joe's patience ran out, as it normally does. Hence why the two of them were having to be kept apart. There was enough trouble as things were without them two going at it.

Me and Sen share everything with each other. Always have done, since we were bairns. I *couldn't* tell her about what had been going on with Jackie and, in turn, Joe and McKenna, though. Christ knows I *wished* I could've talked to her about it. A problem shared, as they say. Only I couldn't share my problem with anyone but Joe and - without any disrespect towards my darling hubby - sometimes you need another pair of ears to bend when you need to talk about something. *Female* ears, to be precise.

It felt wrong, keeping it back from Senga. *Especially* when I had the horrible nagging feeling that it was all going to come out eventually anyway and she was going to be left looking at me and asking the question 'why' I hadn't told her - my closest confidant - about any of it to begin with.

Away from the more pressing issues like the imminent jury duty. We just sat having a general chit chat from what happened in Eastenders the night before to what we were having for our tea later on. As we did, I started getting myself ready for going into the court. Most of what Senga was saying was just going in one ear and out the other, though.

'Oh my god, Hannah. You're shaking, look at you.' She said, as she watched me lift up my cup of tea and almost spill some of it through my trembling.

'Tell me about it,' I self depreciatingly laughed.

'Maybe I can just call the court and say that I've started to be violently sick and that I can't attend?' I said, hopefully.

'You think that they've not heard that one before, down there? I'm pretty sure that there's been hundreds of people who - for some reason - thought that pulling a sickie would sound authentic. When it obviously doesn't. Aye, people get sick. Of course they do, sis, but to get sick on the morning of an event that - let's face it - not one single person would *ever* want to be involved in. Stinks more than the seafood kiosk at Morrisons. You're going. Even if *I* have to take you there myself.'

I was glad that she was there because - otherwise - I'd have probably just gone ahead with calling the number on the letter and saying that I wasn't feeling well and couldn't come. Which, I imagine, would've landed me in trouble with the authorities at some point down the line.

Thanks to that moron of a husband of mines. I *still* managed to achieve that, anyway.

'So good morning, everyone, and thank you for all coming here today for jury selection with regards to trial ED6597, scheduled for this coming Monday.'

The man in the suit that looked like it had seen previous decades and who had greeted us all when we were showed into the room - having checked that everyone was now in attendance - stood up at the front of the room and got things started.

'Now I appreciate that being selected for jury duty will be novel to everyone of you and I will be here to address any questions that you may have on the subject but first. Please allow me to give you some information regarding the case itself. It is in connection with criminal charges brought against a member of the public for attempted murder, last year, in the Pilton area of the city. The trial is expected to run from one to two full weeks.'

The reaction to all of this news around myself and the rest of the jurors was a mixture of excitement and disappointment. The man in front of me muttering a *'fuck's sake'* under his breath at the news of a potential two week gig. I wasn't too happy at the prospect of two weeks going to court either. Imagine being the defendant, though, I thought to myself to try and find the bright side of things. Attempted murder, though? Pilton? Pretty much *everything* that I'd been stressing about since the day that letter had came through the door.

Joe's words, that night, when we did that role-play, came into my head. Could I though? There were around twenty of us in the room and from what I'd picked up that far. Not all would be making the final cut. It would've almost been like I was 'helping' them out by narrowing things down for them. Even I would've admitted that I was hardly a shy and retiring wallflower. It had only been weeks before that I had been running around The Grassmarket with a makeshift flamethrower in my hand.

Making a fool of myself, though. In a premeditated and thought out way? Something like that is not such an easy thing to do. I didn't know any of these people sat all quiet as mice around me from Adam but that wouldn't have stopped them from all going home that night and telling the story of what had happened at their jury selection. And, of course, that story would be passed on and on until the *whole* of Edinburgh knew about it. It didn't matter that this woman - that they would all be speaking about - would be nameless and that it wouldn't be linked to me, and even if it had? You'd have had Ninety Nine point Nine Nine Nine Nine percent of the city who wouldn't have known who 'Hannah Carson' was, anyway.

I would, though. That they would all be talking about 'me.' Sometimes, if you're embarrassed, you're embarrassed and that's *all* that really matters.

So it was with extreme hesitance that I - straight out of the blue - shouted out a 'F F F F FUCK WANKER FLAPS,' into the room of people.

Due to how unsure I was about even saying it in the first place. The first part was a little timid and to try and counter balance that. I ended up shouting 'wanker flaps' extra loud. This, interrupting the gent at the front.

'The offence in question took place on the night of ...'

You might think that you've experienced a moment in life where you just wanted the ground to open up and swallow you alive, even if it was the devil who was taking you down there, but believe me. *This* was 'that' moment. And it only got worse from there.

The man from the court stopped dead in his tracks and looked out over the room, to try and establish who it was that had shouted out. Didn't take him long to work that out considering all the other would be jurors were looking squarely in my direction. Me sitting there with a face that felt so hot from burning I could've done with applying some after sun onto it.

'I do apologise.' I said, while throwing in a fake involuntary wink and then - inexplicably - quickly cocking my head to the side. Like a dog would do when it hears a high pitched noise. What the actual FUCK was I doing?

Taking a second to assess this. He chose not to say anything back and, instead, took another look at his notes to catch up with where he was before I'd interrupted him. The woman to the side. This smartly dressed older woman in a business suit looked at me with a mixture of pity and concern.

'You ok, doll?' She whispered to me, reaching across and grabbing my hand and squeezing it for support.

'Aye, I'm fine. thank you for asking, though. Normally I can keep my condition under control but I think the stress of coming here today has got the better of me.' I replied and then gave her the strangest look at the end of the sentence where I screwed my face up at her, exposing the top row of my teeth while I blinked three times.

I'd be the first to admit. I had *no fucking idea* of what the actual symptoms of Tourettes were, apart from the swearing and even then that was only because of that famous programme on the BBC when we were younger. I knew it wasn't *just* swearing, though. That about the *only* thing that I knew.

I was sitting there, barely able to believe that I'd taken Joe's advice and was - in court - trying to fake a medical condition. It was too late to go back now. All eyes were going to be on me at that point and - I'd felt - that meant that I would need to now display further examples of my condition. One outburst alone would've seemed like nothing other than a piss poor attempt at someone getting out of jury service. There had to be more examples to go with.

I felt like the worst person in the world, to be pretending that I had something that I didn't. I always see that kind of behaviour as if you're tempting fate. When Joe was driving he never got away with that parking in a disabled spot shite with me. Park in one of those spaces and the next thing you know you're using one for real. You don't tempt fate in such a way. I'd panicked, though, and *regretted* it straight away.

I wasn't in any way poking fun at the Tourettes community. It all kind of made me sound like a Nazi but I was only following orders. Orders from the lunatic otherwise known as Joseph Carson. I'll fucking Tourettes him, I thought, as I felt all of those pairs of eyes fixed on me.

'Now on the screen behind me, in a second, I'm going to show a current picture of the defendant which was taken upon the time his arrival at Her Majesties Saughton Prison when placed on remand. If any of you recognise or think you know who he is please raise your hands now. Please take all the time you need to look at the picture before you make your final decision, however.'

The picture went up on the whiteboard behind him. Showing what I could've classed as just your average North Edinburgh radgey. Scars on his face. Simple Roman Crop haircut. I didn't recognise him but it really wouldn't mattered much if I had. I wasn't going to be doing anything to put him away.

Looking at the picture of him. I decided to squeeze in another sign of my 'illness.' This being a couple of quick nods and a wink. Government guy at the front just happened to see this though and shouted out to me.

'Do you recognise the person?' He stopped and asked me.

Once more, all eyes on me. 'No, no I've never seen him before.' I replied, having backed myself into a corner that I was now trying to pretend to be someone with Tourettes who was now *embarrassed* about their condition. The depths of deception that Joe had sent me down knowing no end. The grim facts, however, being that I'd have doubted that Helen Mirren would've been ale to pull off such a role, never mind an acting novice like myself.

In the end, no one's arms went up in the air. Clearing the way for the last part of the selection process. The interviews. And where things went drastically wrong from there. I'd had to sit and wait my turn while everyone was called up to the front of the room, where the man had a couple of chairs and desk set up. Far enough away so that private conversations could still be had.

I got chatting with the woman beside me, while we waited to be called out. She was telling me about how this two weeks of jury duty couldn't have come at a worse time as she was about to close this big deal with some American investors. They were due to fly in next week and - it looked like - she was going to be turning up at Edinburgh Sheriff Court instead of the big meeting and that - should she end up being selected - she was going to have to ask them to cancel coming over and that it might well be enough blow the deal. Apparently, millionaires not being people that took too kindly to being messed around. I didn't really have much in the way of anything back to share. What? Oh being here for two weeks will get in the way of my life of part time working at The Co-Op while also trying to ensure that my family doesn't set itself on fire. *More* important than her business deal but even I'd admit, not as impressive.

'Got any plans to try and get yourself out of it, then?' I asked. Through speaking to her. I'd felt safe about bringing up such a serious subject, in the setting we were in. Still, though. I didn't *know* her - never mind trust her - so while we sat speaking. I treated her to the occasional facial tick, so as to keep my cover.

She discreetly looked around at this, just to make sure that there hadn't been anyone who had been listening to my question, or what her answer was going to be.

'You know? This contract, if I can get it over the line for my company, is going to make me a *very* rich woman. Why should *I* have to lose out thousands because of some schemie battering another one?' She asked. Confident - by then - that she had a sympathetic, and understanding, ear in who she was sitting talking to.

Maybe I'd surprised her in that someone from Muirhouse could be so well turned out for a date, such as jury selection, so I didn't really appreciate her sentiment, even if her point kind of was valid. Why should *anyone* be impacted if two radges had a fight and one landed off worse than the other? Whether they were from a scheme or not wasn't the point.

'Well you've *still* got time.' I assured her. 'You had a good chance there when the picture was up on screen. You should've taken it.' I flashed her my biggest scary monster face yet. Following it up with a stifled 'HAIRY MASSIVE BALLS' with my fist in my mouth in an attempt at muting myself to everyone around.

'Well you can't play the race card, with the boy being just your average Edinburgh boy. If it had been someone Asian or black you could've told him that you were racist. That would've got you off the jury, no worries.' I said, going over any options that she could've used.

'But, I'm not a racist.' She said with her hand up to her chest as if she was trying to protect herself from such an accusation, which - obviously - wasn't an accusation at all.

'I'm not saying you *are* a racist. Neither am I. But for five minutes of an interview you could've *pretended* to have been one. All I'm saying. *Neither* am I saying that it's - ethically - the correct thing to do, though.'

Christ, I was as bad as Joe. He's telling me to feign having a health condition while I'm telling others to be cutting around like white supremacists.

'*MRS HANNAH CARSON*' Came the cry from down front.

'Ok, well good luck.' I smiled to her then theatrically pulled one side of my face up and held it there for a second before letting it drop again, as I stood up to go down to the front of the room and join the man in the suit. 'With a bit of luck, neither of us will be back here on Monday.' She brought both her hands up into a praying position and smiled.

'*So then. Carson, Hannah. Martello Court, Muirhouse.*'

He said without looking back up from the file with my details on it.

'Shite, fucking, big bull shite,' Was the reply which, aye, got his attention.

'*Excuse me?* If the information contained on there is incorrect in any way then I apologise but I will not stand for language like that.' He said, less than impressed.

Completely shriveling and dying inside. What else could I do other than keep going. Sitting there looking for some kind of a response from me. All I gave him was three rapid blinks and a quick smile up one side of my mouth before letting my face rest again.

He continued just looking at me. It started to make me nervous, like. You know? As if he was staring into my mind and was able to read that I was putting all of this on and was about to confront me about it.

'Look, if you don't mind me asking here, Mrs Carson, but are you feeling ok? Do you have any underlying health conditions that I need to know about before progressing your selection? It's just that, I've noticed ...'

Here we go, I thought to myself taking a deep breath and hoping that whatever I was going to say was going to come out - at least - close to semi convincing.

'Well, I'm sure that you've noticed a few examples this morning but I have Tourettes. It's only a slight diagnosis that I was given and is handled, generally, quite well, day to day. I've been really nervous about coming here this morning, however.'

'Yes, that's quite common,' he interrupted as if me bringing up my nervousness wasn't anything worth even mentioning.

'I think that with my nerves in here it's ended up with my condition getting the better of me FANNY LIPS - sorry - What I was trying to say there was that this isn't generally how bad the condition is. I think it's more the stress and anxiety of coming 'here' than anything else.'

I was treading a fine line between looking like the very *last* person that you'd put on a jury team and someone who looked genuine about their condition and that while they knew their limitations they weren't letting it stop them in life. The way I felt, how I was appealing to him. It was in danger as if I was coming across as someone who really *wanted* the gig. Maybe he was someone with a big heart and seeing me - against all odds appearing on a jury team - enthusiastic about being part of my civic duty would end up thinking. 'Good for her, not lying down to her condition. I'm sticking her on the team.'

To try and suppress any sympathetic feelings that he might've been left with. Right after my heartfelt appeal to him - and while he sat there taking in what I'd just said to him - I then let out a loud 'Bollocks, THE QUEEN'S AN OLD BOOT.'

I didn't want him to give me the sympathy vote. I wanted him to *be* sympathetic towards me but only enough to the point where he had to use his common sense and see that I was not going to be the ideal candidate for jury duty on something so serious as an attempted murder trial.

Suppress any sympathetic feelings from him? I needn't have bothered.

He wasn't impressed, and not because I had dissed Elizabeth the whatever number she was.

*'Mrs Carson? You 'do' realise that it is an offence **not** to report any health reasons for why you may not be applicable to be used for jury duty?'*

I had no other option than to plead ignorance. Aye, I'm sure the letter *had* said something about if you had reasons not to attend, to provide them, but I hadn't actually *intended* on taking Joe's advice seriously so - because of that - never phoned them about it, in advance.

'I didn't reali ... ' I tried to say but was blocked off by him.

'This is an 'extremely' important trial and the selection of the jury is paramount to the crown providing a fair and proper trial. We need to ensure that all members of the public selected to be shortlisted are of fit and able body. This SHOULD have been reported in advance of today, well in advance.

Meanwhile I'm sitting there winking across the table - as if I was some deranged woman trying to pull him - while trying to apologise. Saying that while I'd read the letter I did not feel that my 'personal' condition was not one that would prevent me from carrying out jury service.

' Mrs Carson? You could - at any given moment - shout out any and all kinds of profanities in a court of law. Were you to be outside of the jurors team you would be liable for contempt of court. 'Inside' the jury, I am afraid that, and I mean no disrespect here, you would be as much use as an ashtray on a Kawasaki.'

So much had I thrown myself into *pretending* to have Tourettes that I actually ended up taking offence at what he'd said about me. Which, at least meant that my response was - for once inside that room - a sincere and perfectly natural one.

'That is such a horribly, insensitively offensive thing to say to someone, I'll have you know.' I said, the smallest of winks following.

None of this registering, or mattering, to him.

'I - and the courts - do not take kindly to having my time wasted. 'Exactly' what you've done today, Mrs Carson. Not only will you be expelled from being selected from jury service next week but I will be forced to recommend that you face further action through your unwillingness to be more forthright with Her Majesties court. You had a legal duty to respond to your initial letter, in kind. This does not appear to have been the case on this occasion.'

'FUCK CUNT BIG PEADO WANKER' I shouted. And I meant every single word of it, too.

'Hmmmmm yes, quite.' He said, choosing not to engage.

'But this isn't fair? You're going to punish me? For having a medical condition?' With him now threatening to prosecute me over some stupid rare as fuck law. It wasn't now a case of me acting just for to get out of jury duty. I was now acting for my own life, in a small scale kind of way.

'Yes, I'm sure you feel this way. You will be given right of appeal when the time comes. Our office will be in touch, subject to an initial consultation we'll have with your GP, regarding your condition. Now if you'll excuse me. I have a lot of people to get through today so if you would be as kind as to vacate the room now and consider yourself as not being required to turn up at Edinburgh Sheriff Court this coming Monday.'

Absolutely busted, no other way to look at it than that. Talk of contacting my doctor who - obviously - was going to tell them that I had *no* history of Tourettes and, in doing so. Letting them know that I was only pretending.

I had that Cher song 'Turn back Time' playing in my head as I left the court to go back home.

'If I could turn back time. If I could find a waaaay. I'd take back those moronic words from my husband and be okay.'

328

When I returned back from the court. I was absolutely livid at him and - on the bus journey back - had formed some carefully thought out plans to set about him as soon as I got through the door, over him and his 'advice.' He was already patiently sitting there waiting on *me* to tell me about 'his' day and what had happened down in Leith, however.

Hearing about what it had involved and that McKenna was now calling in the favour, and as soon as the weekend. As angry and utterly embarrassed over the show that I had put on down at the Sheriff Court and one that was now going to leave me in a bit of trouble, legally speaking. Something I was still going to have the joy of informing Joe about later.

Me making a complete arse of myself took a very distant second place when placed beside Joseph and what *he* - which meant 'The Carsons' - now had to worry about.

Chapter 33

Jack

'I know that some cunts from elsewhere might look in our direction in the Naughty North. Say that some of us are fuck all other than criminals living in squalor but you know what, Jackie? Some of the very fucking BEST people come from Muirhouse. Salt of the earth folks. Some of the most warm, loyal, generous and loving human beings.

There's no need for you to be reverting to type. Turning out who *they* - those snobby cunts from elsewhere - want and *expect* you to be *because* you're from this part of the city. Don't make it so simple for them, son.'

Is there anything worse - *or* more boring - than a lecture from a parent who is completely off on one? Aye, there is, actually. When it's coming live and direct from a complete hypocrite. And one that you can't say anything about it to. When it's your dad, and someone that you're not exactly on the best of terms with, as it already is.

I'd been sitting bored to tears in my room. Watching the telly but not really *watching* it. Had fuck all *else* to do, otherwise. I had 'I'm a Celebrity' on just because I'd heard that Shaun Ryder was on it so thought it would be a laugh but once I started watching it I began to overthink things. First of all. With the title of the show having the word 'celebrity' in it. I didn't have a fucking clue who half the people were, and a quarter of them - who I knew - I still didn't have a clue what elevated them to being on the show. What the fuck does being Paul Gascoigne's ex wife have to do with being a celebrity, I pondered, as she sat there around a camp fire. Spraffing with Linford Christie, Shaun Ryder and this blonde woman called Britt Ekland who - after a google search - I'd found out used to go out with Rod Stewart. I thought the show would be a bit more interesting or funny, like.

Thought that Ryder would've been cracking the jokes and telling them all of his radge stories but nah. They were all just sat around this fire all talking about life, and stuff. Was a bit boring, if you ask me.

It went to the break and when - the show - came back on it was going to be the part where they did things like eat kangaroo bollocks next up. That's all you heard cunts at school talking about. The eating of the bollocks. Who the fuck wants to watch someone who isn't even a celebrity *pretending* to *be* a celebrity, eating some animal's cock or balls? I reflected. Fuck, I miss my X-box, the follow up thought.

Even if I'd *wanted* to have watched that segment of the show, I wasn't given the chance.

'JACKIE, CAN YOU COME DOWN THE STAIRS.' Dad shouted to me from the foot of the stairs. I sighed before pulling myself up off my bed. Nothing ever good happened when one - or both - of your parents shouted that they wanted to see you. Maybe other stuff is happening with kids elsewhere, of course, but I've never yet experienced being shouted on by my mum or dad only to find that they wanted to give me a pat on the back and words of encouragement over just what a fucking good job I was doing as a son and that I should keep up the good work, amongst other compliments.

'Mon, we're going out for a walk. You, me and Stanton.' He was already standing there with his coat on and the dog's lead in his hand. Stanton jumping up and down around him with that demented look on his face whenever he sees anyone with that lead in their hand.

I'd literally thought that me and dad walking the dog 'together' had ceased to be a thing anymore. We'd never done it in years. Making sure that Stanton got a walk was seen as a chore and one of the things that you just 'have' to do in life than it was as an event or pastime, as such. Something that the family would participate in.

He'd never asked me to go with him in years so I didn't even bother trying to protest and say that I was staying in my room. I wasn't getting any say, anyway. I quickly slung my Air Max on and my hoodie that was lying on the floor after my earlier attempt at throwing it at the pegs in the hall - from a distance - and hoping the hood would catch onto one or more of them had failed.

'Would rather take Stanton out than sit and watch someone eating eyeholes, earholes and arseholes.' Dad said - indicating that *he* was downstairs watching the same programme as I'd been - as we travelled down in the lift. I wasn't sure whether to laugh at the like father like son example I'd just been given or to be scared shitless at the thought of being *exactly* like my dad when I was older.

'Aye, I was watching it too, dad. Nothing else to do, without my X-box, like.' I replied while chancing my luck with a wee dig about the fact that he'd sold it. He just looked back at me. If I'd had a guess of what the look said it would be that he was saying 'You sure you want go down that road?'

Turned out, we were going down it anyway and *that* was the reason for our mysterious and surprise late night walk with the dog.

'So, now that I've had a wee while to calm down. It's time you and me had a wee chat, Jackie. Wouldn't have done you or me any good before because I'd have wanted to rip your head off the minute we got onto the subject. You might act like a daft wee cunt at times but you're a smart kid so you might well have picked up just *how* pissed off you had your dad this time around.'

He passed the lead to me for a moment while he cupped his hand from the wind around his cigarette to light it. Stanton, meanwhile, pulling at the lead like one of those police dogs that have picked up on a scent.

I just gave him a short and non committal 'aye, dad,' as I resigned myself to the next ten to fifteen minutes being a complete cringe off.

He went on to tell me half of what he'd already said at the time. Only this one was the extended version. Like how you get the directors cut DVDs with extra content to it. Aye, well I was getting the remake of the lecture I'd already had weeks before, only heavier, but - weirdly - without the underlying threat of violence towards me coming from him.

He done pretty much all of the speaking and me the listening. A father to son chat rather than father *and* son.

'I never expected you to be a choir boy, Jackie. Fuck, growing up around here. Me *and* your mum would've been surprised *if* you'd grown up as one.' He lifted one arm and pivoted it around to highlight the tower blocks of Muirhouse around us.

'And neither does your mum and me *expect* you to be one, either. There are levels that you should never raise yourself to, though, and lines that you don't cross and you need to learn them at this age or else it's going to be a lot harder lesson if you have to learn them when you're older.' He said - without looking at me - as we walked side by side. Stopping - what felt like - all the time for Stanton to do his dog stuff.

'Like a few months ago when you put that Hash into those cakes. I stuck up for you, though, and made sure that you didn't get punished because I saw a wee bit of myself in you that day. Just a wee prank, eh? Hardly like you're Howard Marks and had shoved a kilo of the old wacky back into the cake mix. Now I know that *other* dads would've made your life a living hell for that but I'm not going to be a hypocrite. Now while it might well be my own and no one else's I happen to think that my idea of right and wrong is pretty much bang on the money, on a moral compass side of things, like. Putting Hash into cakes? Well that's one step up from something Oor Wullie would've done.'

'Aye, dad. Like that time we were driving through Gorgie and we saw Michael Stewart and you put my window down and told me to shout that he was a wanker when we were driving past him?' I said, smiling at the memory of it and picking up on his vibe that he was giving in relation to examples of me being a wee dick but not getting any actual grief over it.

'Right son, stick your self out the window and call that ginger prick a wanker.' He'd said that day - pointing ahead - as he spied him walking towards us along the road in his Hearts shell suit, carrying his leather kit bag.

'HAWWWW MICHAEL STEWART YA JAMBO WANKER WEEEYYYY' I shouted, almost taking my head off the side of a lamp post due to being hung out the window so far. The look on his face was classic, like. By the time that he'd have had any kind of reaction - if any - we were long past him down Gorgie Road. That was a good day, that.

'See that's the thing, Jack. Stuff like that is harmless. You think that's the first time that Michael Stewart had been called a wanker? Or the last? Nobody's getting hurt with things like that. Do you think that random insult from a stranger impacted on Michael Stewart for the rest of his day and caused him a lot of pain and heartbreak? Course it fucking never. How impacted do you think he'd have been, though, to come back home from training and find that his house had been broken into and his medals and caps had been turned over?'

I stayed silent even though I was dying to make a wideo reply about the burglars not having too many medals and Scotland caps to steal.

'Like I've told you, though. There's levels, Jack. Levels, son, and you need to *remember* that.' He tapped the side of his head while fishing his packet of cigarettes and lighting up another one.

'They expect half the cunts from around here to be junkies housebreakers and thugs - and we both know that's not the case, if you live here you see both sides - so don't go giving them the satisfaction. You've got your whole life ahead of you. Next few years are going to shape your future, mark my words. You got yourself a pass *only* because of through a simple stroke of luck of being my son. Next time you won't be so lucky but there's not going to *be* a next time, is there, Jackie?'

'Trust me, dad, after all that's went on recently. There's not going to be a next time.' Whether that was going to go on and be true - in my future - or not. I didn't know. I meant each and every word of it in my reply to him, though.

'Actions have consequences, pal. *That's* why you're sat in your room watching people eat genitals instead of playing your video games.'

He *had* a point. Especially when he put it in that kind of a way.

'I'm not making any promises here so don't be going getting any of your hopes up but if you keep the head down and out of trouble - stick in at school as well, mind - me and your mum will see about getting you another X-box for your Christmas, ok?'

He'd spent the last ten minutes telling me about myself, where I was going wrong in life and what I needed to do to improve that. I'm sure people pay to get that from others but dad was giving it out for free.

Isn't nice, like, when all the shit that you've done gets laid out in front of you like that. Definitely makes you think. Yet at the end of this lecture he's dangling the possibility of getting another Three Sixty for me. Classic dog to owner technique where the dog knows that if it behaves it'll get a treat. For another games console? I would've *gladly* given him a paw on demand, rolled over to get my belly rubbed and walk devotedly back from Azan's - by his side - with his copy of the Evening Times in my mouth, and anything else that a dog does.

'I promise, dad. I'll be good.' I couldn't hide my excitement over what he'd said.

'Aye, I'm sure you will.' He laughed, knowing he'd pressed the *exact* button that he needed to.

'Aye, actions equals consequences, son. And not just for you and your Call of Duty ranking, either.' He said but seemed to be miles away as he came out with it.

'And *that's* the reason I've brought you out to talk to you tonight.'

Fuck, so *all* that he'd said up to that point hadn't even been the 'reason' for asking me to go out with him? I thought.

'I know you're only fourteen, Jack, but you're soon going to be a man and I - your mum as well - *especially* your mum, are going to need you to grow up, use the head, think of the family, like.'

'I will, dad,' I tried to let him know but he was too into things and kept talking.

'If I was to go away for a while you would literally be the man of the house. And to be able to *fill* that position, one of the main skills required is for you to *actually be* a man. Your last escapade was hardly head of the house material.' He shook his head at me in disappointment.

'If it was just you and your mum you'd need to step up BIG TIME.'

He mentioned the subject of him not being around more than once and by doing so only made it stick out all the more.

'Are you going to jail, dad?' I just came out with it. It had felt like he was buttering me up and preparing me for some heavy news and I couldn't take the slow build up that it was feeling like. I'm not going to like this next part so you may as well as rip the plaster off and be done with it, I was thinking, but still bricking it for *what* I thought was coming next. Aye he gave me a hard time *half* the time but that didn't mean that I didn't love my dad and would've been absolutely devastated if he went to jail. Who wouldn't?

'Who? Me? Jail?' He stopped, Stanton and me having not much choice other than to do the same. 'Not in this life, son.' He laughed and started walking again.

That laugh turning out to be completely put on with him going on to tell me the *real* reason that he had taken me out on the walk. Well, his version, at least. Without actually *telling* me what he was going to be doing - instead, saying that the less I knew the better - he let me know that - with actions having consequences, remember - this McKenna guy was needing dad to do a favour back, to pay for not fucking me up like the other three.

Dad was right, though. As in what he'd said about how I'd grown up *because* of where I was from and how I *should've* been a few levels away from a model child. Because of that I was able to read between dad's lines so that he didn't have to properly come out with the words which I couldn't decide on whether he was trying to find a way to say or actually *couldn't*.

He was basically saying that he was going to have to do something for this man - whose house I'd 'been in - and that, due to how illegal it was, he'd be going to jail *if* he got caught over it.

'You'll not get caught though, dad, will you?' I asked, just really looking for any kind of assurances from him that would replace the massive guilt trip that was starting to sink in. He was only standing there almost - I was getting the impression - as if he was planning for being in jail *because* of me. I can only imagine the stuff that dad *didn't* tell me or mum so the fact that he was even telling me this, in advance, made me feel that he thought that it was a real possibility and that he was genuinely worried about it.

'No, of course I won't but that doesn't change what I've been saying to you out here tonight. If you need to be the man of the house *I* need you to be ready for it. Mon, let's get ourselves back in. You've got school tomorrow.'

The assurances of 'no, of course I won't' from him didn't exactly fill me full to the brim with confidence. *Especially* the way that he said it. Probably the exact same way he'd have done when I was younger and more easily fooled I'd have been.

I went back upstairs to my room to get ready for bed as soon as we got back, guilt tripping out my nut. *Whatever* dad was roped into it was *because* of me. I'd taken the extreme heat that breaking into McKenna's house had brought me. Kept my head down and took my punishment in all ways. As the weeks had passed, they'd stopped talking about it and - Muirhouse, being Muirhouse - there had been about a hundred *other* things for people to be talking about so the subject of the four of us robbing a house, and the reprisals that it brought, had started to drop off people's radar. As it started to be mentioned less and less I'd started to think that it was something that was all behind me.

I hadn't realised that mum and dad had kept some of it back from me, though. I'd thought that it had been because Davey McKenna and my dad knew each other that I'd escaped a paggering. This kind of *was* the truth, I suppose. It's just that mum and dad had neglected to tell me the bit about where my dad would have to do something in return for the man to pay off the debt. It had all been half truths and carefully selected words in front of me.

Actions and consequences, like dad said. *My* action, of going along with that stupid cunt, Dynamo, and all of his nonsense leading to the consequence, now, of dad landing up in whatever it was that he was knee deep in.

Aye, night night, Jack and sweet dreams, eh?

Chapter 34

Strings

'OOH, TO, OOH TO BE, OOH TO BE A HIBEE'

Three quarters of Easter Road were singing and bouncing around having - a few minutes earlier - witnessed an absolute screamer of, easily thirty years, a goal from Ian Murray past the Hearts keeper. Absolute bedlam all around. Me? Well any other Edinburgh derby I'd have been going as ballistic as everyone else but that afternoon, inside the ground. I was left motionless. Almost could've been taken for a sly Jambo who hadn't been able to get a ticket for the away end so had stuck his scarf in his pocket and went in with the home fans. I had other things on my mind that day other than Hibernian versus Heart of Midlothian.

There was less than twenty four hours to go until the Kwik Save Challenge Trophy final.

A group of police - up the other end of the stadium - in fluorescent yellow jackets went running up the touchline - from the tunnel area - and down towards the corner, where the Hibs and Hearts fans respective stands met each other. Murray's goal seemingly sparking something between both sets of supporters. I thought I'd seen a seat thrown from the away end but like I said, it was bedlam. I was in my own semi-conscious state of mind, though, and had been since Han had woken me up earlier in the morning, doing the hoovering down the stairs.

Derby day at Easter Road comes but twice a year. Well, it does, depending on various circumstances due to the Scottish Professional Football League and their radical views of how a league campaign should finish, that is. Their whole splitting the league up - into to halves - with five games to go capers, kind of dictating things. At home. Once *or* twice a year, though. The Edinburgh Derby is an occasion that should be treated like one. And I normally did.

Generally any derby day would see me springing out of bed like a bairn on Christmas day and - after a shite, shower and a shave - I'd have been kissing Han goodbye before the Saturday post had arrived and telling her that - depending on how the game went - she might not see me until the end of the day. Aye, there was always a Violet match the next day but your commitment to a cause can only stretch so far at times, eh? If you can't make an exception for the Edinburgh Derby and take to the pitch the next morning completely breathing out of your arse from through having just getting yourself changed in the pavilion, then I'm not sure the point of anything.

Felt differently that morning, though. First thing that popped into my head, the very first thing, was that the cup final was the next day. The next one *after* that was that it was derby day. You could have worse starts to a day when you open your eyes. The prospect of playing in a prestigious cup final *and* before that you're going off to the fitba to watch your team go up against their - and by extension, your - hated rivals. One of those games that mean *way* more than just what takes place during the ninety minutes. The amount of Yams that I, and the rest of us Hibees, will bump into the following week that - depending on the result - will be fucking lording it over me.

I'm never sure if the players actually *get* that side of things. Aye, they're playing to win the game and get the three points and aye, of course. I'm sure they'll get an extra buzz about winning the derby, professionally, like. None of those cunts have to co-exist with Jambos *after* the game though so don't have to go through the pish that we will if our team loses the match. Can't beat a fucking derby, though. Even if half of you doesn't actually want the game *played* for fear of getting beat in it. Like sometimes, the fear of losing a derby outweighs the hope of winning one, when it comes to me, personally, like.

Still, you wouldn't miss it for the world, though. Was a good thing to have ahead over the day. That positivity only really lasted, though, until the third and final thought - before I fully came to lying there in bed with the splitting sound of the hoover attacking my senses - popped into my head.

What was sandwiched in between the Hibs match and the Kwik Save Challenge Trophy final. Fucking felt like I'd been pinned down in bed and someone had dropped one of those big medicine balls onto my stomach at the thought of this job for McKenna that lay ahead.

I didn't waste any time in getting myself ready and out the door. Telling Han that I was just going to get something for my breakfast down at The Gunner.

'Champagne breakfast, aye?' She said, raising her eyebrow at the news that I'd be having my breakfast along with a pint.

'Derby day, Han. You know the rules, eh?' I replied, using my get out of jail free card.

'Aye, that there *aren't* any.' She laughed as she started winding the hoover cable up and wrapping it around the outer clips on the body.

Her and I had already spoken about me having to go to Manchester - and why - so she already knew the reason that I was heading out the door that morning with a wee travel bag over my shoulder and not coming out with my 'you'll see me at the end of the day' patter I'd normally hit her with on derby day. She'd basically see me *when* she saw me and that was as good as I was ever going to be able to promise her. With what time of train McKenna had put me on from Waverley there was no point in me going back to Muirhouse from Leith - after the match - only to have to turn back around and head *back* to Waverley to get on the train to Manchester.

Figuring, instead, that it would've made more sense for me to just head into The Albion for a couple of pints while all the crowds made their way out of the area, and by then, it would've been time for me to jump in a taxi up to Waverley Station, anyway.

When I kissed her on the way out. I had the quick thought of 'what circumstances would I next see her' pop into my head but kicked it right fucking back out again. Could've well done without any of that negativity shite in my head. Not then. Especially not *that* day.

I slung my scarf around my neck and lit up an Embassy and headed off down to The Gunner.

'Gies a pint of Tennents, please, Erika.' I shouted to her over the noise inside the place. Still wiping the pastry remains - of my sausage roll from the bakers - from my stubble.

'You have to watch this video first, Strings.' She said handing me her phone and telling me to press the play icon on the corner of the screen.

I could already see from the still of the video that Jock Hunter was in it. The bar of The Gunner in the background.

'What's this, like?' I looked up and asked, rather than just press play on the thing.

'Jock's already been in this morning. Asked me what time I was on until and when I told him all day he asked me to tape him and that if any of the team was in today - and going to Easter Road later on - they were to watch this video *before* I served them a drink.

Sepp, Terry, The Monk, Daz and Mr Benn (mostly a mix of both Hibees and Jambos) were already sitting in the corner. Loud and animated with a table full of booze on it.

'I take it the rest of them have watched it, aye?' I asked, tipping my head in their direction.

'Oh aye, every single one of them. You know what Jock's like when it comes to the team. He finds out that I served any of you drink without showing you the video I'll get as much grief as you all will *for* drinking before a big game.'

Knowing Jock, like we did, I knew she wasn't even exaggerating.

I looked back down at the phone and pressed play. It had Hunter standing at the bar with a freshly poured out pint of stout sat beside him. He wasn't the best when it came to technology, Jock. His own mobile still had a fucking aerial on it that you had to pull out to make a call. This showed with the video because, despite the record button having already been pressed, it took him around another few seconds before he *knew* that he was actually being recorded. Once he did, though, he took on this serious tone to things. Cunt looked like he was presenting Panorama or something. Or at least *thought* that he was looking like that.

'Right, cuntos. Now while it might be Hibs and Hearts today you don't need me to fucking remind you what day it is TOMORROW? Some fitba players can go their whole career and never come close to a whiff of silverware and you lot are ninety minutes away from experiencing what it feels like to KISS it, never mind catch a sight of

it. Now I'm not a fucking daftie so don't go taking me for one. I know you're all going to have a drink today. I've been in charge of enough fucking Violet games on a Sunday morning following derbies to know otherwise. Tomorrow's different, though. TOMORROW you have a chance to be local fucking HEROES. There's going to be loads of other Edinburgh derbies that you can all get mortal over, but today? Think about it, eh? Don't be a bunch of selfish bastards. Put The Violet first. You think Niddrie will be all out on the piss today? Nut. And another thing ...'

He looked like he was about to go off on his high horse about something else but - off camera - the singing started around him. Drowning him out and diverting his attention away from the camera.

'GLORY GLORY TO THE HIBEES. GLORY GLORY TO THE HIBEES'

The video ending with him shouting and gesturing at - whoever it was - to quieten down. Still, his point had been well made. Not *sure* it was going to be entirely followed through to the letter of the law by all of the starting eleven, mind. *Especially* going by the early start that almost half the team had made already. I wasn't judging anyone. Soon as the video ended I handed Erika her phone back again.

'NOW can I have a pint, please.' I said, like some kid that had wanted to leave the dinner table but wasn't allowed permission by his mum and dad until they'd eaten their greens.

I joined the rest of them, where we sat for the next couple of hours having a scoop. During that time about three quarters of the squad had come in for a lunch time drink. Despite the banter flying back and forward - in relation to the derby - there was only four of us that even had tickets - two Jambos (The Monk and Terry) and then Benji and myself - so we shared a taxi down to Leith around two. Leaving the rest of them still in The Gunner where - if we were going to have *any* chance against The Paddock the next day in the final - I hoped that they'd have taken Jock's words in the video to heart and kept their Saturday a quiet one.

'Quiet' is not what you would have been able to call Easter Road, following Murray's goal.

'Pick that one out of the fucking onion bag, eh, Strings. Their keeper didn't even see it.' Benji screamed, with his arm around my shoulder bouncing but finding me fixed firmly to the ground. *I* didn't see it coming either, to be fair. Looking onto the wet and muddy pitch but miles away deep in thoughts over how fit the lads were going to be the next day, or how 'hungover' to be precise. There *was* a few injury issues that we had though that I was also praying would work out. Bungalow had put his back out picking up a bag of cement at work through the week. Backs are no joke when you put them out and you could take years to live with the pain, never mind hope that it passed inside the space of a few days. With him being such a vital player for us and someone that would be 'key' against a team of nasty bastards like The Paddock - Jock had said he would be giving him right up to the last minute to prove he could play.

We couldn't have passengers in such a vital game. You're either one hundred percent fit or you're nothing at all. As far as going into the trenches, and who you'd want with you, though. Bungalow is one of the first names I'd select so - for our chances of winning the cup -was hoping he'd make the starting eleven.

'We need to put someone else into midfield. They're running all over us.'Benji said, around ten minutes later. Hearts having changed their tactics to try and get themselves back into the match. This comment, though, only then making me think about *our* tactics and when I say our I don't mean Hibernian Football Club. I'd had The Paddock watched for the past couple of weeks. Was all unofficial, like. Jock didn't even know about it. I'd been noticing their results had began to improve over the weeks. Their goals conceded when up against scored was a clear indicator of 'something' having changed with their side. Conceding very little while scoring for fun up the other end.

I hadn't thought much more of it than that but once I knew that we were going to be playing them in the final. I thought it would be a smart idea to get them watched to see *what* was different to when we'd last played them.

Apparently, they'd ditched their manager and this young boy had taken over. Never played a serious game of fitba in his life - the lad - but talks a good game because he's played Championship Manager in his bedroom for twelve hours a day. Was bringing in his laptop before games - with some fancy software on it - to show the starting eleven how he wanted them to go out and play. The reports that I got back were that The Paddock, out of Niddrie, were playing like fucking Barcelona. Tippy tappy tiki taka stuff. Maybe there was something in this new approach?

'They fucking passed Roseburn to death.'

The stick out line that had been the one that had chilled me the most.

There's *nothing* worse than not having the ball. Tires you out, double quick. Chasing it around like a fucking Jack Russell. Add that to the possibility of most of our players (post Edinburgh Derby) being rough as a bag of spanners and - if we weren't taking to the field with anything less than full focus - it gave me a chilling vision that not only was there the possibility that we *wouldn't* win the final but that we'd be given a complete lesson at the same time. An embarrassment you'd rather be spared in something as high profile as a cup final.

They had that Brian Narey in their side. Good fucking player and someone I *hated* coming up against every season, which in itself, is a mark of a decent fitba player. Like me, he'd played with his side for years. In with the bricks. Season upon season. I'd tried to tap him up, - to come and play for the Violet - a couple of years before when, coincidentally, we'd found ourselves in the same Edinburgh Airport departure lounge that summer me and the family went to Salou.

I was serious, like, when I asked him to come and play for us. Didn't have any authority to *do so,* in terms of acting under the capacity of a member of Muirhouse Violet, but if I'd come bak from Salou saying that I had Brian Narey from The Paddock wanting to play for us there wouldn't have been any cunt complaining about it, either.

'Nah, thanks for the offer, Strings, but I'll not be playing for anyone other than The Paddock. One team man, me.' He said before he boarded his plane to Palma with his wife. Wishing Han, Jack and me a good holiday.

I knew where he was coming from. Being the same type of player as him. I'd rather hang up the Copas than pull on anyone else's strip on a Sunday morning.

He was going to be a danger the next day and - as much as I respected him for both his loyalty towards his side and his actual playing ability

- I hoped that one of the boys were going to take one for the team and let him know that they were there early doors. If I didn't do so myself.

'This Skacel's running the fucking show. We need to do something about it. Benji fretted. By this point the match well into the second half with us still leading from that first half goal. They say that derby matches go so fast that they fly by for a player. Well that was applicable to me there, inside the stadium. One minute it was us going one up and the next there was less than ten minutes to go and I'd have barely been able to tell you another three things that had happened during the first eighty minutes, other than the goal.

Getting my hands around the Kwik Save Challenge Trophy - since we'd got through to the final - had become an obsession of mine so it was natural for it to be able to vie with an Edinburgh Derby for my full attention but, in reality, all it was had been a welcome distraction over more pressing matters.

I was probably the least arsed Hibee inside the stadium when Ryan Stevenson scored right as the referee had his whistle in his mouth to blow for full time, and causing a mini pitch invasion at the Hearts end of Easter Road. This, temporarily at least, bringing an instant short lived angered response around me, which replaced the feeling of crushing disappointment to be so close to winning a derby. At odds with any other derby that I'd ever been to in my life. I felt all a bit lacking in emotion, over the events on the pitch.

I had that train journey to be thinking about.

And 'whatever' waited at the other side of it.

And anyway, as Jock had said in his video - There would be *other* Edinburgh Derbies. Well, for me, I hoped so, anyway.

Chapter 35

Strings

'Who's the fucking wideos that sets the prices for products on a train, anyway, and *where* the fuck do they get them from? Just draw the numbers out of a tombola and whatever comes out they slap on a fucking can of beer with a pound sign in front of it?' I - borrowing some of Benji's patter - asked the woman sat facing me and, as already semi expected, was ignored by her. I was already in possession of Benji's drivers license so may as well borrow his patter too, eh?

The poor cunt that was pushing the trolley up and down the aisle through the carriages was just standing there looking awkward. Wasn't his fault, like - and I'm sure that he'd have rather been doing something other than having me nipping his head on a Saturday night - but if you're going to ask someone to pay the equivalent of three pints in The Gunner for the one - barely cold - can then you've got to expect some kind of a blowback from some people, eh?

Could've bought a four pack for the train at that price from the offie, I thought to myself as the guy handed me back my change and can of Heineken. Not that I could've done that, anyway, though, mind. Couldn't have a proper drink due to the driving I'd be doing later. If the cunts hadn't all been so secretive about *what time* I was doing the collection it would've at least given me a ballpark time so that I'd have known if I'd been able to have a few scoops or not but - due to it being all this cloak and dagger stuff - I had to settle for just the one can on the way down.

I knew that she was going to rubber me when I spoke to her. *That's* why I even said it, of course. When I'd got on the train and - after a bit of fucking about - found the seat with my matching ticket sitting above its headrest. 'Here we go then, eh!' I said to the woman who was already sitting in the bank of two seats facing another two, with a wee table separating them. I was just trying to be friendly, like. Fuck's sake? You're going to be sitting facing each other for the best part of fuck knows how many hours. May as well try to be civil, eh?

You could tell that she'd already pre judged me from the moment that I sat down beside her. I'd had a few drinks, nothing mad, like, over the day so was probably stinking of bevvy - in such a confined space with not much in the way of ventilation - and green and white fitba scarf sitting around my neck. One look from her and you could almost see her trying to prevent herself from spontaneously combusting at the thought of sharing - potentially - an Edinburgh to London five hour train journey, with a fitba supporter. I wasn't the only one on the train with either Hibs or Hearts colours. Was actually surprised by how many there were dotted across the train carriages when I'd been trying to find my seat.

I tried to sip that can from Edinburgh to York. Knew that if I drank it, chances were I'd have had *another* one. By the time I was getting off at York I still had around a quarter of it left. Undrinkable by then. I spent the two and a half hours journey thinking about match the next day. Wondering what kind of states the rest of the squad were going to be in by that point of their Saturday, and if they'd taken Jock's advice or not.

Realising that I had been that caught up in everything else, I hadn't checked to see what the weather was going to be like. If it was going to be raining overnight or not. I *always* checked that, too. I can't lie. I LOVE a slide tackle, the type that you can see the proof of on the ground trailing behind you afterwards. If I could pick a condition to play a game of fitba. *Every time* would be with a wee bit of light rain having fallen before the match. Helps with a good wee sliding on your knees celebration as well. Not that I ever got much chances to do any of them, mind. That time Rossi tried one and the ground wasn't wet enough and he ended up with his knees stuck in the ground while he face planted it? Still gets the piss taken out of him about it yet.

Obviously, I knew what I *should've* been thinking about but I'm good at that, though. Bottling up shite. Well, not literally putting shite into a bottle but you know what I mean? It's like, for me, the serious things that I should be thinking about. Well they can get tae fuck. All that negativity and stressing about stuff? Puts fucking years on you. Aye, I much prefer taking all of those kind of thoughts, stuffing them all into a jiffy bag and sticking it into the postbox. That's the thing about that method, though. The jiffy bag *always* comes back return to fucking sender in the end.

With around a quarter of an hour until my connection I took the chance to lum a couple of Embassy before having to get on the second of the two trains. It was only at that point where I started to get a wee bit nervous. You can get nervous, of the unknown, like, though. I think it was the fact that the train, *my* train, on the board now said 'Manchester' as opposed to York. York - on a train timetable - was just non threatening, quaint, never done fuck all to anyone, York. Seeing Manchester, though? Well Manchester represented the place where I was heading for to carry out some cross border highly illegal shite that - no doubt - was going to result in me making my TV debut on 'Road Wars' at some point in the yet to be determined future.

For around about eleven at night. The platform was packed with an assortment of all walks of life. As I stood there having a smoke, a teenage lad, who was standing along with his mates, asked me if he could have a light. As I gave him one, and to pass the time, we stood having a chat. I asked him where him and his mates had been for the night. Boy just laughed at me. That's when I clocked his eyes and how big they were.

He told me that *this* was the first of them all going *out* for the night to 'Warehouse Project' and that this was the last train into Piccadilly.

'You're some boy,' I said shaking my head at him. 'Most people are getting ready to leave the pub by now, - if they've not already left - and you're just going out! Aye, good luck to you, pal. Wish I was joining you.'

'You should come, mate. I'll get you fixed out with some gear. You'll need to ditch the scarf though.' He replied back, already well under the influence because, well, you're not going to go around inviting cunts that have just given you a light on a night out with you, are you?

'Nah, I already have another prior engagement tonight. You have a good one, though.' I replied to the boy while wishing that I could've just went and got smashed in a warehouse. That's not even my thing either, like, but I tell you what, though? I'd take that over driving hundreds of miles on a collect and deliver job for one of Scotland's most notorious underworld figures.

It was touching one on the morning by the time I was taking myself back off the second train and down the platform of Piccadilly and trying to find the exit and my way to the hotel. I didn't even get *out* of the train station without having McKenna on the phone to me. At first - because of it not being *my* phone - I hadn't realised that it was the phone I had on me. Didn't recognise the ring tone and McKenna hadn't called it once since he'd given it to me the last time I'd seen him. It was only when it had continued to ring and ring - while the sound of it didn't get any louder, or quieter - that I eventually twigged that it actually coming from my bag.

'*What took you?*' The first thing that McKenna said, once I'd finally answered the call.

'Aye, sorry, Davey. I'm in the middle of Piccadilly Train Station, pal. It's not exactly a library in here with all the tannoy announcements, eh.' I replied, thinking this was easier to explain than the actual reason.

'Well that's my question answered before I even ask it. I know the train from York to Manchester just arrived at Piccadilly. I just checked. I wanted to make sure that *you* had got off it. Now, I've got a nine o clock tee time at Bruntsfield tomorrow morning so I'm heading off for a few hours sleep so before I do I just wanted to make sure you know the score down there. Just wait on the call. If you don't get a call by six 'then' you can call the number you have. Soon as you make the collection get yourself right up the road, no fucking about. My men will be there at the drop off where I told you. And, Strings, if this goes wrong, mind.'

Maybe I was only able to stand up to him because we had hundreds of miles put between us but I chose to cut him off before he said anything else on the subject.

'Look, Davey. There's no need to say that stuff. The threats and that. I *know* the score. I don't need any *motivation* from you to get the job done. I've already got the motivation to get it done and back to my family. You don't need to go threatening me, or them.'

'I'm just saying, though, Joe. I'm placing a lot of faith and trust in you, with this wee job down there. I'd hate for that to be misplaced and you ending up letting me down. That's all I'm saying, here.'

'Right, I need to find this hotel and get checked in and that'll be me set.' I tried to engineer the end of the call. It wasn't helping, the chat. Only put more pressure on me although - I do believe - that was the whole 'point' of McKenna's call in the *first* place.

'Well if you leave by the correct exit from the station you'll be able to practically piss on the hotel, it's that close to the station.' He replied. 'Anyway, I suppose I better go and get a wee bit sleep. Need to be fresh for my eighteen holes, don't I. Playing with a couple of counsellors tomorrow. Need to be fresh for such esteemed guests, when it comes to greasing the old palms. As a rough guess we should see you back up the road for around eleven, twelve-ish.

Fresh? Was he taking the piss? No doubt, the fat bastard would've been getting driven from hole to hole on the course the next day. If there was one out of the two of us who needed to be fresh, it was my good self. After being up all night and then the stresses and strains of a five hour drive the very *last* thing that I was going to be ready for was ninety minutes chasing a ball around a fitba pitch. Fresh? Aye, right.

He hung up and left me to navigate my way to the Holiday Inn that I'd been booked in to. McKenna hadn't been joking. While he might've been exaggerating about the hotel being close enough for me to urinate on, from the station, it was easily close enough for me to have thrown a half brick at. Convenient.

With it being gone one in the morning by the time I arrived at the front door to check in. The main entrance was locked and you had to talk to a girl on an intercom - I could see her through the glass, sitting behind the reception desk, looking at me as she spoke - and give her your details before the doors would be unlocked to let you in.

'Well here is your key, sir. Check out is eleven am in the morning. Seemed daft that I was checking in at that time of the morning only to be booked to leave again hours later, and it showed on her face.

'Had a bit of issues with trains being cancelled on me. Should've been down here hours before.' I said, making up something vague on the spot that would've explained someone checking in so late for their room.

Frowning on my behalf over this. Her facial expression changing straight away as she remembered about the Enterprise Vehicle Hire envelope that was sat behind the desk for me.

'Oh, this was dropped off for you earlier on from the hire company.'

Thanking her and taking the green and white envelope. I asked if she'd have any clue as to the van's whereabouts might be.

'Take a left when you leave the front of the hotel and walk around five hundred yards and you'll see the sign for the NCP. We have a arrangement with them for parking for the hotel so they should have parked it there for you.' She said, as I opened the envelope in front of her and showed her the car park address that was written on the card and her nodding her head to confirm that it was exactly where she'd assumed it would've been.

'Have a good night, well, morning!' She said as I headed off in the direction of the lifts to go up to my room.

'Aye, you too as well.' I said back to her, thinking that it was probably going to be a competition to see who fell asleep first between her - at her desk - or me, up in the room. Not that sleeping was an option for *either* of us. Both had our own wee jobs to be carrying out, eh.

Didn't fucking STOP me from falling asleep all the same, though. All I did was take my trainers off and sit up on the bed, watching the telly. Since the room was being charged to McKenna's card anyway. I helped myself to a 'wee' watch of a porno - Milfs Next Door 2 - and then paid for that film 'The Hangover.' Aye, we've all been there, like. Sessions that leave you feeling like you've been to hell and back by the end of them. Never managed the whole film. Couldn't even remember where the film had been up to when I passed out. Only realising that I *had* crashed when the phone started going off. Leaving me in a panic when I realised that I'd drifted off and - for the first few seconds at least - didn't know *what* time it was, or if I'd missed other previous calls.

'Hello,' I said, pressing the green icon on the phone as quickly as I could but while trying to sound like anything *but* someone who had just woken from a sleep.

'Yeah, Jock?' A Mancunian accent asked.

'Naw, mate. I'm Strings.' I replied, looking around me and seeing that I was still in the exact same position that I'd been watching the film. Sat upright with my back against the headboard.

'No, by Jock, what I meant was, oh it doesn't matter. You the Edinburgh connect that our mutual friend sent down tonight, yeah?'

He replied. As if he was going to say something but then decided that he couldn't be arsed in the end. Now that I was a bit more alert I had picked up that - exactly like McKenna when he'd called me on getting off the train - he wasn't for using any *actual* names. Making me feel a bit of a dick for saying *mines*.

'Oh, *that?* Aye, I'm the guy.' I almost asked him if he was Wes, which I'm well sure would've went down like a lead balloon, but managed to stop myself at the last moment. All I really needed to worry about was to keep things simple. McKenna told me I'd get a call - having picked up my own phone I had noticed that it was almost half four - and this was 'the' call. In *theory,* all I needed to do now was drive to where the boy on the other end of the line told me to. Get the van loaded with *insert illegal product or products* and drive up the road while not getting stopped by law enforcement and found to be driving while disqualified - and along with - transporting - most likely - Class A drugs.

Piece of piss, when you put it like that.

Despite feeling sick to my stomach at the prospect of it all and the possibilities where it might go wrong. When I'd clocked that the call had came through still kind of early-ish it, at least, gave me a bit of hope that things were going to work out for me getting back to Edinburgh with plenty time to spare before the match. Maybe even sneak in a couple of power hours back at the house, I thought to myself as I got my things together to leave the hotel room.

Wes(?) had given me directions to a residential address in an area called Cheetham Hill. Telling me that it was around twenty minutes from the city centre. I'd half joked to him that it would probably take me longer to find the rental van in the car park so not to stick a timer on me getting there but that I'd be there as soon as I could. I could hear the urgency in his voice when he met that by telling me that I needed to be there straight away. McKenna had hinted that it was all going to be as instant as this - when the call came - and this English boy was living up to that.

I'd heard of Cheetham Hill and - from memory - it had a bit of a reputation to itself. I wasn't too concerned about that side of things, though. Why would I be fazed with going into a notorious part of one city when I *lived* in just as notorious an area of my own? Fucking busman's holiday, that.

'Phone me on this number when you get there and I'll pop down and get you. Tarrrraaa for now, mate.' He said before he hung up.

To be fair to 'Kim from Enterprise' - who had personally signed my drop off card with a single kiss for me - Her written down directions to find the van so clear and concise I reckon a blind man would've found the white Volkswagen Transporter that had been parked for me earlier on prior to my arrival.

After a wee bit of fucking around - due to not knowing the area - that saw me going around the city centre in a complete circle before seeing Piccadilly again, I was on my way. It felt well weird, to be back behind the wheel of an automobile - of any shape or form - never mind a large heavy goods van. I was a wee bit rusty at first and almost took the van into the side of a parked Saab before I'd even made it *out* of the NCP.

Like a bike, as far as remembering what to do. It felt liberating, though, and it wasn't until I was making my way out of the city centre that I realised just how much I'd missed being able to drive. It would've been a lot better had I not been sat with the absolute fear of blue flashing lights going on behind me during every single fucking centimetre that I drove, though. I tried to put that shite at the back of my mind and make the best of things.

Not knowing my way around the van, other than how to turn the key and drive the thing. I turned on the radio but left it at the station that was pre set. Be just my luck to have a wee bump into another car while fucking around with a stereo while I'm banned, I thought to myself. Choosing, instead, to just let the station to play.

Had you not already known what it was that I was on my way to do - and the background story involving me being banned - there's not a chance that you'd have believed that I was driving while disqualified and on my way to a likely drug deal. Singing along to that 'Don't mess with my Toot-Toot' song from the eighties. Tooting the horn in quick succession every time the woman sung 'toot toot' in the lyrics.

Maybe it was just my coping mechanism, to pretend that things are just swell and fucking dandy - when they're not - but peeping your horn as you're driving along the road at five in the morning probably isn't the best way to go about things, when you're trying to remain undetected.

Couldn't help but laugh, though, at the couple of pissheads (or ravers) who had mistaken my peeps as a sign of me knowing them while I passed by them on the road. Both giving me a wave back. I actually gave them an extra toot back, just to say an *official* hello back, like.

Once I got to Cheetham Hill. Despite having never been there in my life before, it had a distinctly *familiar* feel to it. Aye it was Manchester but it could've easily been the north of Edinburgh. The familiar feel to my surroundings wasn't enough to stop me from getting myself lost and having to call the boy back on the number, though.
'You outside, fella?' He answered.

'Well, no, not exactly, well, I *might be*, I suppose, for all I know. To be fair, mate, it's the middle of the night and I don't know where I'm going. Not exactly working with Tom Tom technology, here, either, like.' I replied.

I'd followed his directions - on coming into Cheetham Hill - as much as I'd been able to remember but due to not being fully awake *when* he was telling me, I'd forgotten some parts to them. I remembered that he'd said something about me looking for a Chinese next to a bookies and to take the next left after that, but hadn't seen either.

'Mate? Yer boss said you'd be on time. Yer gonna miss yer fookin slot.' He said, kind of in a fluster. Should've been *me* who was doing the panicking, not him. And what did he mean by 'slot' too, either?

After a quick confirmation of where I was parked up, he managed to issue me with some amended directions. Telling me that I was only a few minutes away.

Making double sure I listened to him, sensing that one more wrong step from me might turn things sour. I pulled up outside the row of houses - that made up a much bigger housing estate - as close as I could get to number Forty Seven, that the guy had given me. With him saying on the phone that he would 'come down' and get me, I'd automatically assumed that he was going to be in some high rise set up. Which then had me thinking that - once again - I had fucked up with my navigation.

I could literally see the name of the street that he'd told me, and that I had scribbled down on the Holiday Inn notepad that was on the bedside table. And the door number matched. I hit redial on the phone and hoped for the best.

'That's me now, I think.' I said.

When I saw the blind slightly open upstairs in the house, enough for me to see the bedroom lights on and for whoever was looking out to see me, I knew that I was at the right address.

'Ok, meet me at the door.' He said before hanging up. The blinds closing again straight after.

I got out the van, unsure what I was walking into. Despite it not exactly being my arena of where I went to work. I think the fact that *any* time I went out stringing and that I wouldn't know what I'd be walking into - or if I'm walking back out - helped as I approached the front door of the house.

I hadn't even really started to consider that *whoever* I was doing business with on behalf of McKenna would be a problem. I know that there's some serious cunts kicking around in England but if you wanted to try and get into things with Davey McKenna, and rip the man off, then *that* would be a fight that you'd be better off not picking. My only worry had been the boys in blue. As far as I was concerned they were the *only* cunts that I needed to be worrying about from leaving Manchester until taking the pitch at Muirhouse Park. I still come over a bit nervous, though, when I knocked on the door. It opening straight away with the boy already having ran down to meet me.

'Alright, fella.' He said, warmly but having a quick peek out of the front door, from side to side, to make sure there wasn't anyone else with me before actually letting me in.

'Upstairs, Jock.' He said, waving his hand to usher me up the stairs - that faced the front door - with him. What struck me first of all was all of the people that were inside the house. Back of five in the morning. It could've *easily* been an afters. Only, everyone seemed to be there working. Moving boxes all over the place. Cunts telling others what to do. It was like a small distribution factory. Only, inside someone's house.

The colour was hard not to notice, either. Boxes and boxes of that unmistakable blue Adidas trainers box. From floor almost up to the ceiling, stacked side by side. And that was just the *one* downstairs room that I'd managed to sneak a look in, as I was walking up the stairs, following behind the Manc lad.

He showed me into an upstairs room and it was the same again. Floor to ceiling in those blue boxes. The wall - that was joining one house to another - had been completely knocked through to offer a massive piece of space and even then, the extended storage was being taken up, mostly, by boxes and boxes of trainers. But they didn't appear to be destined to sit there for long. Being carried away in droves by several bodies, at a fast pace.

I felt a right fucking fanny. All that stressing I'd done since McKenna had handed me the job. Fucking drugs and weapons, potential Eastern European girls for his strip clubs? And - *instead* - all it was were pairs of Adidas. McKenna had that sports shop in West Tollcross, mind, I thought to myself as I started to put two and two together. *And* managing to come up with *anything* other than four in the process.

There had to have been a good twenty plus gadgeys spread across the room, all coming and going. Carrying as much blue boxes as they could without dropping them. I couldn't get my head around the fact that all of this was going on at that time of the morning, on a housing scheme. There was a boy who was sat a big table and wasn't speaking to anyone. Just sat shoving stacks of notes into one of those money counters that you always see the drug lords using in the films. I'd never seen as much money in my life. I'd also - in the flesh - never seen an Uzi before. Well that's what it looked like. Sat on the table beside him. I'd seen enough front covers of Hip Hop albums in my life to know what an Uzi looked like, though.

It was, also, a gentle reminder the level - and mentality - of people that I was dealing with. Normally your average JD Sports staff aren't strapped when they're sorting you out with a new pair of trabs, like.

The boy - who I still didn't know if he was Wesley or not and by then, it wasn't important. All that *was* was that I got my van filled with what it was meant to be loaded up with and I got on my way - left me to stand there in the middle of it all. I did a three hundred and sixty degrees turn and there was, at no point, a moment where there was a break in the Adidas boxes. Was almost like it was wallpaper in the house. Well. Three D wallpaper of Adidas boxes popping out at you, like.

'Ok, we need to get the Jock sorted next and get him gone.' The boy, who'd let me, in said to the moody looking chap at the table with the Uzi. Without even saying a word he looked up and did the slightest of nods to the guy which had seemed enough to get the show on the road.

The boy, at the table - who I couldn't help but take as the boss - didn't look like he was English. Albanian, possibly? Anyway, wherever he was from. He was commanding the respect in the room. Fair dues. I'd have been expecting all the respect in the room if *I* had been the one with the Uzi, as well.

'Right, fella. Chuck us yer keys.'

The original boy - who was wearing a pair of Zx's and, due to being a short arse - a pair of jeans that had it's hem taken up on the inside, so he could wear them. An Umbro Manchester City sweatshirt tucked into his jeans. I'm no fashionista, like, but I've never understood that sweatshirt tucked inside jeans look, myself. The boy even had the trademark Martin O'Neil sleeves pulled up over his elbows look but I think that was more down to the graft that he was putting in. I'd been given the impression that there had been a whole lot more of those boxes of trainers at the start of the night. *That* was what he was originally on about with my 'slot, I reckoned.' Cunts had, evidently, been picking up boxes of before I'd got there and it appeared that this was a 'pop up' kind of operation and that they were going to be keeping going until the house had been completely cleaned out.

'I'll get some of the boys to fill it up for you, mate.' He said as I handed the keys over. Still in my hand from getting out and locking the van.

'How much for the Jock collection?' He shouted over to the boss guy at the table who done fuck all other than point towards the sheets of paper that were stapled against each other, lying on the table.

The guy walked over, picked it up and had a quick look before putting it down again and shouting across the room. 'Hayzo, a hundred and seventy pairs of Sambas. White VW Transporter parked outside. Come on boys, ten boxes at a time. Chop chop.' He dished out the order that looked like having an immediate effect. 'Hayzo' getting *his* team sparking into action. Half a dozen of them reaching for the stacks of boxes, picking them up and all exiting the room with the sound of footsteps - like an army - going downstairs.

'Not sure what the fuck the big man up the road is going to do with a hundred and seventy pairs of Sambas, like. Maybe a few years ago but you don't see as many wearing them, these days.' I said, just trying to break the silence and the feeling of me standing there like almost a ghost while teams of men all scurried about the place, past and around me.

This comment, though, seeming to stop this Wesley (I'd decided it was him) boy in his tracks.

'You think you're picking up Sambas, fella, yer?' A smile crept onto his face at this.

One of his team was walking past, carrying a stack of boxes as he'd said this to me. I stopped and grabbed him and took one of the boxes off his pile and opened it up. There was a pair of Sambas inside.

'Well, there *is* a pair of Adidas Sambas inside the box so…' I didn't think I really needed to say much more when it came to proving my point to the boy.

'Well, yer, there *is* a pair of Adidas in there, but. You mean? You don't know?' He looked around to a few others who had been watching and started laughing. 'You really thought you were down from Scotland to pick up pairs of trainers?' He asked - almost for one last piece of confirmation - once he'd stopped laughing again.

'No, mate. I thought I was down here on a drug run.' I replied back.

'Ah, so you *do* know why you're down here, then. I was going to fookin say there, for a moment.'

Now I was just plain confused. I came down pretty much accepting that I'd be bringing a load of drugs back over the border.

I'd felt that to have known more details of *what* I was bringing back to Scotland would leave it harder for me to *lie about* if and when I got the van stopped by police. Easier to just be ignorant. Knowing that it was going to be drugs or weapons of some description was *enough* to know.

Instead, I find myself surrounded by boxes of Adidas trainers, that I'd looked inside and seen with my own eyes to actually *be* trainers, while he's trying to tell me that they *weren't* trainers.

As some of the workers went back and forward with boxes to the Transporter. He then went on to tell me that aye - as I'd already kind of accepted was going to be the case - I was taking a shipment of Ching up to McKenna *inside* the pairs of Sambas. An ounce inside the sole of every single one of them. Two ounces per box. One hundred and seventy five boxes. There'll be fucking flying cars by the time you get out if you get caught, I thought, when dealing with the twist that saw the confirmation that I was going to be transporting drugs *just* as I'd started to think that it was a wee bit lower down the scale, with me driving stolen trainers around.

'It's a long story why I'm even down here, pal. I'll just be glad when I'm back *up* the road and dropped off the van again.' I said as I watched almost a quarter of the room empty in front of my eyes. Someone else was standing beside the guy at the table. I heard him say something about 'Birmingham consortium and also Wrexham' and the boy with the Uzi nodding his head and pointing in another direction of the room. A few of the lads all then starting to take boxes from that particular pile.

'We'll get you on your way soon, fella. Van's about loaded up. Long drive ahead, haven't you? What's it? Like five six hours or summit?' He said as he took a cigarette - offering me one too which was gladly accepted - out of his packet and lit it up.

'Aye, something like that. It's not just that, pal. I'm playing fitba later on for my team. Been up half the night and have to drive back to Scotland.' I said, enjoying the strong early morning knock of the nicotine.

'Oh, yeah? Sunday league stuff?' He enquired.

'Aye, kind of. It's a final though, so not just your standard run of the mill league match, eh. Kwik Save Challenge Trophy final, like. Decent, man.' I looked at my watch. It was getting on for almost seven in the morning by that point. I thought ahead to early afternoon and kick off time. I'm stood there inside a converted house slash distribution centre on a Manchester housing estate while the rest of the team were still lying in their beds from the night before.

'Fookin Kwik Save trophy, eh? Fookin ell, lads. We've got a potential Balon D'Or winner in our midst, here.' He shouted out, pissing himself laughing. I wasn't too chuffed, like. On account of him taking the piss, you know? Was never going to be a good move to let the cunt know this though, obviously, so instead I laughed along with them.

'Aye, word is Barca, Bayern, Juventus AND Man United are going to have scouts there today to watch me.' I joked back which had them laughing further.

'Be lucky if I last the first twenty minutes before I'm breathing out my hoop, though. Hardly the best pre match preparation, this. Telling me Cristiano fucking Ronaldo spends the morning before a match away picking up gear for someone.' This was the reality of it. While I would've fucking DIED for The Violet. There was no was that I was giving up my place in the starting eleven to someone who would be a lot more fresh and fit for the occasion. Call me selfish if you like but Kwik Save Challenge Trophy finals don't come around too often and I wasn't giving up my spot to no cunt. How long I'd be able to *last* out on the pitch really was debatable, though.

'Eyyyy, do you get drug tested, fella?' He asked me, like he was pondering on something.

'Drug test? Nah, pal. It's not that high a level, no pun there, like.' I answered while thinking about Montana and the fact that if we were to have ever been tested for drugs while playing for The Violet he'd have been banned from the game fucking years ago.

'Well get a bit of this down you, fella. That'll help give you a bit of energy. Just like Red Bull, really, only probably better for your health,' He said passing over a small bag of this dirty looking whitey yellowish compressed powder.

'Nah, mate, I'm not really into drugs. Not exactly *anti* them, either, like. We're all free to do what we want to our own bodies. No for me though, like.' I said to him but he wasn't for listening to this.

'Nonsense, fella. It's just a bit of Billy, eh? It'll perk you up for the drive back to Jockland and you'll be fresh as a daisy for kick off. Best of stuff, too, fella. Base. I couldn't pull off an all-nighter, myself, like tonight without a little bump now and again.

Just as he had forced the bag into my hand I heard the screams from downstairs.

'DIBBLE'S COMING.'

On hearing this, my man sparked into panic mode.

'GET EVERYONE BACK IN AND THE FOOKIN SHUTTERS DOWN, NOWWW.'

It was the most animated I'd seen the boy at the table with the Uzi be from when I arrived. One mention of the police, all it took. While cunts were running all over the place. Some grabbing weapons. This boy at the table stopped the process of counting the money and grabbed his gun.

One of them, standing by the blinds had opened them slightly enough so that he could look down the road. The same direction as I'd driven down.

'No sign of them yet.' He said, to no one in particular. I heard the slamming of doors and went and had a quick look out, myself. It was the back doors of the Transporter being closed while two of the boys who had been loading up the van quickly ran back into the house. Then I heard the sound of the metal shutters coming down. I'd never noticed them when I'd originally entered. Probably because they were on the *inside* of the house - actually behind the front door - as opposed to the outside. The kind that you'll see business premises use.

'Best get yourself comfy, fella. We might be here some time.' The boy, who had been dealing directly with me, said as he rushed about the place. Making a couple of calls and asking for updates.

'IF THOSE FUCKING BASTARDS TRY TO GET IN HERE YOU FUCKING DEFEND. LIKE FORTRESS.'

The boy with the Uzi spoke up for the first time. Adding to my theory that he was of Eastern European descent.

Admittedly, being stuck in a house with fuck knows how many kilos of drugs stashed inside it *was* something that I should've been concerned about. With how some of the boys inside the house were equipping themselves, though. The police were going to have a hard time ahead of them actually getting their hands on them. Could've been doing with *not* being in the middle of it all though, mind.

It didn't exactly look practical for me to say 'Excuse me, lads. If you don't mind handing me the keys to my VW and I'll just slip out the door before you all engage in that whole gangland warfare that you're getting ready for.' so I just ended up taking a seat for the first time since entering the room. Nervously puffing on another cigarette while I tried to gauge what was really going on.

You can normally get a handle on things by the reactions of others and while the 'hired goons' in the room had their hands around a range of weapons from hand guns to proper automatic rifles, standing on alert, it was only because they'd been *told* to. The reaction of the Manc that I'd been dealing with from the get go more put me at ease as - apart from the initial orders to abandon filling the Transporter and to get everyone back inside the house - he seemed to be quite chilled about it all.

Eventually he explained to me that this was all precautionary and that the chances - unless they were acting on a specific tip off - of the police actually having *any* interest in the house, and more importantly what was inside it, was practically none. Still, when you've got millions of pounds worth of product on you. No chances can be taken. He'd told me that they had the whole of the housing estate sewn up in terms of look outs and that the police could never enter or leave without them being seen. Parts of Cheetham Hill, apparently, were practically no go zones for law enforcement.

'Amount of Ye-Yo that we've had dropped off here tonight, fella? You carn't be too careful, eh. By the time we've emptied this gaff there won't be a bit of the fookin British Isles that won't have our Charlie showing up by tomorrow.' He said, with a bit of pride behind it. As if his staying up through the night to send Ching off in all directions of the country was something that he could sit down and tell his grandchildren about.

'Excuse me a second, fella.' He said, his phone going off while he was in the middle of telling me about some of the dirty police that they had in their pocket, which tended to help them when it came to the free and easy movement of their operation.

'Yer fookin kidding? When did that happen? Ah for fook's sake, that'll set things back. We've still got around half a dozen pick ups before we're clear. No, no, I know, fella. Not your fault, yeah. Appreciate you finding out for us. Tarrraaa for now, yeah.'

'RIGHT, SOME UNLUCKY FOOKER'S BEEN FOUND LYING STABBED ACROSS THE WAY SO YOU KNOW WHAT THAT MEANS? WE'RE GOING TO BE KNEE DEEP IN DIBBLE FOR AT LEAST THE NEXT COUPLE OF HOURS. THE REST OF THE COLLECTIONS WILL NEED TO GO ON HOLD AND NO FOOKER LEAVES HERE UNTIL THINGS DIE DOWN OUTSIDE.'

He shouted across the room to everyone.

'OH, oh naw, naw, pal. That's not going to work for me. I need to get back up to Scotland. I've got the final later on, eh?' If I'd had the chance to again, I wouldn't have said it. Surrounded by millions of pounds worth of drugs, and what that - and the money that it entailed - meant to everyone. Someone playing in an amateur fitba final? Well it didn't really register, when you put it like that.

'Fella? *I* want you out of here and on your way as soon as possible but the place is going to be swarming with dibble looking for a suspect. No go zone or not. They still need to be seen to be doing their job when there's something serious like a stabbing. You really want to chance being stopped driving on your way out of Cheetham Hill when you've got over a million pounds worth of Cocaine in the back of your van?'

'You're right, pal. Doesn't sound too appealing, like.' I shrugged my shoulders pragmatically.

'You know what it's like. There'll be a whole clean up crew on the scene in the next few minutes. Police team, ambulance, forensics. Let's just pray that it's not a murder or else the cunts will be there for fookin days. He said, while offering me another cigarette which I knocked back, having just stubbed one out.

'Should be cool, though, fella. My man on the inside - on that phone call - told me that the lad was still alive when he was found up the close over the road. Tell you what. Why don't you get yourself a bit of kip? May as well, since you're not going anywhere for the next couple of hours.

The thought of me passing out, while I sat inside a house full of Manchester gangsters guarding a pile of Ching while half of Greater Manchester police were outside, along with an Enterprise rental van full of drugs and my prints behind the wheel, was preposterous.

Instead, I sat in the corner and tried to keep myself to myself while clock watching and stressing the fuck out over the fact that the longer I was kept back from leaving, the more difficult it was going to be for me to make kick off. Priorities all wrong, as always. Missing being in the starting eleven of Muirhouse Violet for the Kwik Save Challenge Trophy sitting right at the top of my list instead of the much more urgent and pressing matters that were taking place right in front of me.

As part of their enquiries. The police eventually knocked on the door of the house. The Manc I'd got friendly with over the course of the previous few hours - casual as you like - opened the bedroom blinds and window and held a conversation with them via that method, as opposed to opening any front doors or anything.

Seemed to have been just standard door to door stuff. Have you or anyone else in your house seen or heard anything. Usual deal.

'Nah, fella. I've slept through it all. Is everything alright, though?' He shouted down to the officer with fake concern knowing that he wasn't going to be given much in the way of information back by the police man other than some sort of stock reply.

There was a *very* iffy moment though when they'd started to sniff around the van, possibly checking vehicles in case the suspect was hiding out inside one.

'You better have locked that fookin van behind you.'

He shouted out but without taking his eyes from outside. I jumped up to have a look, myself. One of the officers was looking inside the front windows while the other one walked around to the back of it. At the time, I'd just thrown them my keys and let them get on with things and had absolutely no idea what they'd done with the van after that. Didn't even have the keys back in my possession at that point.

'Emmmmmmm' One of the lads standing across the room said, looking unsure of whether he had or hadn't in the whole rush to get inside before the police had appeared on the scene.

We're going to fucking find out in a second, I fretted, as I watched him try the door. While they were - specifically - looking for a suspect in a stabbing. I imagined that a VW Transporter full of boxes of trainers would not be an average find in somewhere like a Manchester housing estate, and would've been treated as such. Due to the angle of the house, and where I'd parked the van you couldn't see whether he had been able to open the door or not but I tell you what, though. It was the longest fucking few seconds of my life until I seen him emerge again and join his colleague as they moved onto the next few cars that were parked ahead. Having a look as they walked down the street towards the next set of front doors.

'Fookin close one there, fella. Bit *too* close for comfort, that.' He laughed but with a very real and relieved look to his face as he closed the blinds again with the subject of the police - who, logically, were always going to be knocking on the door at some point - now dealt with.

Now it wasn't exactly like that Stockholm Syndrome thing you hear about because it wasn't like I'd been held hostage inside that council house but - in situations like that - it's mad how you can end up getting on with cunts, like.

This boy eventually confirmed that he was, indeed, Wesley. Season ticket holder of Manchester City and someone who had been into the whole flares and Kickers / Hacienda Manchester scene. When I'd told him about me being a Hibee he laughed, kind of like self depreciatingly. Telling me that my team had cost him Three Hundred and Fifty quid through conceding that injury time goal in the derby. Aye, it's funny how you can find yourself bonding in such situations, like.

Fair play to the GM Police. They didn't fuck about. The last patrol car pulling away from the scene around half eight in the morning. Maybe they just didn't want to be there any longer than they needed to, I suppose. Knowing the police like I do, though, it was probably more to do with the fact their piece break was coming up, than anything else.

'Right, lads. Finish up with the VW out there and lets get Hot Shot Hamish on his way.' Wesley said, clapping his hands in a chop chop fashion.

I thanked him for his urgency on the matter. With what time it was. I was still going to be able to get up the road in time, drop off the van and then get myself sorted and away to the game. But only *just.*

'Well it's been a pleasure meeting and doing business with you, fella. Hope to do so again in the future, Jock.' Wesley said as he handed me the keys to the van and attempted to give me some kind of idiots guide on getting out of Manchester and back onto the motorway.

'Don't take this the wrong way, pal, but while it was a pleasure meeting you, considering what's went on the last couple of hours. I hope I *never* see you again in my life.' I joked.

'Good luck in the final, by the way, fella. I hope you win.' He said patting me on the back as the two of us left the upstairs room.

'Right now, a win, for me would be to get myself (and the Adidas') back up the road in one piece. Lifting the Kwik Save Challenge Trophy at the end of the journey would be a mere bonus.' I said as he unfastened the industrial sized locks at the top middle and bottom of the front door to let me go.

'Be safe, fella and tell the big man up the road I was asking for him. Me and McKenna go way back.' He said waving me off.

'Aye, me too. *That's* why I'm here, unfortunately.' I said, knowing that he had no idea the ins and outs of that particular statement and didn't really need to know.

He'd told me to follow the directions for Salford and then I'd see the signs for getting myself onto the M6. The roads, while quiet, were relatively busier than they'd been when I had travelled through the night from the NCP to the house in Cheetham Hill. The darkness had provided me with a bit of a false sense of security. As if the night sky was able to hide the disqualified driver from everyone's view.

Driving my way out of Manchester though, at around nine in the morning and in the daylight? It felt like the *opposite* of my last journey. That *every. single. car,* who either passed me or was sitting behind the van, *all* knew that I shouldn't have been behind the wheel. It was going to be a long journey with such a paranoid mindset.

I suppose I should've been thankful. It took my mind off the life changing amount of Cocaine that was in the back of the van that was being driven up the road. Paranoia is paranoia, though. Wherever you manage to find it from. It was not an easy drive as a result. Thinking - *expecting*, actually - that I was going to be getting pulled by the police at any given moment.

I thought the radio would take my mind away from things. Stick some tunes on, eh, I assumed as I switched it on. It was some woman presenter on Radio Two who had bagged the misfortune of an early Sunday shift. She was saying the she had an hour left of her show which left me thinking of all the capers that were taking place back in Cheetham Hill while her shift was probably just starting.

After she'd done a wee bit of blethering she introduced the next track. A Simon and Garfunkel tune, 'Somewhere they can't find Me.'

I'd never heard it before, quite like them as well, but couldn't help but see the irony of the lyrics as they came from the speakers.

'But I've got to creep down the alley way. Fly down the highway. Before they come to catch me. I'll be gone. somewhere they can't find me.

Oh baby, you don't know what I've done. I've committed a crime. I've broken the law. while you were sleeping and just dreaming of me. I held up and robbed a liquor store.'

Sometimes you get those weird wee coincidences, where a lyric in a song fits your own personal situation - apart from robbing an offie, like - so I had a wee laugh about it. Wasn't laughing so much - or my own personal paranoia doing much better - when the next song come on from Adam and the Ants and Adam's on there singing about being the 'Dandy Highwayman.'

What the fuck are all these songs about highways or highwaymen? I thought to myself while looking in the side mirrors behind me for the millionth time. It was a bit of a stretch to even ask but I'd hoped to avoid any sightings of police vehicles on the M6 but for such a major stretch of road, that was *never* going to be possible. I'd passed three - in some shape or form - since leaving the house back in Cheetham Hill with my arse convulsing each and every time until I'd felt that the danger was past. I'd seen one pass me. Another one parked up on a raised lay-by beside the motorway on my side and, for all of a couple of nervously arse dropping minutes, had a BMW X5 yellow and blue marked police car traveling at a smooth sixty behind me who, naturally, was not risking anything by going even one mile per hour over the speed limit from A to fucking B.

The police officer in the passengers seat even giving me a friendly nod as they overtook me. Me smiling back at him while inside praying to fuck that they weren't about to stick their lights on and pull me over. Instead - looking like they'd just taken a call - they went from their steady and smooth slow speed to sticking their lights on and tearing up the outside lane of the motorway.

I pulled in at the nearest services from there. Just to get my head together, more than anything else, because just from the reaction I'd had from them driving behind me for a couple of minutes. I had showed myself that *had* they actually decided to pull me over I wouldn't have had a fucking chance of negotiating my way out of things without them thinking that there was something 'off' about me.

Fuck, I was knackered though. Felt like I was ready to mentally and physically drop. I'm one of those 'needs his regular eight hours' types or I'm all out of sync and no good to no cunt, never mind myself. This wasn't even *close* to having had eight hours. A couple, at best, while sitting upright on a hotel bed doesn't even fucking count in my book, at all.

I came back out of the service station bathrooms and went to get myself a coffee for driving up the road, figuring *that* would at least keep the wolves from the door when it came to me falling asleep behind the wheel and crashing a million pounds worth of Ching into some farmer's field. I went to pay for it at the till and - sluggishly as well as sleepily - pulled out both a tenner *and* the wee bag of yellowish powder that Wesley had given to me *right* as it all kicked off when the shout went out about the police coming. I'd forgotten all about it - due to the instant panic that fell over the house - but, subconsciously, in that moment I must've just shoved it in my pocket.

'I've seen worse at this time of the morning in these services.' The woman, around her late forties early fifties, behind the till said as I presented her with both a Ten Pound note and a bag of 'Base,' as Wes had called it.

'Aye, I suppose you only take legal tender as payment though, eh? It's not the apocalypse, yet.' I joked, making no attempt to rush the bag back into my pocket. Well and truly busted. But if that was going to be the biggest bust I'd experience from Kendal to Edinburgh then I'd have snatched your fucking hand off at that.

Getting back to the van and sticking my cup of coffee in its holder. I sat staring at the bag of powder that Wesley had given me.

'Do I?' From what he'd told me. Take some of that and I'd *fly* back up the road, and still be alive and kicking to play the game of my life in the final. I'd had 'Speed' before, back in the day, like. Who hasn't? The way Wesley had spoken about *this* stuff though, it was as if it was like some weapons grade strength stuff.

You know what, fuck it. It's been that kind of a twelve hours, why stop now, eh? I decided, prising the plastic lid from off the top of the coffee cup before tipping in the contents of the baggie. Didn't know how much - technically - I'd put in but thought it would make a difference to things.

By fuck it made a difference to things. It was a task to keep my van going at seventy going up that motorway. The amount of times I had to correct myself because I'd caught myself creeping up. I couldn't help it. Once it kicked in, my journey changed. I felt my own confident self again. Full of thoughts and ideas. My mind was all over the place but it was *far* preferable to how it had been *before* I'd stopped at the services.

The hundred and seventy five boxes of pairs of Adidas' that were in the back with ounces of Ching inserted under their soles? A mild side note as far as I was concerned. Barely even remembered about them behind me as I drove up, continually watching the distance to Edinburgh decrease while my mind began to fix on the fact that there was a certain Kwik Save Challenge Final trophy only hours away now.

Those earlier thoughts about how fucked I was going to be for the match? What were they all about? I thought to myself. The way I was feeling, breezing up that road. I felt that - despite not really having a sleep since going to bed on the Friday night - not only could I absolutely boss a midfield for ninety to one hundred and twenty minutes (plus pens) in a Kwik Save Challenge Trophy but could then go on and do a fucking twelve hour shift *for* Kwik Save, themselves!

That stuff, the Base, *was* strong, though. I was talking away to myself on the drive up. Giving myself some Jock Hunter style pep talks before the match. Obviously wasn't as conventional as *any* player would choose before a final though, to begin with.

By my reckoning. They'd all be starting to arrive at the pavilion for the game when I'd be dropping the rental van off at McKenna's drop off point in Portobello. I'd already phoned Benji - much to Benji's annoyance although I reminded him that he should've been up by that time, anyway - when I was driving up to say that he had to be ready for picking me up around one and getting me to the pitch in time for the match.

The Base must've showed in me because about the first thing he said to me was 'You been fucking taking something?'

'Benji, just you fucking be there to pick me up. You won't believe half of what I tell you later on but for now make sure you get me to the game. MUIRHOUSE RULES YA BASSS' I shouted merrily before hanging up on him.

Knowing that he'd have been up for hours with excitement. I called Jock Hunter next.

'This better not be a fucking sickie getting pulled,' The welcoming way he answered the call.

'Quite the opposite, Jock. I just wanted to let you know that I'm fit and raring to go.' I replied enthusiastically. Maybe *too* enthusiastically.

'Is this a new thing? This pre match fitness update, Strings?' He asked, sarcastically.

'Naw, Naw. It's just that I wanted to give you advance warning that I'm not going to be turning up until just before kick off but just wanted to make sure you don't go doing anything daft like sticking someone else's name in the starting eleven because you think I'm not coming. I'm down in England on business but not long and I'll be over the border. I've had a good night's sleep though so don't worry about the drive up.'

'England? What you doing down … Actually I probably don't want to know. Just you fucking be there, ok! This is the big time today, mind, Joe. You worked hard to get to it. Don't go missing it. If you're there a minute after kick off then you've blown it because I'm not wasting a sub after a minute.' He said, letting me know the score upfront, as always.

'I'll be there, Jock. Don't you worry about that, mucker.' I said, confidently, before hanging up and continuing on with the drive.

I put in one last call to Jack - also waking him up - to tell him to meet me at Muirhouse Park with my boots and shinpads. I rested after that. Now satisfied that all ducks were now in a row for the rest of the journey back up in Edinburgh.

I could see the signs for Penrith up ahead and just over a hundred miles to Edinburgh. Couple of hours and I'd have made it and with that fucking Base it felt like it would feel like an hour and a half would've been shaved off the time, anyway.

For the first time since before McKenna had given me my orders. I felt good. I felt like things were going to work out. And as far as the small - and aye, fucking massive - matter of the Kwik Save Challenge Trophy? That trophy was in the bag already. Like how you pick something on Amazon and it goes into your basket but you've not paid for it yet? Aye, that particular piece of silverware was already sitting in Muirhouses 'cart.' We just needed to go and make the payment by taking care of Niddrie.

That's always how life works though, isn't it? Just when you're feeling good about your self and life's going to go your way, for a change. I'm driving - in silence - smiling away to myself at the prospect of getting McKenna off my case again *and* getting the chance to kiss some silver. Fuck your Sky Sports 'Super Sundays' *that* would be a fucking Super Sunday, and a half. But, aye you're driving along - speeding out your tits - happy as a fucking sand boy and *that's* when the blue lights go on behind you and bring you crashing back down to earth.

I hadn't seen any danger. From the moment I'd left Cheetham Hill I had looked in the rear view mirrors *way* more times than is probably safe for a driver of an automobile but that had been led through the insane levels of paranoia ripping through me. From Manchester to Edinburgh there was not going to be a chance that a police car was going to end up behind me and me not know about it.

Undercover PI cars, though?

Chapter 36

Jack

'NOW DON'T YOU FUCKING LET ME DOWN HERE, SON. LET ME DOWN ON THIS AND YOU CAN KISS THAT ARSE OF YOURS GOODBYE TO *ANY* FUCKING X-BOX.'

Dad sounded manic. Like a record playing where it's speeded up a couple of notches. Only in dad's case a lot *more* than just a couple. Wasn't quite chipmunk pitch but he was on the way.

Mum had already woken me up, hours earlier when she'd got up to get ready for her shift, and it had only seemed like I'd managed to get myself back to sleep again - What else was I supposed to do on a Sunday morning? - when the phone went, downstairs.

I just dingeyed it to begin with and let it ring out. Only it rang again, and wouldn't stop. Of course, it stopped by the time I'd managed to get myself out of bed and down the stairs to answer it. I wasn't even given a chance to put one foot on the first stair to go back up to bed when it rang for the third time.

'Oh, I'm glad you could surface ya wee bastard.' It was dad on the other end of the line. It was a bit of a bad reception and you could tell he was in a car somewhere. With it being the derby the day before, I'd not seen him come home and - up until answering the phone - had thought that he was still lying through in bed, sleeping off whatever he'd been doing for the derby.

'Thought you were still sleeping, like I should be.' I said, not even sure *what* time it was but sure it was still well early.

'Wish I fucking was, son.' He replied.

'Listen, I need you to do something VERY important for me, Jack. You're going to the cup final later anyway, aren't you?' He asked.

I knew that he had this cup final with The Violet. He'd not stopped banging on about it once they won the semi final, that Sunday. I hadn't decided if I was going to go or not, though. Mum - being at work - couldn't go and had been saying to me that I should've went, just to lend dad a bit of moral support on his big day, and that. Not that that emotional blackmail stuff works on me. Especially when I couldn't exactly ever remember much in the way of dad putting in *any* appearances when I was playing for the primary school. If you wanted to reverse the roles.

Putting me on the spot like that, though? Well I could hardly say I *wasn't* going. I'd envisaged no cunt mentioning it and me then just happening to not appear by kick off.

'Aye, of course, dad.' I lied.

'GOOD well I need you to do something SUPER important for me, Jackie. I'm out doing a wee bit of earning this morning and I'm not going to have a chance to swing past the house before the match to pick up my boots and shinpads. Stick them in a bag and bring them down to Muirhouse Park. Go to the pavilion and hand them into the home dressing room for me. They're inside the cupboard in the hall.'

'Aye, dad.' I simply replied. Pissed off that I'd been brought out of my bed and double pissed off that I was having my Sunday afternoon picked out for me before I'd even had a chance to have any breakfast.

'Kick off's half one but have them down there by one at the latest.' He barked. His over enthusiastic shouting along with the noise coming through travelling was enough for me to hold the handset away from my ear and still hear everything.

"NOW DON'T YOU FUCKING LET ME DOWN HERE, SON. IT'S A BIG DAY FOR YOUR DAD. LET ME DOWN ON THIS ONE AND YOU CAN KISS THAT ARSE OF YOURS GOODBYE TO ANY FUCKING X-BOX. FUCK THIS UP AND YOU'LL BE GETTING A SEGA MASTER SYSTEM.'

He hung up on me after that. Maybe cut off through a bad connection? My orders were understood, though. Didn't have a fucking clue what a Master System was but had a feeling that I'd have still preferred an X-box, going by the way he'd implied it.

I ended up back in bed again. For the few moments that I'd been down the stairs. Stanton had been stood beside me with that tail of his going in expectation but I couldn't face taking him out so early.

'In a wee while, pal. Go back to your bed for a bit, it's Sunday, ya daftie.' I told him, as I started going back up to my room. Never sure what it is that dogs actually 'hear' when you speak to them but he seemed to take the hint and skulked back through to his bed in the kitchen.

Not thinking to set any alarm on my phone. Through all the sleeping and waking and sleeping and waking *then* sleeping again. I didn't wake up the next time - the one *without* mums or dads being the enablers - until around lunch time. Slept a bit later than I'd planned but that's the stuff that you tend to get away with when you've not got a parent nipping your head.

Another thing - that your parents are brilliant at getting you to do - is to get a move on, when required. I could've probably done with it, that Sunday. I had a whole hour to get myself ready, give Stanton a wee walk, and then myself down to the pitch to drop my dad's kit off to the team. Plenty of time.

Obviously, that was why I found myself unleashing my inner Usain Bolt. Leaving Martello Court *well* after one o clock - and in fact - so 'after' I was now beyond the half past cut off and kick off time. Bolting down the street with my dad's boots and shinpads stuck in my rucksack. He was going to go completely fucking radge at me when I got there. All that dominated my thoughts as I ran through the street, almost getting myself ran over by some cunt in a Mondeo when bolting across the street without looking where I was going.

Things like basic pedestrian road safety couldn't compete with the grief that I was going to get from the old man. Fuck's sake? You'd almost rather *take* getting hit with a car than having him on your case. For the big game of fitba that he'd not stopped talking about for weeks. Better late than never, though. That's what dad had said when he'd got the times of the film that night at the Odeon mixed up and we ended up only seeing the second half of our film.

The best bit was, though. For about the first fucking time in living memory. This time it wasn't actually *my* fault. It was dad's more than anything although I was pretty sure he wasn't going to see it that way when I turned up late with his Copa Mundials.

As much as he was going to be stressing about things. I was going to have them down there before kick off time and *that* was all that really mattered at the end of the day, anyway, as far as I was concerned as I got myself ready to leave.

I was just sticking his boots and pads into my rucksack - kind of rushing by this point having realised that I was a bit late - when the front door went. I tried to have a look through our peephole but whoever it was on the other side had deliberately put their finger over it so I couldn't see out. That made me a bit hesitant to open the door after that because, what kind of a wideo *does* that when they're knocking on someone's door?

The second, much louder and harder, knock spooked me, though. It sounded like it had been delivered with a bit of threat to it and - naturally - it would make you think twice about finding out who was on the other side. It was how ferocious the knocking was, though, that was the reason I *did* open the door. Like they had intimidated me *into* opening it for fear of what would happen if the person had to knock again for a third time.

'Awright, wee man. Is yer da in?'

I stood there staring back at two mountains of men. To look into their eyes I had to tilt my head up slightly. I'd seen a few of dad's 'associates' over the years come to the door. Some frequently, others you saw them once and never again. These two were new ones. Hadn't seen them kicking around Muirhouse - at all - never mind at our front door before.

One of them, with slick back hair - and a dirty looking black stubble that almost looked like it had been drawn on with a Sharpie - dressed in a Hugo Boss tracksuit while the other one - who had more of a crewcut that had started to grow in and, as a haircut, didn't know what it wanted to be - stood there in this fucking radge sheepskin coat that, while looking warm as fuck, didn't exactly make him look the height of fashion.

'Emmmmm, naw.' I said. Trying to strike a balance between looking at either of them.

'That didn't exactly sound too sure of a no, there. Did it, Lawser?' The man in the sheepskin jacket looked at the other one and said.

'No, didn't sound too sure of himself, the wee man, there, did he?' He replied. The both of them speaking as if I wasn't physically standing there.

'You sure he's not in, aye?' The one in the Boss top finally said, but trying to poke his nose over and past me, in case he could detect any other signs of life inside. With me having switched the telly off and ready for leaving, there was no sounds at all.

'He went out yesterday morning to go out to the Hibs match and hasn't been home since.' I said. I wasn't sure if it was the truth but with me not having seen him since then. It might've well as been.

'Hibs?' He replied, like as if he wasn't too impressed by this and at the same time letting me know that he didn't know my dad. Otherwise he'd have already known this.

'Hear that, Jazz? Fucking Hibs.' 'Lawser' said to his mate.

'The cheeky bastard.' The other one seemed to mutter under his breath.

'So when do you think he'll be back again, then?' Asked sheepskin man.

There was something about the pair of them that I knew to be wary of. And to tell them absolutely fuck all. It helped, there, that I didn't know much to start off with. Straight away I thought that it might've been in connection with what I'd done. They seemed the kind of boys that would've hung around scrap yards grinding your bones to make their bread.

'Your guess would probably be as good as me or my mum. If Hearts win then he's back in the house by tea time. If Hibs win then we see him when we see him.' That wasn't even a lie.

They both took a second's pause before any reply.

'Aye but, the derby was a draw. I watched the highlights on Sportscene. Good goal from the Hibs boy, but.' The guy in the Boss tracksuit said.

'My dad pretty much does what he wants.' I said. Once again, not without a whole lot of truth behind it. This made the pair of them laugh.

'Aye, you're not wrong, there.' The man in the sheepskin coat said which then had me - for a few moments, at least - thinking that maybe they *did* know my pops, after all.

They then went on to ask me all kinds of questions about my dad which soon confirmed that, actually, they didn't know after all him but, without a doubt, were *very* interested in meeting him.

Which boozers he drank in.

Takeways that he would've used while out on the piss.

Names of mates that were out with him.

I played the dumb kid who doesn't know what his dad is up to when out on the piss and they never questioned any of it.

The longer that they stood there at the door, though, the slimmer the chances were going to be that I would've been at Muirhouse Park in time for kick off. I pictured my dad standing down there in the dressing room. Decked out in his Violet kit pacing the floor of the dressing room calling me every name under the sun while the reality of it was that I was standing - at the time - lying my arse off for *him*.

'Is it alright if I can go, misters?' I eventually plucked up the courage to them to say. Pulling just enough of my dad's boots out of the bag - but without showing them how big they were - to show them what was inside.

'I'm getting picked up for my game. Away to Penicuik' I added.

I swear, sometimes dad doesn't give me the credit that I deserve. Before saying that I was playing fitba I'd already second guessed that they would've - completely wrongly - assumed that my dad, being *a* dad would be there to watch his son play fitba. I'd thought that if I'd said I was playing locally then where do you think these two men - looking for my dad - would've went looking? Muirhouse Park, obviously.

'Oh aye, no worries, wee man. We'll get you back down.' The one in the sheepskin said as they waited on me closing and locking the door.

Despite giving up the idea of being any kind of a serious fitba player - once I'd reached Craigroyston High and found out that there were a *lot* of boys better at fitba than me - I then had to invent my own persona of a fitba player - and who I played for - for the duration of waiting for and then travelling down in the lift to the bottom of Martello Court.

'What position do you play?' The man in the Boss said as the other one pressed the button in the lift to take us to the ground.

'Emmmm goalie.' I said, without thinking. I'd quite enjoyed being a goalie when we needed being a stand in but had never been my actual position (at primary) so it was a weird position to choose, even if it was only made up.

His eyes lit up.

'Same here, let's see your gloves, then. If they're not Uhlsport you'll be getting marked down a score.' He said, already with his hands out in expectation of recapturing a piece of his youth by seeing a pair of goalkeepers gloves.

'Emmmmm I don't have them on me. They just go with the rest of the kit after the games. One of our teachers takes care of that stuff.' I hoped to fuck that even a fraction of this was convincing because - without them really giving me any kind of a reason - they didn't look like the kind of men that would appreciate being lied to or fucked about.

'Oh, wee man. Who the *fuck* is coaching you?' He said, shaking his head while - regardless of the 'No Smoking' sign *or* that we were in the smallest of metal boxes, his mate in the sheepskin lit up a cigarette.

'Look, yer da will already know this but, what age are you?'

'Fourteen'

He seemed to think about this for a second and then said 'Well, I think it was probably before you were born but Hibs had a keeper, John Burridge, more clubs than Captain Caveman, probably someone else you don't know who I'm on about, but. Anyway, Burridge? Was so invested, as being a goalkeeper, that he SLEPT in his gloves at night. WORE them when he was in his living room watching matches on the telly. You should treat your gloves like Greg Norman with his putter. Don't be leaving them with some teacher who doesn't give a fuck about them.'

He was well into this but, anything to fill the time of an awkward lift ride and I was happy enough to go along with. Inside I was bricking it and was trying to keep it from showing. What did I have anything to be scared of, after all? Just a kid on his way to play fitba. If I'd displayed anything other than that then it would've stuck out a mile.

I made sure I was first out the lift when the doors opened.

'Do you want me to pass on a message to my dad from you next time I see him?' I asked, trying to appear helpful before I took off at speed and away from them.

'Naw, you're alright, wee man. We'll catch up with him at some point, no worries. Hope you get a clean sheet today.' The man in the Boss gear - who had actually seemed to be quite sound by the end - said as I told them that I needed to get a move on as I was late for being picked up from my mates house down the road.

I never looked back after that. Just took off in the direction of the pitch, knowing that the game had - by now - started and just really wanting to get there as soon as I could. Figuring that dad would be able to do a quick pitch side change of footwear and that it would've been all forgotten about. *Especially* if Violet won the cup.

As I approached the pitch I was well surprised by the amount of people who were there to watch it. Way more than your normal Muirhouse Violet match. 'Glory hunters,' as my dad would've called them. With the amount of people lining the side I couldn't see any of the players on the pitch but could hear that that the game was already underway.

Noticing a wee break between two groups of men stood there by the touchline. I squeezed myself in between them and looked for dad to get his boots to him.

Chapter 37

Strings

I'd been super vigilant on the journey back up from Manchester. I'd seen the occasional police car or van but none had posed any threat to myself. When the blue lights starting going off on the front grille of the Audi behind me - reminding me of the car from Knight Rider when it would speak - it completely caught me off guard. I'd actually thought that it was a doctor on call, at first. With me being on the inside lane of the motorway there wasn't anywhere else I could've went so just stayed there at a steady speed and expected it to pass me.

After a few minutes of it staying behind me though, flashing its headlights intermittently at me, it then pulled out to overtake me. Once it had got alongside me, though, it held back from completely passing. This, catching my eye and having me look across the cab and outside and into the next lane.

Inside the dark blue Audi, two police officers. The one driving, looking past his colleague and at me for a moment with an angry and contorted look on his face while pointing to the side of the road. While I would never claim to be skilled in the art of lip reading it looked very much like he was shouting

'Pull the fuck over.'

It felt like my whole world had had a claw hammer taken to it, seeing him - with that uniform on - looking back at me and knowing that in a matter of seconds I was going to have to negotiate being stopped by traffic police - as a banned driver - while transporting kilos of Ching. You wouldn't have guessed this from the reaction that I gave him back of apology for having them behind me for those previous minutes.

Pointing to myself with what (should've) was meant to look like a baffled look on my face as if to say 'Who? Me?' Him nodding angrily and me giving him a quick wave to say sorry and then a thumbs up to indicate that I was going to now pull over onto the hard shoulder of the motorway.

Right, composure here now, Strings, I said to myself - spoken like a Jock Hunter - as I glanced at myself in the mirror - fuck, my eyes looked manic - before then switching to the side mirror and seeing the doors to the Audi opening. Me opening the drivers door to the Transporter and getting out to meet them.

'Can I help you officers?' I said, taking advantage of the fact that I was staring directly into the strong morning sun by looking at them while squinting my eyes. Hiding how bulbous they looked, in the process.

One of them - the one who had been sat in the passengers seat - completely ignored me and walked right past and started to have an inspection of the van. Starting at the passengers side rear tyre. With it being a rental van you'd have already assumed that everything would be in fit and legal order so I hadn't checked any of that side of things, myself. Understandably, I had more things on my mind than the legalities of the vehicle I was driving. There was fuck all else legal going on so who gave a fuck about something like the tyre wear on the van, anyway?

If it was just going to be one of those random police spot checks that they do - probably have some target they've got to get through in a day - then this, in itself, was not going to be a problem.

Me being able to pull off the role of someone who hadn't just been stopped by the police - speeding out my head on this crazy stuff the Manc had given me - while transporting an obscene amount of Cocaine while - himself - not even legally allowed on the road as a driver.

That was the problem.

'It's a rental van from Enterprise, pal, so everything should all be roadworthy. Better be for the price that they charged.' I joked nervously over to him but once again was ignored.

'Sir, do you know why we've pulled you over today? The other one stood and asked while the other one carried on having a look around the van.

'No, officer.' I replied, cupping my hand over my eyebrows from the sun while hoping that it would also detract from my eyes - which had reminded me of that Real Madrid player, Mesut Ozil - 'Is there something wrong with the van? It's a rental one.'

'More something wrong with your driving, mate.' He said, all cocky as fuck, like you get with some that get a piece of authority and pure lap it up. I didn't know what he was talking about. Aye, there had maybe been a couple of times that - due to the Base - I'd caught myself just creeping above seventy but would bring myself back down again straight away. As much as I could've been doing with taking the van up to the fucking tonne up that road. I wasn't as stupid as to do it with kilos of drugs in the back.

'What did I do wrong?' I stood there with arms outstretched while I practically closed my eyes completely to the glare facing back down at me.

'Back down the road you failed to slow down to the temporary fifty miles per hour speed limit that is in force on this stretch of the motorway.'

Truthfully? I hadn't noticed it. If I had then there's no doubt I'd have complied with it. As far as I was concerned. It was like my driving test all over again, that drive from Manchester. The thing was. Even if it *had* been there, the temporary sign, it was there for a reason that hadn't actually existed. There wasn't any crash. No roadworks, Fuck all. Just the same motorway that I'd been on since leaving Cheetham Hill.

'Oh, I'm really sorry, officer. I'm from Edinburgh and didn't realise that the seventy miles an hour speed limit didn't apply, there. I must've not noticed the sign for fifty. Just seems like any other stretch of motorway, eh?' I appealed to *any* sense of fairness that might've been there and that maybe - had he not have been a police officer patrolling that neck of the woods - he'd have seen it from someone else's point of view travelling on that road.

I was doing my best not to start to shake. The nerves definitely starting to get the better of me, however. I'd hoped for some kind of a quick interaction with them that would've seen us all parting ways as quickly as we'd come together. The longer I was around them the more chance that they'd notice there was something not quite right with this driver that they had stopped. They can pick up on that shit like a sniffer dog.

It could've been only a few more moments away before I gave the game away.

I knew how the rest of this was going to go. I'd already been there, hence the ban that I was serving. I started to see prison bars in my future.

What was going to happen next was that the two of them were now going to take me and stick me in the back of their car and take down my details, while we dealt with the paperwork to go with my three points and obligatory fine after me answering all the relevant questions. While *inside* the close confines of their Audi *that* was when one, or both was then going to clock that I was 'on something' and then it was all going to spiral disastrously out of control from there.

I'd taken Benji's drivers license with me to Manchester just in case I was stopped. Hoping that it would be a quick and easy way to get around being - in the eyes of the law - a disqualified driver. They'd started to bring in the cards with people's photo on them but, thankfully, Benji hadn't got around to the point where he'd had to renew his old paper version. Fucking Osama bin Laden could've driven around - with Benji's license - and claimed to be him and would've been good as gold as far as I was concerned.

Now, the use of his license really was meant for nothing else other than just to prove who I 'wasn't.' I definitely hadn't planned on committing any road traffic violations with all that gear in my possession so Benji landing up in any trouble - by proxy of having a mate like me - had not ever been a consideration.

Now I'm finding out that I've been driving twenty miles an hour over the speed limit for a couple of miles which is going to be an instant three points. And that - in itself - presented a problem. Benji was already on nine points already, himself. Another three and he'd be landing up with a ban, too. And I'd just earned them for him.

And *that* was the BEST case scenario?! Landing my best mate with a ban and - as a consequence - leaving myself with no cunt to drive me around stringing. Fuck, the worst case wasn't even worth considering. The only plus that would've come out of the worst case scenario would've been that - at least - Benji would've kept his license. And as far as *I'd* be needing one. He'd have been as well keeping the fucking Ibiza, permanently.

'Edinburgh? What has you down in England.' He asked as he started to take his notebook out of his jacket.

'Emmmm, Business.' I replied, cautiously. 'You know what it's like for us drivers. Most of the country are still sleeping while we're getting their goods across the country for them.' I tried to be chatty with the officer but not *overly* talkative as that in itself is always a bit obvious to a police officer. That 'skill,' in itself, though, proved to be tough to master, with that Base inside of me. While I was just about managing to hide the size of my eyes from him, keeping my fucking trap shut wasn't so simple.

'Can you please open the back of the van for me, sir?' The other one, who had ignored all of my attempts to speak to him up to then, said from behind me.

Now *there* was a question to end all questions.

"Could" I open the back door? Well, aye, of course I could. A fucking toddler could.

Did I *want* to? Fuck, god, no.

I felt like I was going to throw up all over the officer that was stood in front of me as I heard the words behind my back.

As far as my actual legal rights? Well I didn't have a fucking clue when it came to driver's rights but what I *did* know was that when a policeman asks you to open the back of a van and you don't do it they're then going to be doing *everything* within their power to make sure that door opens, whether it's with your cooperation or not. I'd had enough experience with coppers in my time to know that if you shone a light in your direction and made yourself *look* guilty of something then they're sure as fuck going to assume that you *are*. Which isn't too Kool and the Gang when you had what I was carrying in the back of the van that morning.

If I said no. I was fucked. If I'd said yes, I was also fucked. Like some Amsterdam red light window girl starting her shift for the day. No matter what happened or the outcome, fucked, one way or the other.

'Emmmm aye, let me just get the keys.' I said, trying to appear keen to help. While on the way back to the front of the van I was actually entertaining some insane thoughts of just jumping in and driving off. The two point five litre diesel van not ever going to stand a chance of outrunning the coppers and whatever horsepower their sporty Audi was packing.

With the subject of the van now taking priority. The chit chat that me and the officer had been having took a back seat, both taking an interest in me returning back with the keys.

The paranoia started to rip right through me as I went to shove the key in and turn it. My heart was beating so fast and hard that I was genuinely worried that the two officers would've been able to hear it. Fucking hell, all it would've taken from either of them would've been a quick stethoscope test on me and they'd have *known* that I was up to something shady.

Opening the door to the traffic cops - while paradoxically closing the door on my immediate freedom, indefinitely - I knew the game was up. I'd been gutted over the fact that - through no fault of his own - I was going to land Benji with a driving ban even though - Benji, being Benji - would've understood and said that he'd have taken a ban over me going to jail for driving while disqualified.

What I'd have done for us to be back at the point where I was going to be taken into the car and officially handed the HORTI. Simpler times. A *lot* simpler than opening up the back of a van that's full of Cocaine.

'Ahhhh the brand with the three stripes, I see?' The one who had ignored me at first, said at the sight of the van being full to the brim with boxes and boxes of trainers.

'Aye, I'm driving them up this morning so they'll be ready for the shops opening on Monday morning.' I said, but to the other officer who had asked why I was travelling on the motorway in the first place.

'Ohhh let's have a look, anything good.' He said, ignoring me and, instead, reacting to what his colleague had just said.

'I'm afraid they're all just Sambas.' I said this but after having giving them a moment to actually start to open boxes - to see what style was inside - after boxes. Both with their backs to me and staring into the fan with their arms inside. I snuck a really low quality picture on my phone of them doing it. Was hardly the best of angles and - with it being without their attention - I just hoped that it had picked up enough. Maybe I was just extremely switched on with the speed I'd had but the sight of the two of them, foraging in the back of a van full of trainers - to the untrained eye - looked a bit dodgy.

They stopped opening boxes at that point, with me confirming that they were wasting their time looking at the same pairs of trainers, time after time. The *first* box that they opened. My legs almost buckled from under me. Maybe these trainers hadn't all been precisely packed with the Ching and that some of them were showing signs of the packaging sticking out from underneath the Adidas insoles?

The first officer who opened up the box just took one of the Sambas out and had a wee look at it as if he was nothing other than a consumer standing in Inter Sport, trying to decide if they were going to make a purchase or not.

Once the first box had closed and the next one opened the nauseous and weak feeling stuck with me. Only lifting when they both turned around, on hearing that all there was inside the back of the van was Sambas.

'Samba, you say, yeah?' The one who had the notepad in his hand, and who had been in the process of starting to write me up, replied.

'You know, Rob? You and me could do with a new pair of Sambas, for the fives, couldn't we.' He said, looking at his colleague.

'You've got a bit of a point, there, Ken. Actually, weren't we just speaking in the car the other day about how we were due a new pair. Weirdly enough, Sambas were mentioned, were they not?' He replied.

'I do believe it was *Adidas* Sambas that we were speaking about. Now *how* spooky is that?' He responded, in the same tone where they were both letting me know loud and fucking clear 'what' they were saying, without having to say it.

'How weird that, days later, we should end up pulling a van for speeding that's got hundreds of boxes of the *same* trainers that we only need a couple of pairs of?'

I was in no way fooling myself into thinking that I was out of the woods yet but the wave of relief that - from the fact that they'd opened and closed a number of those boxes - the realisation brought that those doss cunts didn't have a fucking clue that I was carrying gear was immeasurable. Almost taking my legs from me as much as the initial fear I'd had of the Ching being discovered.

'You know, sir. We really would appreciate the contribution to our work team of the donation of a couple of pairs. Nine and ... what's your size again, Ken?' The one who had asked to see inside finally stopped dancing around things while, technically, not asking outright.

'Eleven' The reply from the other one before following up with 'You may have noticed, I didn't actually write a word in this.' Holding up his notebook. 'It can go back into this jacket again just as easily as it came out.'

The two of them stood waiting on an answer. Just knowing that they were staring at me - making me feel like I was under the microscope - leaving it difficult for me to make a decision. Probably *the* biggest and potentially life changing decision of my life.

Say no to what they were more than hinting about and take the three points, well, Benji, anyway. But who was to say they they wouldn't have ended up being dicks anyway *because* I'd knocked them back. Maybe they would then start asking questions about 'where' the trainers had come from, possibly suspecting that they'd fallen off the back off a lorry and *right* into the back of my VW.

The fact that I was stood parked on a hard shoulder with the doors of a van that I was driving - open to police - while enough drugs to get me twenty years sat in the back was the overriding factor here. The absolute *one* thing that I had feared when being forced to get behind the wheel. *This* situation. The one that would dwarf the whole driving while banned issue.

Anything to end it all, I thought. And - picking up on things said and both unsaid - they were giving me an out.

I couldn't help but smile inside while I was rifling through the boxes in the back of the Transporter, to try and find a size for each of them. I'd been bricking it over all permutations over how much shit I was in when I'd seen him angrily gesture to me to pull over ten to fifteen minutes earlier. And yet - instead - there I was trying to find a pair of Sambas for each of them as part of a shakedown.

For all I'd known. The trainers had been nothing more than for show. As a means to simply disguising the transportation of the Ching - aye, they were proper Sambas, though - in that there was no real choice in sizes with the main point of them being *not* for wearing. And at first it was looking like there was only a couple of 'token' sizes out of all the boxes. I'd found one of the nines but yet to find the bigger pair for the other copper.

Despite still being racked with nerves over what I knew, and what they didn't. I wanted to start laughing at just how farcical this was. Right under the noses of these two officers was the biggest bust of their life - and they were settling for a pair of trainers - which wouldn't so much as be under their nose as under their fucking feet!

If I was to get away from 'Ken and Rob' clean as a whistle and up the road there was no doubt about that I was going to piss myself over this episode.

There would be time for that, much later.

Just when I was about to admit defeat and say that I couldn't find any size elevens I managed to spy a few boxes with that size marked on the end of the box. Obviously, they'd been one of the first pairs that had been loaded into the van back in Manchester.

'Good trainer, the Samba.' I said - like I was a salesman trying to punt pairs to them - while the two of them stood there clutching their blue boxes, chuffed to bits.

'I play as well, got a match later on this afternoon. Cup final, like. Kwik Save Challenge Trophy. I don't know why I was even telling them this because *due* to them I was now perilously late for said cup final.

One of them whistled - sarcastic, like - as if I'd just told them something absolutely massive.

'Kwik Save, yeah? Sounds a big one.' The other one chipped in, giggling.

Dicks, I thought, but dicks that - through their own corrupt ways - had managed to miss out on both a banned driver (they hadn't even reached the point of asking me my name or to see - Benji's - my drivers license) and an unlimited amount of blow jobs from their Drug Squad back at the station. So aye, they might've been wideos but they - when all actions had been taken into account - were quite sound cunts into the bargain.

I didn't want to just go on and make the assumption that by giving them the trainers I was getting off with the speeding. I mean, you'd have fucking hoped so, like. What did a speeding fine cost? Sixty quid to a Hundred, tops. From what Wesley had informed me, back at the house. I had just handed over the best part of ten grand, five in each box, to them. Bit steeper than a Hundred quid, like.

I needed one of *them* to tell me that I was free to go, though. That's how it generally works and let me assure you that's how it *definitely* applies when you're standing by the side of the road with kilos of Ching standing talking to two coppers who have pulled you over.

Next, one of the cunts was wanting to talk to me about Edinburgh. Saying that he was going to be booking a city break for him and his wife.

'Oh aye, you'll love it, pal. Just remember to remortgage your house before you go if you're going to go our for a drink in the town centre, though, eh.'

I said, while saying fuck it to myself and taking a cigarette out of my pack and lighting it up. For one thing, it wasn't looking like they were about to let me go, all be it in an 'everything's cool' way and not looking like I was getting done for anything, either. Almost as if they felt that because they'd shook me down for something that by then hanging around for a friendly chat it would make the act seem less illegal? I wasn't sure but they weren't peeling soles out of the pairs of Adidas' inside the back of the van so it was sound on my end.

No denying it, though. I hadn't planned for this extra delay. Well, not so much as not planning for it but having *no spare time* to accommodate it. The more pish the two of them stood and talked to me, the more my time window was closing on me reaching Muirhouse Park before that first whistle went.

'Same for any city though, really.' Said the other one. 'Take New York, last year. I took my Jan there for our wedding anniversary. All I'd ever heard was that America was so cheap to go to and you got so much for your money.' He stopped for a second. Almost as if he was unable to believe what he was about to say next. 'Central Park, one of those vendors that you always see on the New York films? FIVE POUNDS FIFTY for a cheese toastie. Five pounds, and Fifty pence.'

What the fuck was going on here? Who was interested in the price of a cheese toastie in a park that I was never going to fucking visit? Could this pair not just let me on my way with my Cocaine and let us all get on with our day? I thought away to myself as I puffed away on my reek.

'Just a cheese toastie? No ham or onions, like?' I asked. In no way able to express my frustration over this really piss poor small talk between a bunch of people who shouldn't have been in the position of needing *to* small talk. I mean, we *all* had work to be getting on with. Anything - whatever the subject - that did not involve the back of my van or who I *actually* was was one that I was happy to talk about, even if, inside, I knew that it was all chipping away at my chances of appearing in the final.

It would work out, though. I'd make it. Niddrie had got the kick off time mixed up and weren't going to appear until an hour late. Muirhouse and Niddrie - without the luxury of top level fitba fan segregation - fans battling with each other on the pitch and delaying the kick off. Something, anything. You tell yourself that because you 'need' that hope. If the hope dips then so do you. It's what keeps your head up, doesn't it?

'Mate? The toast was barely cooked. The Americans don't understand toast, for some reason. Barely any of them even have a toaster in their hou… '

He never finished his sentence. The radio strapped to the outside of his jacket crackled into action. I never understood any of it but whatever was said was enough for him to look at his partner, rattle out some police numerical code signal (to describe the call they were taking, I assumed) and mention five miles up the road and them jumping in the Audi. The driver, bringing his window down before he pulled out onto the motorway and shouted 'Good luck in the Aldi Cup.'

The two of them laughing at this before the window went up and him pulling off. Leaving me stood there, barely able to believe what had just happened. The fucking van was now missing two "pairs of Adidas" from the back. If I needed *any* evidence that it had happened.

The fact that the cargo's value had decreased by around ten grand was all the proof needed.

With them long gone up the motorway. I just stood there, finishing my cigarette, kind of like I was in a daze. Over the amazingly lucky escape I'd had. I could've been picking up a bag of Ching marked **"Cocaine"** on the side of it for all I'd known driving to Cheetham Hill. It was only through the professionalism of McKenna and the Manchester link that had been the difference between me sitting in the back of a patrol car by then or standing like a doss cunt by the side of the road smoking a cigarette like he had all the time in the world when *that* was the one thing that he 'didn't' have.

I snapped myself out of it and got back into the van and started off on the Hundred and fifteen mile drive. The issue about making the Violet match was one to start thinking about once I got nearer to Edinburgh. There was no point in worrying about it until then. Especially when I had the issue of four ounces of McKenna's product now missing and sitting inside pairs of trainers that - I presumed were not designed for actual wearing, what with an ounce of Cocaine sitting underneath the insole - were going to be soon tested out during a police team five a side match.

It made me laugh, just thinking about it. Those two officers turning up for their five a side match, through the week. New Sambas ready to get their debut. Only a few minutes into the match, both of them realise that they're running a little funny. Trainers feeling a bit strange. Let's take the insole out of one to see if there's any issue there.

If only you could be a fly on the wall for those moments. I was chilled about what would happen *when* (not if) the Ching was discovered inside their trainers. The officer hadn't taken down any details of the van, or me, so I wasn't seeing any way that they were going to track me down. Tracking me down would've probably been the very *last* thing they'd have wanted to have done, anyway. I imagine it wouldn't have been too good a look on them if cunts were to find out that they'd been kicking around in pairs of Adidas that had ounces of Coke in them, that they'd extorted from a member of the public. Aye, that side was cool and nothing to worry about and, when I stopped to think of it - almost Shakespearean - and *VERY* funny.

I actually ended up seeing them tending to a two car smash at the side of the road, a few miles into the journey. The one lane delay not exactly winning a fan in me either. The officer recognised me as he was waving the line of traffic through and I gave him an enthusiastic thumbs up from behind the wheel and big smile while pissing myself at the boldness of it all.

What *wasn't* so funny and, in fact, something that was considered as worthy of worrying about was having to tell McKenna that two pair of trainers had needed to be sacrificed along the way and hope to fuck that he was going to understand that the difference had been going to be him receiving *none* of the shipment while *I* was going to be in jail for possession.

That was going to have to be a chat for another day, however. I had now crossed the border and back in the motherland and edging my way to unloading not just a shit load of Ching but a shit load from my shoulders. Being in Scotland by then. Thoughts started to turn to Muirhouse. With it being a cup final there would've been cunts down there a lot earlier than they'd normally have been seen. Soaking up the occasion, like.

It wouldn't have been long before people started mentioning my name and asking where I was as - on a normal basis - I would generally be one of the first down there, at the pavilion. Helping stick the nets up amongst other minor duties that only those with The Violet truly at heart were ever arsed about doing before a match.

Passing the Livi slip road, I got back on the phone to Benji to give him a status report in that I was just past Livingston and around twenty minutes out from the drop off point at Portobello.

'Fuck took you?' He asked, genuinely annoyed and I knew why. I was impacting on *his* cup final experience too. He should've been standing around the park. Watching the lads warm up and being part of the all important pre cup final team talk.

'Look, just all kinds of fucking wild stuff that I'll tell you about *after* we've won the trophy. But with me twenty minutes away, are we going to make it back up to the pitch for kick off?' I asked, managing to cross my fingers while regaining hold of the steering wheel.

'If there's not any other delays, then we should do it. Bawhair, though, like. He replied candidly.

'Right well, you know the address. I'll see you in twenty. I'm driving a big fuck off long wheel base white VW Transporter. Oh and tell Jock that I'm going to make it but that I literally won't be there until a few minutes before kick off.'

'Comprende,' he said before hanging up.

With the scent in the air of a cup final. For the first time, part of me wanted to speed and get myself to Portobello. I did, for all of five minutes before common sense kicked in again. I'd went through so much. From being locked in a Manchester housing scheme for hours· and then shaken down by two five aside playing traffic coppers. To fail now would've been of 'disaster for Scotland' proportions.

Benji's few words had been enough to pull me back from the brink. Just hearing him saying that he thought we would still make it to Muirhouse Park had seen a transformation in the man who was, only minutes before, almost smashing the drivers side window in frustration.

I already saw Benji sitting there in the Ibiza, waiting on me when I came swinging into the yard and heading towards the small warehouse at the far end of it. Giving him a quick flash of my headlights and getting the same back. It was hoped that I'd be running back over to the car a few minutes later, jumping in, and getting ourselves up to the Naughty North.

Admittedly, the Base that Wesley had given me had done *exactly* as he'd said it had on its tin. Medically and technically, I should've been on my fucking arse - by then - with the possibility of going on to play a game of fitba considered laughable.

Yet there I was. Jumping out the van and banging on the metal shutters - that I'd been told to knock on - with such strength and enthusiasm that did not reflect a man who'd had the previous twelve hours as I'd just been through.

'Come on, hurry up.' I shouted with absolutely no idea who or what was inside. The desperate *need* to get this done and up to the park, more important than anything else.

The big metal roller doors eventually sparked into action, slowly rising up from the ground. From about half way I could make out the figure of someone who was standing to the side and pressing down on the button that operated the doors. While still with his finger on the button, he just stood and stared at me. Me shouting from the outside in the way that I had, possibly not to his liking.

'Emmmmm I'm the guy. McKenna told me to come here with the delivery.' I said, hesitantly, aware that I shouldn't give out too much in the way of information until I knew I was, at least, dealing with the correct person.

'*You* should've been here fucking hours ago. We've been here for ages waiting on you.' He said, not exactly impressed, now that he was realising who it was that he was exactly - and eventually - faced with.

'Aye, I'm fully aware of that.' I replied, less than chuffed with his response. ALL I'd had to do to get there and *that* was the appreciation I was getting. 'You want me to drive it right in?' I asked, noticing that the door was now raised high enough for the van to now drive into the warehouse.

'Well, either that or we just unload the shipment in broad daylight. What do you fucking think?' The cunt replied, sarcastically. I hated him, instantly. I'd never seen him around McKenna before and I was already counting the minutes until I didn't see him again. He looked quite a tidy cunt, though. Looked like he had the backup to go along with the way that he spoke to people.

All I was interested in was getting up to Muirhouse Park, to be honest. Aye, I could've appreciated him being a bit off with me if McKenna had told him to be there for a certain time and I roll in around three hours late but, for fuck's sake. It wasn't as if I'd taken the fucking coastal route back home from England to Scotland. Maybe stopping off somewhere for an ice cream at North Berwick, that kind of thing. *None* of this was either my fault, *or* choosing.

To engage with the boy would've only meant that I'd have been wasting my own valuable time. What meant more to me? A cup final appearance or standing arguing with someone - who if they wanted to could've snapped me in two - about the reasons I was late with a van full of Ching?

Ignoring him. I jumped back into the Transporter and drove it all the way into the warehouse. Him closing the door behind me again. Once I was inside it was only then that I really noticed how big the place was. There was half a dozen cars parked inside, all with their boots open. There was enough bodies inside there for each car. The drivers didn't seem to be too chuffed with me, either. Obviously, they'd all been waiting to get their cars loaded up and away to whatever parts of the country they were destined for. McKenna's tentacles reaching far and wide in Scotland since back at the start of the Nineties when he made that move against one of the bigger dealers through in the Weeg. It was all on the news at the time because when his competitor had been busted - no thanks to McKenna - it involved a hostage situation when one of the police officers had been taken hostage by one of the couriers with a knife. Some radge from Dundee, I mind.

'Right, pal. There you go.' I said 'I'll be in touch with Davey later on about everything. He told me just to leave the van here and he'd get it sorted.' I said, as I threw the keys at the boy who had let me in as I started walking towards the metal door. This catching him completely by surprise and leaving him scrambling to catch the keys before they hit him in the face.

'And where the fuck do you think *you're* going?' He said, arrogantly.

'You're going fucking nowhere until we've checked that everything's there.' He added.

'Mate? Have you heard of Muirhouse Violet? Course you fucking have. Well I just happen to play a pivotal role in the side and in under half an hour's time. The whistle is going to go for the start of the Kwik Save Challenge Trophy against Niddrie and I *need* to be on that fucking pitch for when that happens.

This kind of threw the boy for a second. He'd stood and told this so called 'daft cunt who only did the driving' how it was going to be only the 'daft cunt' ended up answering him back. The rest of the boys who were hanging around the cars stood watching him, to see what his response was going to be.

'I'll tell you upfront right now - and I'll be speaking to McKenna about it personally - but it's all there apart from two pairs. They put one hundred and seventy five pairs into the van down in Manchester but there's only one seventy three in there now.'

'Whoooah whooaah whoooah, wait a fucking minute. Where's the other two boxes, like?' The boy's tone changed from arrogance to something a lot more on the threatening and explosive side.

I - as briefly and concisely as I could - explained to the boy that I'd been stopped by traffic police near the border. Thought I was getting busted and instead had them extort a couple of pairs of trainers from the van, while having absolutely no fucking idea what was actually *inside* them.

Even then, amongst what was a bit of a dicey situation and inside a world that I wasn't used to, all I was thinking about was what was going on back in the pavilion. Jock Hunter's team talk. Benji - outside - would've been having fucking kittens waiting on me emerging back out of the warehouse so that we could make the kick off. I *should've* been focussing on what was right there in front of me but, in my defence, this *was* the Kwik Save Challenge Trophy that we were talking about, here, mind.

'And you expect me to fucking believe that?' He laughed, looking round at the others, producing a bout of sycophantic laughter from a few of them.

'Pal? With the greatest of respect, I probably wouldn't believe it, either, but it's the fucking truth. Trust me. The choice of being busted with a van full of Ching or bunging a couple of pairs of "trainers" to two bent coppers, it wasn't exactly a toughie, like.'

Then the picture I took popped into my head. Fuck, through my situation multiplied by the strength of that Base powder stuff, my head had been racing with an outrageous amount of thoughts flowing through it. I'd forgotten *all about* the wee picture I'd snuck when the two traffic cops were rifling through the Adidas boxes in the back of the van.

'Actually, I've got proof for you.' I said, confidently, as I dug my N95 out of my pocket to open up my picture folder on it.

I walked back towards him to show him the evidence. Only there *wasn't* any. It had been a rushed picture as in I'd pressed the button to take the picture without actually *seeing* what was on the screen of the phone.

'What do you say to it now then?' I said - literally preparing myself for his face dropping when he looked at the picture - as I opened it only to find a blurred picture of two men's bottom halfs, wheels of the van, the rest taking up the picture, asphalt.

'And that's your proof? Is it?' He raised his eyebrows at me.

'Well I was hardly in a position to ask the cunts to say cheese to me, could I.' I tried to defend the quality of the picture. 'Look, if you zoom in you can 'just' see a wee bit of one of their fluorescent jackets creeping into the picture.'

'You're fucking reaching, there, pal. That could've been any cunt with a vis-vest, ya fucking chancer.' He said, shaking his head.

'You know what I think happened? Here's what I think,' he followed up with.

I didn't have the fucking time to hear what he 'thought,' even if I'd been interested in his theory of the missing Ching or not. Already knowing the reality of it. Who gave a fuck about any cunt and their 'theories.'

'I think that - what's happened - is you've met up with someone on your journey and you've passed them onto them and *then* you've came here to drop off and have come up with some fictional story about two of the filth shaking you down for FUCKING SAMBAS. You should be a writer, pal.' He laughed but there was no spark in the eyes to go with it.

Know what? I thought to myself. Fuck this. If I was going to miss the kick off it was going to be through not physically being able to walk back out of the warehouse. I had fuck all to lose so just let rip at him.

'HAW, listen here, pal. Me and McKenna go back. It's *because* we go way back that I've even done this fucking favour for him. I'm not a bag man, or a courier. I'm a stringer and a fucking good one, at that. Since agreeing to do this favour for Davey I've been locked up for hours on a Manchester housing estate along with cunts with fucking Uzis. Driven enough Cocaine - to put me away until my sixties - hundreds of miles WHILE UNDER A DRIVING BAN. Stopped by traffic police and having to stop my fucking arse from collapsing as they had me open the back of that van so they could see what was inside. ALL of this getting in the way of the preparation for the biggest game of fitba I've ever played in my life. And *you* stand there and accuse me of fucking skimming from the van. Trust me, the only thing I've got out of my work over the past twelve hours is some grey hairs and a head full of speed. Like I said, full disclosure. There's two boxes missing. Call it collateral damage, if you will.'

'I'm not sure McKenna's going to see it quite that way.' He replied. A wee bit less threatening now that I'd said my piece. It must've come across as impassioned or something but he seemed to be less hostile, as a result.

'Aye well if there's anyone who'll know how or where to find me, it's him.' I said, not really up nor down. Aye, I'm sure that there was going to have to be a 'chat' with him, when he found out that there was a couple of boxes light from the delivery, but that could come later.

'Now if you'll excuse me. I've got a cup final to win.' I announced, turning and heading towards the side of the metal doors and, specifically, the door button that I'd seen the boy use to let me in. Turning around one last time I saw that a couple of the boys, who had been stood around, were now already getting fired into the back of the van and stacking boxes of trainers into the boots of the cars.

'Right, driver. Muirhouse and don't spare the horses.' I said, jumping into the passengers seat of the car. Benji already having the engine running and ready for pulling away. He'd *also* had the piece of mind to bring my Muirhouse kit - so that I could get changed on the way back up there - to ensure that I'd be ready for taking the field, on arrival at the pitch.

'You think we'll make it?' I asked him, as he tore out of the yard. Already pulling my top off and grabbing my Violet shirt to replace it with.

'I'd stick your seat belt on if I were you, mate' His answer.

Not even having been told just how close he'd come to getting the last set of points to land him a ban hours earlier, he hoored off down the road. Risking copping his *own* three points. At some stages going double the speed limit. Overtaking cars when you really wouldn't normally have. This *was* an emergency situation, though. Fuck, it deserved a police escort, really.

Due to the fucking about inside the warehouse we'd - technically - been left with not enough time to get us to Muirhouse in time for kick off. Technically. *That* didn't account for what 'speed' our method of transport was going to be travelling at, though. It's all relative, that stuff.

My 'stickman' - through some manic and death defying driving - had made up a bit of time and sat there - dressed in my full Violet kit minus my boots, which wee Jackie was taking care of for me. For the first time, I was starting to dream. Believe that - despite all the capers since I'd first arrived in Manchester - it was all going to work out. Mentally - thanks to that Base - I was fresh as fuck and raring to go. 'Mentally' I felt like, once on that pitch, I'd have been three steps ahead of everyone, despite not even having been to my bed.

Rather than fill Benji in on all that had went on. The journey was spent mostly with me asking questions related to the side. Was everyone fit? Anyone fucked it the day before through going too far when it came to the Edinburgh Derby?

'Nah, everyone's good and reported for duty. Who had arrived up to the point that I left to come down and get you were all buzzing and up for it. Some buzzing more than others though, eh?' He laughed.

'Hey, what could I do, Benj? If I hadn't have taken that stuff the boy gave me down in Manchester I'd have probably fallen asleep at the wheel and be waking up handcuffed to a hospital bed somewhere. Plus, I wouldn't have had a hope in hell of being fit to play a game of fitba.' I said, justifying my actions.

'I'm not just talking about you, either. It's a toss up between who's more flying out of you and Montana. He appeared at the pavilion, earlier. Fucking dancing to music that wasn't even playing. Like it was only in his own head, or something. The daft cunt was at the Liquid Rooms until six this morning. Some DJ playing there, Selecao I think his name was, Brazilian DJ, or something. You know? Like the Brazilian national fitba squad?' Hearing that Montana was still wrecked from the night before was not in the way of anything novel.

'And how is Jock setting the team out? Mind, it's not the same Paddock side that we played last time, eh?' I asked, fretting that me having had them watched a few times and finding out some valuable intel on them was going to be for fuck all.

'Don't worry about it. He's got a plan for those tippy tappy pass you to death bastards.' He replied.

'Would it involve us receiving a plethora of coloured cards, I'm going to take a punt?' I asked, realistically.

'Aye, something like that,' the reply.

We were tearing along West Granton Road, towards Pilton, when you saw the build up of traffic up ahead. Benji, upon seeing it, edging himself out onto the other side of the road to try and see what was going on.

'Ah, fuck. No cunt's moving any time soon.' He said. Telling me that it looked like one of those Travis Perkins delivery HGVs, the ones with the hydraulic pumps to them had somehow managed to tip over on its side. Blocking one side of the road while the contents of what had been on the back had tipped out over onto the *other* side of the road. Cars were getting through but a lot slower and as a result, the traffic had started to build up.

'Right, Plan B. We'll need to approach from Pennywell Road.' He said as he took the turn off West Granton Road and a wee diversion through Pilton to get us back on track. Good thinking from the Benji boy because to have sat there in that traffic would've been as well as waving the white flag of surrender, as far as getting to the pitch for kick off.

It wasn't exactly cool, how fast he was driving - in a built up area - like. If a bairn had ran out at any point they'd have been a goner. I wanted to tell him to slow down but - due to the time constraints we now had - there had been a kind of tense silence that had fallen over the car. Had we been able to just carry on along West Granton Road then, aye, chances were that we were going to make the kick off. I don't know *how* but we were. With this diversion that had been thrown at us, though? Well it was all in the laps of the gods, eh.

Maybe it would've served me better to have been a regular at church up to that afternoon because when I saw the

"ROAD CLOSED - FOLLOW DIVERSIONS"

Sign on West Pilton Street I knew the ball was burst. We followed the diversions - which initially took us in the wrong direction - until it got us back on track and, eventually, onto Pennywell Road with a clear path into Muirhouse for Benji to speed down.

'You know what its like, Strings. Sometimes it's two or three minutes late kicking off. Hardly like we need to be coordinating ourselves with Sky Sports for their ad breaks or anything, eh?' Benji said, knowing by the look on my face that I'd given up the ghost. Providing me with nothing other than a wee bit lip service and telling me what he 'thought' I'd have wanted to hear.

He *did* have a point, though. Our games on a Sunday were hardly what you would have called 'tightly regulated.'

Approaching Muirhouse Park. I could tell simply by the extra cars, that were parked around the area, that there was a decent crowd that had come along. Once we were close enough I was practically jumping out the car and running in the direction of the pitch before Benji had even parked in his spot.

First thing I heard, though, was a ref's whistle, followed by a few jeers and shouts.

We were too late.

As dramatic as this might sound. The confirmation that I hadn't made the starting eleven - on the biggest day of my playing career - left me sinking to my knees. Like the boy on the front of the poster for that film, 'Platoon.'

'MAN ON, MAN ON'

'THAT'S IT, VIOLET, GET STUCK IN.'

'REFE - FUCKING - REEEEE? YOU NOT SEE THAT?'

I could hear Hunter's voice screaming out above every cunt else.

'Mon, Strings, mate. Lets go over and see what the craic is.' Benji said, standing over me, squeezing one of my shoulders to try and coax me back up onto my feet again.

Chapter 38

Strings

Muirhouse Violet had only reached one cup final in all the time that I'd played for them. Seven years before. Against Oxgangs in the final for some trophy that had been sponsored by Hilton Exhausts (long gone now) and due to my own immaturity - at thirty - I had conspired to get myself banned from the final.

It was just high spirits, having just won a semi final, like. We were walking back off the pitch and I was high as a kite. Had never sampled *that* feeling before. It was a pretty stupid thing to do, like, but I knew the ref, - Alan McKenzie - personally. We used to hang around with each other when we were teenagers. Anyway, we were all walking victoriously back to the dressing room and Alan was walking ahead of us, with his linos on either side of him.

'Watch this.' I said to Dean Anderson - 'Deano,' who played for us back then - as I crept up quietly behind Alan and before he had even realised that I was behind him. I'd grabbed his shorts and pulled them down. Went too far, though, didn't I? Ended up - accidentally - pulling his scants down *along* with this referee's shorts. Leaving him stood there bollock naked.

'**WOYYYY OIIII**' I shouted out, pissing myself along with everyone else.

I didn't know that you could get a red card *after* the match had ended. Found out that day, right enough. Once Alan had managed to quickly get his shorts back up around him he was right into his pocket and out with the card.

I actually laughed, to begin with, because I thought he was just having a wee joke with me. When I clocked the look on his face, though. *That's* when I knew he was serious.

Fair dues, he came round to the house that same night for a word when he didn't really have to. Told me that he couldn't have cunts saying that he was a soft touch or - even worse, according to him - a ref that was known for letting his mates away with offences that *other* cunts would be going in the book for.

I was heartbroken, the day of the final, like. That's when it *really* sank in. That I was going to be standing watching the lads from the side of the pitch and not able to play any part myself.

It hurt me, to miss out that day. The lads won the cup and we had some fucking sesh afterwards but I couldn't feel properly one hundred percent involved, 'because' I hadn't played in the final. I used that feeling, though. Told myself that as long as I played for Muirhouse Violet. If we were to reach another final, I wouldn't be left with that same feeling of loss and deep regret. It spurred me on, some seasons. The thought of capturing 'that feeling' of satisfaction. The one where you right a wrong and find the redemption that you were looking for in the process.

Not one cup game that I played in - following that Oxgangs final - did I not think about the bitter taste that I'd been left with back then.

And a lot of fucking good all of that did me, as well. Standing there - the Kwik Save Challenge Trophy final now into the second half with the score sitting at one apiece. It had been a tasty first half. Jock's 'masterplan' to combat the free flowing fitba that The Paddock were going to be producing against us had, indeed, been to knock their players as high up into the air, as possible, as *early* into the match possible. To give them the message. Set some sort of precedent, like.

At first, it looked like it had worked. Despite me only being two or three minutes late I'd already missed the first example of Muirhouse's approach to the more dark arts of fitba tactics. The Paddock - apparently - had got the ball down on the floor from kick off. None of our players getting a sniff of a kick. And you know what it's like? Seeing that ball getting sprayed around and not being able to 'get' to it? *That* would test the fucking patience of a saint. Bungalow (definitely *not* a saint) Had caught one of their players with a 'stray' elbow when trying to track back with him. Off the ball, like.

Me and Benji were just getting to Jock Hunter on the sidelines when I saw one of their players getting led off the pitch. Blood streaming from a cut above his left eye. One of the coaches of The Paddock leading him off while the player was more concerned about seeing where Bungalow was so that he could let him know that he'd be looking for him when he came back onto the pitch again.

'I'm not going anywhere, pal.' Bungalow said, blowing a kiss towards the boy.

'Fuck me, looks like the fuse has already been lit.' Benji said, taking in what was going on.

I wasn't interested in him or what he had to say, Bungalow *or* the random cunt that had blood pishing down his face. Seeing those twenty two players out on that pitch, and me not being one of them. I wasn't in the best of places for the first part of the half.

'I gave you up to the *very* last minute, Strings.' Jock Hunter said when he clapped eyes on me approaching the touchline in my full Muirhouse kit. 'It wasn't fair on Mikey, either. Telling him that he needed to be ready for playing but that if you appeared he was back out the team. You can't be doing that with players minds, especially cup finals, pal. Need them to be focussed.'

I hadn't even noticed *who* had taken my place in the side up to that point. Knowing that it wasn't me had been enough. The irony, though, of me giving Mikey that pep talk. The night that he'd taken me and Han into the town centre. Telling him to keep his head up because Daz had been suspended for the semi final. Only, Mikey ended up getting *my* place, instead.

It's a fanny old game, eh? As Greavsie used to say.

'Where the fuck were you that was *so* important that you couldn't be here in time for kick off, anyway?' He asked before launching into a tirade at the referee over missing a clear push from one of their players on Terry.

'You fucking blind, ya cunt?'

'Grafting, Jock. Couldn't turn it down. Good money, like,' I lied.

'Well I hope it was worth it because fuck knows the next cup final we'll get to. You're not getting any younger either, Joe.' He said, coldly. Wounding me way more than he could've ever believed, or intended.

I spent most of that first half in a bit of a malaise. I felt like I was being a bit of a bairn, like. Pure spitting the dummy because I hadn't got what I'd wanted. Couldn't stop myself, though.

Even when Rossi opened the scoring - following an opening fifteen minutes of Muirhouse players systematically and calculatingly taking it in turns to clean out any of The Paddock players at every opportunity. This, eventually getting to the Niddrie boys and knocking them out of sorts - I didn't celebrate. Fuck, if we'd scored a goal in a meaningless league match at the end of the season I'd have celebrated it like fucking Marco Tardelli so a cup final goal for Muirhouse? I should've been doing laps round the pitch but, instead, just stood there with my arms folded while Rossi lay underneath a pile of bodies, all celebrating on top of him. All our subs running onto the pitch and piling on, too. Well, not *all* subs.

Don't get me wrong. I was *happy* that the wee man had scored. Fuck? We were up in a cup final. Nothing shabby there, like. I was just in my own wee zone of negativity, like. If Rossi's cheeky wee lob over their keeper and into the net hadn't been enough to bring me out of my mood then The Paddock scoring an equaliser, a few minutes before half time, was hardly likely to help restore my parity.

Their big number nine - who had looked a danger all the way through the half - managing to find that vital wee yard of space to get to their cross before Wullie and knock it past Sepp who was stood rooted to the spot.

It took a quiet word from Jock at half time to knock some sense into me. Having given all the outfield players their talk, he took me to one side.

'A wee word with you, Strings.'

We went into the corner of the dressing room. Jock putting an arm around me and moving in closer so that he could bring his mouth to my ear.

'Look, I know you're disappointed that you're not playing today but you need to pull yourself out of whatever the fuck it is that you're in right now, son. This is about Muirhouse Violet. The *team* comes first. Not you, not me, but the fucking Violet. Now, unless you weren't paying attention. We're already on four yellow cards by half time PLUS I don't expect us to have it all our own way the second half. The amount of pressing we did there in the first half. Not easy to keep that high tempo play up for a whole match so there *will* be subs getting made in the second half. Whether it's to protect any of our boys that are skating close to the wind when it comes to a second yellow or just because they're fucked from all the work they've put in.'

I wanted to laugh at his analogy as I was pretty sure he'd got sailing close to the wind and skating on thin ice mixed up and ended up giving me a combination of the both of them.

'I can't be putting you on that pitch in that frame of mind, though.' He said, taking his index finger and pressing it into the side of my head.

'I only need *full* focus out there. Not any cunt that are felling sorry for themselves. No passengers, Strings. You know that. *Especially* today.'

I just nodded my head to him, indicating that he was correct. Telling Jock Hunter that he's right, about *anything* was always a good start when it comes to currying favour with the man. From a man management standpoint. It worked a charm. I walked back out with everyone else, a new man. Standing and cheering on the boys. Kicking and heading each and every ball from the sidelines.

While Jock's words had been on the inspirational side they'd also ended up being a bit double edged as it had then led to me over his shoulder and whispering in his ear, following any incident involving any of our players. No matter how minor or innocuous they were.

'Tell you what, Jock, Coffee's leg's look a bit heavy do they not, think he maybe overdone things last night, eh?'

'Looked a bad challenge on The Monk, there. Maybe better taking him off. Precautionary, like.'

'You need to keep an eye on Terry, Jock. He's already on a yellow and him and their number seven keep nipping at each other. You know

Terry's temperament. He'll snap sooner or later. You really want to risk us going down to ten men, in a cup final?'

'These cunts are starting to run over the top of our midfield. We need to get another player put in there to shore things up.'

There wasn't one of our players - apart from Sepp - that was sacred when it came to me trying to steer Hunter into making a subbie. Well, every player apart from Sepp and Montana. I couldn't have been as much of a hypocrite by commenting on Montana being full of the drugs, when I was as well. And I sure as fuck wasn't going between the sticks, either.

'I can see what you're doing, Strings.' Jock said, having finally had enough of me chipping and nip nip nipping away at him.

'I'm just saying though, like.' I replied, making no apologies for the strategy that I'd adopted to try and get myself on the pitch.

While the score was still one all, it wasn't exactly reflecting the general play. They had created quite a few chances that - on another day - they'd have put away. Hit the post twice, as well. One of them rebounding right to their player from two yards out who completely fluffed his lines and ballooned the ball over the bar. The second occasion the woodwork was struck. One of those time standing still moments where the ball had beat Sepp's despairing dive and hit the inside of the post. I thought it was in, most did. Their player was almost away celebrating. Instead, though, the ball came off the inside of the post, rolled *along* the goal line before hitting the *other* post and rebounding out to The Monk who booted it away to safety. Fuck, I think he booted it that far the ball eventually ended up in Pilton.

'Right, go get yourself warmed up, Strings.' Jock said. It couldn't have sounded sweeter had he sung the words to me in a lullaby.

'Oh I love it when you talk dirty to me, Jock.' I replied, a man reborn at the realisation that I was getting on and taking my place in a cup final for the first time in my playing career.

I went for a little jog up and down the touchline. Done a few stretches - for nothing other than appearances sake - just to fill in the time until Jock got ready to make the sub. Terry, it was, who got the hook. He'd been an injury doubt anyway but had given the side a good hour before it started to tell on him. Jock had made the correct decision, though. An hour of Terry giving his all for the cause is worth more than a full ninety minutes from most others. Plus, The Violet were hardly downgrading by swapping my good self for Big Tel, eh?

'See that number seven of theirs? Fucking smash the cunt for me, ok? I couldn't touch him because I was already on a yellow. Fucking ref told me that next time I breathed on anyone I was getting cairded.' Terry's request as we double high fived each other when he left the pitch.

Sometimes that's all it takes to change a game and turn a team's fortunes - making a sub - and after only a few minutes on the pitch you saw the impact of that. Only it wasn't the 'spark' that we'd been looking for that Jock probably had in mind when he'd made the change. The Paddock going two one up. Me being directly at fault by taking one touch too many in midfield and their nippy wee winger taking it off my boot. His mazy run past a couple of our boys before he done this wee clever disguised pass to a team mate that left him with just Sepp to beat. Doing so with style by completely out-psyching our keeper by leaving him on his arse while he strolled past him. Taking the ball and sliding it into the empty net.

All I'd wanted was to play in the cup final but as I watched The Paddock players celebrate, while I heard the comments thrown my way from both crowd and team mates. I'd have swapped a cup final for just about *anything* else. Fuck, I'd have stood all day and spoken with those two traffic cops about the price of fucking cappuccinos in Rome rather than be stood there on that pitch knowing I'd cost us a goal.

I had two choices from there. Either go back to the feeling sorry for myself state I'd been in during the first half or I was going to go the other way and dig my team back out the hole that I'd put them in.

'Nah, fuck this,' I said as I watched the Niddrie boys all finally creeping back into their own half again. Rossi and Montana already standing there with the ball on the centre spot waiting to go. 'It's not ending like this.' I coached, myself, determined.

'THIS ISN'T FUCKING OVER YET, LADS' I shouted around the players closest to me with a clenched fist.

We had something like twenty five minutes left to get ourselves back in the game - or throw it away altogether - and we reacted in the way that I'd hoped we would. Taking the game back to them. We threw everything at them but the goal just wouldn't come. Their keeper pulling off one save - in particular - from Daz that had it been a keeper for one of the big teams in Europe who'd made the save, they'd be showing the clip until the end of time.

There was that undeniable feeling, though, that as time wore on the match was slipping from our hands. The Paddock - naturally - decided to try and defend what they had and had abandoned any actual ambition towards going up the other end of the park. Their back four so deep they were almost *behind* their goalkeeper.

By then, Han had come down to the pitch after her shift had ended. I'd spied her and Jackie standing with each other behind the Niddrie keeper. Her noticing me looking in her direction and giving me the same clenched fist that I'd given the rest of my team mates, following us conceding the second. I just nodded back to her, cool, like. Meant a lot to me, her coming down because she *never* came to watch the Violet when I was playing.

'TWO FUCKING MINUTES LEFT, VIOLET. PLENTY OF TIME TO GET BACK INTO THIS.'

I heard Hunter shouting from the sidelines.

I'd heard his shouts far louder than normal, having found myself out on right midfield and near the touchline. While out there Coffee and one of their players went in for a good old committed fifty - fifty where it would've probably taken a dozen looks at the slow-mo replays just to establish which one of them got a touch on the ball first out of the pair of them.

The ball deflected away from them - both players lying in a heap - and into the bit of space ahead of me. With no one covering ahead, I had a bit of freedom to take the ball on and run into. Reaching the outside of the box, I pulled one of their defenders away from the middle who had come out to try and block me but in doing so left a huge area of space for Rossi to run into.

'SQUARE IT, STRINGS. FUCKING USE ME.'

Rossi screamed, pointing ahead of him to indicate exactly where he wanted me to put it. I just needed to hit it low and hard - and beyond the player who had come out to meet me - across goal and into the path of Rossi and leave him with the simple task of tucking it. It didn't take the skill and precision of a Zidane. Just hit the fucking ball in pretty much a straight line.

Looking up one last time to check where Rossi was, I glanced back down at the Mitre and - trying to be as measured as I could - hit it low and hard.

'You stupid fucking fanny,' I said out loud - instead of sending the ball across the box and into the path of the incoming Rossi - I'd sclaffed the ball, sending it flying towards the direction of the side netting.

This was *THE* chance. And I'd fucked it.

If you can't even put a simple ball across and into the box you shouldn't even be playing the fucking game, I criticised myself, as I put my hands over my face to blank out the monstrosity of my attempt.

Hearing the ref's whistle go I'd assumed that it was for to signal the goal kick. When I took my hands from over my eyes, though, the ball was nestling in the back of the net.

For the next couple of minutes, confusion ruled over Muirhouse Park.

I *knew* I hadn't scored. I'd pretty much watched the ball heading in the direction of the side netting. The Paddock *also* knew that I hadn't scored. The referee - somehow - hadn't though and - seeing the ball in the back of the net - had whistled for an equaliser for Muirhouse. Once the penny had dropped, and that he'd given the goal. Well, I went fucking radge. As you'd expect for a last minute cup final equaliser. Being the goal that Han and Jackie were behind. I went to run and celebrate with them but - and it was as if everyone all realised it at once - there was a rush of Muirhouse fans who invaded the pitch, bringing Han and Jackie onto the pitch along with them.

It was chaos.

Anyone connected to Muirhouse was on the pitch. Dancing and jumping around with relief that we'd saved the game. Meanwhile the whole of The Paddock - manager and assistant included - were surrounding the referee going - and quite understandably - off their fucking tits at him.

Maybe it was the speed that I'd had in me - because I *definitely* shouldn't have been as fast and free thinking by that point of the day, following my night and morning - but I grabbed one of the fans who had come onto the pitch and screamed at him to go and check the side netting and if there was any pegs loose then to get the fuckers stuck deep into the ground. There was too many fans still on the pitch for it to be as obvious as what he was doing. The other prong to my doubled pronged moment of self preservation was to get some players over to 'protect' the ref. Have some of the boys run interference on things.

I decided to be one of them. Figuring that the longer we made of things the more chance the side netting was going to be secured *if* there was going to be some kind of inquest to follow.

'BUT THE BALL *DIDN'T* GO IN THE FUCKING NET, THOUGH?' The Paddock manager was screaming in the ref's face. Eyes about popping out through the seethe that he was experiencing.

'HOW THE FUCK DID IT NOT GO IN THE NET IF THE BALL WAS LYING THERE ... *IN THE NET*, THEN?' I joined in to give the 'other opinion' that was there, just for the benefit of the referee to hear.

''I MEAN, IT'S KIND OF HOW FITBA HAS BEEN WORKING FOR A WHILE NOW. BALL CROSSES THE LINE AND THAT NORMALLY MEANS IT'S A GOAL.' I added, sarcastic as fuck while still unable to believe that we were even standing in this position.

'IT WENT THROUGH THE FUCKING SIDE NETTING, WE ALL SEEN IT.' Their big centre half steamed in shouting and pushing me and getting a couple of pushes back for his cheek.

'SIDE NETTING? YOU STILL PISHED FROM LAST NIGHT, YA CLOWN?' Bungalow jumped in.

Referees don't change their minds, anyway. No fucking way was he going to now go back and chalk the goal off. Not in Muirhouse, he wasn't. He'd never have left town alive. Half our team would've thrown him off the top of Martello Court, never mind the Young Team who had come down to watch the game under no other provisions other than the hope that some of their Niddrie equivalents had come along, looking for something similar in the vein of some regional based violence packaged up as them 'innocently' being there to watch their local teams and nothing else.

I'd broken away from - what was verging on a mass brawl with all the pushing, shoving, harsh opinions and threats being dished out and, somehow, managed to lock eyes with the kid I'd grabbed and told him to check the net. I couldn't remember his name but knew his face from around Muirhouse so assumed it would've been likewise. He gave me a wee nod and a thumbs up. It was all I needed to see.

'RIGHT THEN, ENOUGH OF THIS SHITE.' I shouted, pushing my way into everyone towards the ref and The Paddock captain and manager, who was still out there doing his absolute dish in.

To be fair, had The Violet been on the other end of such an atrocity I'm not so sure that we'd have been so reserved as the cunts from Niddrie and, being fair to them. They weren't exactly shy and retiring about taking the referee's decision in the corinthian spirit of the game of fitba.

'THESE CHEATING BASTARDS ARE TRYING TO SCAM YOU OUT OF GIVING US A GOAL, THAT WE'VE CLEARLY SCORED. TALKING PISH ABOUT THE BALL GOING THROUGH THE SIDE OF THE NET, EH? LET'S CHECK THE NET THEN, FAIR'S FAIR. IF THERE'S A HOLE IN IT THEN YOU CAN CHALK IT OFF. CAN'T SAY FAIRER THAN THAT?' I shouted directly at the referee over top of around another dozen voices.

Their manager and captain - who had been close enough to hear this - reacted positively to my suggestion. The captain applauding in appreciation of my sporting gesture. Meanwhile, inside I couldn't believe that I'd had the ability to lie - in such an impressive way - inside me all that time and was only finding out there on the Muirhouse Park pitch. The fucking nerve of me. I wasn't giving a fuck. Kwik Save Challenge Trophies don't just drop into your lap. They have to be earned, my friend. By hook or crook.

I led the mini delegation of players and officials over towards the side of the goal that my mishit cross had went flying into.

'Right, you're the ref. I'll let you do your thing.' I said, confidently, while standing beside Montana. Taking a rest and leaning on his shoulder while we stood speaking as the inquest took place around the side of the net.

'What's happening, Strings?' Montana said, white foam on either side of his lips and a set of manic eyes staring back at me. The product of, by the looks, a cocktail of *all kinds* of drugs leading up to him taking his place in the team, that afternoon.

'We're about to be awarded an equaliser out of a cross that I fucking sliced into the side of the net. Whatever daft cunt set up those nets this morning didn't put the pins in properly. I could kiss them.' I laughed.

'Aye, that was me, like. I hadn't been to bed after going out to see DJ Selecao - only Scottish date, like - so ended up coming here earlier than I needed to. Had fuck all else to do. Jock chucked me one of the nets and told me to stick them on the goals. Haven't done it in all my time playing for the side, never mind trying to do it fucking wired. I played the first half with my shorts on the wrong way around before some cunt told me about it, for fuck's sake. Probably wan't the best person to be handing out the tasks to, like.' He said, bashfully.

'Well your lack of skills at putting nets up has just saved our fucking arse, you beautiful wired to the moon bastard.' I said, grabbing his head and kissing it. Instantly regretting such a move due to how drenched in sweat he was through the combination of running around a fitba pitch after a night of dancing to a House DJ and the drugs in connection with this that were all trying to escape out of him after serving their time, and purpose, over the night.

The ref - who was crouching down to inspect the side of the net - was obscured by a crowd of both Niddrie and Muirhouse players, everyone surrounding him. All trying to influence his decision.

I just stood there praying that the young lad had fixed the side netting *better* than Montana's original attempt had been.

'YOU FUCKING ROBBING BASTAAAAAARD.' I heard their manager scream out, which was a bit of a spoiler ahead of the ref standing up and blowing his whistle - yet again - and pointing to the centre circle. This sending the Muirhouse players running all over the place - anything other than back to their own half - while the whole of the Niddrie players, along with their beyond incensed gaffer chased the referee back up the pitch.

Took a good few minutes before any kind of order had been restored. The Paddock manager having to be physically dragged off the pitch by some of the Niddrie contingent that had come across to Muirhouse to support their team.

'How the fuck did we just get away with that?' Bungalow whispered into my ear as we stood waiting on the two Paddock players kicking off. 'Hey, there's been bigger injustices on much bigger stages, mucker, eh?' I said, shrugging it off. Well, *pretending* to shrug it off. No one yet aware over just how Machiavellian I'd sunk to in captilising on my shocker of a cross.

'Just ask that daft curly headed cunt, Shilton, eh?' I continued. 'Then again if you're a keeper and you let some cunt that's Five foot Five out-jump you then you deserve all you fucking get, in my opinion.'

Niddrie didn't look like a team who were going to use such an injustice to fuel fire to their bellies. The goal had broken them. Their two strikers hadn't even taken centre yet - despite the ball being there at their feet - due to being more interested in pointing and shouting at the referee. Issuing all kinds of threats of what was going to happen to him after the match. The kind of stuff that would get you a six month ban in the English Premiership but just another part of the game at Sunday league level.

'You're fucking dead, ya cunt. Soon as the final whistle goes.' One of them shouted towards the man in black. Doing the throat slit gesture to back up the words.

'Hey, no need for that stuff, eh? The boy comes down here to do this in his spare time. No money in it for him or fuck all. Doesn't deserve stuff like that, pal.' I said, and admit, was on the wind up with him. Standing there giving him a wee cheeky smile that let him know that I knew it wasn't a goal.

'And you can fucking shut it, as well. You'll get it too, ya cunt.' He turned his attention to me.

'Aye, you'll do fucking lots, mate.' Rossi shouted, to back me up. 'Yous cunts won't even leave Muirhouse if you want to start with that shite so fucking grow up and take centre, ya wee fucking dwarf.'

The boy - who *did* look around five three, five four at a push, and resembled one of those wee yapping dugs that are all full of it when they're behind their gate but if you were to open it they'd do fuck all - was considered as 'telt.'

'Right, come on, lets get into these cheating cunts.' The other Paddock striker said to the wee man as they took centre. Niddrie's heads had gone, though. While the phantom goal had only been an equaliser. Coming so late in the game - and in such controversial circumstances - it looked like it had been felt like a winner from us.

'These cunts' heads have gone, Strings.' Wullie said as one of their players booted it up the pitch and out of play for a goal kick. He was pointing up the pitch where a couple of their defenders were arguing with each other, the ball still up our end. Another one of their players still running after the ref. Proper Michael Ballack against Barcelona in the Champions League stuff.

Their two central defenders were *still* nipping away at each other by the time Sepp had taken the goal kick. Due to being more concerned with their argument they'd completely lost their sense of positioning. Us, benefiting from their lack of discipline through Daz flicking Sepp's kick on and over top of both centre halves who, positionally, were way too high up the pitch. This, leaving Montana running onto it and with a free run in on goal. One of those attacks where the rest of the team just stands still and watches. Hoping that their man is going to do the business and not choke.

While the central defenders had been woefully caught out of position, one of their midfielders had been tracking Montana's run and - while most definitely second favourite to get to the ball - looked like he wasn't giving up the chase while pretty much all of the other Paddock players had stopped to watch.

Even with all the stoppages in the game. We *had* to be almost at the end of injury time. Stick it away, son, and we win the cup, I stood there with my hands on my hips watching him running in on goal with their number six hooring after him.

'MAN ON, MONTANA.' About - what sounded like - a hundred voices shouted out all at once.

Take the shot, for fuck's sake,' I thought, worrying that maybe the boy had been given too much time to think about what he was going to do. Almost as if he had taken that thought from me telepathically and acted on it. Opening up his body and shaping himself to shoot.

This, drawing - from the Paddock midfielder - just about the best example that you could've ever seen of a 'professional foul' regardless of it being on an 'amateur' football pitch. He knew that he wasn't going to get to Montana in time to play the ball, or even get close to the fucking thing. Montana, though? Well, aye. *He* was close enough.

With absolutely no fucks given. Their boy took a massive swipe at Montana's standing leg. Completely clearing him out and leaving the ball to trundle its way towards the waiting keeper. To be fair to their midfielder. He didn't even wait on the red card coming out. He just turned around and walked off the pitch. The ref holding the red up more for official confirmation than anything else.

This all coming so soon after our 'equaliser' ignited things again. Sparking more handbags amongst the two sets of players.

'YOU'D GET SIX MONTHS IN SAUGHTON IF YOU DID THAT AWAY FROM A FITBA PITCH'

Jock Hunter was hardly helpings things from the sidelines with his own input.

While everyone was having their own mini arguments around me. How it was or wasn't a red. Where the tackle had actually taken place and where the free kick was going to be taken from. I checked on Montana who was now sitting up wincing and rubbing at his leg. Benji had ran on with the old Ralgex and magic sponge. I thought a stretcher might've been more appropriate with the sheer level of viscousness that the Paddock player had assaulted Montana with.

'You can put that fucking thing back down again too, by the way.' Montana said, looking up to Rossi, at the sight of him with the ball in his hand. Looking poised for taking the free kick, once he was free to do so.

'I won it, I'm taking it.' He said while Benji sprayed his leg with the aerosol in his hand. Montana and Rossi arguing over who was taking a free kick was, by no means, a new phenomenon. Barely a game went by without them having a wee tantrum at each other over who got to take it. The best part was that they were both fucking honking at them but the way they made out you'd have thought that they were a pair of Juninho Pernambucanos.

At any moment, *especially that one*, Muirhouse comes first. Not personal glory of any kind. Aye, Montana had won the free kick but the lad had almost broken his leg in doing so. Maybe just maybe it would've been better to leave the job to the guy who was able to stand on both legs. I suggested as much to Montana.

'Ohhhh please.' He said, as he held his hand up in the air for me to grab and help him up again. 'Never underestimate the power of Ketamine, Cocaine and a wee morning top up of Amphetamine Sulphate.' I helped him to his feet and he wasted no time in grabbing the ball back off Rossi and placing it on the deck.

'If you hold any religious beliefs, whatsoever, then prepare to give them up after you see this, mate.' He said, picking up and re-placing the ball again to suit how it sat on the turf.

'Montana, literally ten minutes ago you were telling me that you were seeing *two* balls, ya fucking mad bastard. And *you* want to take the free kick?' I asked.

'As long as I hit the ball that's actually *there* though, I'm good, eh?' He winked before pushing me aside. Telling me to 'watch and fucking learn.'

Him and Rossi stood close together, whispering. Montana pointing towards the top corner of the keeper's right. This, I'm sure, more to give the Niddrie players something else to think about than anything else because it was certain that Montana was taking it. The Paddock keeper having his wall lined up and with Rossi stood beside the ball. Montana waited for the ref's whistle.

It had been a noisy ninety minutes. Both on *and* off the pitch. That split second or two, though - waiting on the referee - I swear you could've heard a pin drop. His whistle, the signal for all the noise and animation to return straight away after a few seconds time out.

Montana took a suspiciously casual, elegant almost, run up to the ball and - looking above the heads of the Niddrie players and towards the keepers top corner - in perfect syncronisation, just as the Paddock players in the wall all rose at the once. Montana having the absolute nerve, and audacity, to hit the ball hard and low *under* the jump of the five men in the wall.

You knew it was in, *once* you realised what it was that Montana had actually done. Some probably only fully sussing it all out *once* the ball was in the net.

I remember the amount of Niddrie players who just collapsed to the ground at the sight of the ball crossing the line. Keeper still standing towards his other post, completely outfoxed by the craftiness of a man who had been up all night dancing to repetitive beats in a sweaty club. That was my first memory of the goal going in. Then came the pitch invasion and I really *do* mean pitch invasion. Celebrating that goal it felt like there were more people on the pitch than there were *off* it.

Montana - in that moment very much looking like a man who had indulged in Ching - stood there lapping up the reception to his moment of genius. I don't think any of us had even noticed that the referee had blown for full time until we'd eased off on the celebrations a touch. Montana's goal leaving there with not even enough time to restart the match again.

What a fucking feeling, though. The feeling of being a winner, like, and I wouldn't have swapped that with the one that the Niddrie players were sat around the pitch with for anything that you would have cared to offer me. I'm not sure they quite knew *what* had hit them. They looked stunned. One minute they're coasting and just about to see the match out and win themselves a piece of silverware. The next, they lose a goal that hadn't actually *been* a goal and then minutes later lose another one that probably only half a dozen players on the fucking planet would've even thought about *trying,* never mind actually scoring.

I couldn't have exactly felt sorry for them, though. Not when I had played such an integral role in completely robbing them blind. Montana's goal had knocked the stuffing out of them so much that none of them looked even remotely interested in taking up the earlier issue with the referee, now that the game was finished. If it hadn't been a case of them having to have hung back for their losers medals I wouldn't have blamed them if they hadn't already fucked off back to the pavilion. You think I would've hung around Niddrie under the same circumstances with the Paddock players and locals all on the pitch celebrating? Aye, fuck that.

Being on the other side of things though? Absolutely majestic and worth *every* year that I'd waited on it coming along. The lifting of the trophy - and the cheers that accompanied it from the locals - getting that winners medal, the look of pride I got off Han and Jack when I saw them on the pitch during the full time pitch invasion, standing posing with the rest of the team - standard team photo with trophy sitting in front of us - for the Edinburgh Evening News. I loved it all if I'm being honest.

I didn't want the moment or the feeling to end and was literally the *last* player to leave the pitch and go back to the dressing room where the day's festivities were about to start kicking off in earnest. Jock - with his mind games - had placed two cases of Bud in the corner of the dressing room and told the boys that it was only for winners and if they came back in at full time with a losers medal in their hand then they wouldn't be getting any of it. No doubt the first case had been fired into before anyone had even hit the showers. It was going to be a day (and night) and a half but there would not have been one cunt that could've said the players, staff and general hangers on of Muirhouse Violet had not deserved it.

As I approached the pavilion I noticed a couple of boys hanging around having a smoke outside the main entrance. It was one of their coats that caught the attention more than anything else.

Fuck, didn't know that the BBC were sending John Motson down to commentate on the match, I laughed to myself at the sight of the boy's sheepskin coat that 'Motty' has had a few digs over the year about.

'Some result, Strings pal. Thanks to the super sub that came on, but.' The boy in the Motty jacket said warmly - and in turn, keeping in tune with the general happy vibe all round - as I got closer to them. I didn't recognise him but thought that maybe it had been a case of the jacket blinding me to everything else. He knew me, anyway, by the looks.

'Cheers, pal.' I said, giving him a thumbs up and a nod as I went to walk past the pair of them and into the dressing room. I felt the tug on the back of my shirt, like an opposing player had pulled me back, out on the pitch. Looking around, it was the other boy - that was standing having a smoke with him - who had a grip of my Violet top.

'Emmmm we need a wee word with you, Josephine.' The one in the matching tracksuit said, in a completely different tone to how the other one had just spoken to me.

I didn't quite 'get it,' at first. I was one of the heroes of the day, for fuck's sake. Should've been getting carried into the dressing room on cunts shoulders on account of my role in our second goal rather than having someone being a dick and grabbing my shirt aggressively like this lad was.

'Eh?' Was all I could come out with while the sheepskin coat one put his arm around me passive aggressively.

'Don't worry, pal. We'll only keep you a couple of minutes, but. Come for a wee walk while we discuss a few things with you. You've been a naughty boy, Joe.' He whispered in my ear.

I felt that it was as if he was trying to ensure that I didn't kick off and make a scene. As you *would* do if you were in deepest Muirhouse and there only being two of you.

Can't I ever have anything fucking nice? I asked myself as I walked away from the pavilion with them. One either side of me. I'd literally just experienced the emotive and biblical feeling of kissing silverware, minutes earlier, and yet was *already* feeling it all being sucked away from me. Just by being in the presence of these two boys.

During our short walk around Muirhouse Park, the two of them went on to inform me that they represented someone from through in the west that owned a chain of amusement arcades. Once they said those two words, I knew I was fucked.

'Now, after crunching the numbers based on an average days takings of the two machines that you played, on the day that you visited his Caledonian Amusements establishment. Our associate, Mr Henderson, has come to the - and what he feels is a *very* fair figure - amount of ten grand that you are due him in compensation. Don't worry, though. Like I just said. He's a fair man. Because of that he's going to - charitably - give you a week to get the money together. Wee bit of advice though, pal. I wouldn't go stringing any of his *other* arcades to gather any funds to pay *off* your debt.' The one in the tracksuit said, as he steered me in a kind of wee half circle, so that we got ourselves walking back in the direction of the pavilion again.

A fair figure? Ten fucking grand? I didn't know who Lloyd Henderson had been up to that point but one thing I could've told you about him was that he, indeed, was the furthest fucking thing from a 'fair man' as you could get. I could see *exactly* what he was doing. Obviously, I hadn't taken that much from his machines but *because* I'd had the nerve to steal from him. *He* was going to set the terms as a result. I was fuck all other than an example that was needing to be set.

There was no point in me even trying to deny any of it so I didn't bother. Between the pair of them. They'd told me enough facts for me to know that it wasn't a case of mistaken identity. To try and make it out to be anything of the sort would've only insulted their intelligence and they didn't look the types that you wanted to be trying that shite with.

They'd mentioned the Rangers gear that I had on that day - like any other work day - and, the boy in the tracky, then telling me that they'd went on to find out that I was a Hibee. Actually tipping his hat towards me over such an ingenious approach.

'Mibbe, need to start doing that, myself too with a Celtic top on, but.' He said, looking like he was considering it before adding 'Aye, fuck that. You'll never see me with one of their tops on my back. I'd rather drink your pish.'

On the subject of the Rangers clobber. The track-suited boy brought up the subject of Benji.

'Now - from the video tapes - it's obvious that yer pal, the 'fellow bear,' he said with sarcastic air quotes 'was in on the rob with you so Mr Henderson feels that it would be 'sporting,' if you will, if he was to share the debt with you. You fly with the crows, eh, pal? And hey, at least it makes it a bit easier on your end.' Now we *could've* grabbed *Benji* as well, to have a word with him, let him know the Hampden too, you know? But while we might not exactly be flavor of the month right now while you're no doubt left here reeling from the news that we've just delivered, we're respectful, too. We do our due diligence and *that* is why we know that your team's just won its first trophy in almost ten years. We don't want to get in the way of your celebrations more than we need to today. We trust that you'll deliver Mr Henderson's message across to your pal? The clock's ticking for the pair of you.'

'Oh aye, that's most considerate of him *and* you, that.' I said with a hint of sarcasm before remembering that - first of all - I *had* stolen from some West Coast character who was a serious enough man to track me down, and let me walk without a limp and - secondly - he was open to reducing the unrealistic target of ten grand to an - equally but - *lower* unrealistic target of five grand!

The one in the sheepskin coat was kind enough to remind me - on the way back to the pavilion - that earlier on that day the pair of them had taken a visit up to the flat and spoken to Jackie. 'Nice lad,' apparently. And that they'd be back in a weeks time to collect.

Ten grand? TEN FUCKING GRAND? Where the fuck were *we* going to get hold of *that* amount of money? Benji had yet to experience the joy of being brought up to speed with events. How I was looking forward to shitting all over his cup final celebrations with *that* piece of breaking news. Ten grand. Inside seven days? Wish I had kept hold of those two pairs of fucking Sambas, I lamented, as I watched them get in their car and drive off.

They disappeared, leaving me stood outside the pavilion with a winners medal in my hand but feeling *anything* but victorious.

Chapter 39

Strings

'Well I have to hand it to you. You're the very *last* person that I thought I'd see this morning. Oh and you've brought that adorable dog of yours, and a mate too. And what do I owe the pleasure? I assume that it's to do with the fact that my shipment was a touch light yesterday? If not then *know* that we 'will' be addressing that particular discrepancy before you leave today.' McKenna sat there. Looking genuinely amused by this early morning visit from me, the dog and Benji. The reference to the missing trainers was not a good sign, though. Not under the circumstances that we were all sat there inside the porto-cabin over, already.

Preferably, I wouldn't have been sitting there, myself, if I'd had any choice. More likely Benji, too. Stanton? Well, he looked none more up or down than he normally did. So, aye, clueless, as always.

McKenna, looking back over his table at us - cogs visibly turning in his head - stroking his chin as me and Benji - me primarily - took him through the delicately awkward predicament that we'd ended up in. That we were sat there looking back at him was a clear sign that we were all out of options and had been left with nowhere else to go.

Giving Benji the news later on, after the match? Aye, *that* was fun.

'OLE OLE OLE OLE MUIRHOOSE MUIRHOOSE. OLE OLE OLE OLE MUIRHOOSE MUIRHOOSE.'

The team, in a manners of dress (and undress) were bouncing around the dressing room with bottles of beer in their hands. Some being drank while others were being used to soak as much of the bodies inside that small dressing room as possible. Proper F1 winners podium stuff.

They looked in their element. I'd never seen the team, my team, celebrate a win like this since the day I first put the Copa Mundials on to play for The Violet. I felt robbed of the moment. I should've been right in the middle of them all. Pouring a bottle of Bud over Jock Hunter's napper. Be as well doing that than drinking the fucking stuff. 'Here, get a fucking swally down you.' Benji said having spied me standing watching everyone singing.

For the purposes of team unity. I took it from him and took a swig from it. Normally you wouldn't have even been able to PAY me to drink a bottle of America's most famous beer. Like I'd always said. If you'd ever wanted proof that the general public's taste is away to fuck and to be avoided from having it steer you in *any* direction then you just needed to look at how popular Bud is.

I'd wanted to tell Benji straight away, there and then. Probably for my own selfish reasons but I wanted him to know what we'd ended up involved in. With it being as personal as it was. Telling Benji would - quite literally - be a case of a problem shared being a problem halved. Not to mention a debt, like.

'Gonnae be some night tonight, Joseph, my man.' Sepp - standing in nothing but his fitba boots, cock and balls flying in all directions - shouted in my face as he grabbed hold of my shoulders and tried to get me bouncing up and down along with him.

'Championes championes ole ole ole Championes championes ole ole ole.'

He sang, along with the rest of them. Me joining in, half heartedly.

I didn't know *what* to think or feel by then, though. There was way too many conflicting factors going on inside me. Physically? It was Sunday afternoon. I'd last had a proper sleep when I'd went to my bed on the Friday night. I'd driven five hours on top of that but taken some drugs to try and balance things out *then* played part of a game of fitba. My head wasn't as fast and alert as it had been once that Speed had kicked in but *neither* was I feeling like I was ready to collapse and sleep for thirty six hours either. I suspected that a heavy and hard crash - one of severe extremities - was going to come, and without as much in the way of notice. Until then, though. I was just going to keep pushing on. I'd had a very brief thought to ask Montana for more speed to keep me going for the rest of the day. Just enough to make sure that I didn't miss out on the day and night instead of potentially passing out in the corner of the pub at four in the afternoon.

And that was just the 'physical' side to things.

Mental? Fucking more ups and downs over the Sunday than you'd find at Alton Towers. I'd went from the stress and mental punishment of driving enough Ching to put me away for years hundreds of miles. Throw in the police side of things, when they stopped me. The potential issues - still to make themselves known- over the two missing pairs of trainers. Fuck? The emotions used up during the ninety minutes of the cup final, alone. To end up feeling so high, so glorious. Only for minutes later to be then informed that you're due a serious figure from the West Coast a grossly inflated sum of money that you already *know* that you won't be able to pay back.

The longer I left it - that Sunday with Benji - the worse it was going to be when I *did* tell him. I decided to tell him when we got back to The Gunner. There was going to be a wee buffet laid out for the victors along with a few quid stuck behind the bar for the team.

The two of us were standing with a pint and getting fired into some tidy ham salad sandwiches when I finally decided to broach things.

'So what the fuck all happened in Manchester? From some of the wee teasers you dropped in on your calls when you were coming back up the road, it sounded a bit radge, like.' He said. Fuck, because of how draining the cup final had been. The whole drive up the M6 felt like it had been fucking *months* ago.

'Aye, it was real, right enough. Doesn't look like they fuck around much down there. That house I was in? The heat that five stars on Grand Theft Auto brings wouldn't have got through that fucking front door of theirs.' I said, as I went into telling him about cunts with Uzis and money counters. While the pair of us were standing talking on our own I took the opportunity to tell him what I'd been keeping back since the dressing room. Asking him if he wanted to come out for a smoke that was going to be nothing more than a prop while he was given the news that our stringing ways had now come back to bite us both on the arse.

'Didn't I fucking say I was worried, that day? Why the fuck do you think that I got us out of there fucking pronto? You don't string for as long as I've done without smelling danger and those two boys that were standing talking to us about Rangers were fucking reeking of it.' I said before taking an extremely long draw of my Embassy while Benji stood there - freakishly - recreating my *exact* pose after I'd given the ball away for Niddrie's second goal, earlier on.

'How the ... How did they know our names or where we're from?'

He asked, as confused as I was on that issue. You *never* use a card when you're in an amusement arcade. Even to pay for some scran for yourself. Cash only. No paper trail left. Simple.

How we'd been caught was something that I'd neglected to ask earlier on. What did it matter, anyway? It changed nothing.

'Fucked if I know, Benj, but they have. I feel bad, mate. If I could take on the debt myself and keep you out of it, I would. You know what gangsters are like, though, pal? They take this stuff kind of personal, eh? Doesn't matter to them that I'm the one with the stringers in his hand and sitting at the puggy. In his eyes you - as my look out - are as bad as me.' I said to him, quite possibly over egging the pudding of how his involvement had been viewed as.

'Oh, no, Strings. You and me? We're a team, eh? We win together we lose together and it's fair to fucking say that we've just taken a metaphorical drubbing, here. *We* were both there, that day. *We* shared the winnings. Wouldn't be much of a mate if I was to say 'aye, good luck, Strings, yer on yer own there,' like. He responded, admirably.

'Not like you sound like you've *got* the choice though, anyway.' I added. Just in case he was to start entertaining any thoughts that he *had* a choice to opt in or out.

After crunching some numbers of our own as we stood outside The Gunner I soon found that Benji's full and frank backing - as a friend in such a situation - was all a bit hollow considering he was as fucking skint as *I* was.

'So, Benji - between us - we have the princely sum of Two hundred and Seventy Eight pounds and Forty Two pence. Which leaves us with a shortfall of Nine Thousand Seven hundred and Twenty One pounds and Fifty Eight pence to find in, now, less than seven days.' I said, sure that I had it down to the penny but whether I had the figure rounded up or not. It didn't take calculator to show that, clearly - as well as - royally. We were fucked.

So fucked that we found ourselves, sitting the next day, in Davey McKenna's Leith scrapyard porto-cabin. We'd had the rest of the Sunday to have a think just where two cunts like us were going to get our hands on ten thousand pounds that did not involve robbing a bank, bookies or post office. None of these remotely close to being an option.

Me coming up with the nuclear option - The McKenna one - sometime later in the evening when - by then - the alcohol had got the better of me. Having chased any remnants of that Speed away to fuck. I'd figured that having just recently done a spot of business for him and - in doing so - no doubt making him a fucking shit load of money in the process. It would've been the optimum time for me to go looking for assistance. I was able to take comfort in the fact that there really was nowhere else for us to go.

McKenna - obviously being already well aware of my talents at a puggy - was spared the ins and outs. Only that we'd been caught with our hand in the biscuit tin and were now being squeezed hard over it.

'You can't blame him. I'd have done the fucking same to you if you'd stolen from me … and we've still to get to the missing trainers, by the way. Just in case you think I'm forgetting about that' There was not much in the way of real understanding, or sympathy, towards our situation coming from McKenna's direction.

'Aye, but I've still to come to that part, Davey. Nobody *stole* the trainers.' I pleaded although no longer as confident as I'd been the day before that he would accept the reason for the shipment being four ounces of Coke light.

For what it was worth. I took him over the story involving the five a side playing traffic cops. Maybe it was the way I told the story but I had both McKenna and Benji sitting there pissing themselves laughing while I told them about me standing there with the traffic officers - without a license - with a VW van full of Cocaine - speeding out of my tits - while we stood there and spoke about the price of cheese toasties in Central Park in New York.

'The way, I read it, Davey. It was give them a couple of pairs of trainers away with them or they were going to take the fucking lot. It was a judgment call that I had to make and you know what? If I was in the same situation I'd be doing the same again, like.' I was so animated, telling them the story, that I was up and out of my seat, walking the floor of the porto-cabin.

'I know you told me that if anything went wrong 'on route' then it was my responsibility, Davey, but I thought that you'd have understood having to lose a couple. There's always some cunt with their palms out to get greased, eh?'

McKenna chose to stay silent and with his silence it almost felt like it imposed an enforced silence upon the rest of us in the room.

I swear, it wasn't a case of *feeling* like five minutes had passed before he spoke. Five minutes DID pass. Benji and me were doing practically anything other than look at him - or each other - by this point. You know those moments where you spy something on your shoe that isn't actually there but you pretend to be looking at it anyway? Aye, that.

It was all appearances and which way you wanted to look at them, I suppose. I thought that having freshly done a favour for McKenna - that, aye, was only because of *other* mitigating circumstances - he was the perfect person to seek assistance from. Well, not 'perfect' as you'd always be better off not getting *any* assistance from a character like Davey McKenna. Period, as the Yanks say. Still, better the devil you know, eh.

Looking at it - from a different viewpoint, though - McKenna, as unpredictable as he was prone to being, could easily have looked on me rocking up that next day looking for help - having already been told about the missing Ching - as a complete piss take of the highest order from me.

He fell somewhere between the middle on things.

'Right then, boys. Here's your facts of the matter.' McKenna finally broke breath while offering us a reek from his packet.

'Me and Henderson have been doing the occasional cross M8 business for about the past ten years and what I *can* tell you, without question, is that if you don't have the money ready for collection next Sunday then you won't get a second chance from him. He's put more cunts under the ground than the Co-Op, Lloyd.'

Benji and I just looked at each other. I think all that was missing was the comedy style loud gulp.

'But maybe I can help you two out, eh?' He'd left the long pause before dangling the possibility of a shred of hope, deliberately.

'Look, we all know that Hendo is taking the piss with the figure that he's asking for but we all know *why*. You pair took liberties with him so he's giving you the same treatment back and, like I said, I can't blame him. His arcade probably doesn't see ten grand in a week, never mind a day, so here's what I'm willing to do for you.'

He picked up his mobile phone and held it up so as to make his point.

'With one phone call I could tell him that you're my associates. That you fucked up, didn't realise who owned the arcade and that had you known you wouldn't have went fucking near the place. That you respectfully apologise to him and, of course, will repay what you stole, plus interest. I'll cover the debt for you and we can work out your 'payment plan' at a later date? What do you say to it? How many folk do you know that would be nice enough to do such a thing as that for you?'

He was loving it. He really was. Ten grand was chicken feed to someone like him but might as well have been a million pounds to the likes of Benji and me. For ten grand he could literally buy and sell our sorry asses. For ten grand he could - well, *would,* actually - be the difference between Benji and me ending up - or not - in intensive care, if we were lucky.

Five grand in debt to McKenna wasn't entirely the *end* of the world. Compared to the alternative, anyway. As long as we paid him what we were due, or worked off some of it. We'd both be fine and free of trips to hospitals and or cemeteries. We'd get ourselves out of it, eventually.

We looked at each other to gauge the other's reaction but as shitty a choice it was to make we both knew it was the *only* one that could be made.

'What do you say, boys? I'll call Lloyd this morning and clear things up.' McKenna said, stubbing his cigarette out despite it only having been smoked to half its length and standing up. He had this Armani body warmer on and while standing up and looking down at us grabbed at each pocket on either side of the zip and pulled them open to show us that there was nothing inside either.

'Room for one of you in each side. Jump in, boys.' He said in such an arrogant way that made me want to tell him to shove his fucking 'assistance' up his arse and that I'd take my chances. It wasn't a moment for pride to be dominant, though. Benji and me having no choice other than to swallow it down and shake McKenna's hand on the deal.

'And a pleasure it was doing business with you pair of fine fellows it most certainly was.' He said with a big smile. Knowing full well that he was going to be profiting out of this in multiple ways.

It's funny how life can be, though. Weeks before it had felt like the end of the world to find myself back in bed with McKenna and, yet there in that porto-cabin. Getting back in with him *again*. It provided an enormous sense of relief which - weeks before - I'd have never felt possible. Aye I was jumping from the frying pan into the fire - in all probability - but I, at least, knew what that particular fire was like.

Benji and me - with the relief written all over our faces - stood up to leave. Business now concluded. The crux of it being that we were in a *lot* worse a position than we'd been in twenty four hours earlier but marginally better than we were going to be come the next again Sunday.

'Ehhhhhhhh and where do you think you're off to, young man.' McKenna said. Looking surprised that I was getting ready for the off. I'd seen no further reason for us taking up any more of his time.

'I don't follow?' I said, still standing up and looking over the table at him. Benji already over playing with Stanton and getting ready for leaving.

'Well now that we've all discussed *your* problem with Henderson. I thought was may as well kill two birds with one stone and talk about *my* problem and the four ounces of product that I was missing yesterday. Do you know that what you so very generously gave away to your two law enforcement pals had a street value of Eleven Thousand and Two Hundred pounds? YOU gave away over Eleven Thousand pounds of MY money, Joe. You didn't actually think that I was just going to write that off, did you?'

He laughed at the thought of it. 'I *do* appreciate that you made a call while under extreme pressure and that you *did* manage to return back to Edinburgh with the rest of the shipment complete so let's round it up to a nice and simple ten k, eh?' He added. I didn't know much about the drug game but knew that if he was saying what the street value of it was then he was paying a *lot* less for it - especially when you're buying VW Transporters' full of the stuff - so even his figure of ten thousand was definitely a mark up on what he'd have paid for it. What really could I do though?

Deflated, I went to sit myself back down again. If I'd felt that my position had been 'marginally better' minutes before. That had been short lived and only a case of some temporary respite from the pain of life. My 'position' at that moment - with everything being taken into account - was now even WORSE than it had been following Jack breaking into McKenna's house to kick start all of the madness.

'Be a good lad, Benji, and take wee Stanton, there, out for a walk around the yard while we sit here and discuss Joe's future and what lies ahead in it. We'll not be too long, pal.'

McKenna gestured to Benji. Indicating that he wanted to have a one on one chat with me only. Benji - naturally - complying and quickly getting Stanton on his lead and away out the porto-cabin door.

Once left on our own. McKenna *did*, indeed, talk about my future. Near enough mapped it out for me through his explaining of what it meant to be fifteen thousand pounds in debt to the man. Had it been an actual 'fortune teller' you'd have been wanting your fucking money back from such a bleak prediction that you were handed to you.

Aye, the future was looking heavy grim, and no mistake.

Then again, though. What made me any different to half the others in the naughty north?

Also by Johnny Proctor

The Zico trilogy

Ninety

A great portrait of a seminal time for youth culture in the U.K. A nostalgic must read for those who experienced it and an exciting and intriguing read for those that didn't' Dean Cavanagh - Award winning screenwriter.

Meet Zico. 16 years old in 1990 Scotland. Still at school and preparing himself for entering the big bad world while already finding himself on the wrong side of the tracks. A teenager who, despite his young years, is already no stranger to the bad in life. A member of the notorious Dundee Utility Crew who wreak havoc across the country every Saturday on match day.

Then along comes a girl, Acid House and Ecstasy gatecrashing into his life showing him that there other paths that can be chosen. When you're on a pre set course of self destruction however. Sometimes changing direction isn't so easy. Ninety is a tale of what can happen when a teenager grows up faster than they should ever have to while finding themselves pulled into a dangerous turn of events that threatens their very own existence.

Set against the backdrop of a pivotal and defining period of time for the British working class youth when terrace culture and Acid House collided. Infectiously changing lives and attitudes along the way.

Ninety Six

Ninety Six - The second instalment of the Zico trilogy.

Six years on and following events from 'Ninety' ... When Stevie "Zico" Duncan bags a residency at one of Ibiza's most legendary clubs, marking the rising star that he is becoming in the House Music scene. Life could not appear more perfect. Zico and perfect, however, have rarely ever went together.

Set during the summer of Euro 96. Three months on an island of sun, sea and sand as well as the Ibiza nightlife and everything that comes with it. What could possibly go wrong? It's coming home but will Zico?

Noughty

Bringing a close to the most crucial and important decade of all.

Noughty - The third book from Johnny Proctor. Following the events of the infamous summer of Ninety Six in Ibiza. Three years on the effects are still being felt inside the world of Stevie 'Zico' Duncan and those closest to him. Now having relocated to Amsterdam it's all change for the soccer casual turned house deejay however, as Zico soon begins to find. The more that things change the more they seem to stay the same. Noughty signals the end of the 90's trilogy of books which celebrated the decade that changed the face, and attitudes, of UK youth culture and beyond.

Available through DM to help support the independents.

Twitter @johnnyroc73

Instagram @johnnyproctor90

www.paninaropublishing.co.uk

Also available through Apple Books, Kindle, Amazon, Waterstones and other book shops.

Printed in Great Britain
by Amazon

33119275R00249